twilight

THE GRAPHIC NOVEL VOLUME 1

STEPHENIE MEYER

ART AND ADAPTATION BY YOUNG KIM

Yen Press

Twilight: The Graphic Novel
Volume 1

Art and Adaptation: Young Kim

Text copyright © 2005 by Stephenie Meyer
Illustrations © 2010 Hachette Book Group, Inc.

Yen Press
Hachette Book Group
237 Park Avenue, New York, NY 10017

Visit our websites at www.HachetteBookGroup.com and
www.YenPress.com

Yen Press is an imprint of Hachette Book Group, Inc.
The Yen Press name and logo are trademarks of Hachette Book Group, Inc.

First Hardcover Edition: March 2010

ISBN: 978-0-7595-2943-4

10 9 8 7 6 5 4 3 2 1

RRD-C

Printed in the United States of America

I love Twilight: The Graphic Novel.

It's simply beautiful.

Working with Young was always very exciting,

but more than that,

it brought me back to my first Twilight *experience.*

She would send me a new set of drawings,

some portrait of Edward or Bella would jump off the page

and suddenly I would be feeling all the same things I felt

that first summer while I was writing their story.

The art made it fresh again.

I hope everyone has that same experience with it.

— *Stephenie Meyer*

◄ ►

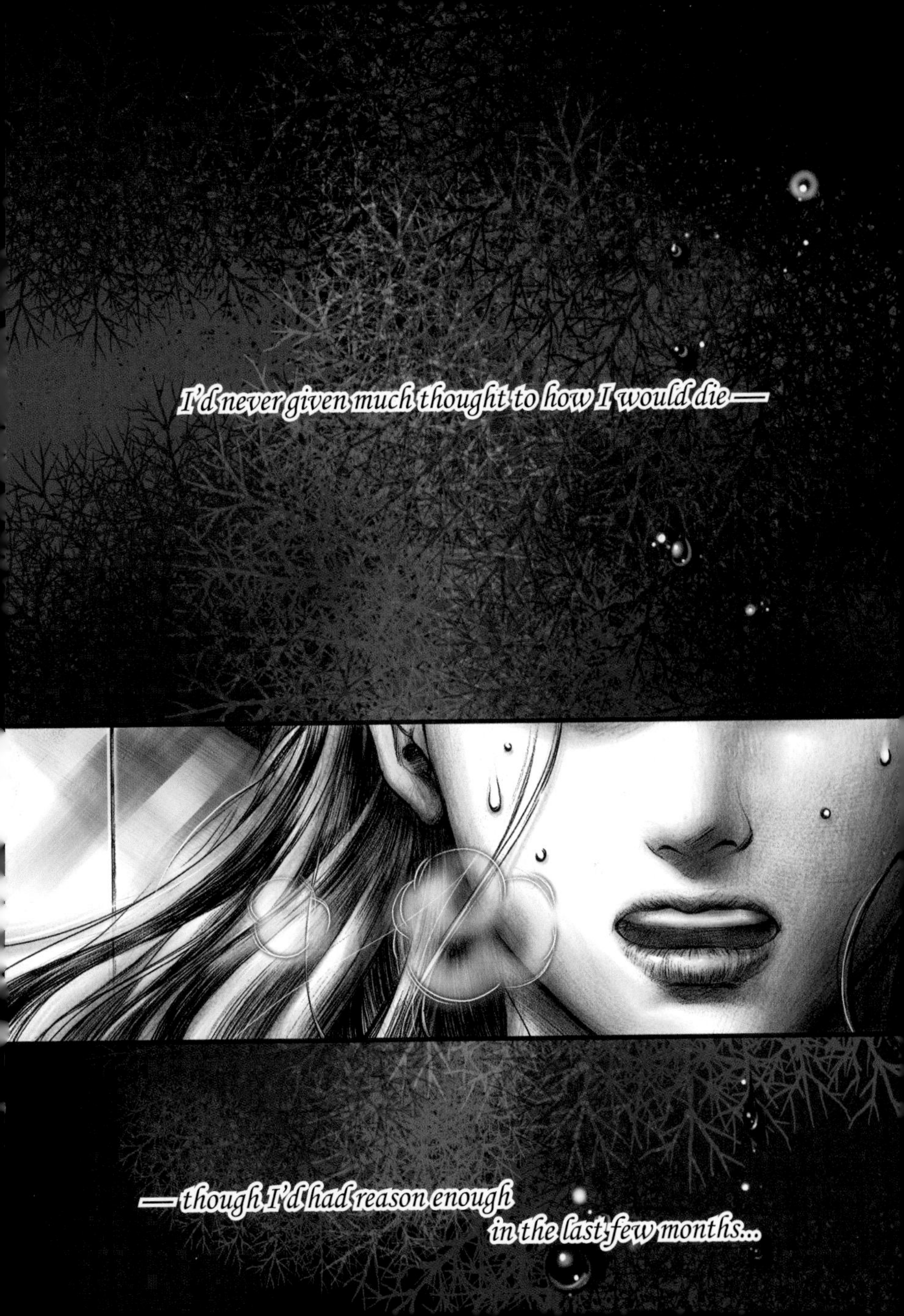
I'd never given much thought to how I would die—
—though I'd had reason enough in the last few months...

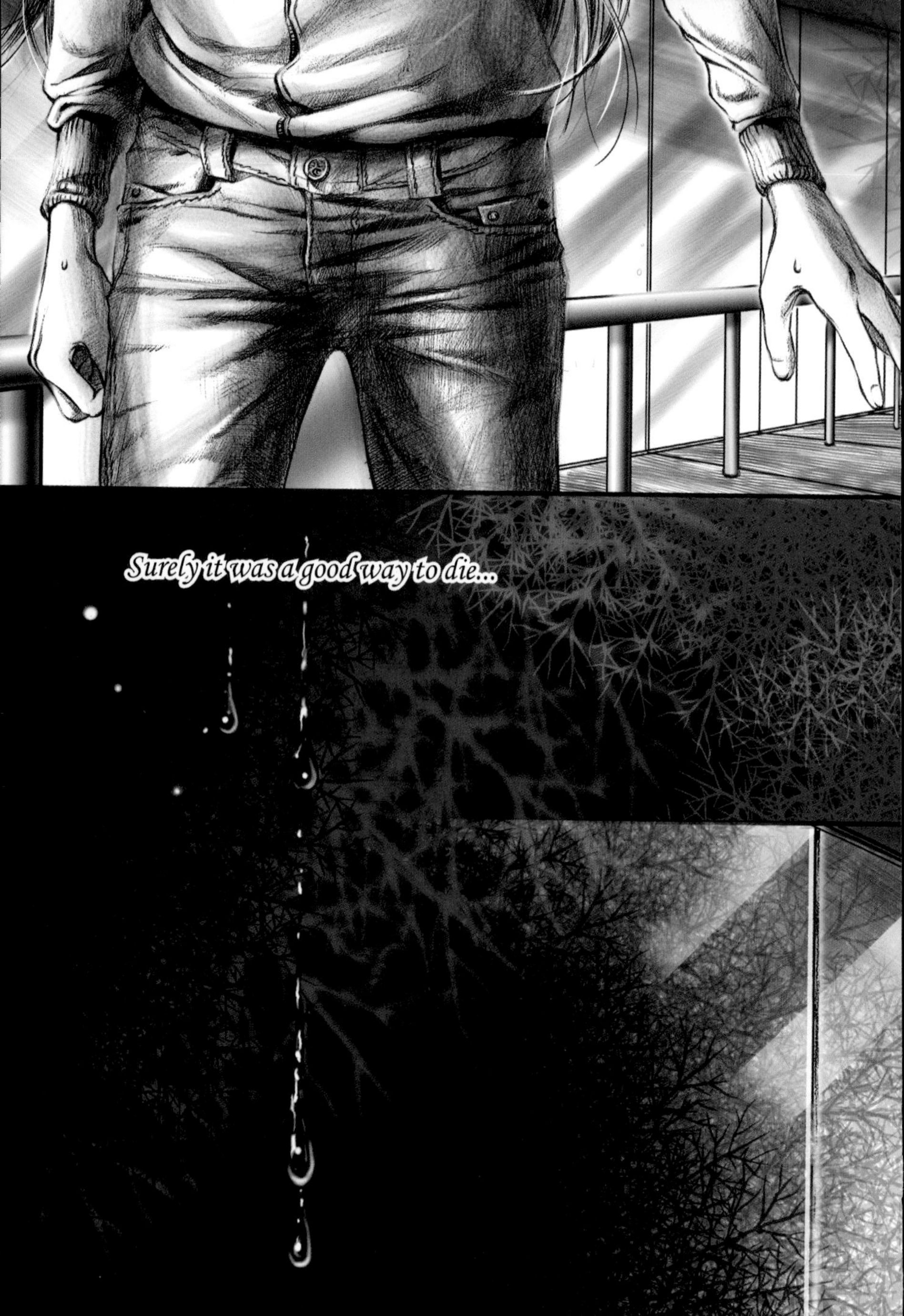
Surely it was a good way to die...

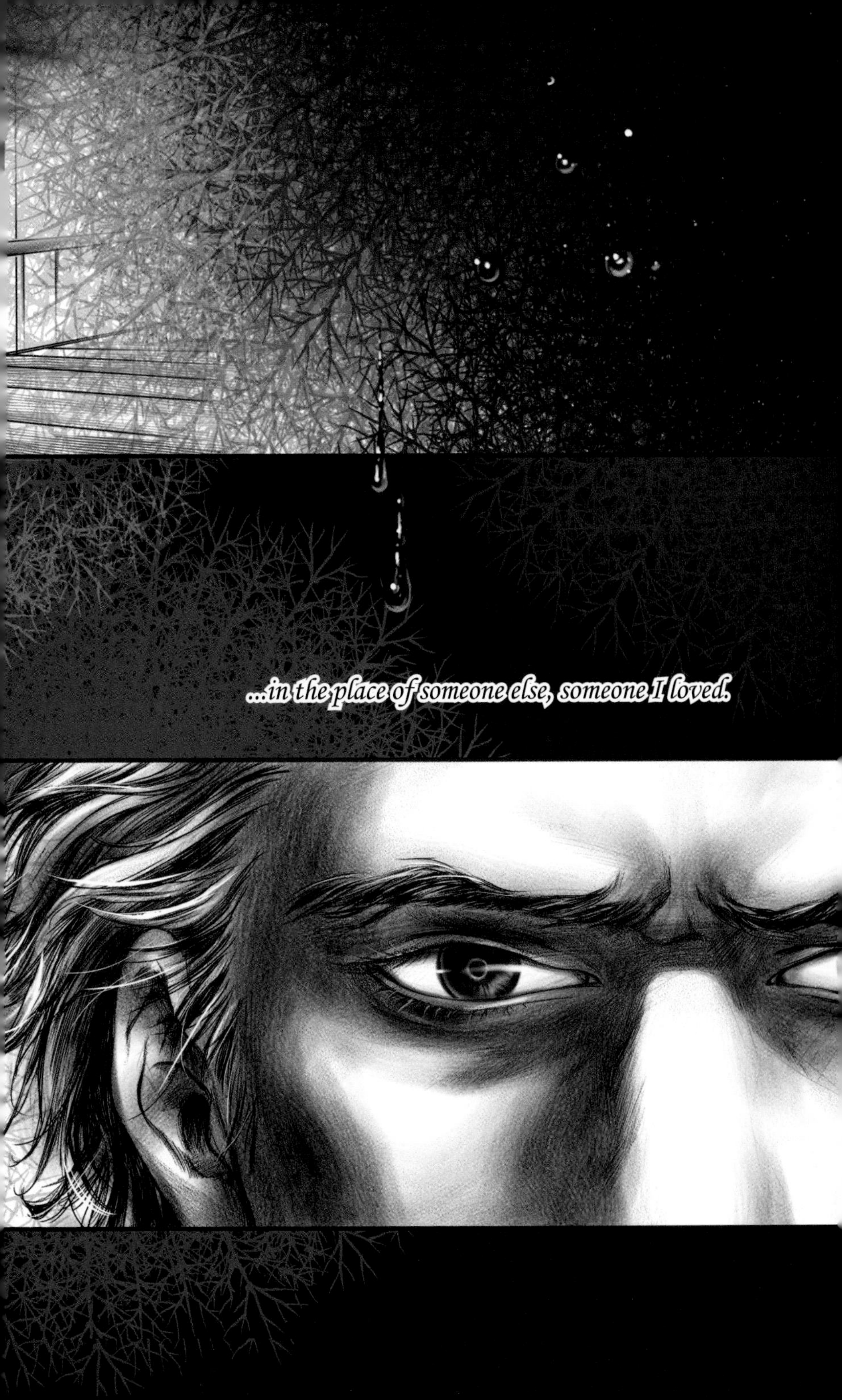
...in the place of someone else, someone I loved.

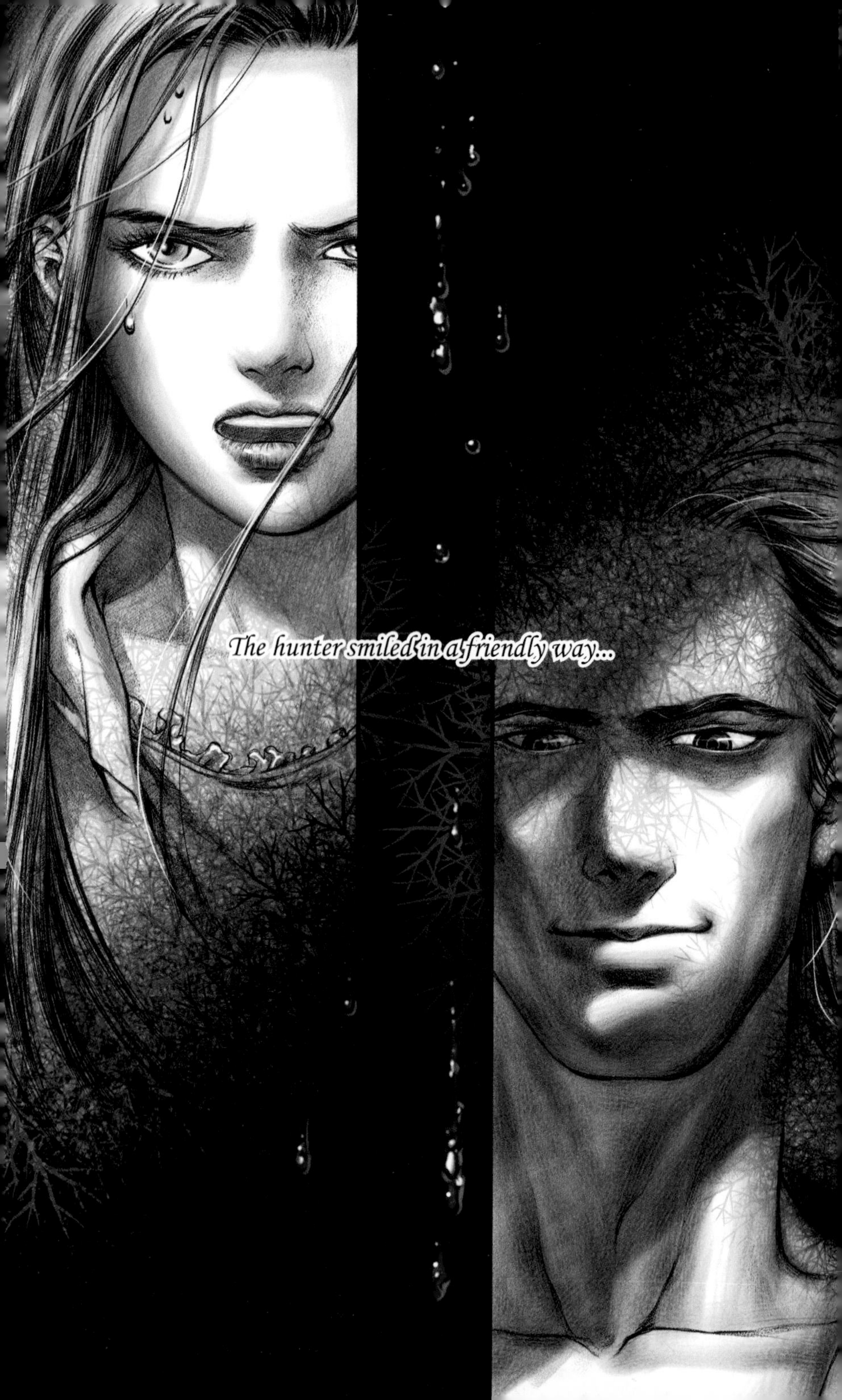
The hunter smiled in a friendly way...

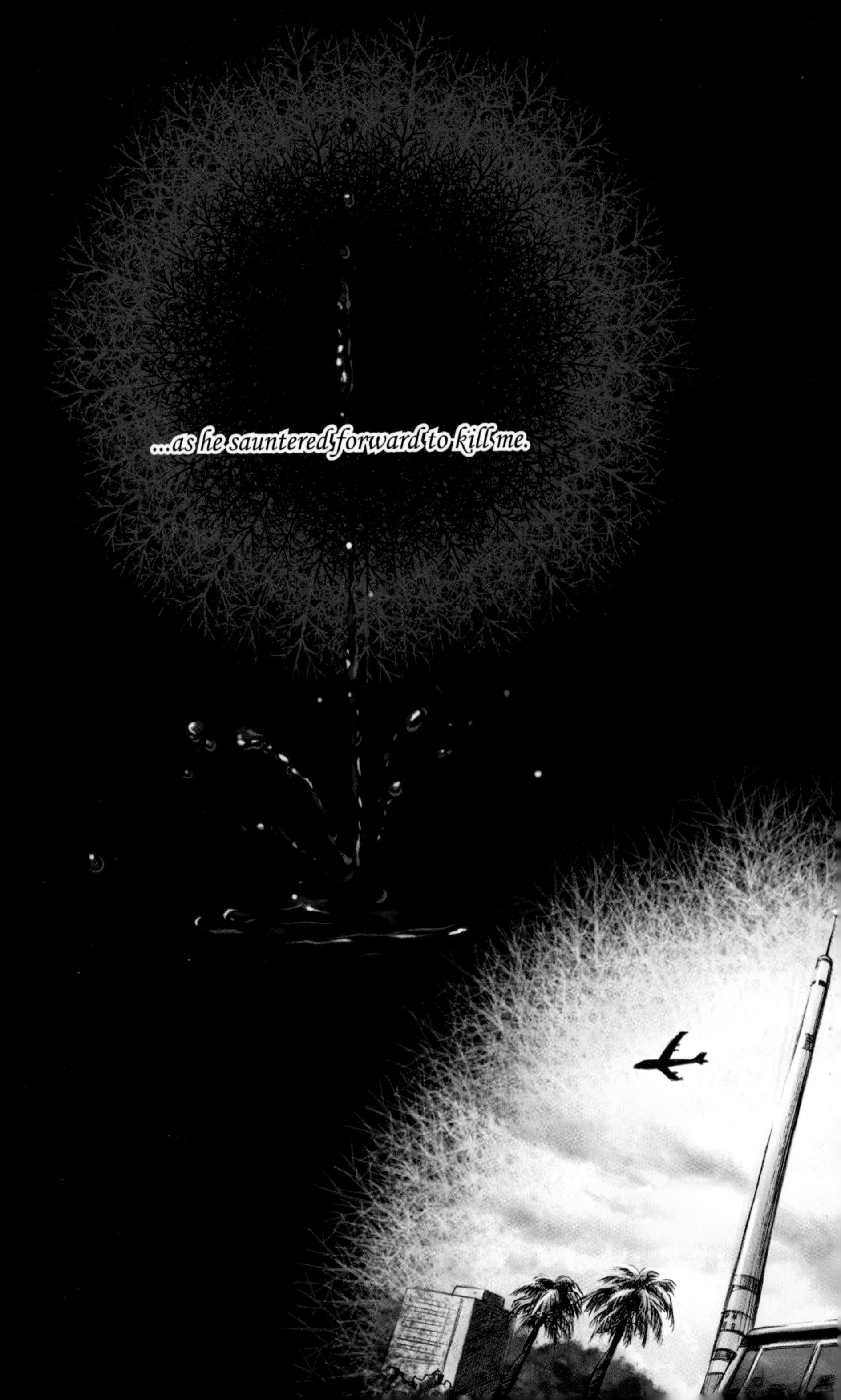
...as he sauntered forward to kill me.

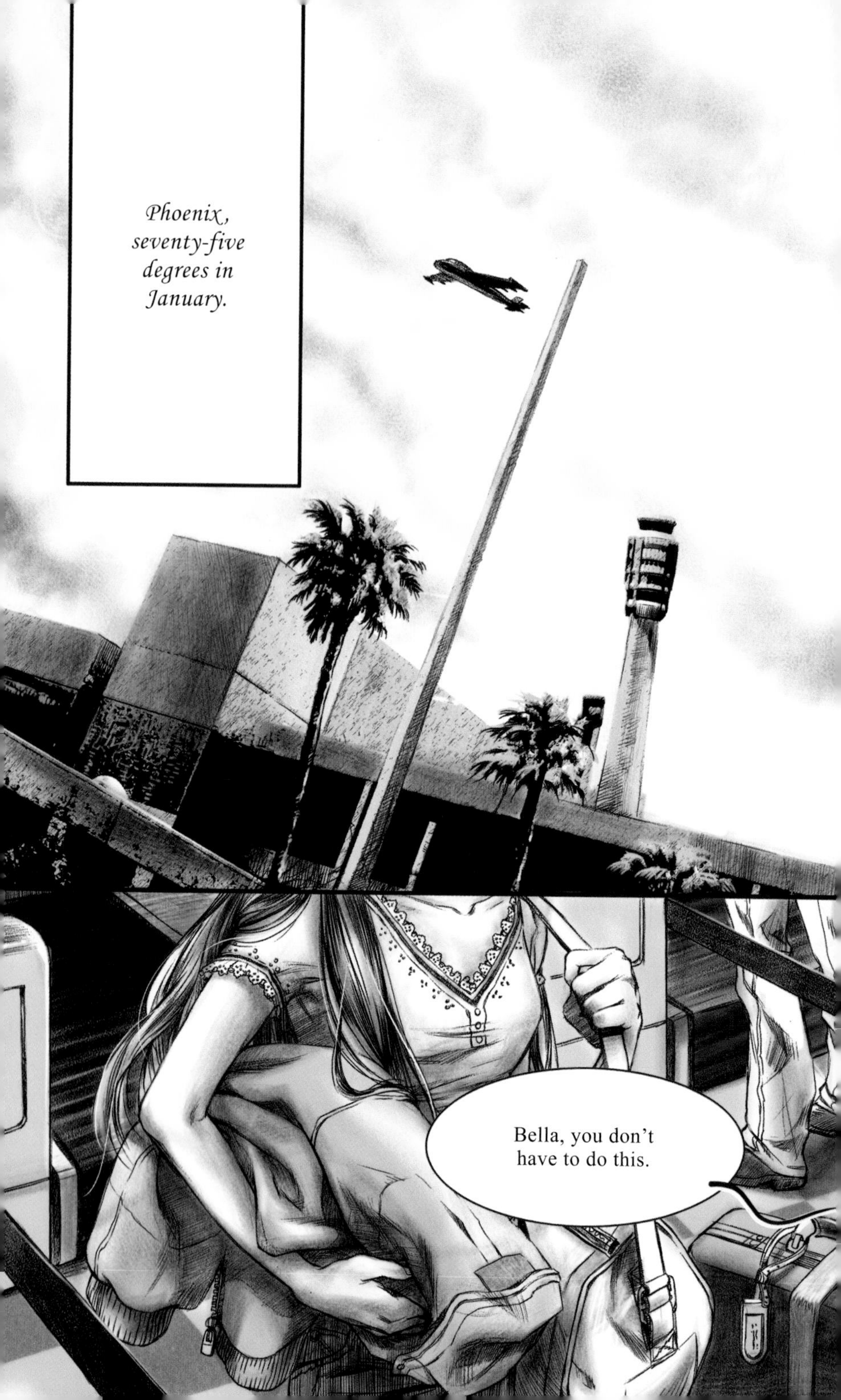
Phoenix, seventy-five degrees in January.
Bella, you don't have to do this.

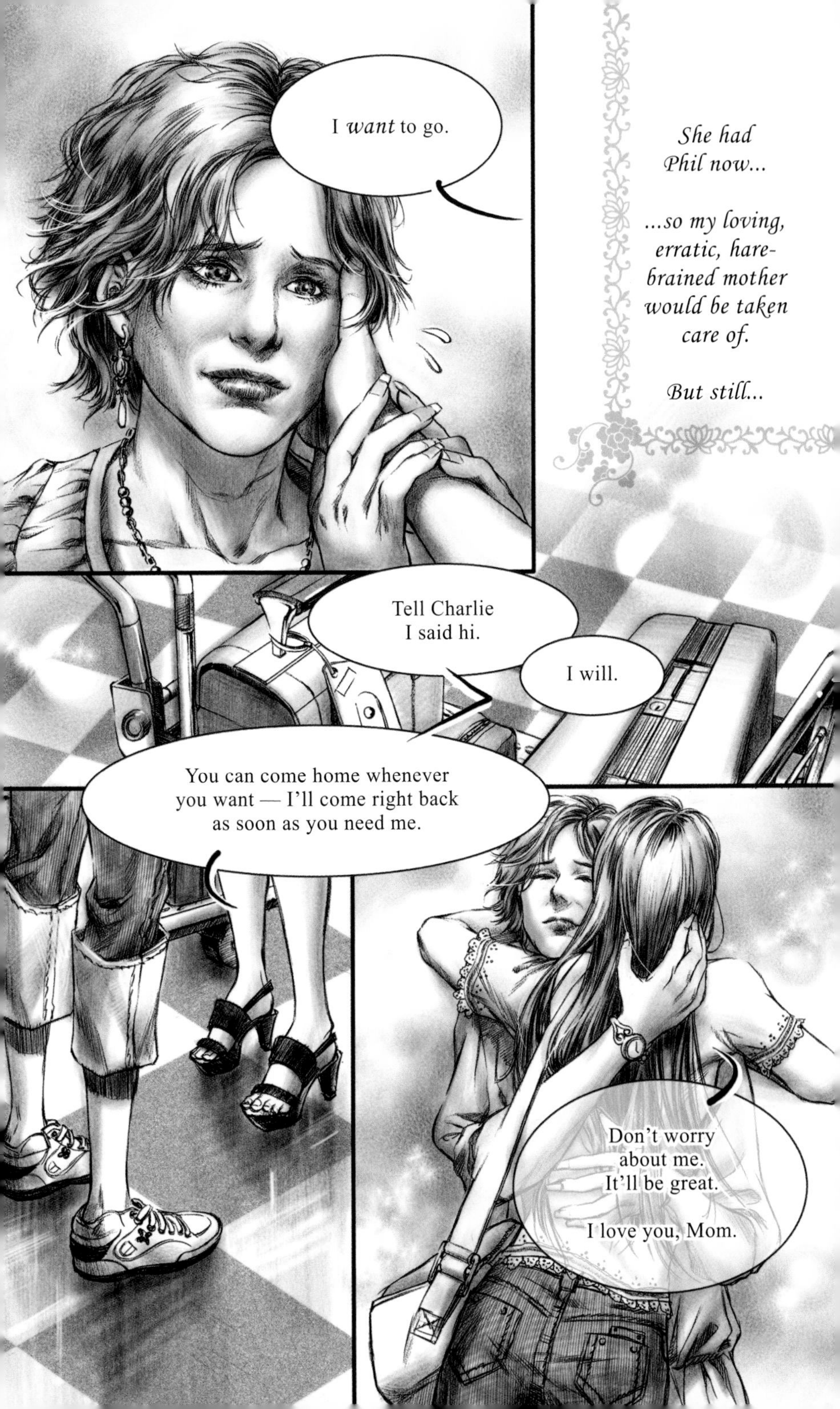
I *want* to go.
She had Phil now...
...so my loving, erratic, hare-brained mother would be taken care of.
But still...
Tell Charlie I said hi.
I will.
You can come home whenever you want — I'll come right back as soon as you need me.
Don't worry about me. It'll be great.
I love you, Mom.

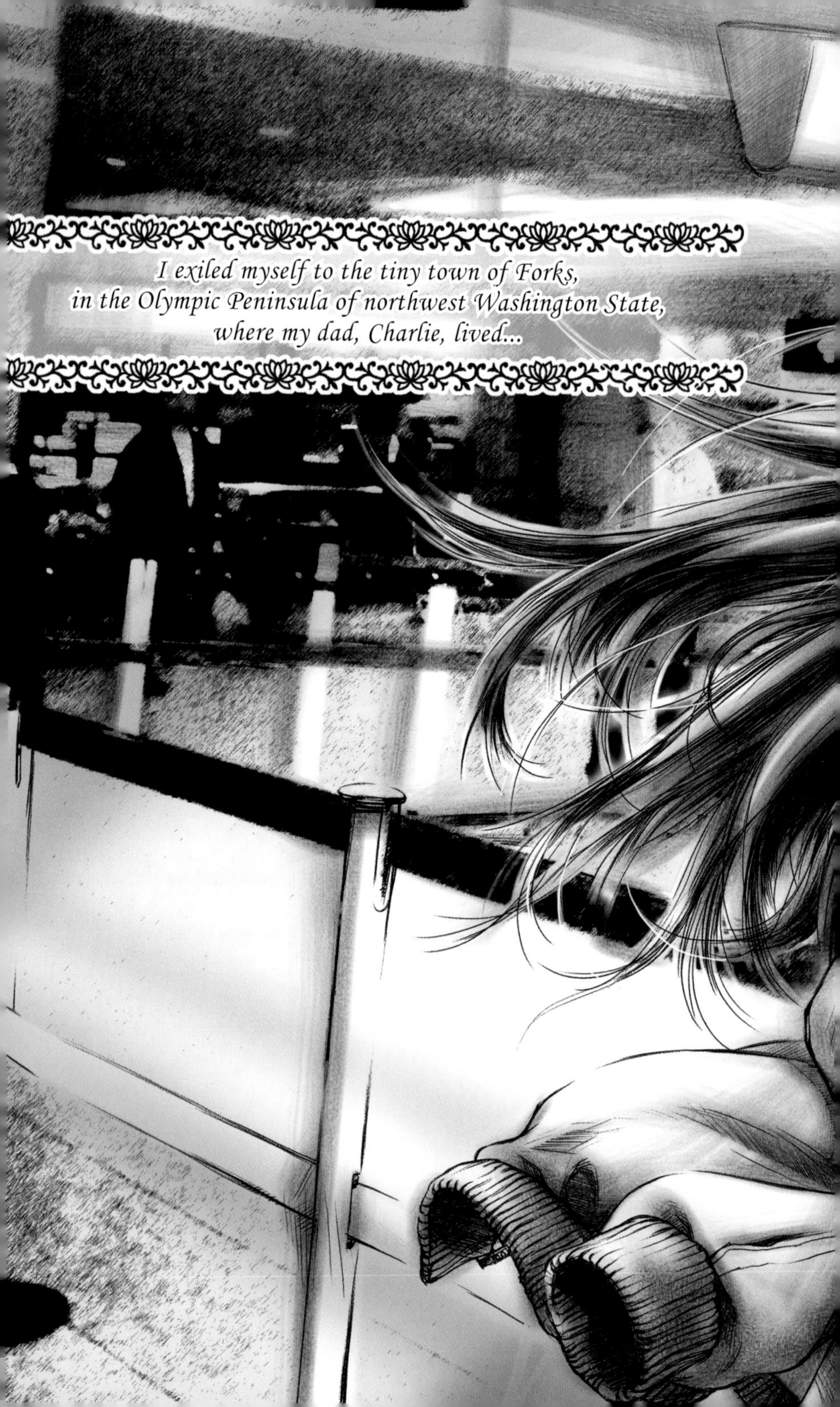
I exiled myself to the tiny town of Forks,
in the Olympic Peninsula of northwest Washington State,
where my dad, Charlie, lived...

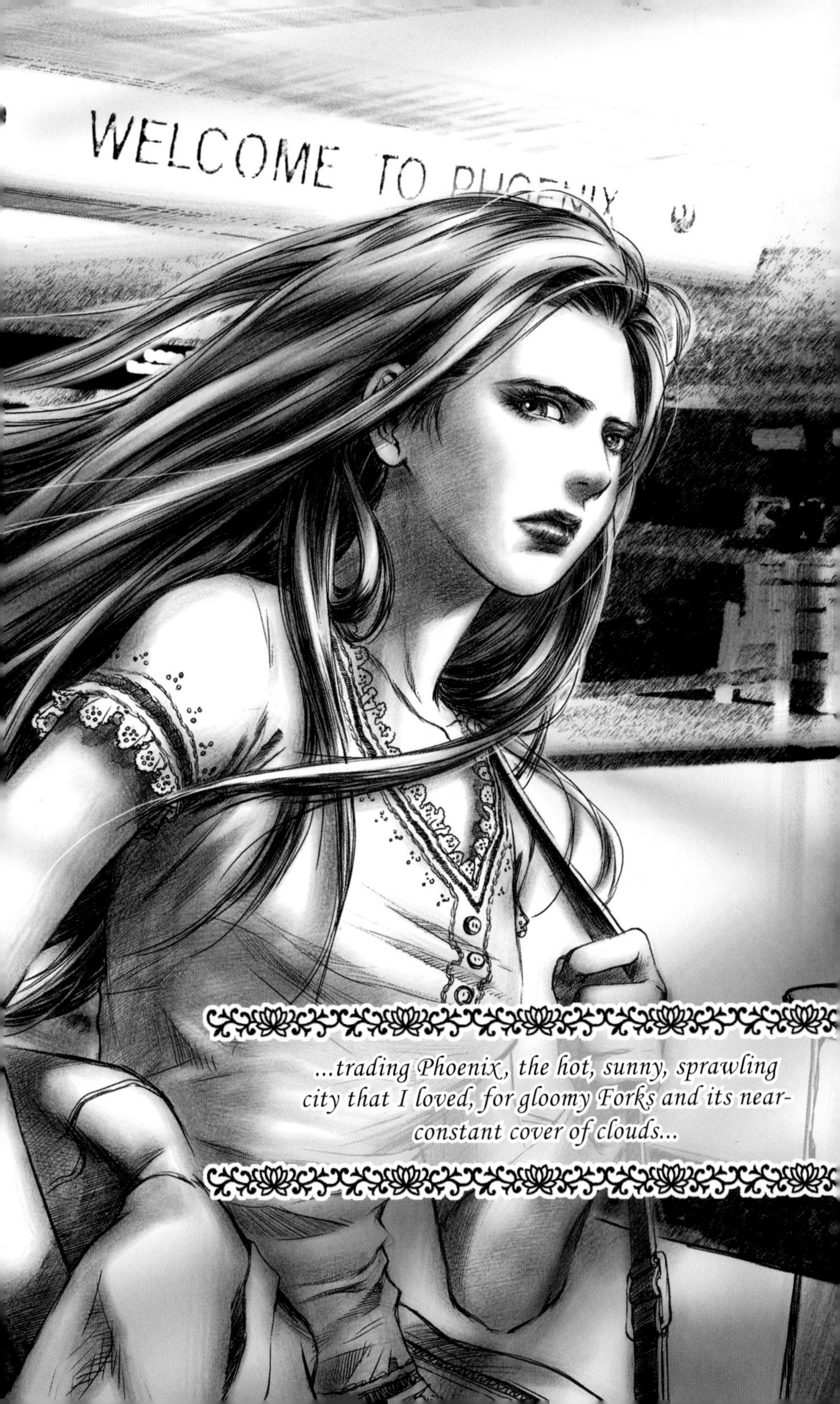
WELCOME TO
...trading Phoenix, the hot, sunny, sprawling city that I loved, for gloomy Forks and its near-constant cover of clouds...

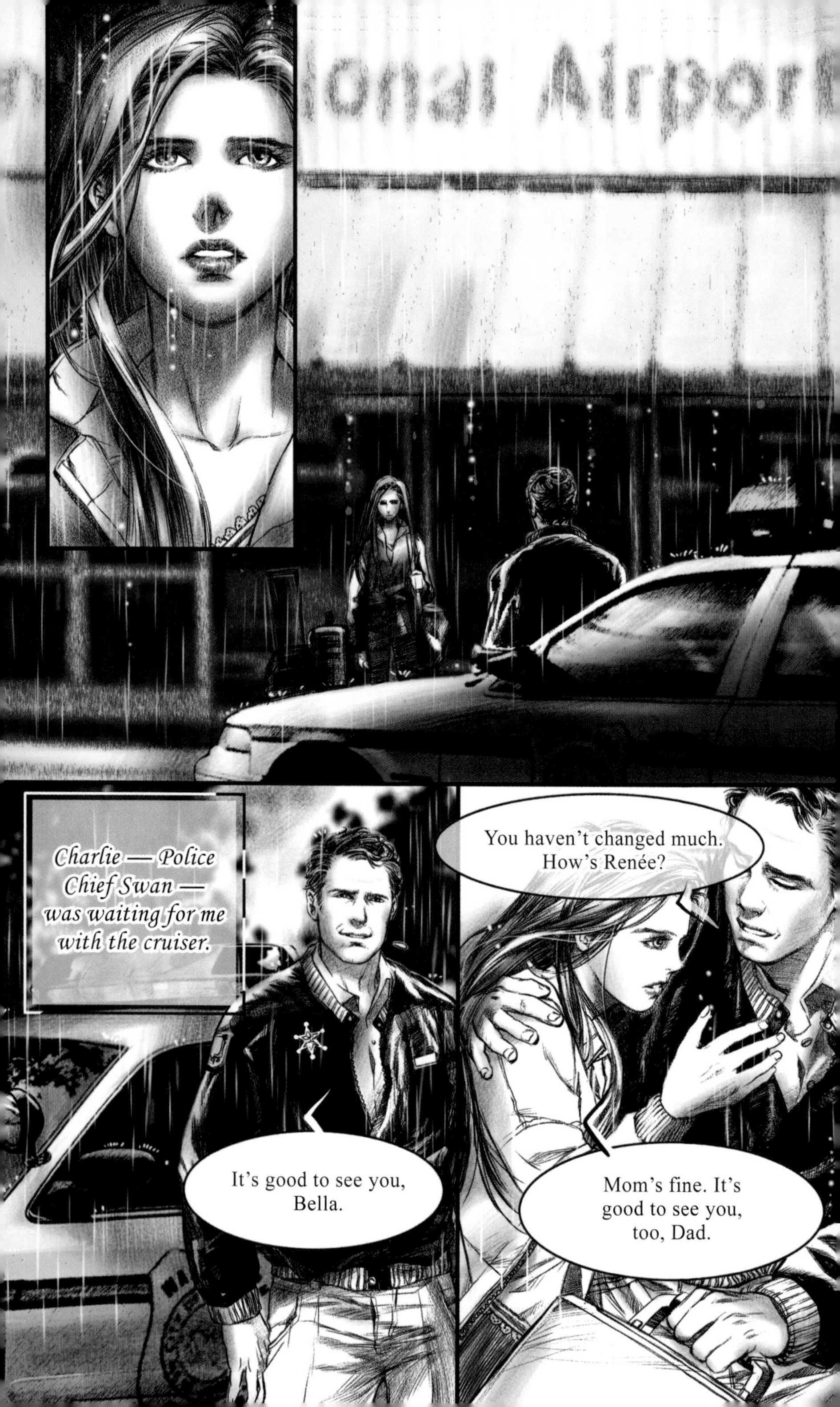
onal Airport
Charlie — Police Chief Swan — was waiting for me with the cruiser.
It's good to see you, Bella.
You haven't changed much. How's Renée?
Mom's fine. It's good to see you, too, Dad.

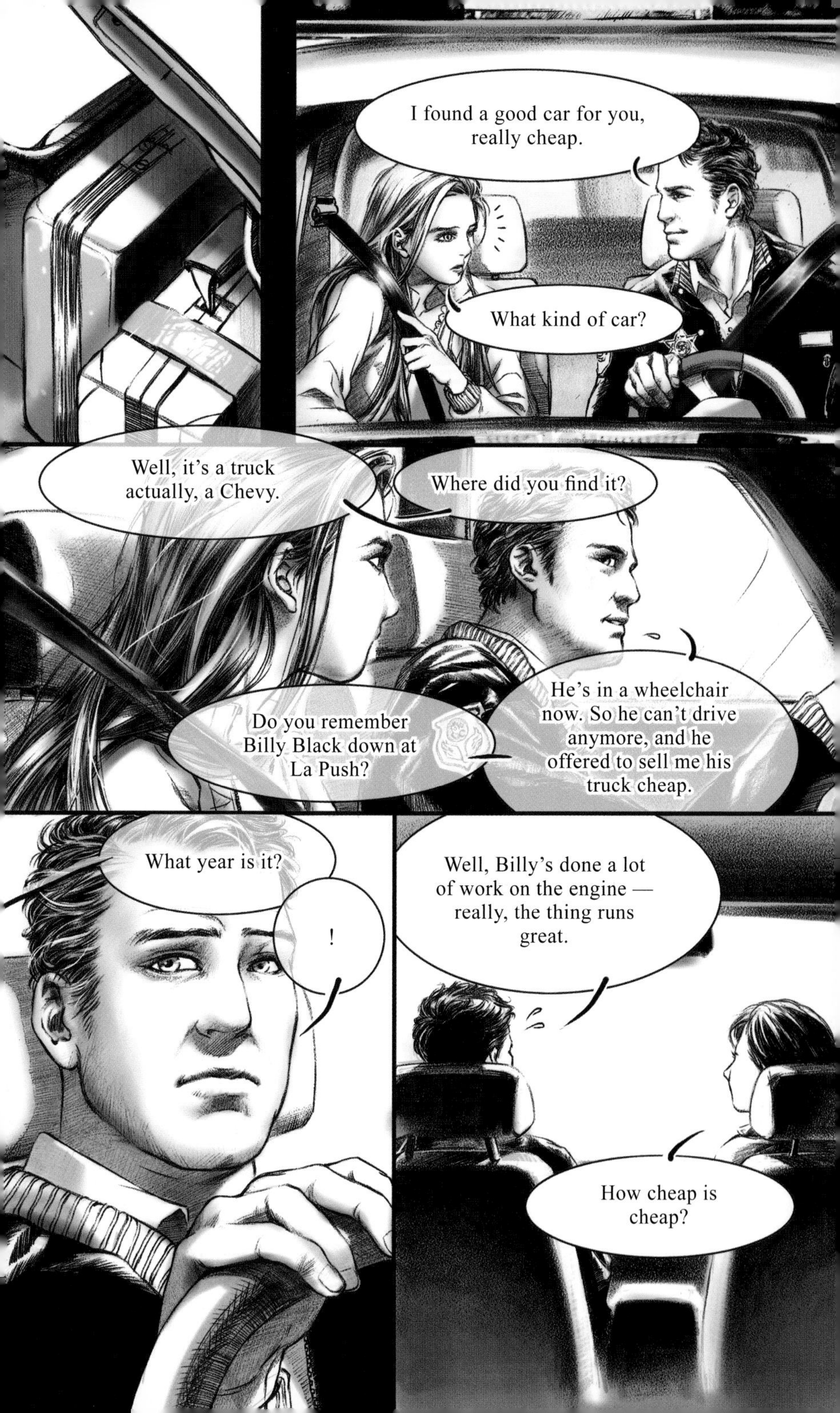
I found a good car for you, really cheap.
What kind of car?
Well, it's a truck actually, a Chevy.
Where did you find it?
Do you remember Billy Black down at La Push?
He's in a wheelchair now. So he can't drive anymore, and he offered to sell me his truck cheap.
What year is it?
!
Well, Billy's done a lot of work on the engine — really, the thing runs great.
How cheap is cheap?

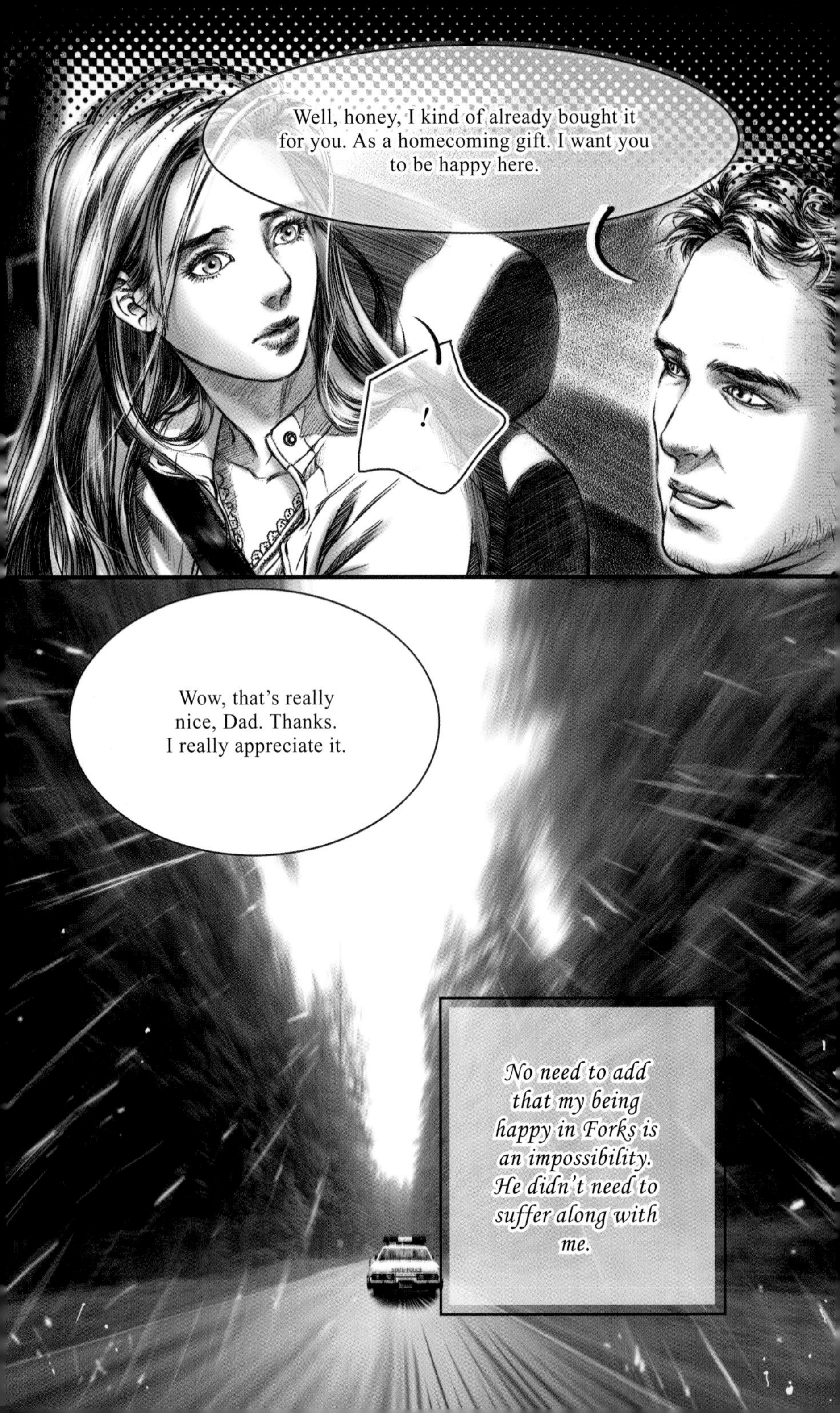
Well, honey, I kind of already bought it for you. As a homecoming gift. I want you to be happy here.
!
Wow, that's really nice, Dad. Thanks. I really appreciate it.
No need to add that my being happy in Forks is an impossibility. He didn't need to suffer along with me.

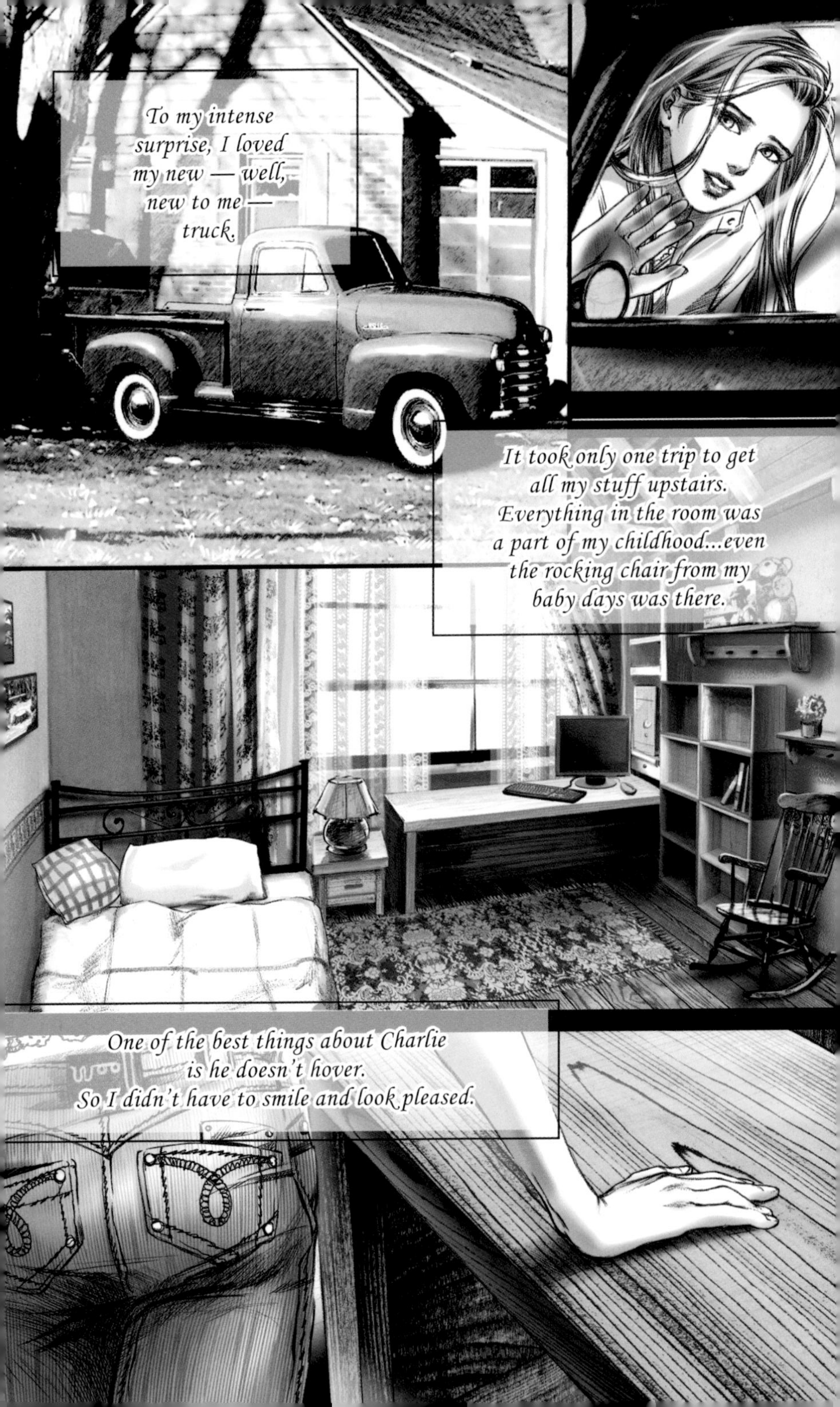
To my intense surprise, I loved my new — well, new to me — truck.
It took only one trip to get all my stuff upstairs. Everything in the room was a part of my childhood...even the rocking chair from my baby days was there.
One of the best things about Charlie is he doesn't hover. So I didn't have to smile and look pleased.

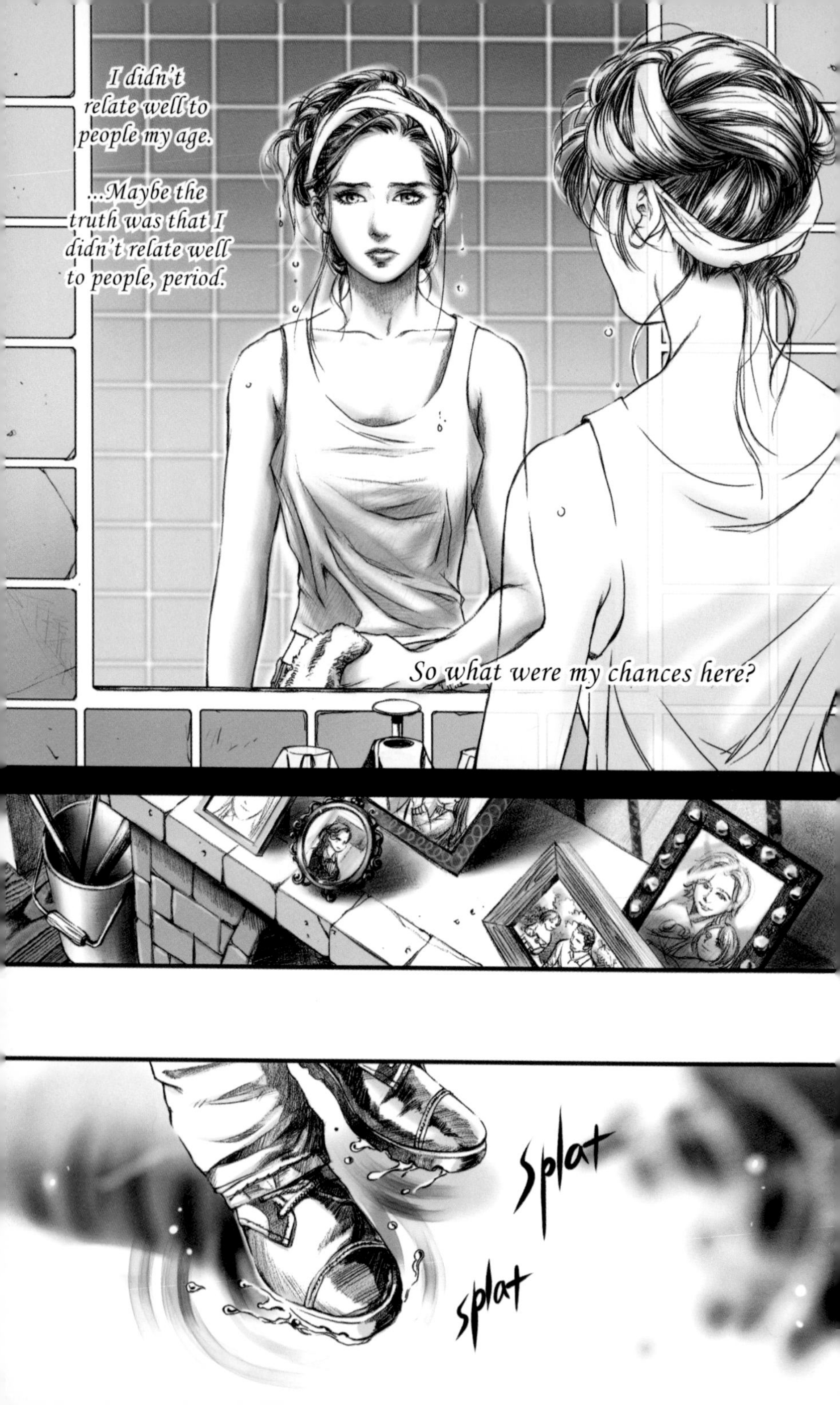
I didn't relate well to people my age.
...Maybe the truth was that I didn't relate well to people, period.
So what were my chances here?
Splat
splat

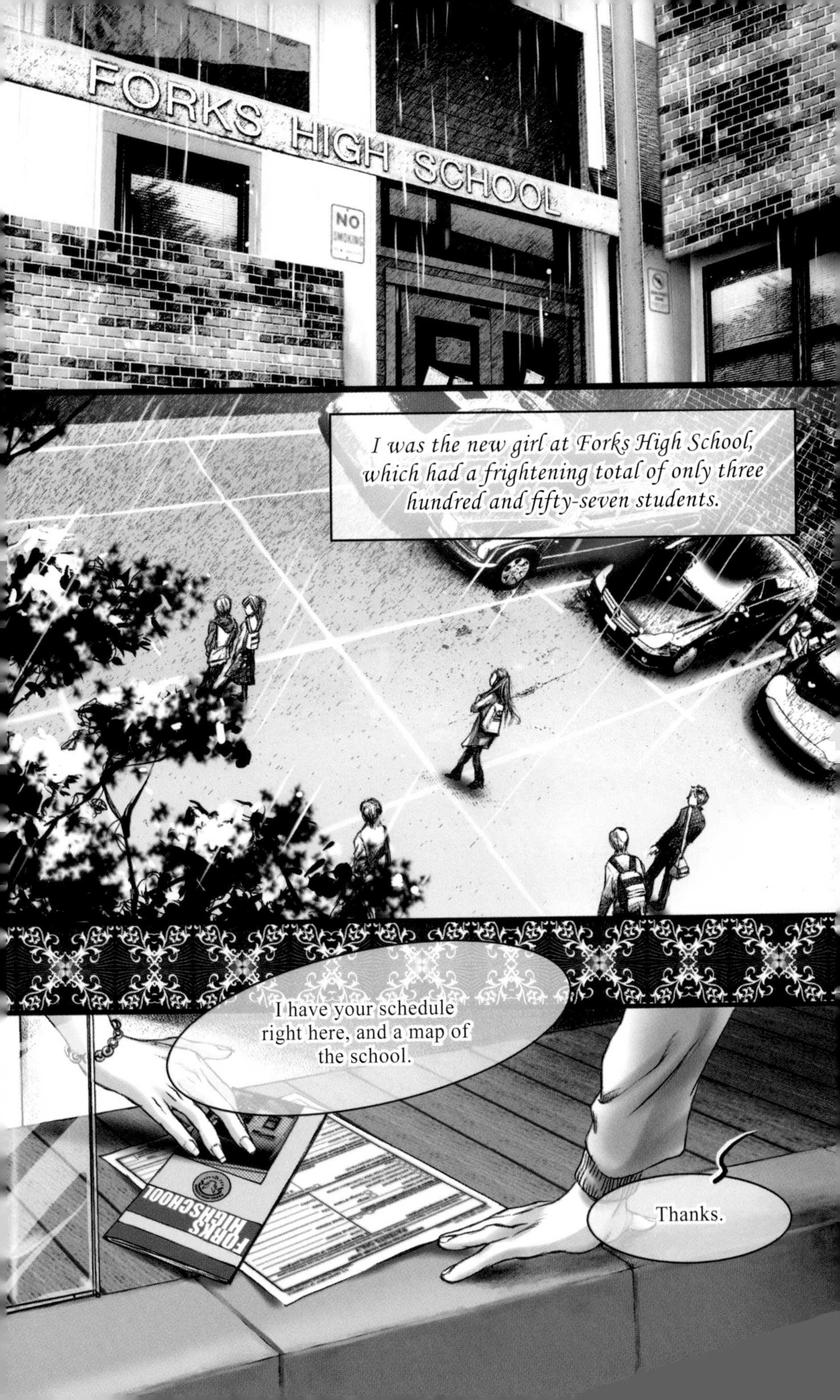
FORKS HIGH SCHOOL
NO SMOKING
I was the new girl at Forks High School, which had a frightening total of only three hundred and fifty-seven students.
I have your schedule right here, and a map of the school.
Thanks.

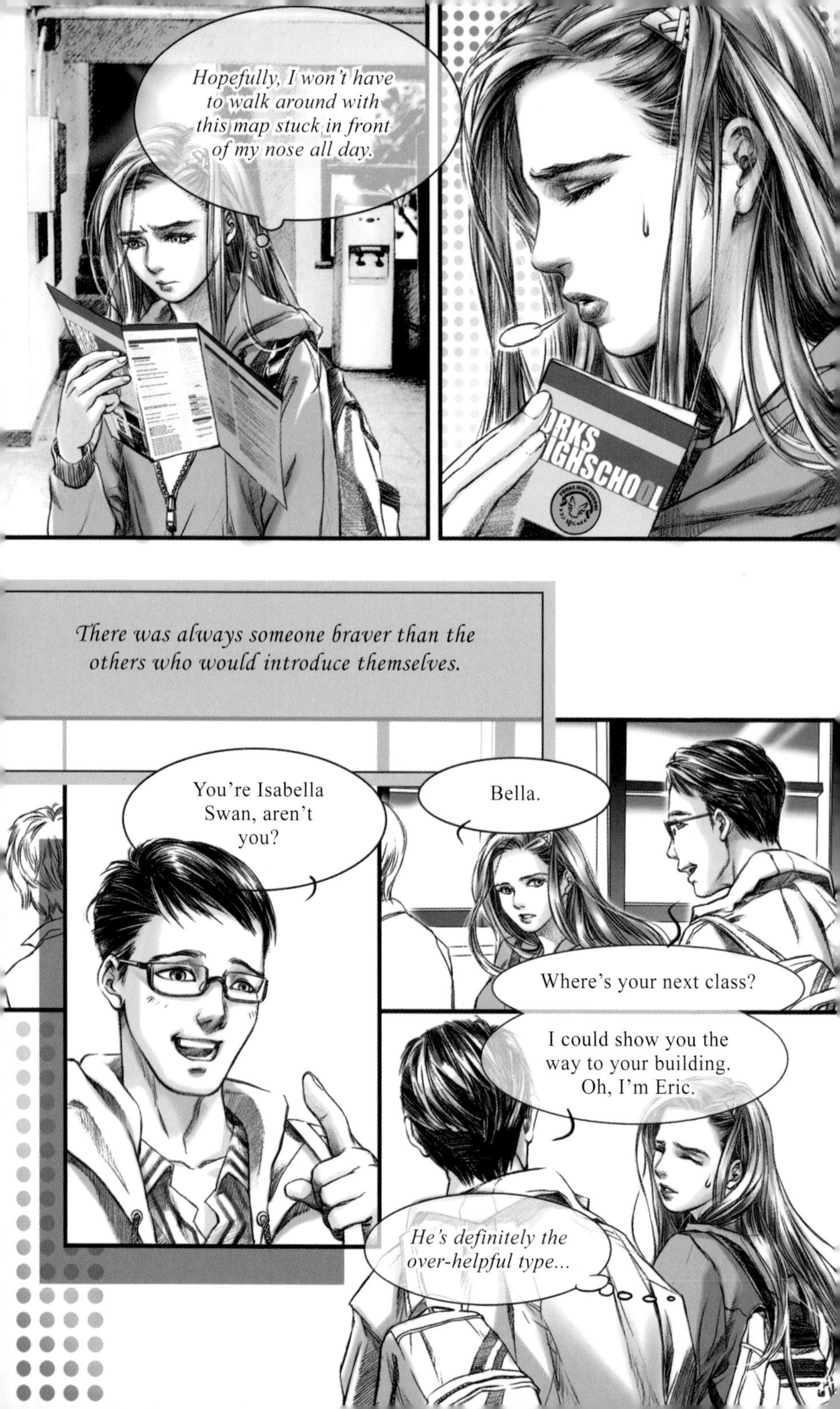

Hopefully, I won't have to walk around with this map stuck in front of my nose all day.
FORKS HIGHSCHOOL
There was always someone braver than the others who would introduce themselves.
You're Isabella Swan, aren't you?
Bella.
Where's your next class?
I could show you the way to your building. Oh, I'm Eric.
He's definitely the over-helpful type...

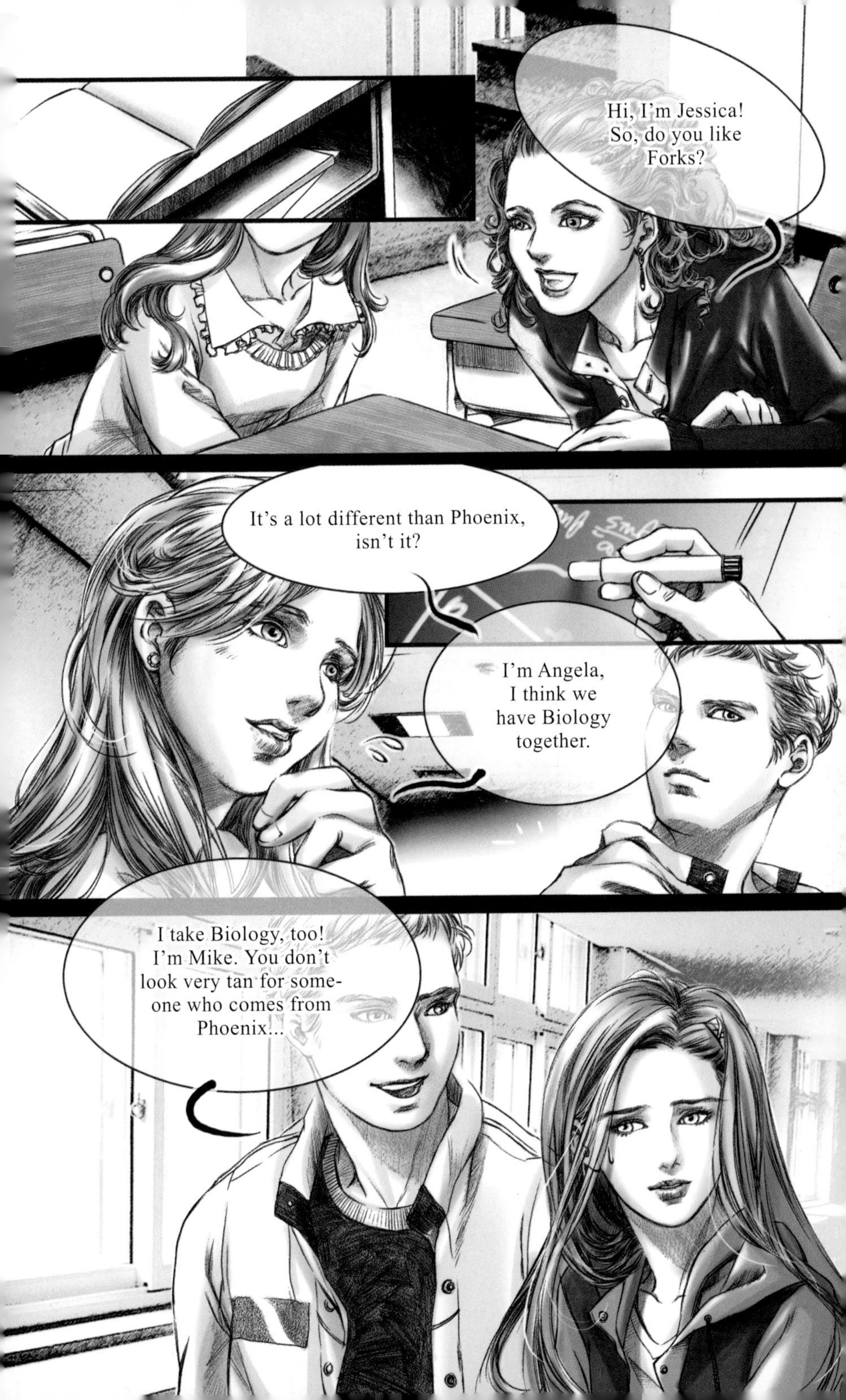
Hi, I'm Jessica! So, do you like Forks?
It's a lot different than Phoenix, isn't it?
I'm Angela, I think we have Biology together.
I take Biology, too! I'm Mike. You don't look very tan for some-one who comes from Phoenix...

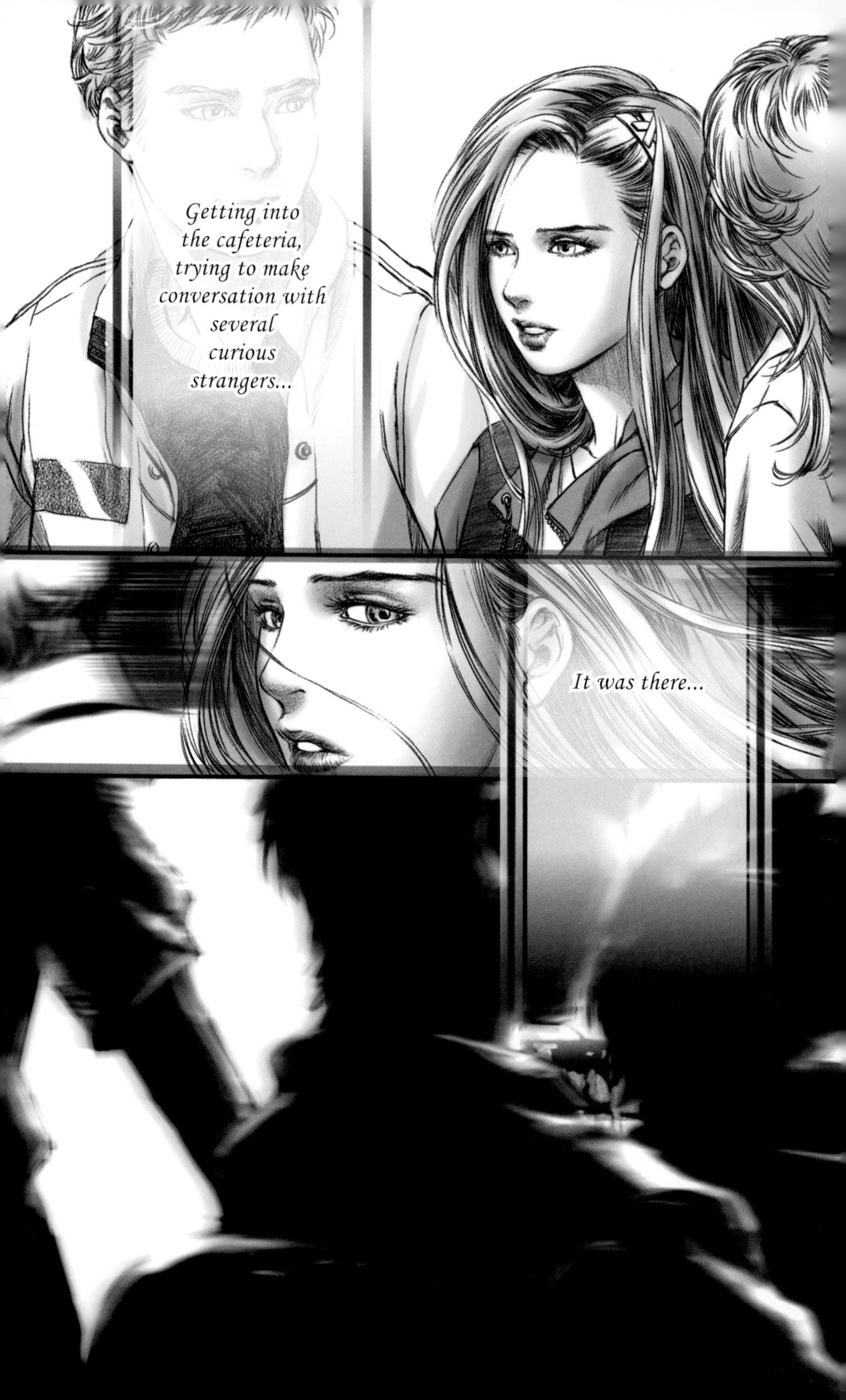
Getting into the cafeteria, trying to make conversation with several curious strangers...
It was there...

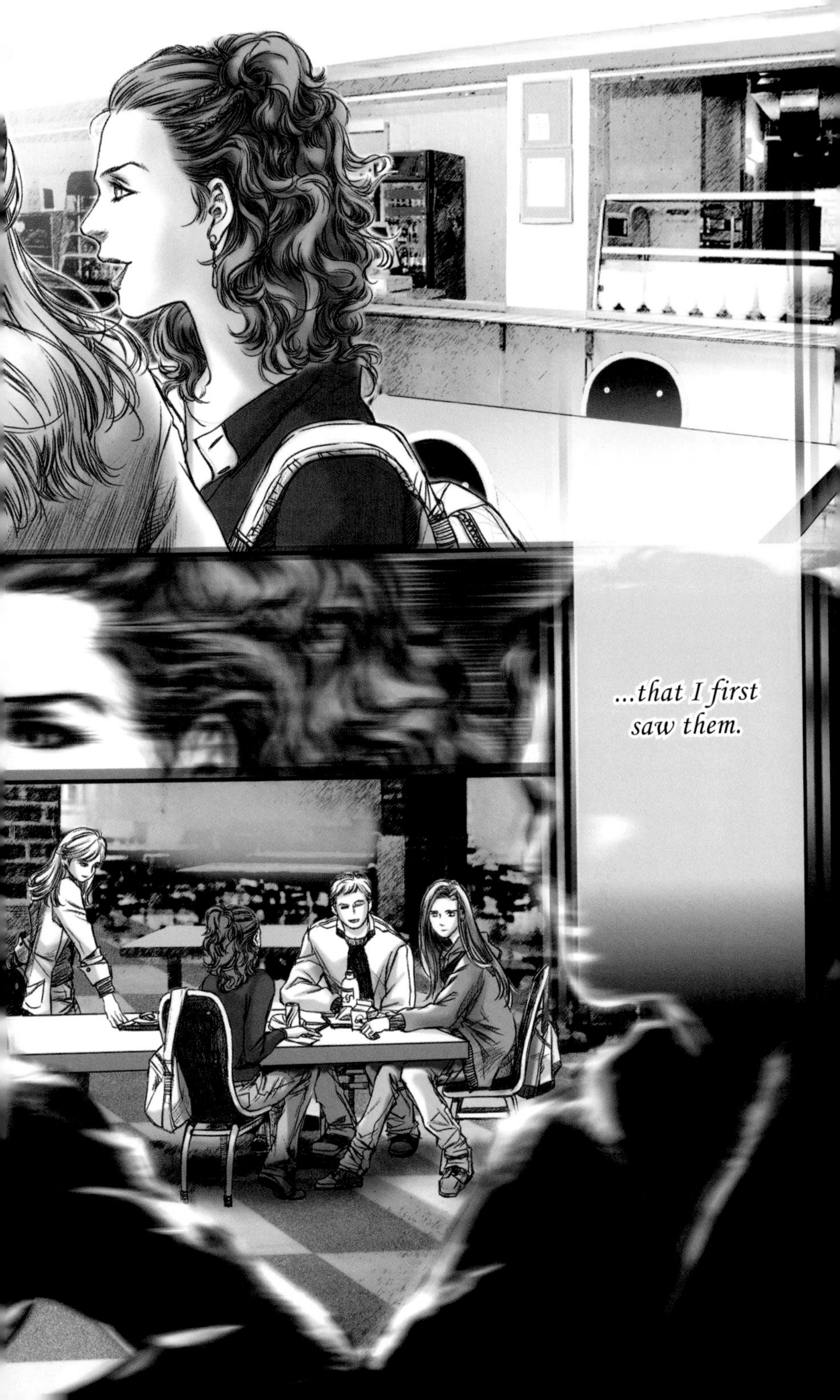
...that I first
saw them.

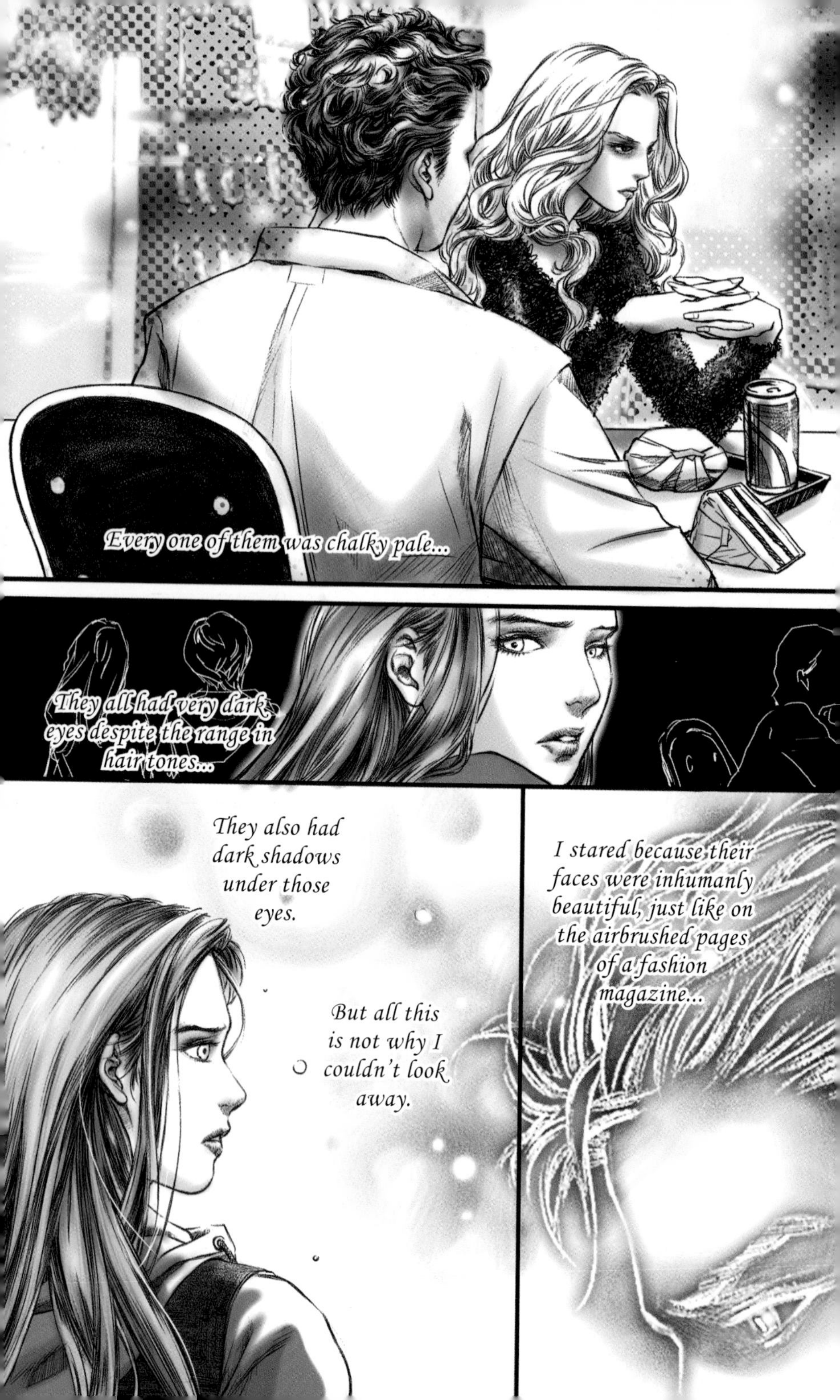
Every one of them was chalky pale...
They all had very dark eyes despite the range in hair tones...
They also had dark shadows under those eyes.
But all this is not why I couldn't look away.
I stared because their faces were inhumanly beautiful, just like on the airbrushed pages of a fashion magazine...

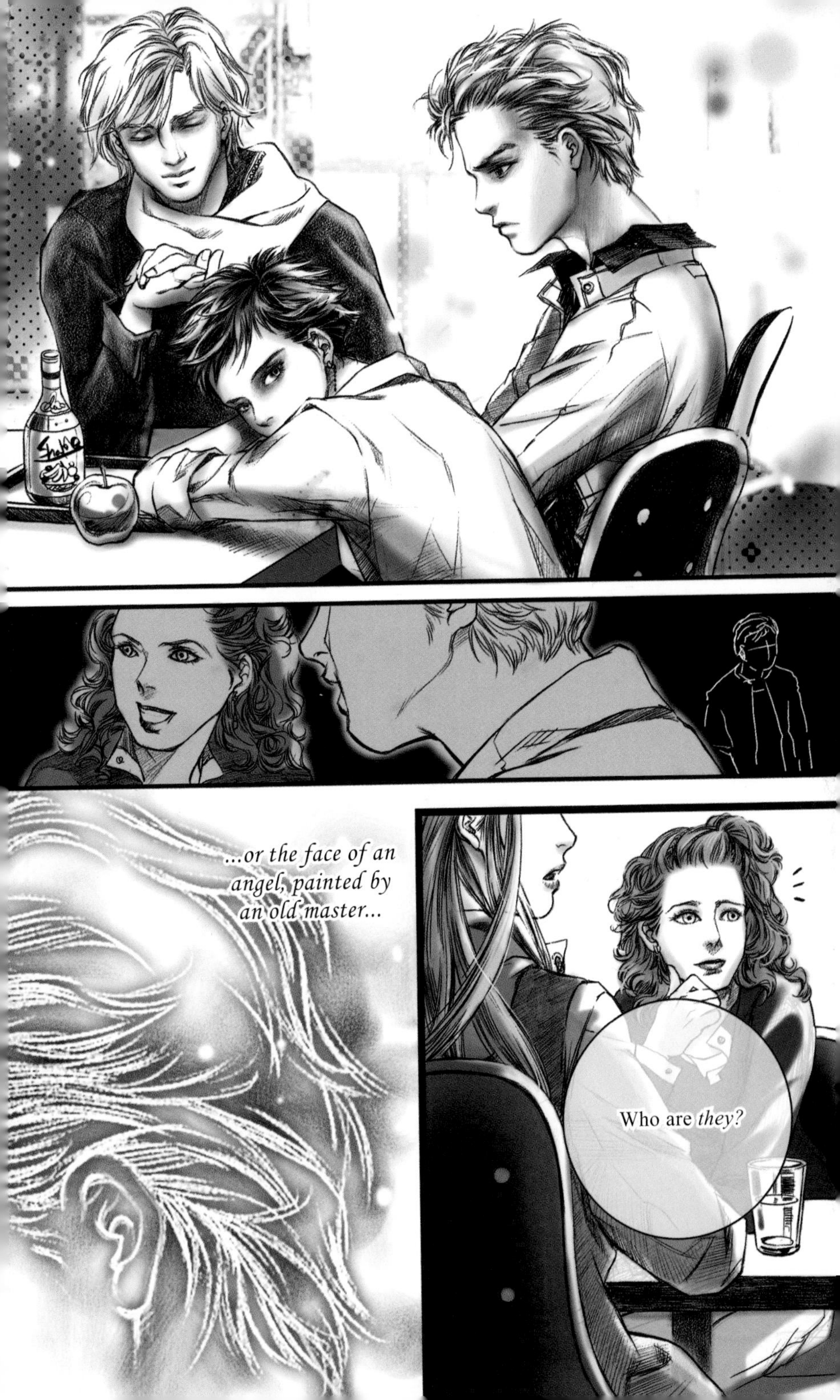
...or the face of an
angel, painted by
an old master...
Who are *they?*

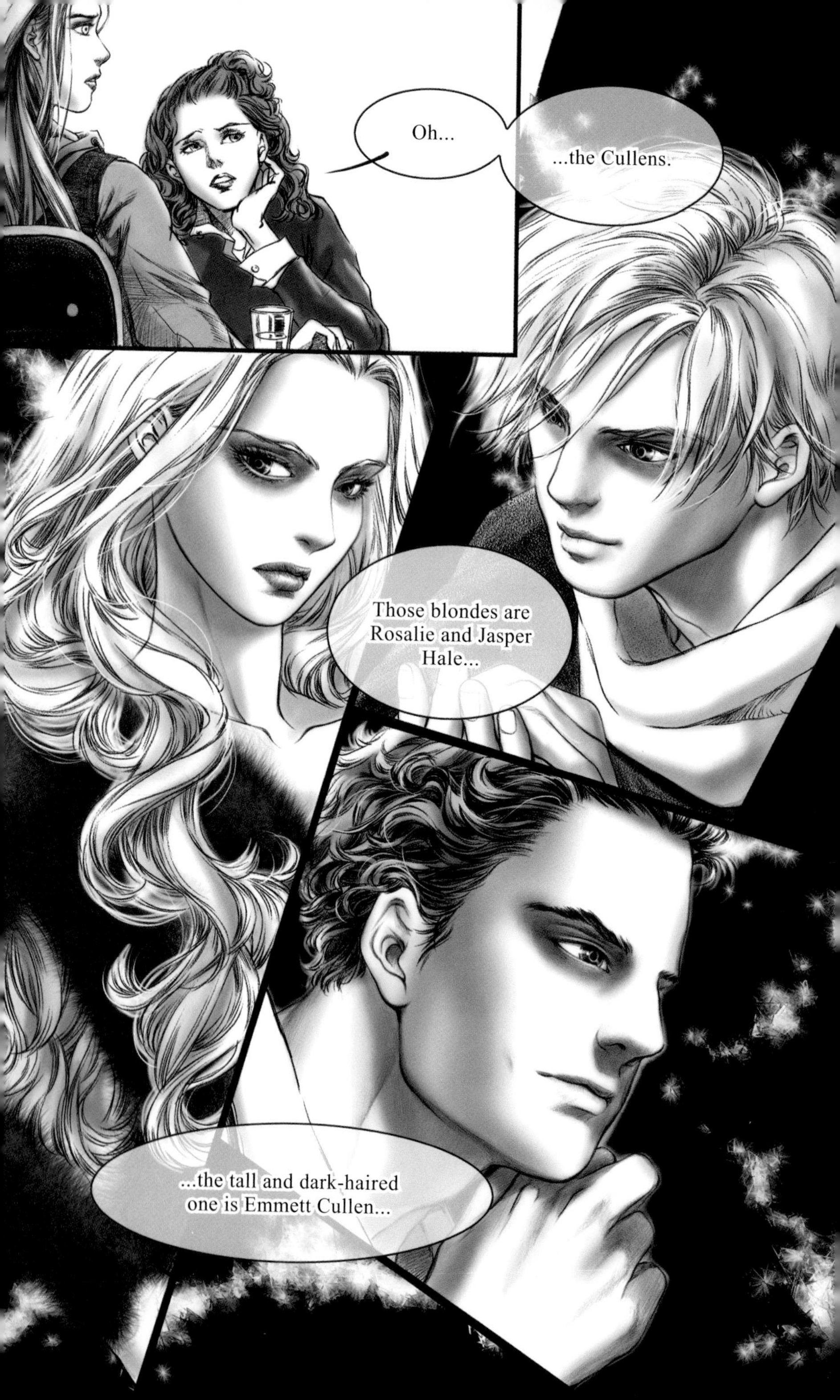

Oh...
...the Cullens.
Those blondes are Rosalie and Jasper Hale...
...the tall and dark-haired one is Emmett Cullen...

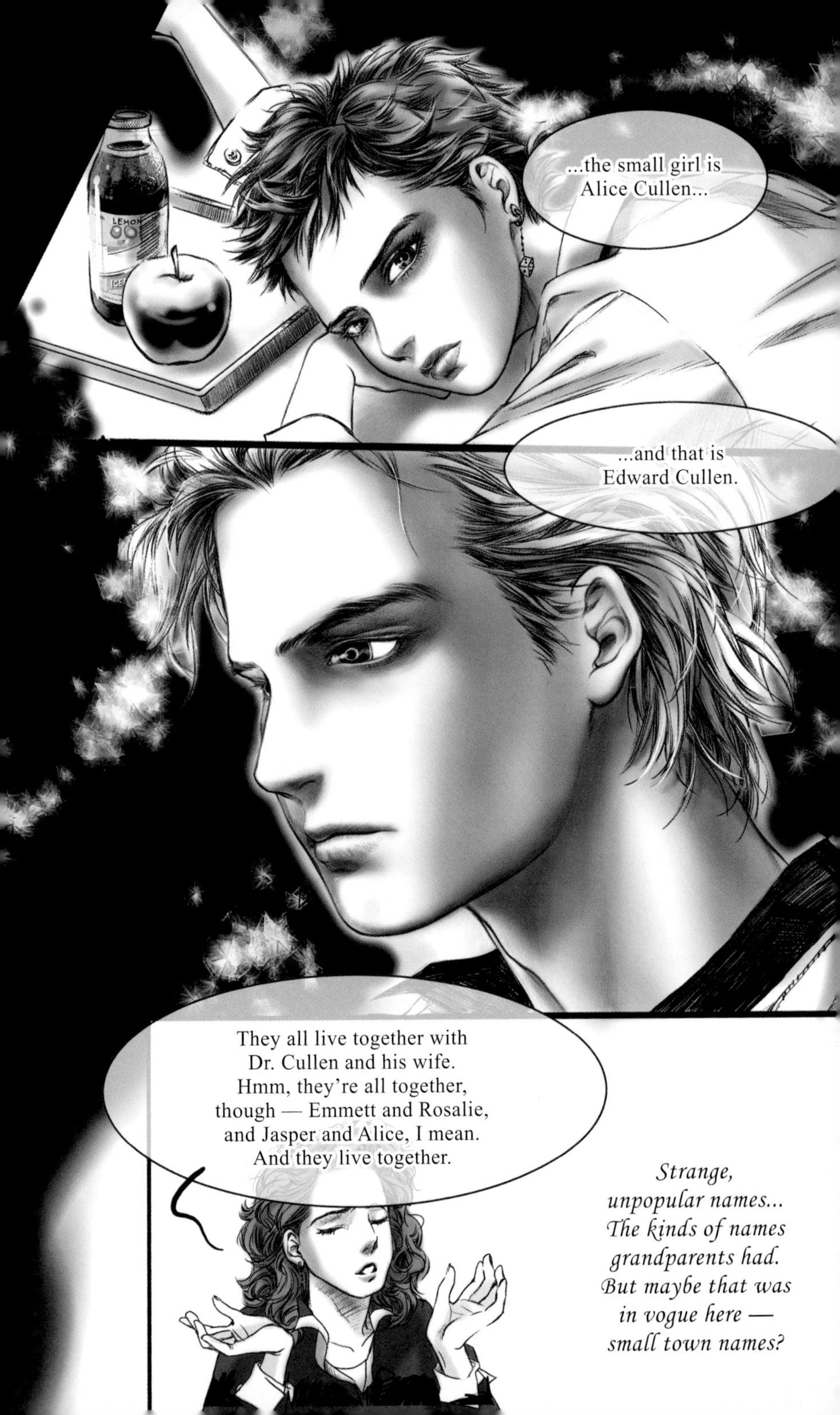
...the small girl is Alice Cullen...
...and that is Edward Cullen.
They all live together with Dr. Cullen and his wife. Hmm, they're all together, though — Emmett and Rosalie, and Jasper and Alice, I mean. And they live together.
Strange, unpopular names... The kinds of names grandparents had. But maybe that was in vogue here — small town names?

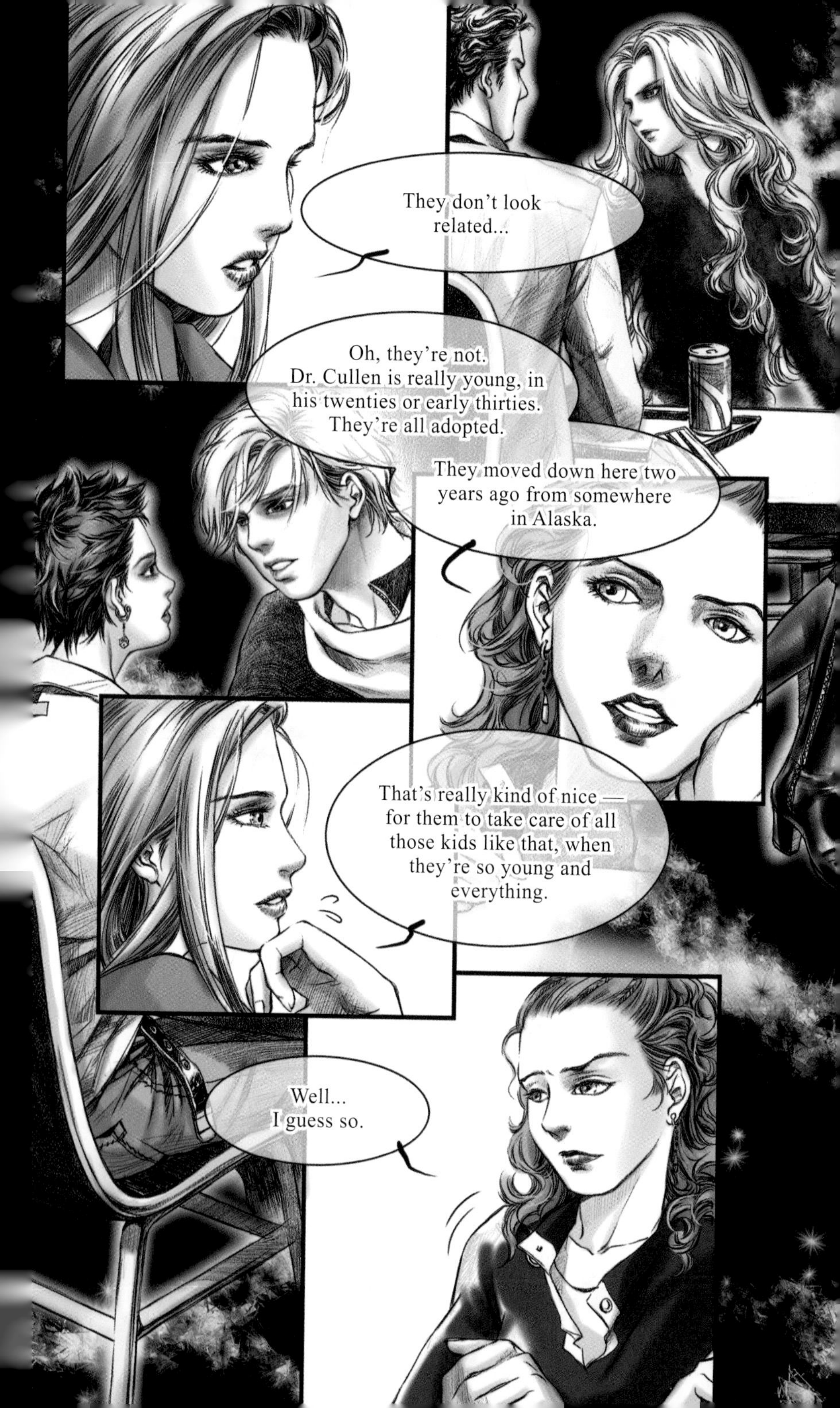
They don't look related...
Oh, they're not. Dr. Cullen is really young, in his twenties or early thirties. They're all adopted.
They moved down here two years ago from somewhere in Alaska.
That's really kind of nice — for them to take care of all those kids like that, when they're so young and everything.
Well... I guess so.

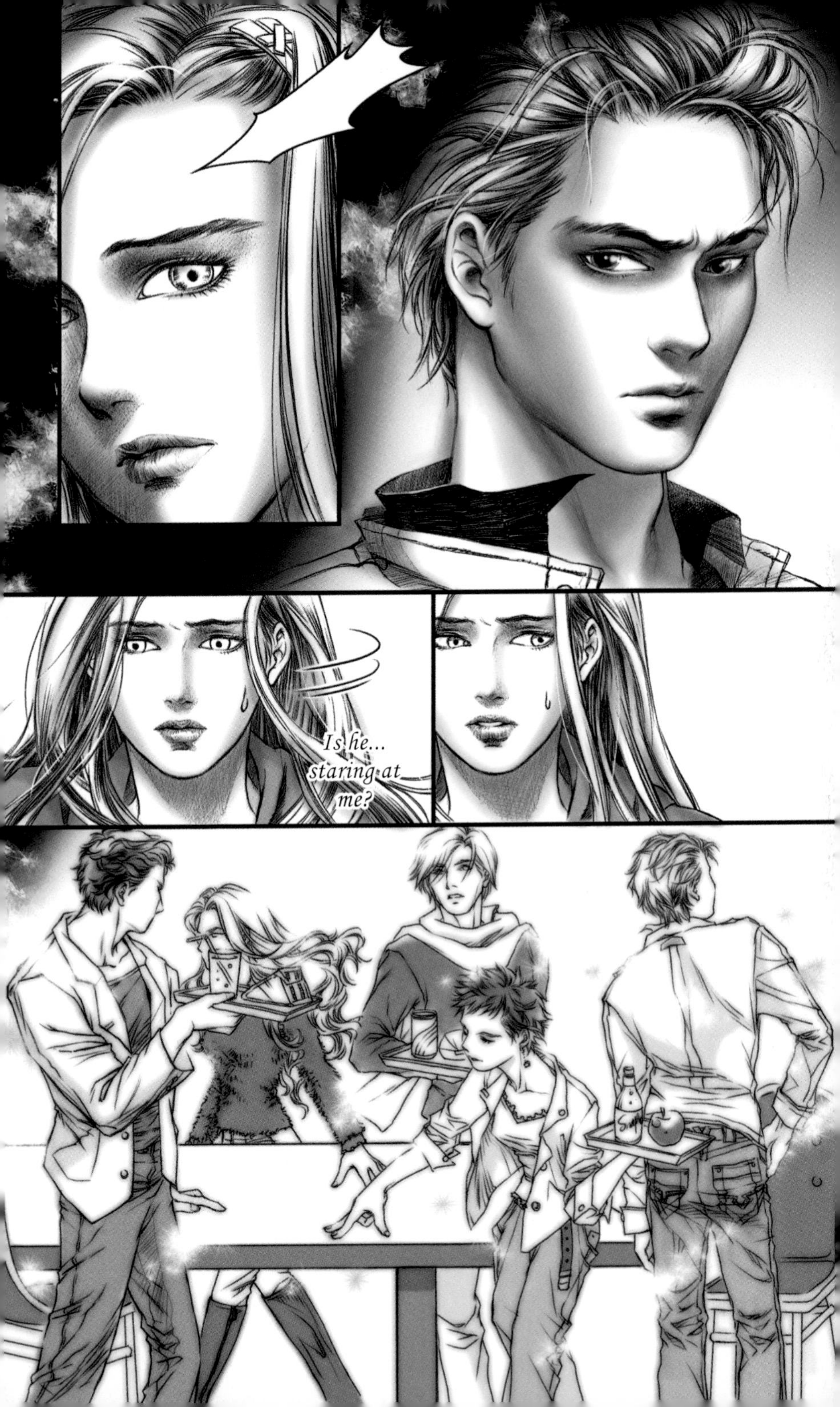
Is he...
staring at
me?

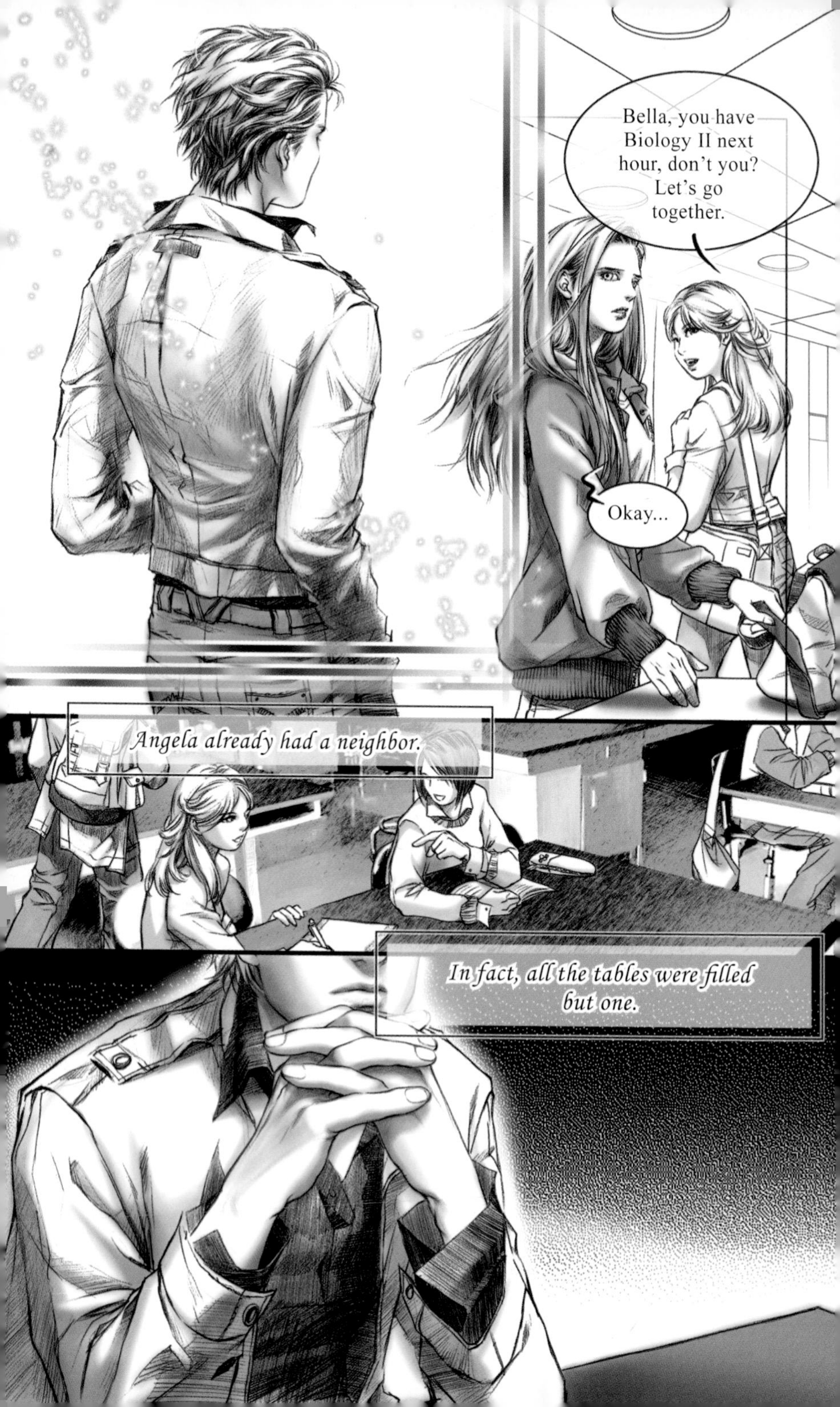
Bella, you have Biology II next hour, don't you? Let's go together.
Okay...
Angela already had a neighbor.
In fact, all the tables were filled but one.

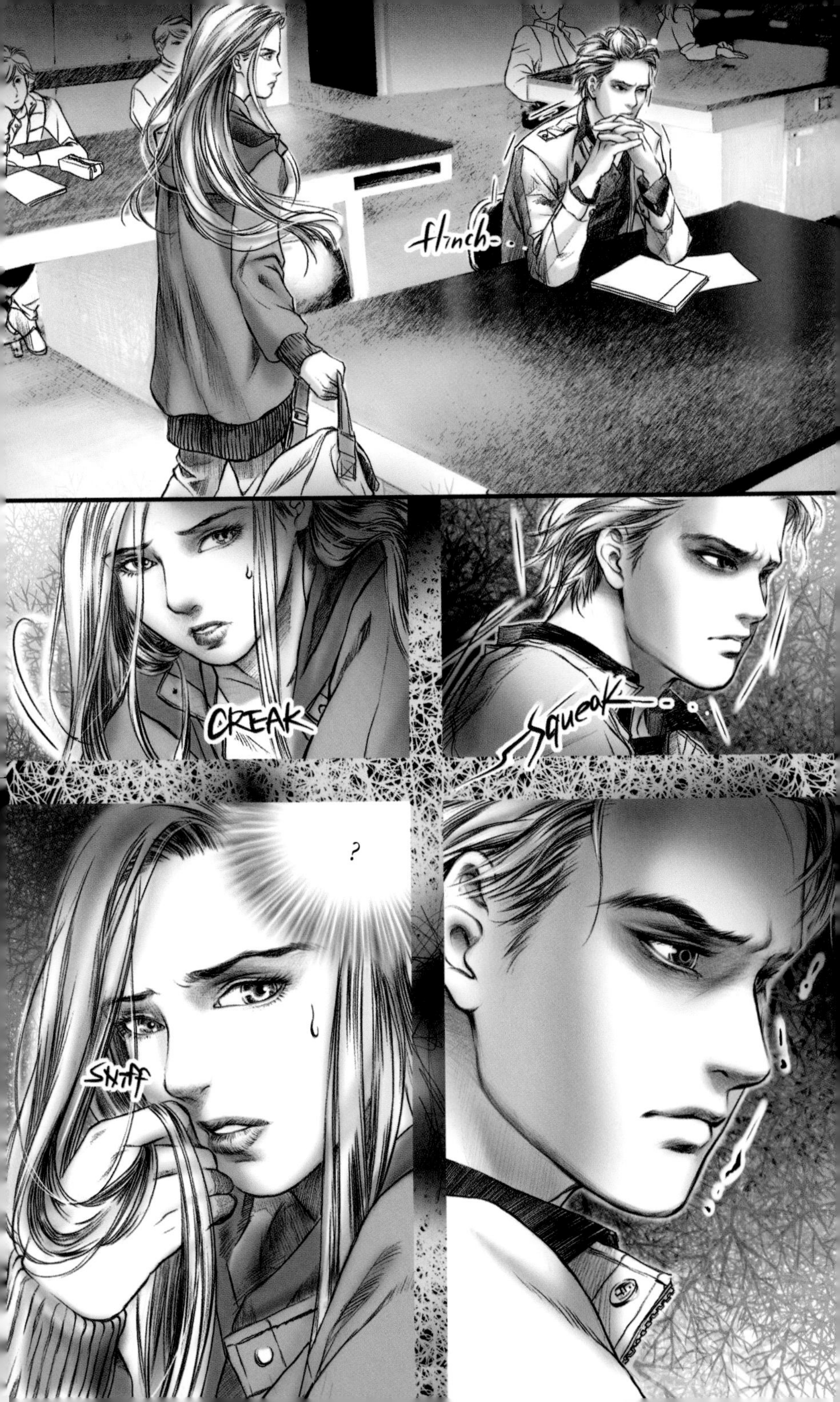
flinch...
CREAK
squeak...
?
SNIFF

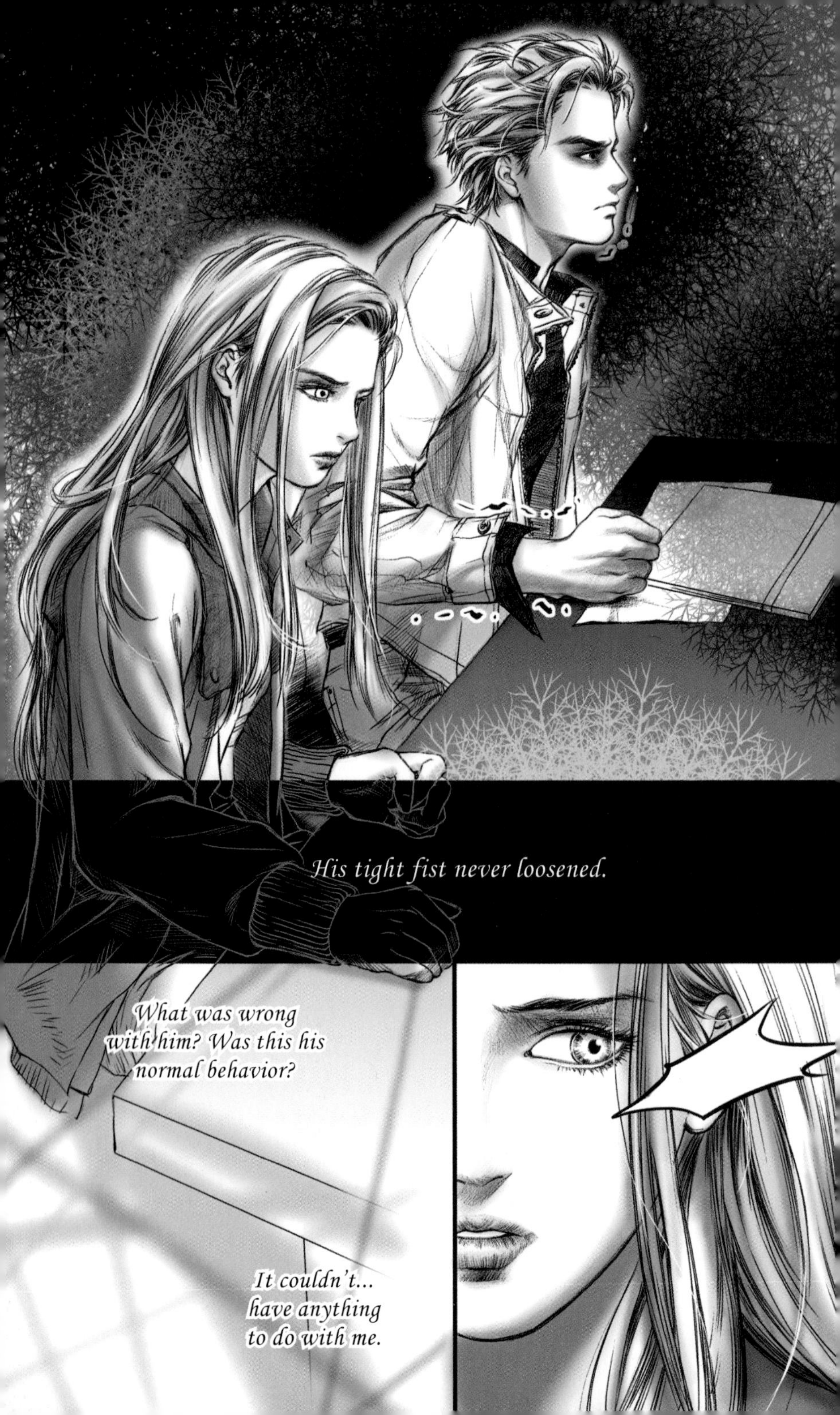
His tight fist never loosened.
What was wrong with him? Was this his normal behavior?
It couldn't... have anything to do with me.

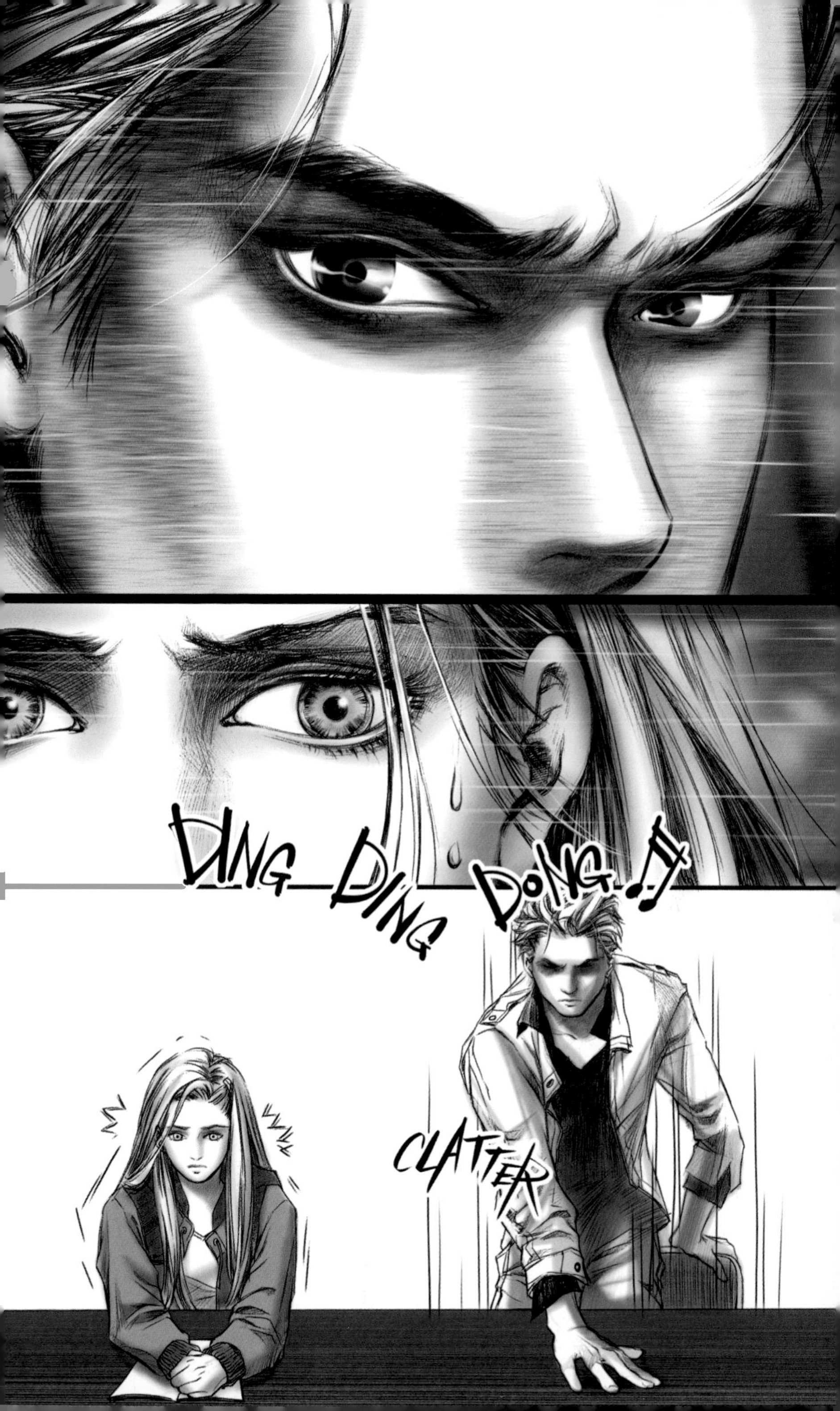
DING DING DONG
CLATTER

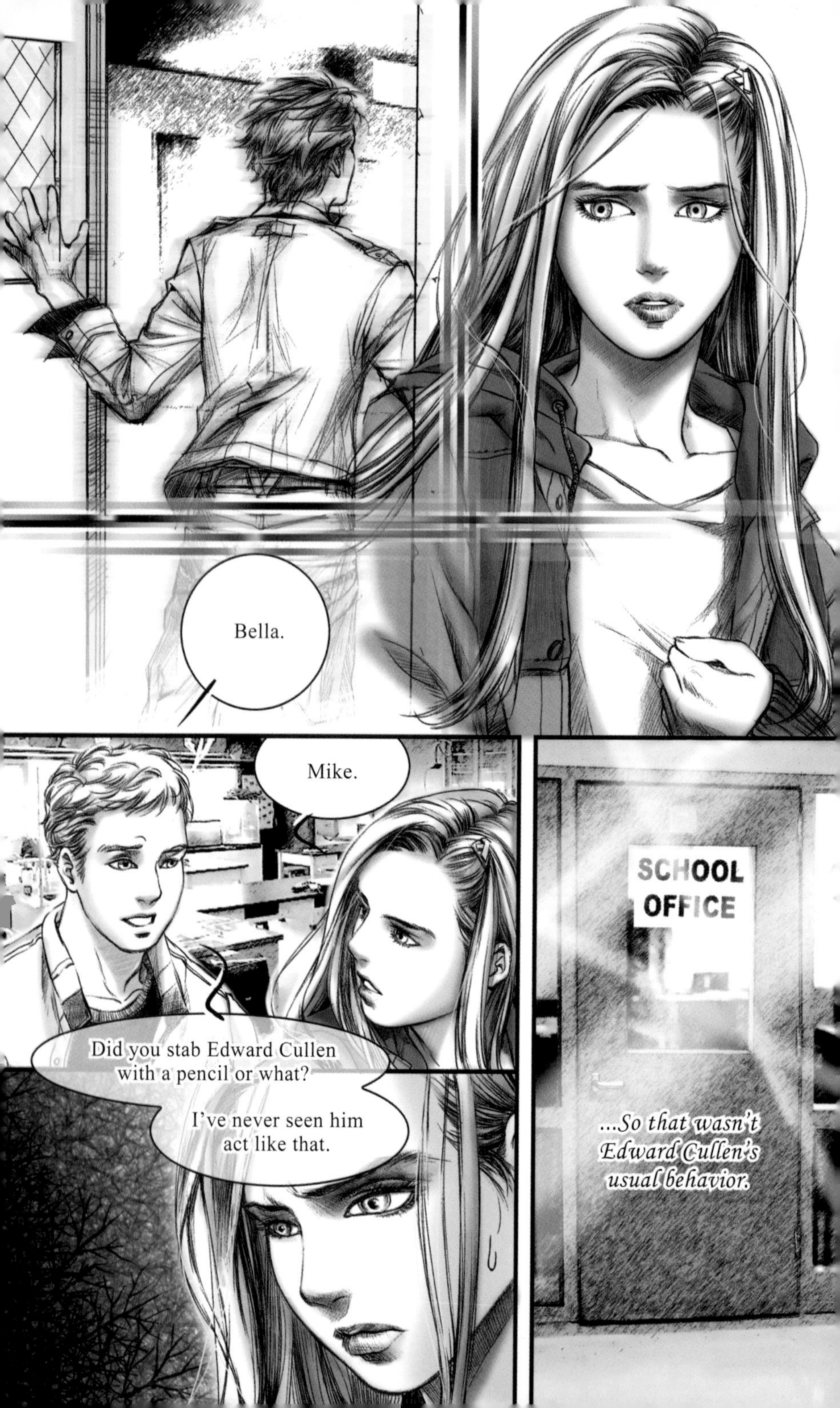
Bella.
Mike.
Did you stab Edward Cullen with a pencil or what?
I've never seen him act like that.
SCHOOL OFFICE
...So that wasn't Edward Cullen's usual behavior.

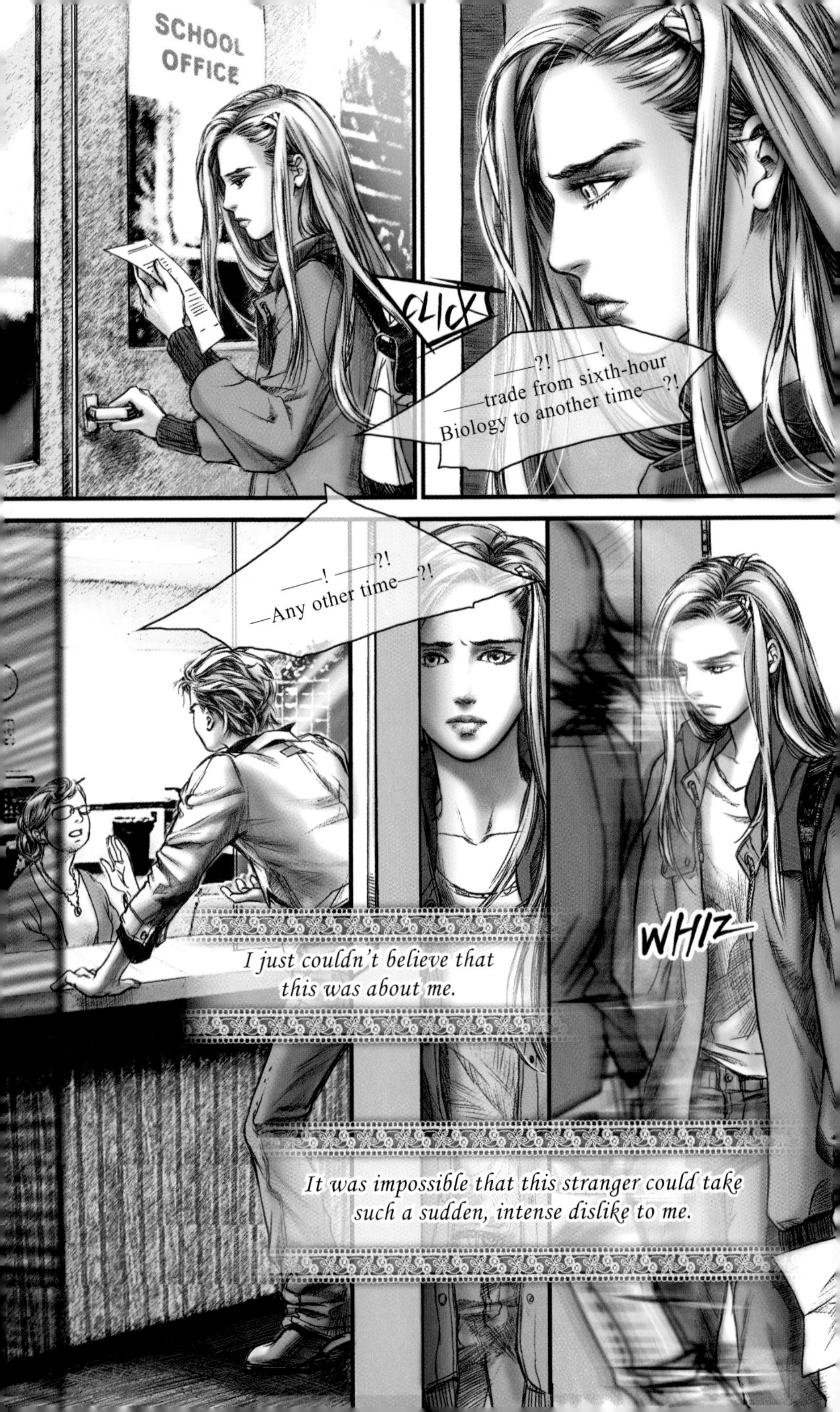
SCHOOL OFFICE
CLICK
——?! ——!
——trade from sixth-hour
Biology to another time—?!
——! ——?!
—Any other time—?!
WHIZ
I just couldn't believe that
this was about me.
It was impossible that this stranger could take
such a sudden, intense dislike to me.

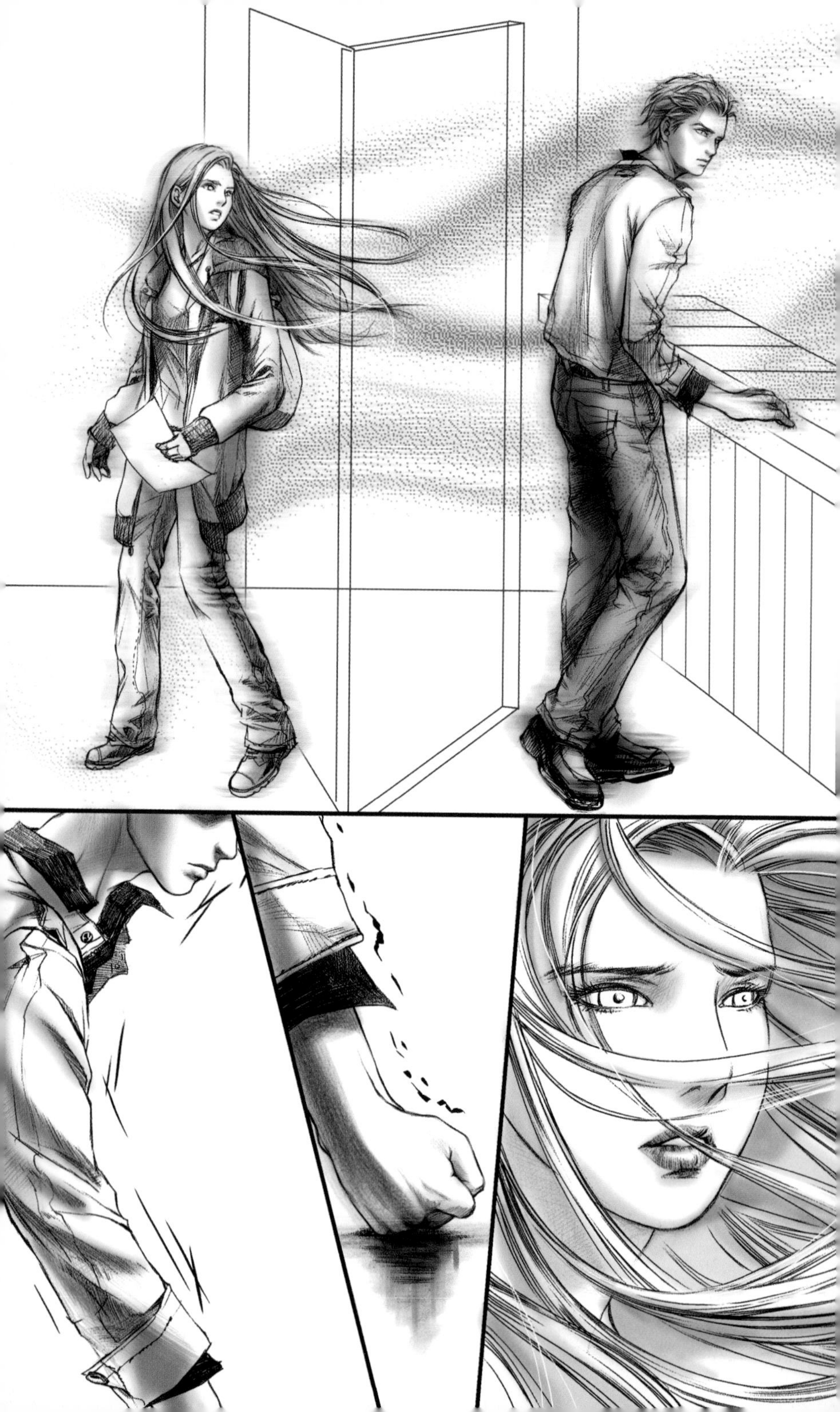

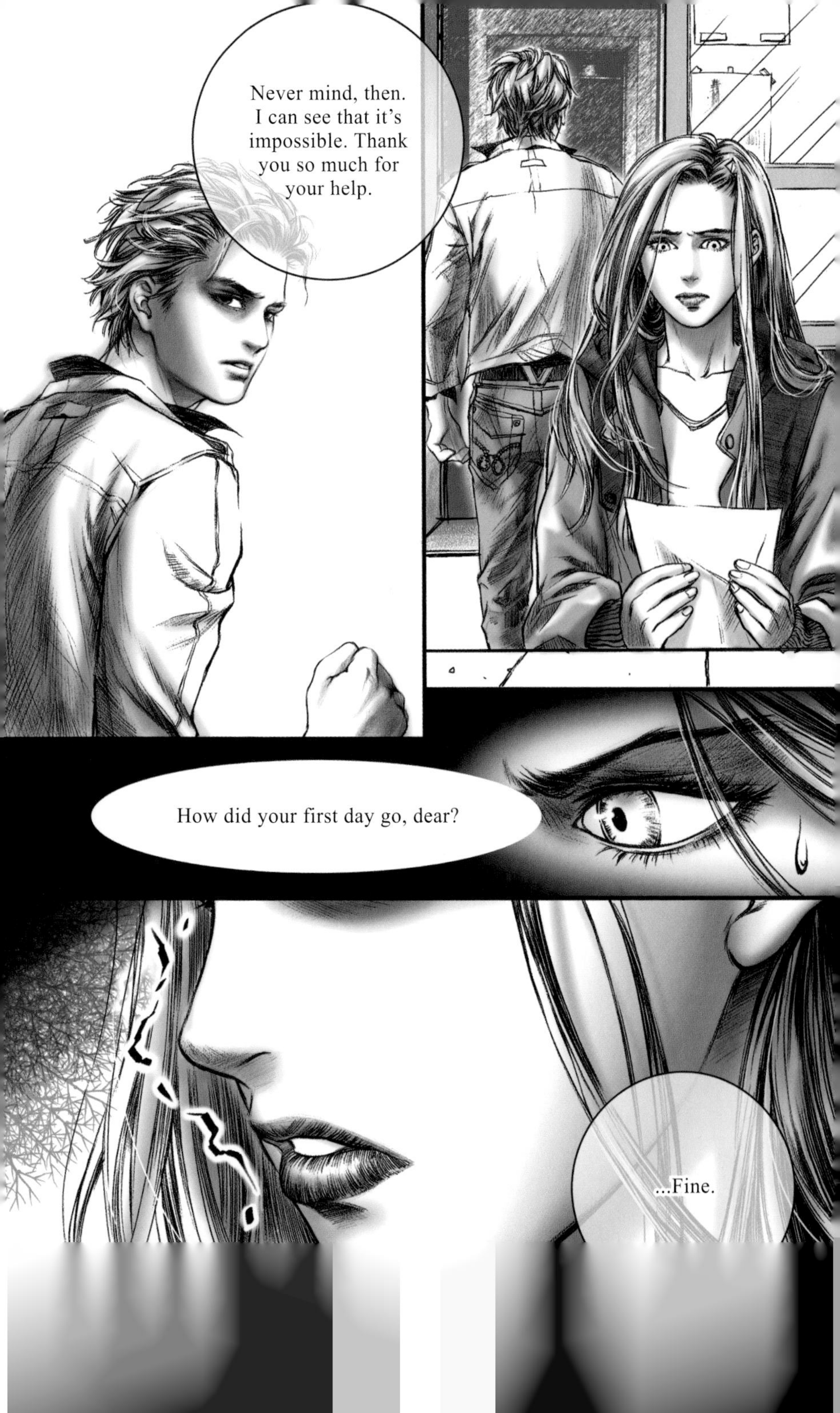
Never mind, then. I can see that it's impossible. Thank you so much for your help.
How did your first day go, dear?
...Fine.

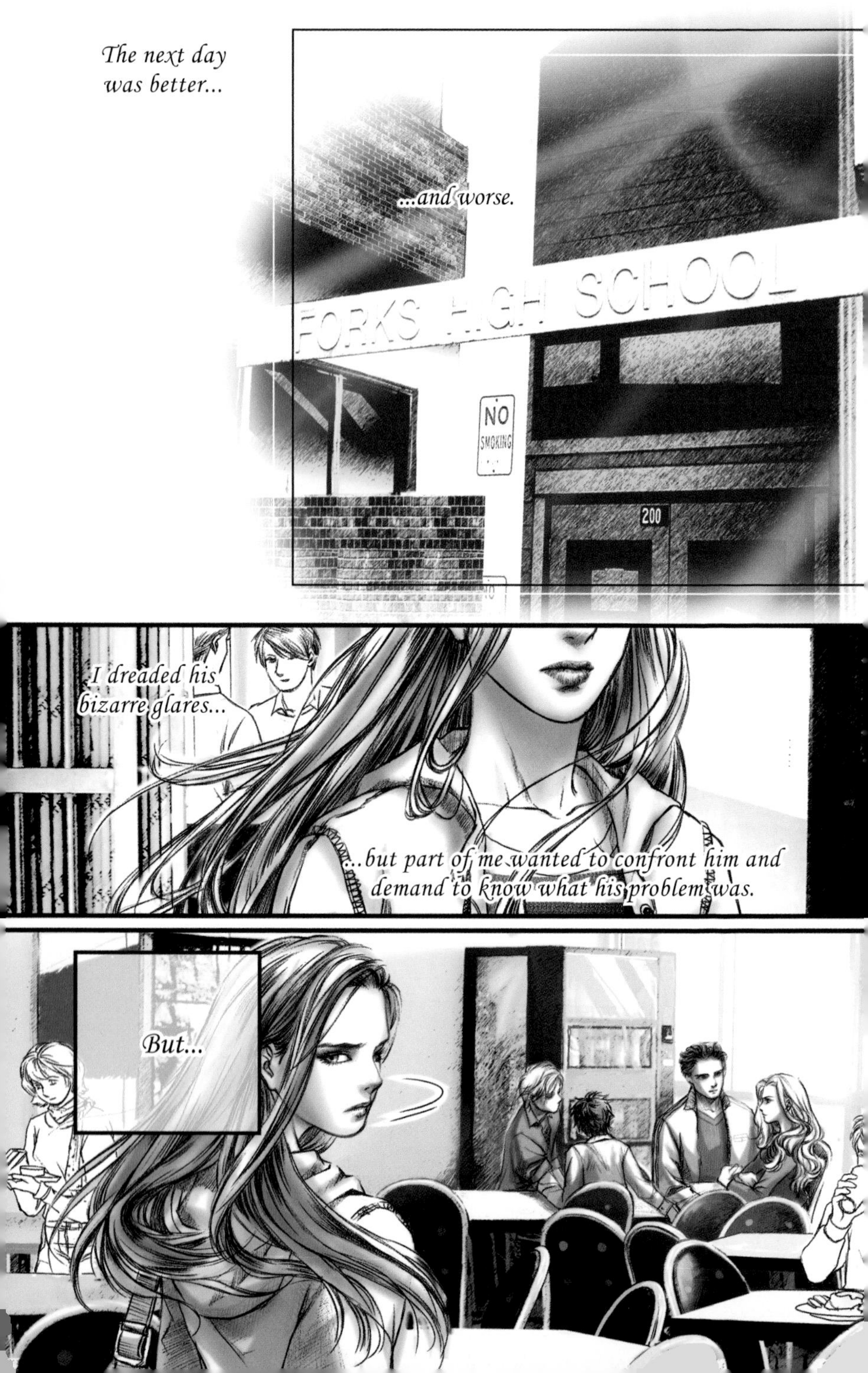
The next day was better...
...and worse.
FORKS HIGH SCHOOL
NO SMOKING
200
I dreaded his bizarre glares...
...but part of me wanted to confront him and demand to know what his problem was.
But...

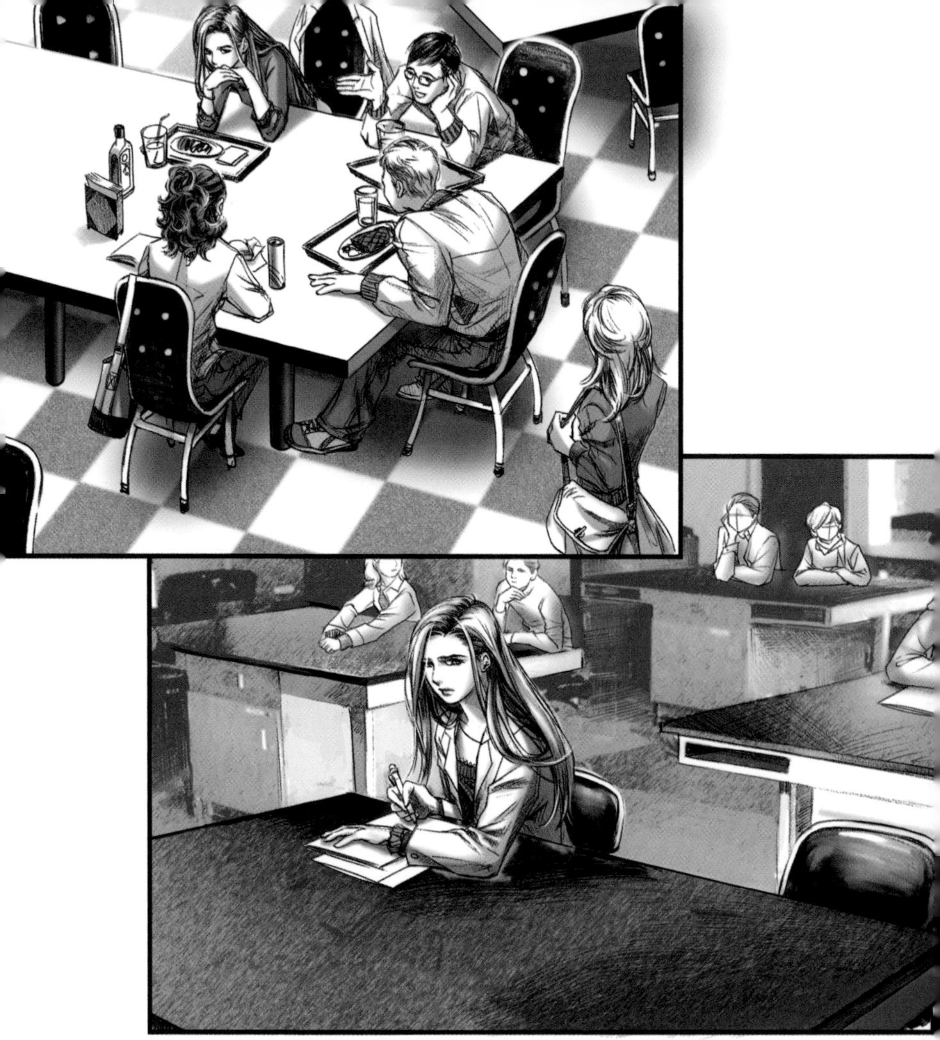

...Edward Cullen wasn't in school at all.

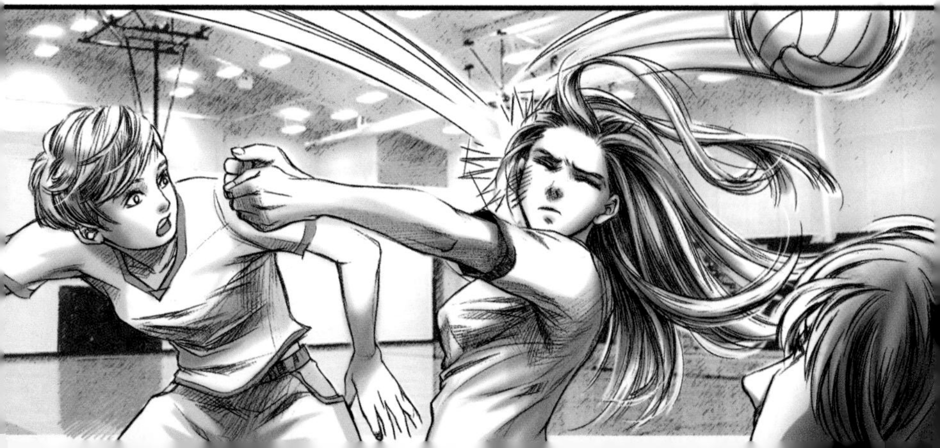

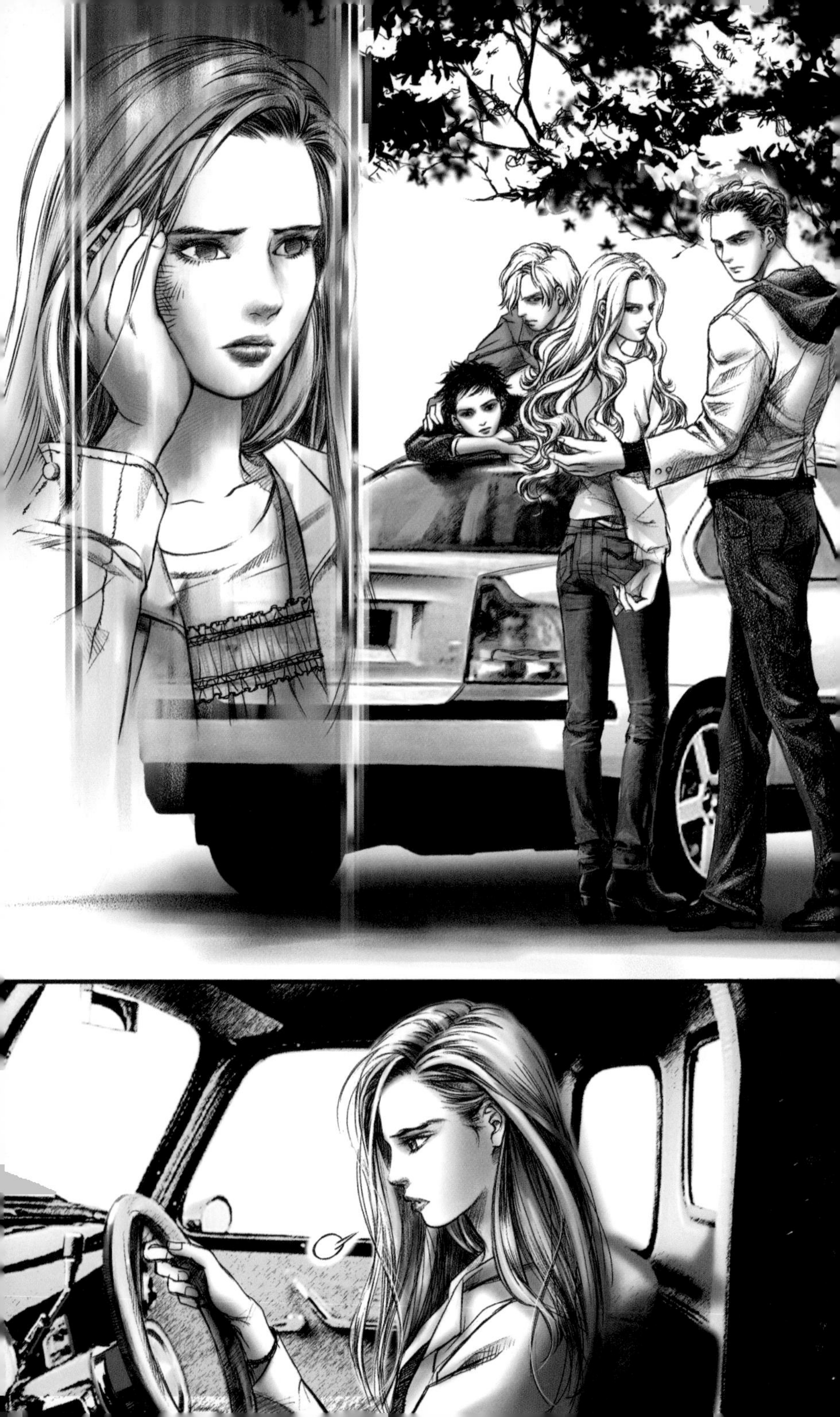

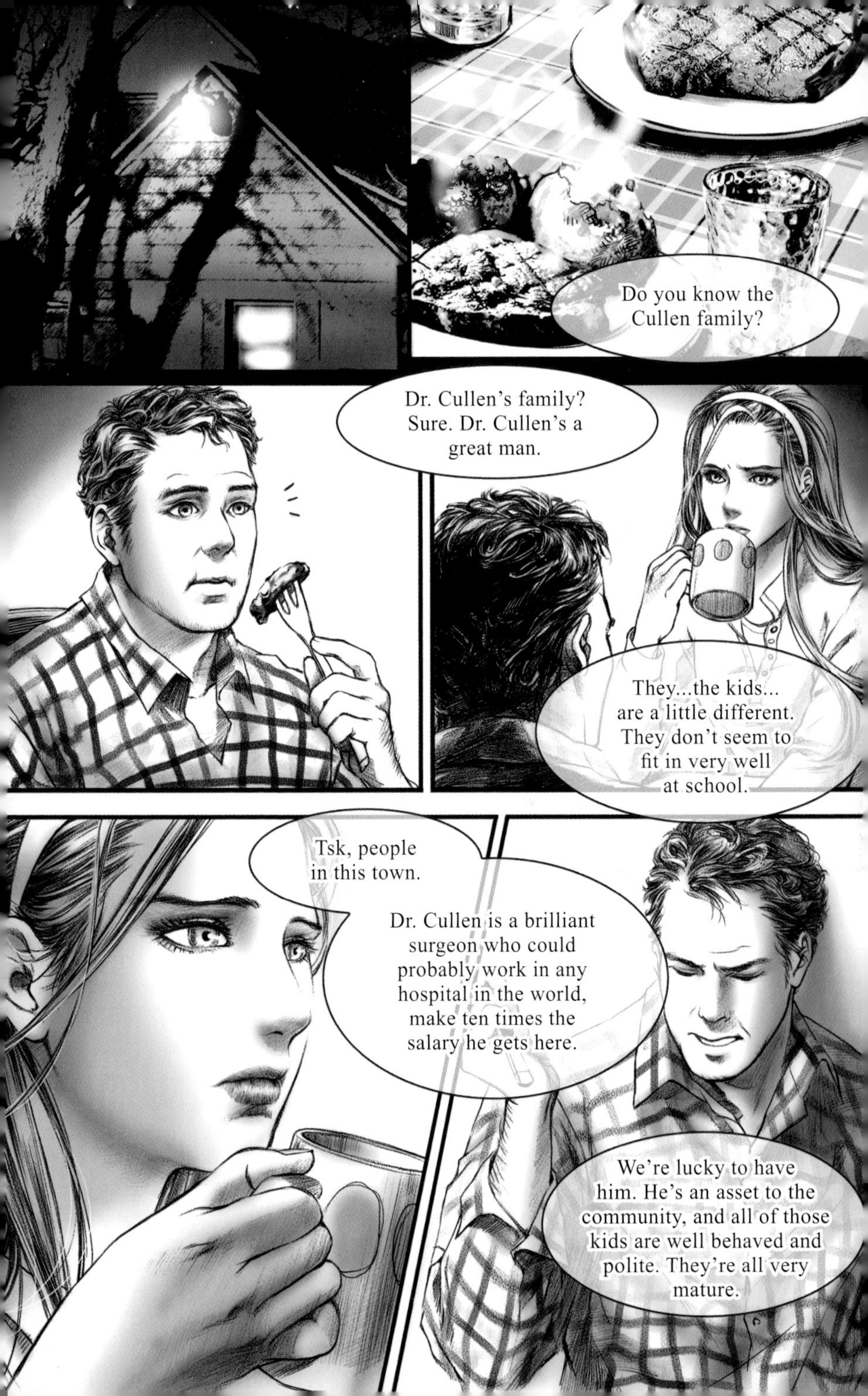
Do you know the Cullen family?
Dr. Cullen's family? Sure. Dr. Cullen's a great man.
They...the kids... are a little different. They don't seem to fit in very well at school.
Tsk, people in this town.
Dr. Cullen is a brilliant surgeon who could probably work in any hospital in the world, make ten times the salary he gets here.
We're lucky to have him. He's an asset to the community, and all of those kids are well behaved and polite. They're all very mature.

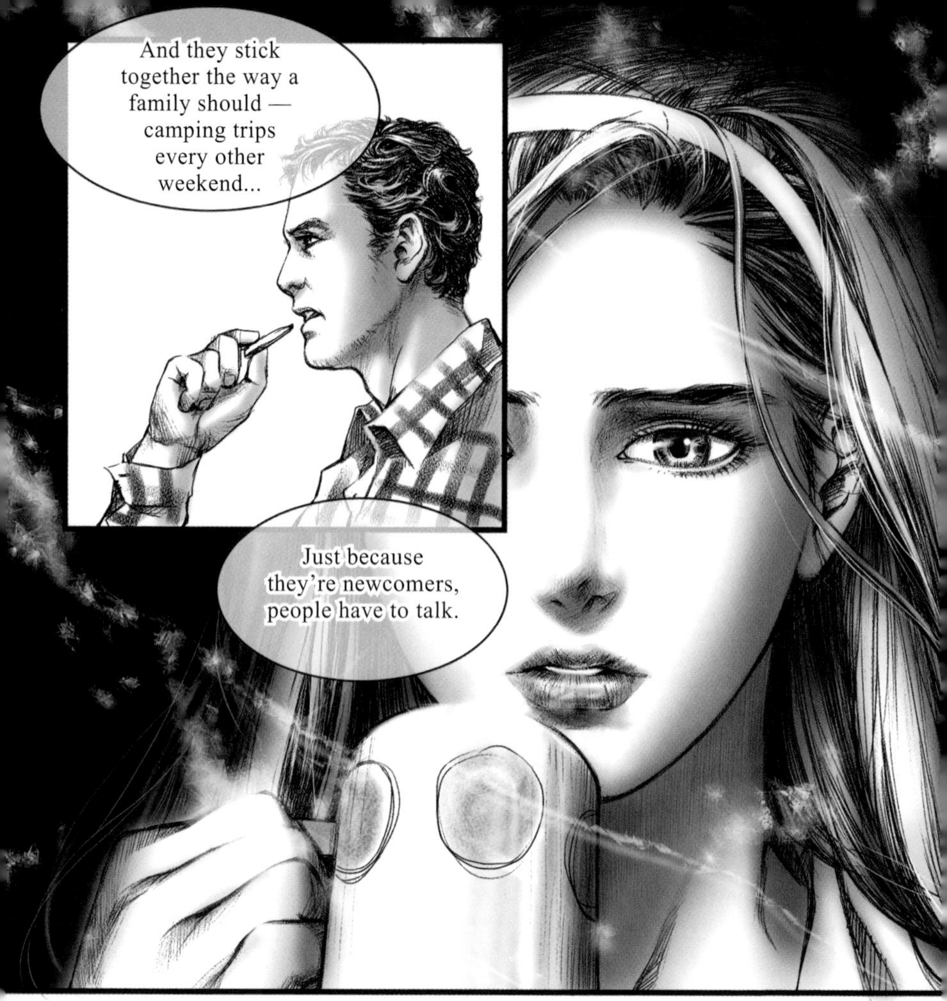
And they stick together the way a family should — camping trips every other weekend...
Just because they're newcomers, people have to talk.

Edward Cullen didn't come back to school the rest of the week.

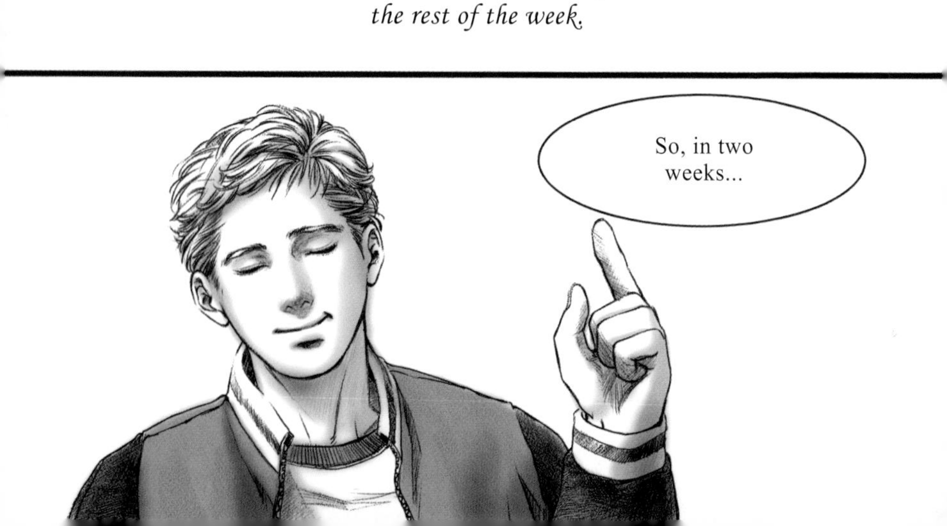
So, in two weeks...

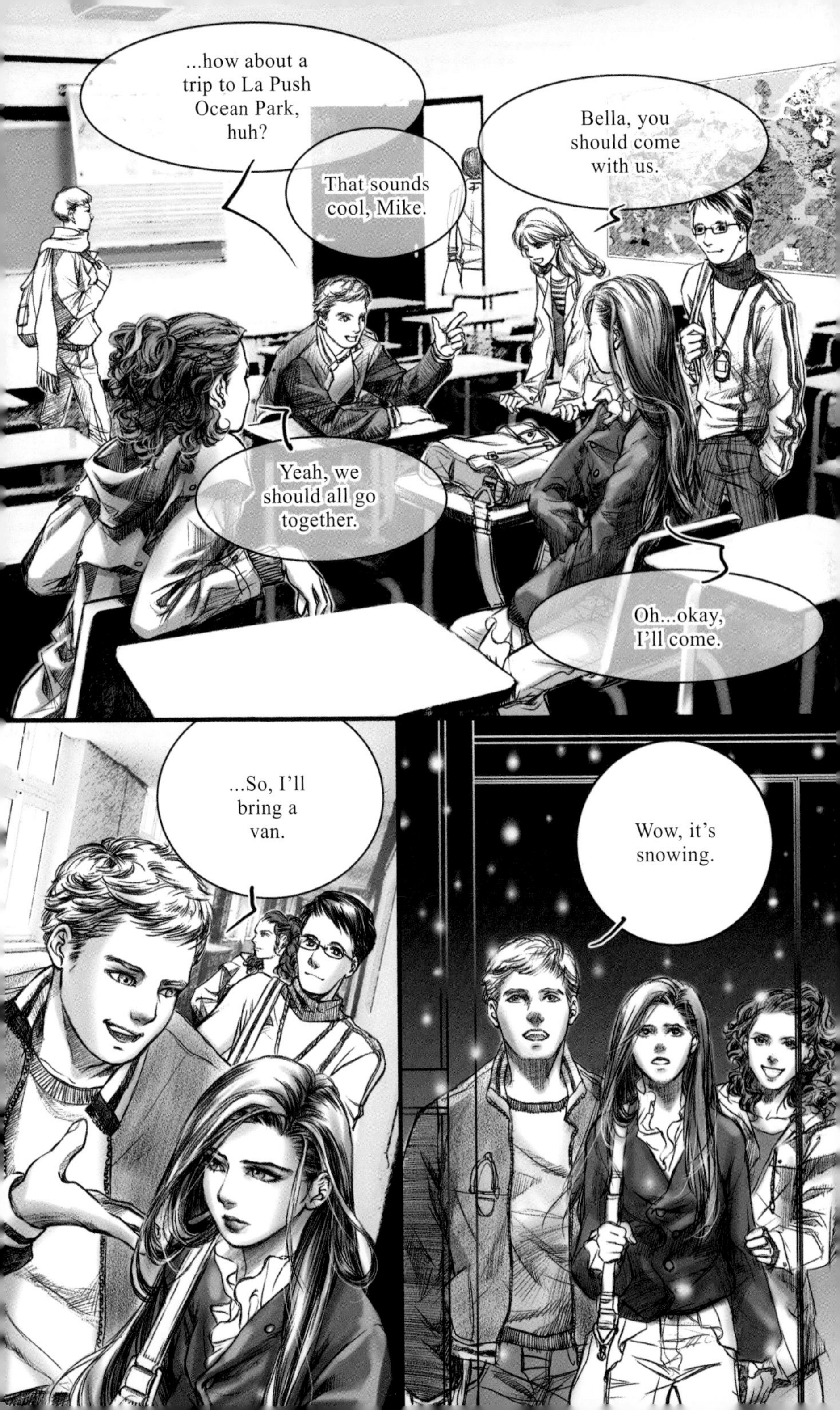
...how about a trip to La Push Ocean Park, huh?
That sounds cool, Mike.
Bella, you should come with us.
Yeah, we should all go together.
Oh...okay, I'll come.
...So, I'll bring a van.
Wow, it's snowing.

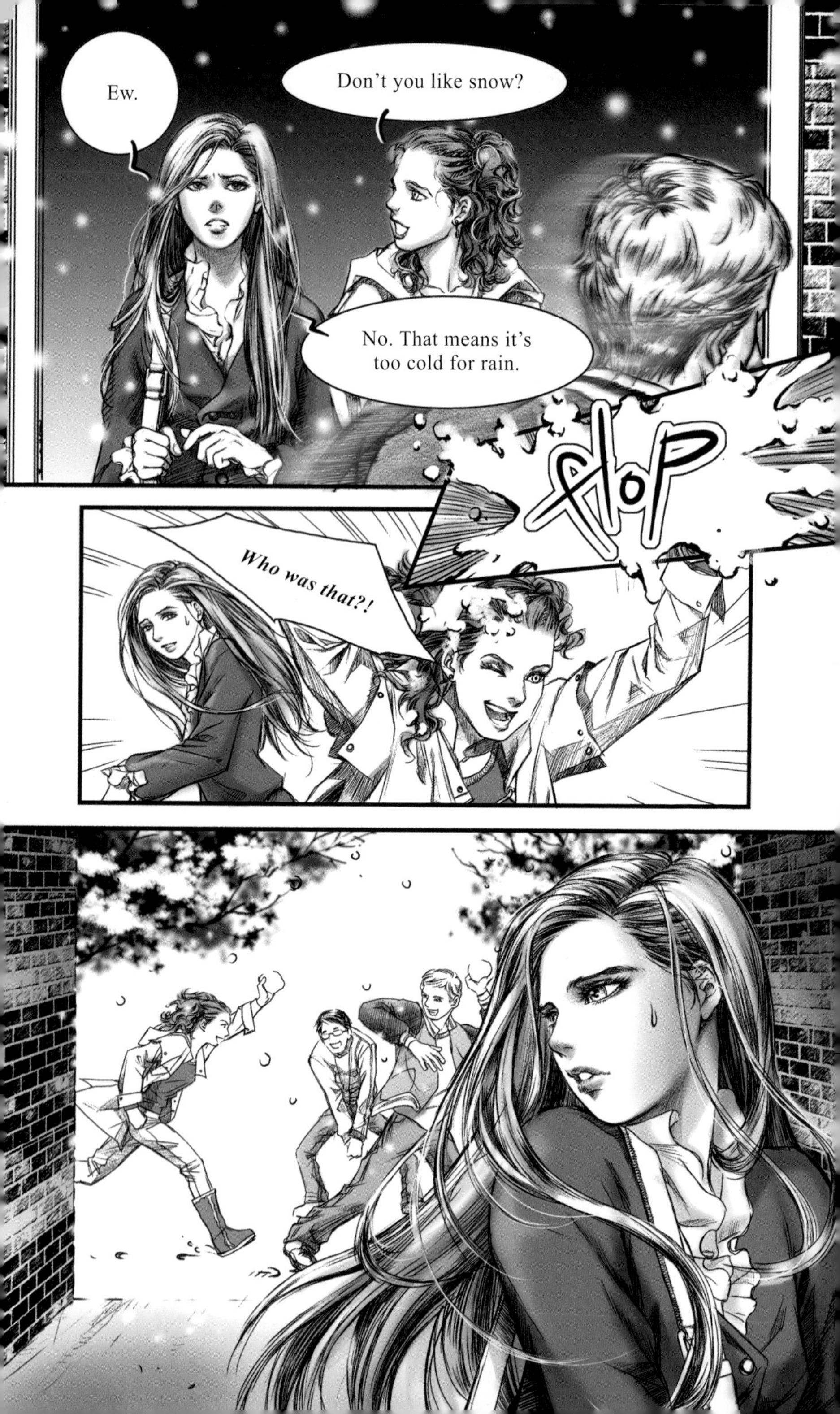
Ew.
Don't you like snow?
No. That means it's too cold for rain.
FLOP
Who was that?!

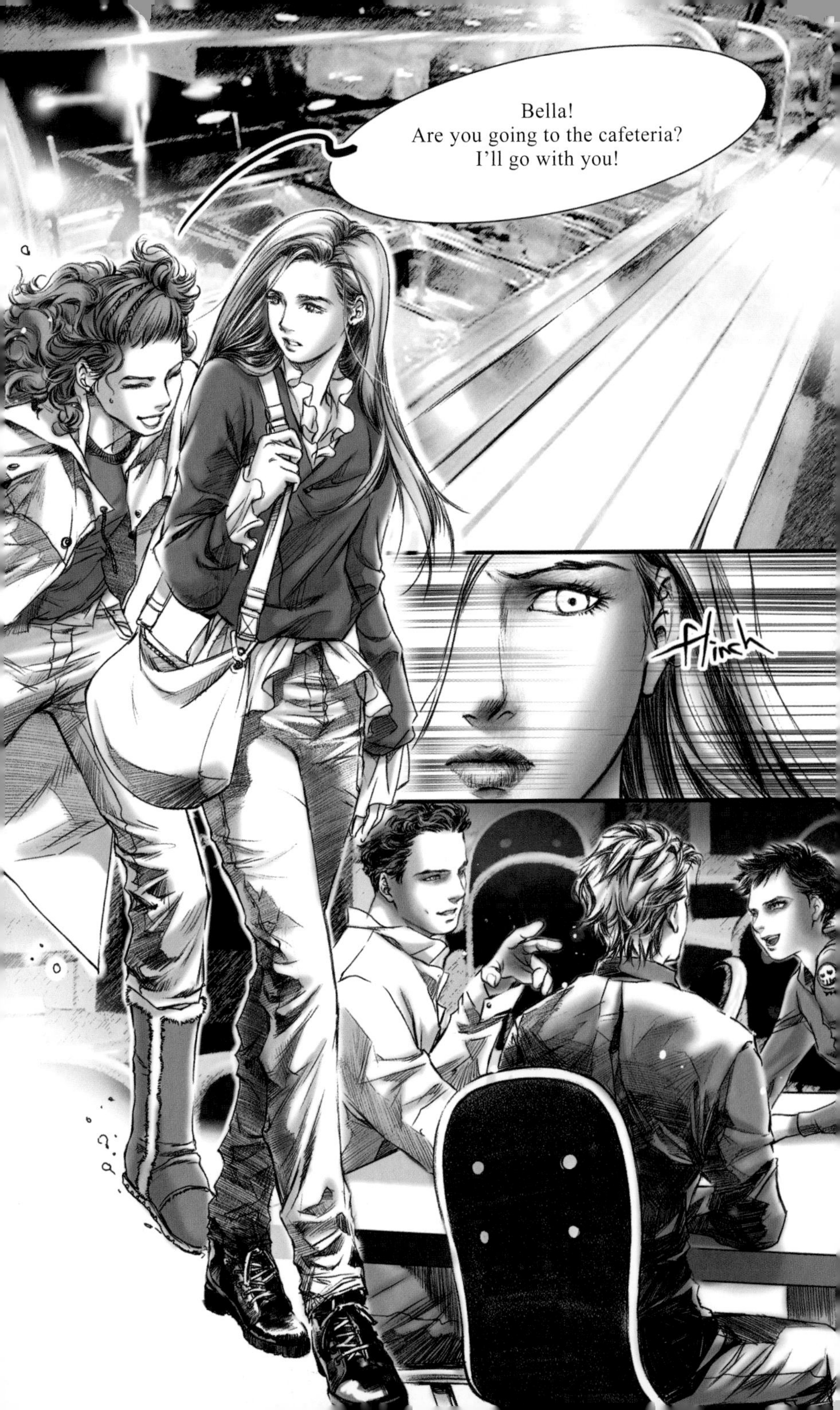
Bella!
Are you going to the cafeteria?
I'll go with you!
Flinch

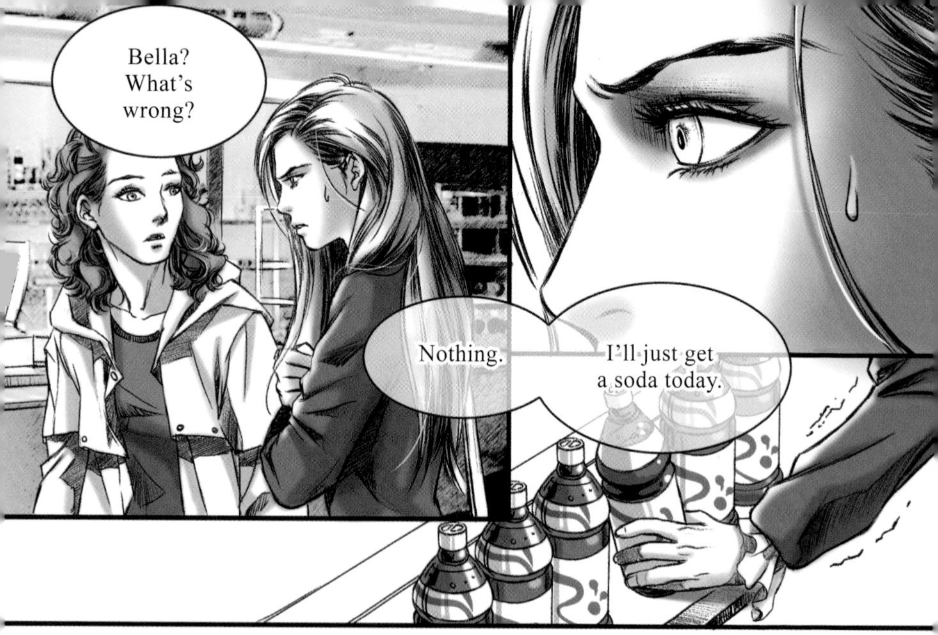
Bella? What's wrong?
Nothing.
I'll just get a soda today.

Ridiculous.
I shouldn't have to run away.

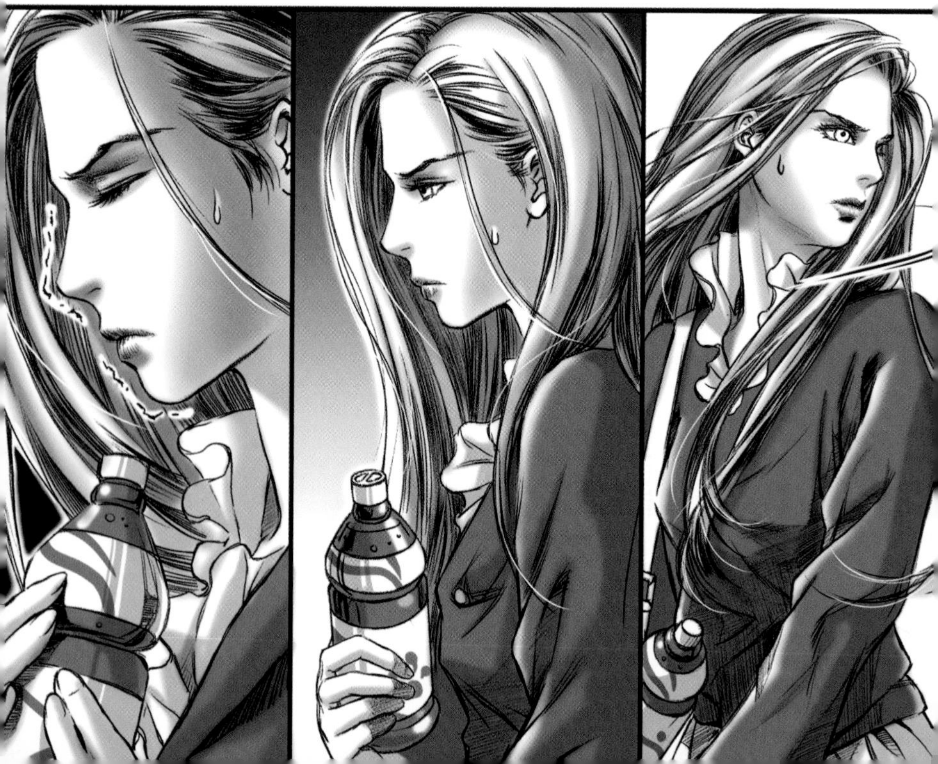

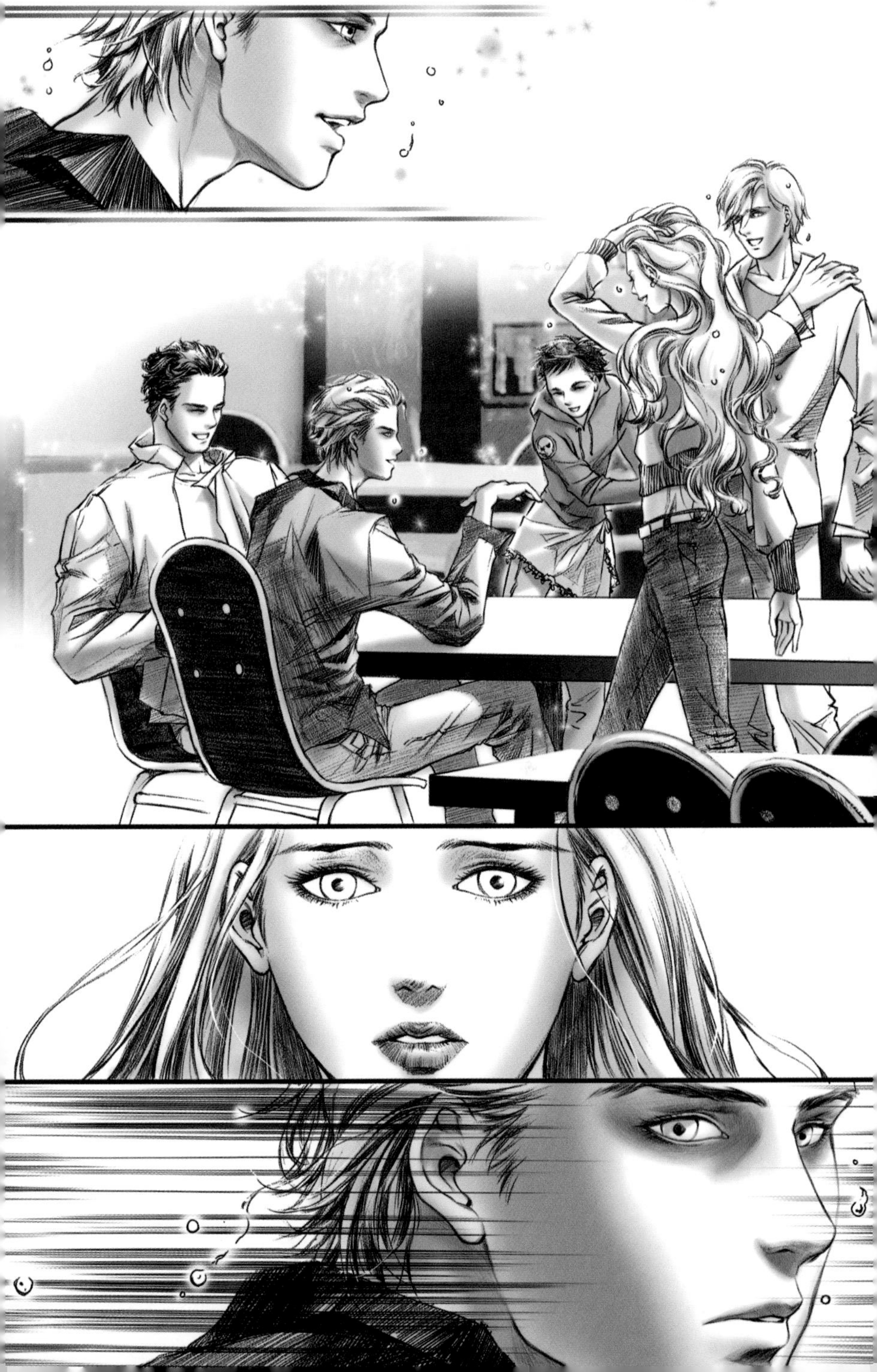

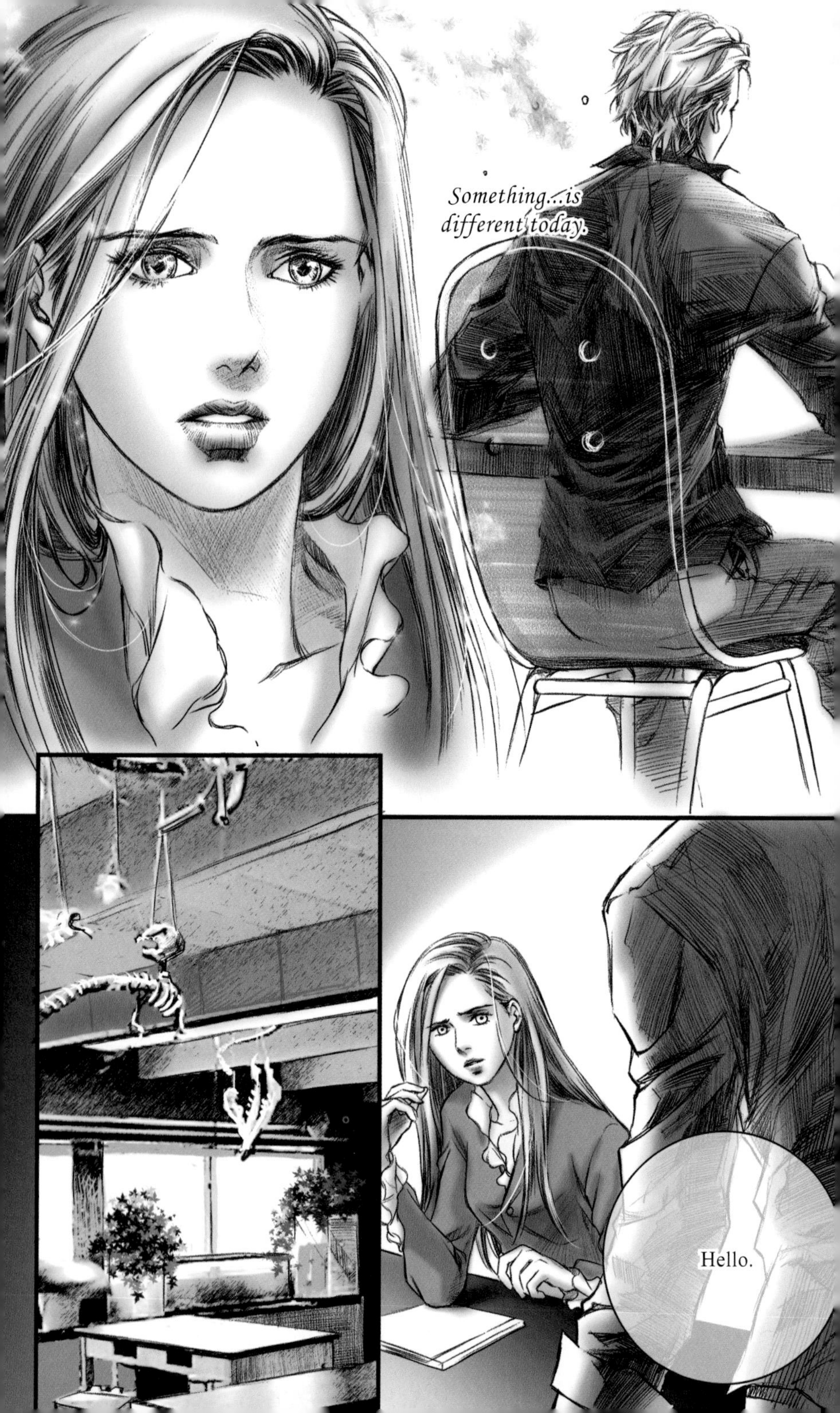
Something...is different today.
Hello.

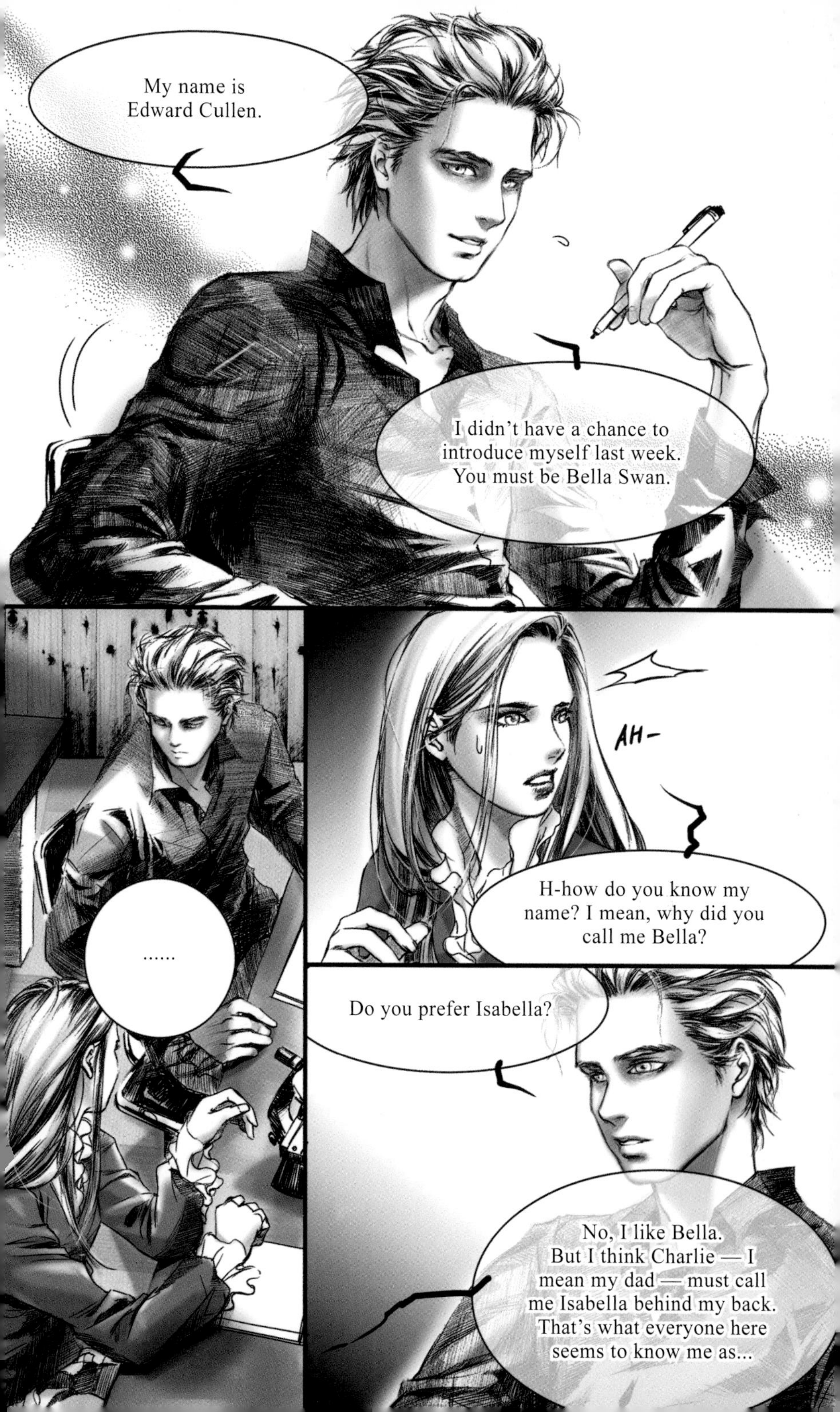
My name is Edward Cullen.
I didn't have a chance to introduce myself last week. You must be Bella Swan.
......
AH-
H-how do you know my name? I mean, why did you call me Bella?
Do you prefer Isabella?
No, I like Bella. But I think Charlie — I mean my dad — must call me Isabella behind my back. That's what everyone here seems to know me as...

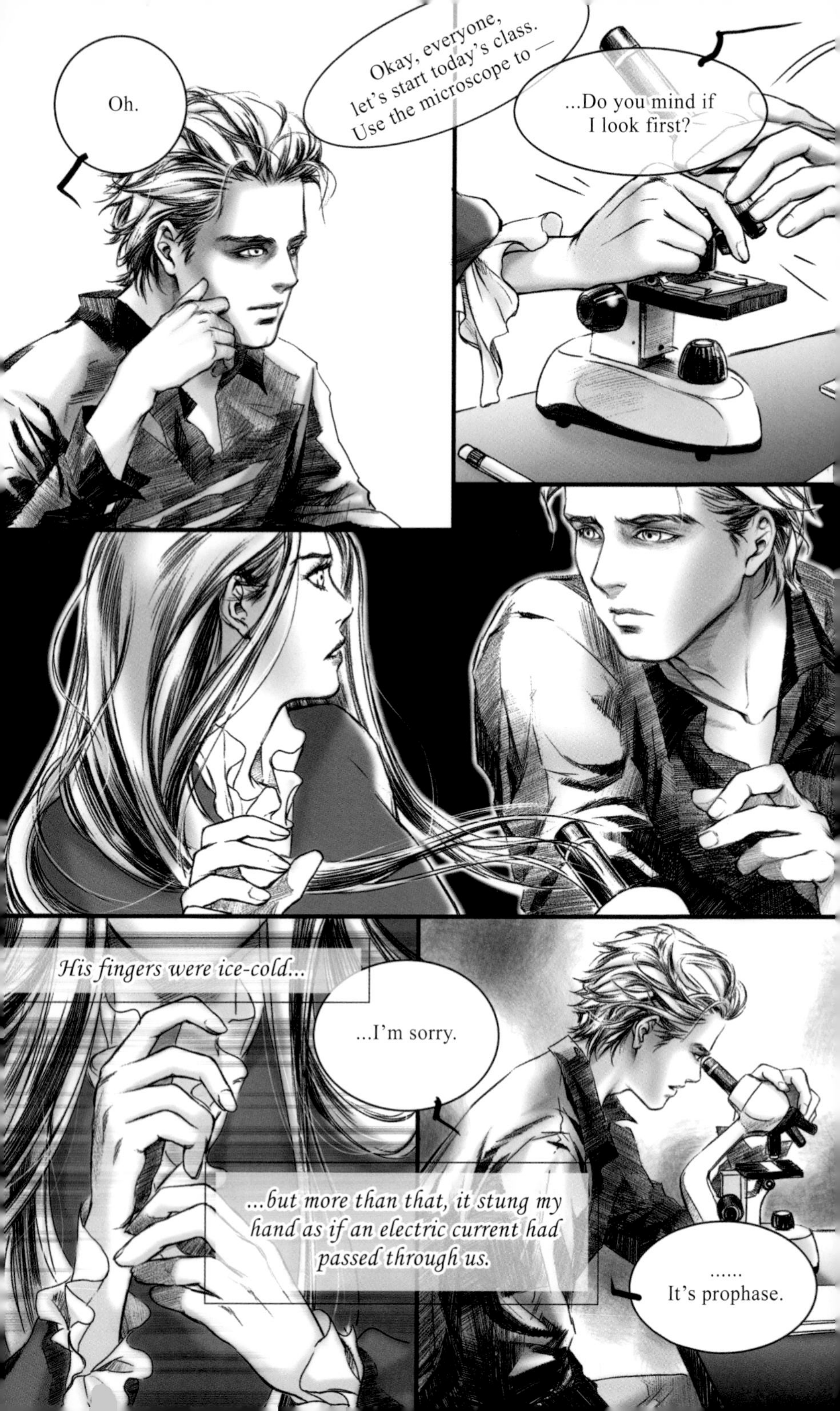
Oh.
Okay, everyone, let's start today's class. Use the microscope to —
...Do you mind if I look first?
His fingers were ice-cold...
...I'm sorry.
...but more than that, it stung my hand as if an electric current had passed through us.
...... It's prophase.

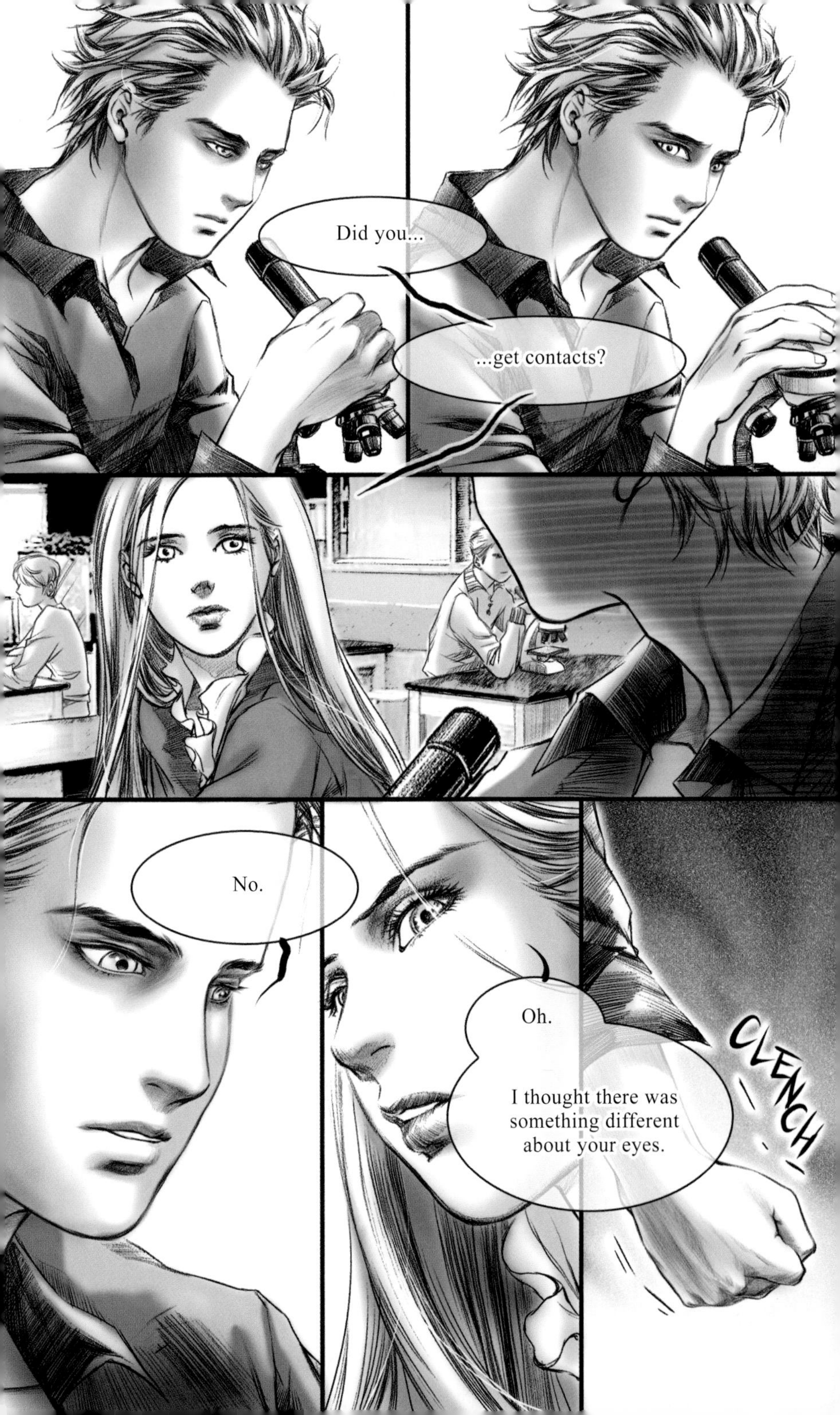
Did you...
...get contacts?
No.
Oh.
I thought there was something different about your eyes.
CLENCH

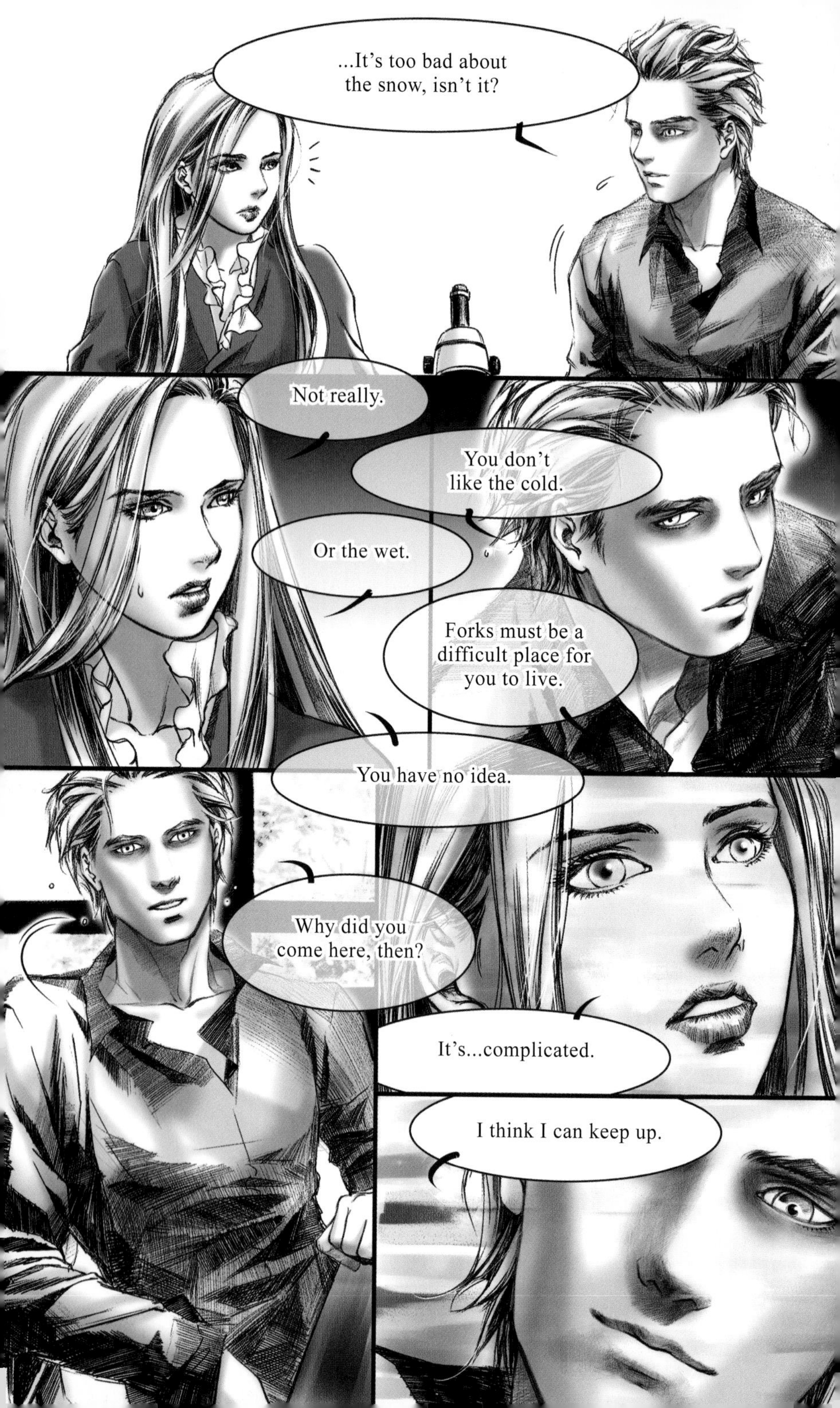
...It's too bad about
the snow, isn't it?
Not really.
You don't
like the cold.
Or the wet.
Forks must be a
difficult place for
you to live.
You have no idea.
Why did you
come here, then?
It's...complicated.
I think I can keep up.

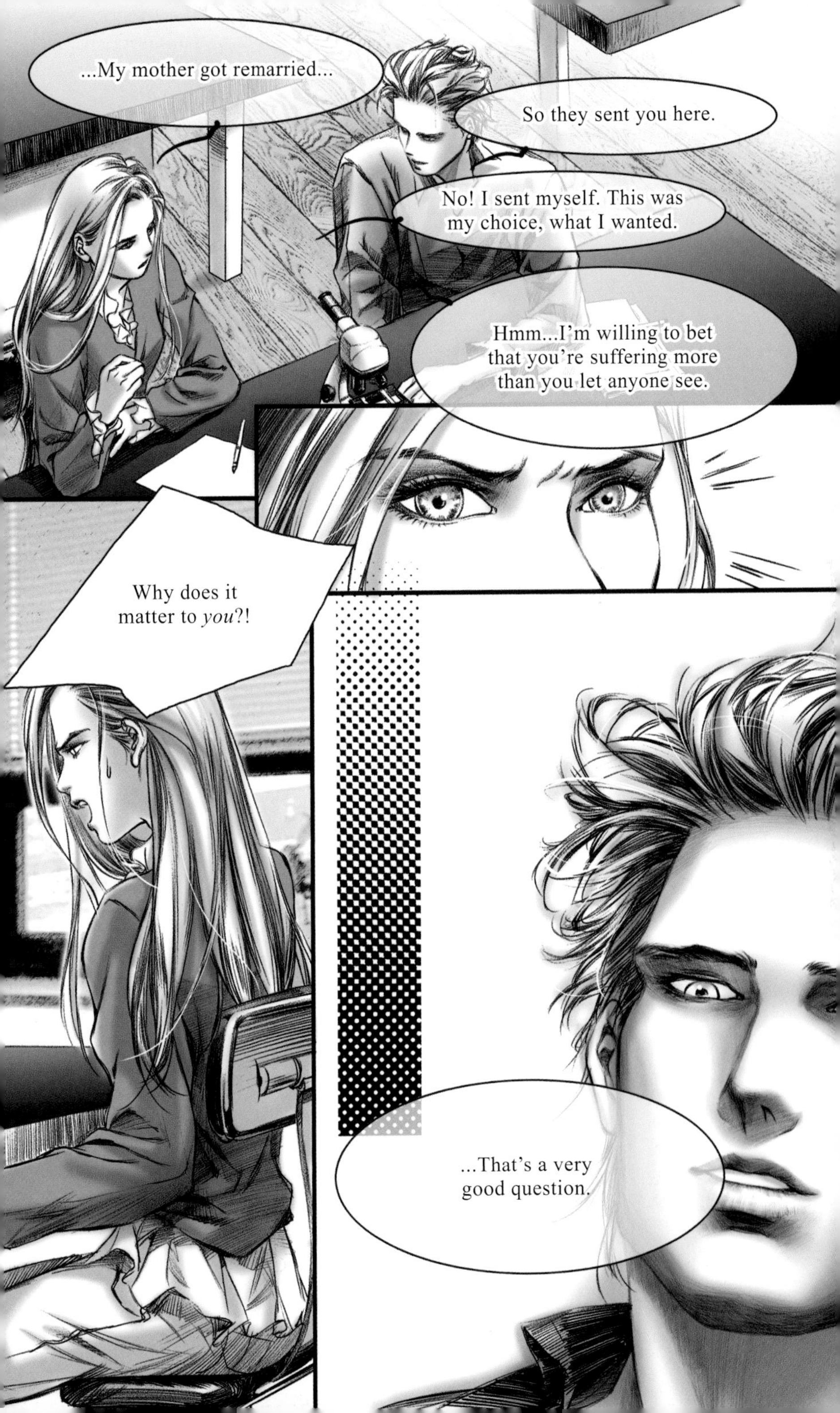
...My mother got remarried...
So they sent you here.
No! I sent myself. This was my choice, what I wanted.
Hmm...I'm willing to bet that you're suffering more than you let anyone see.
Why does it matter to *you*?!
...That's a very good question.

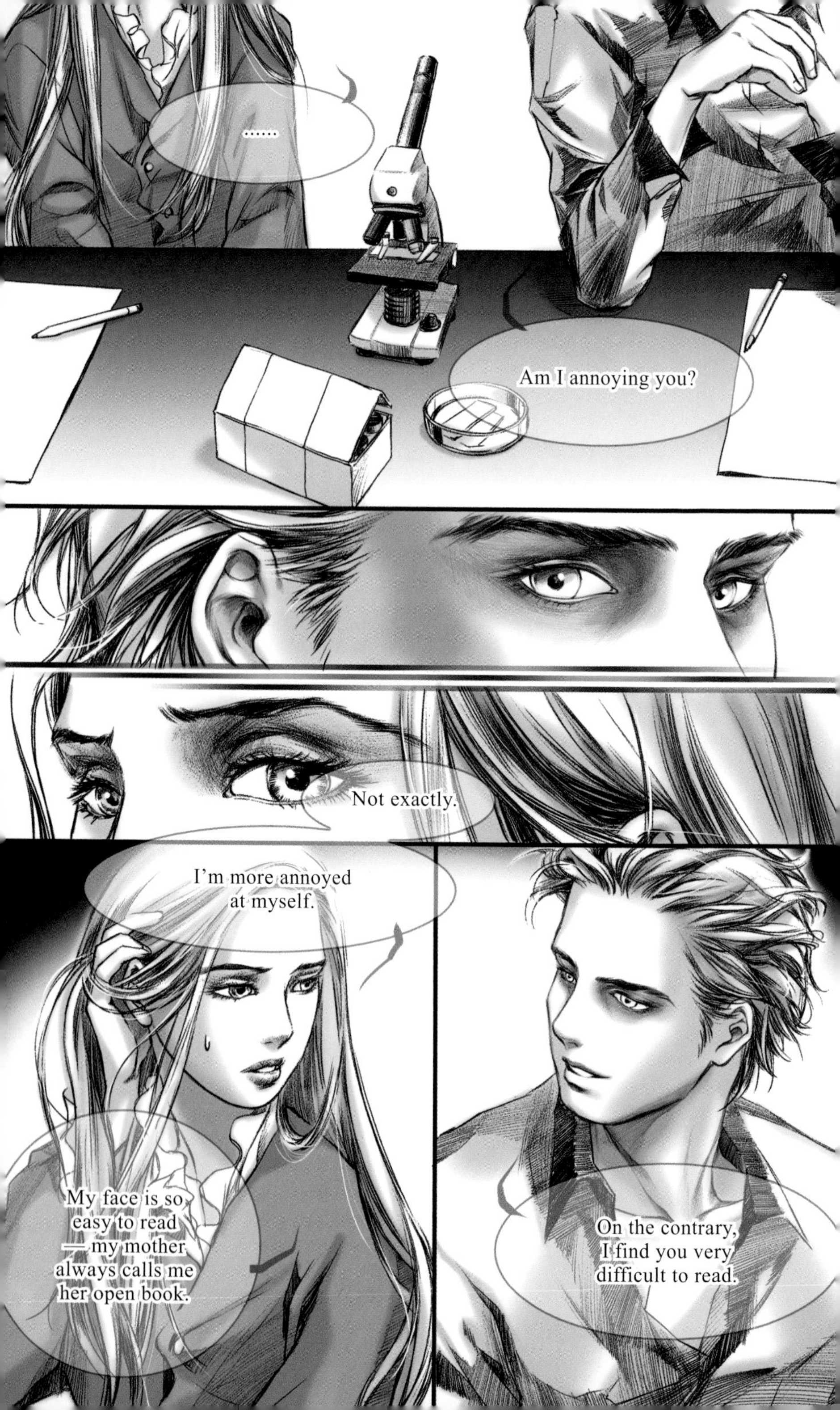

......
Am I annoying you?
Not exactly.
I'm more annoyed at myself.
My face is so easy to read — my mother always calls me her open book.
On the contrary, I find you very difficult to read.

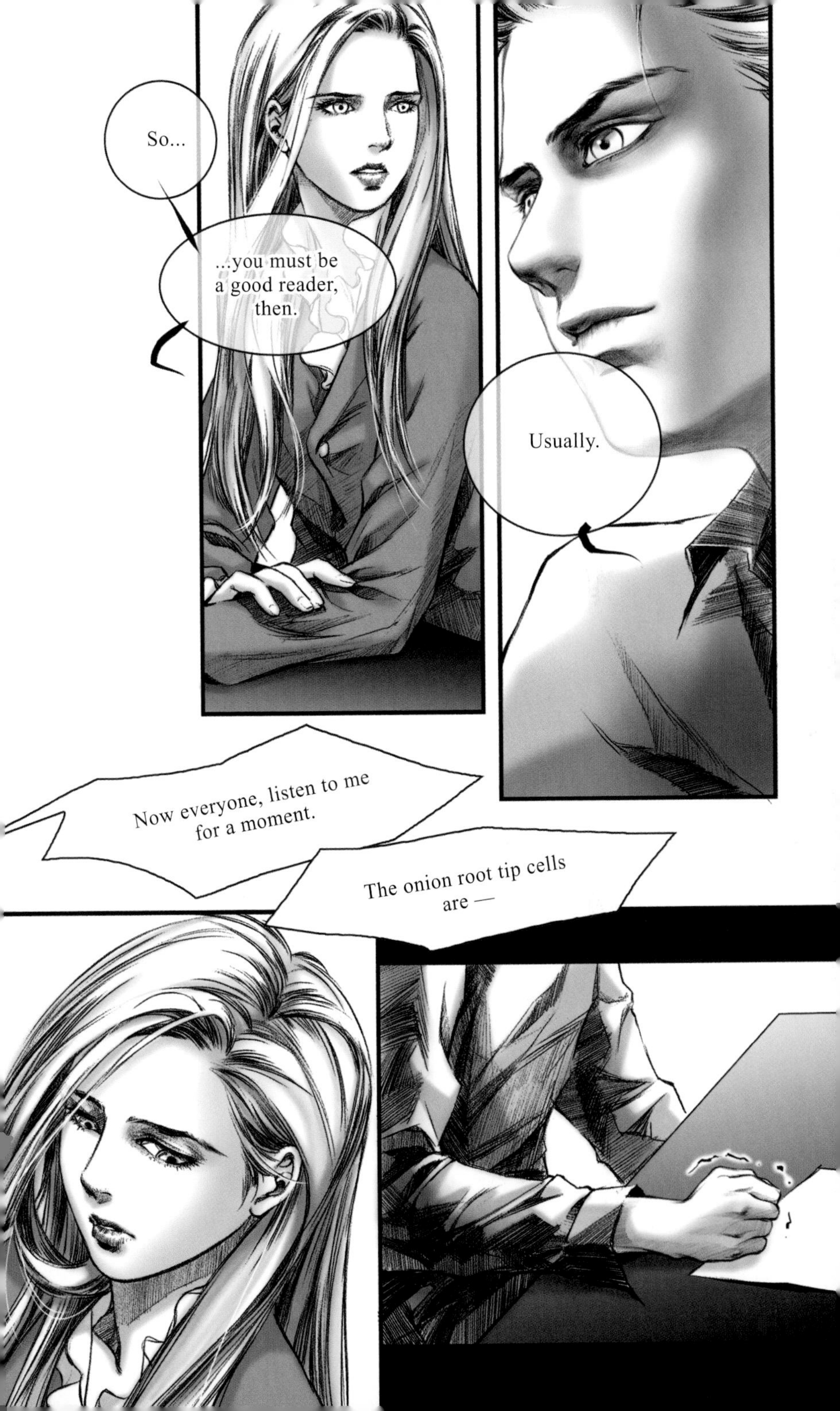
So...
...you must be a good reader, then.
Usually.
Now everyone, listen to me for a moment.
The onion root tip cells are —

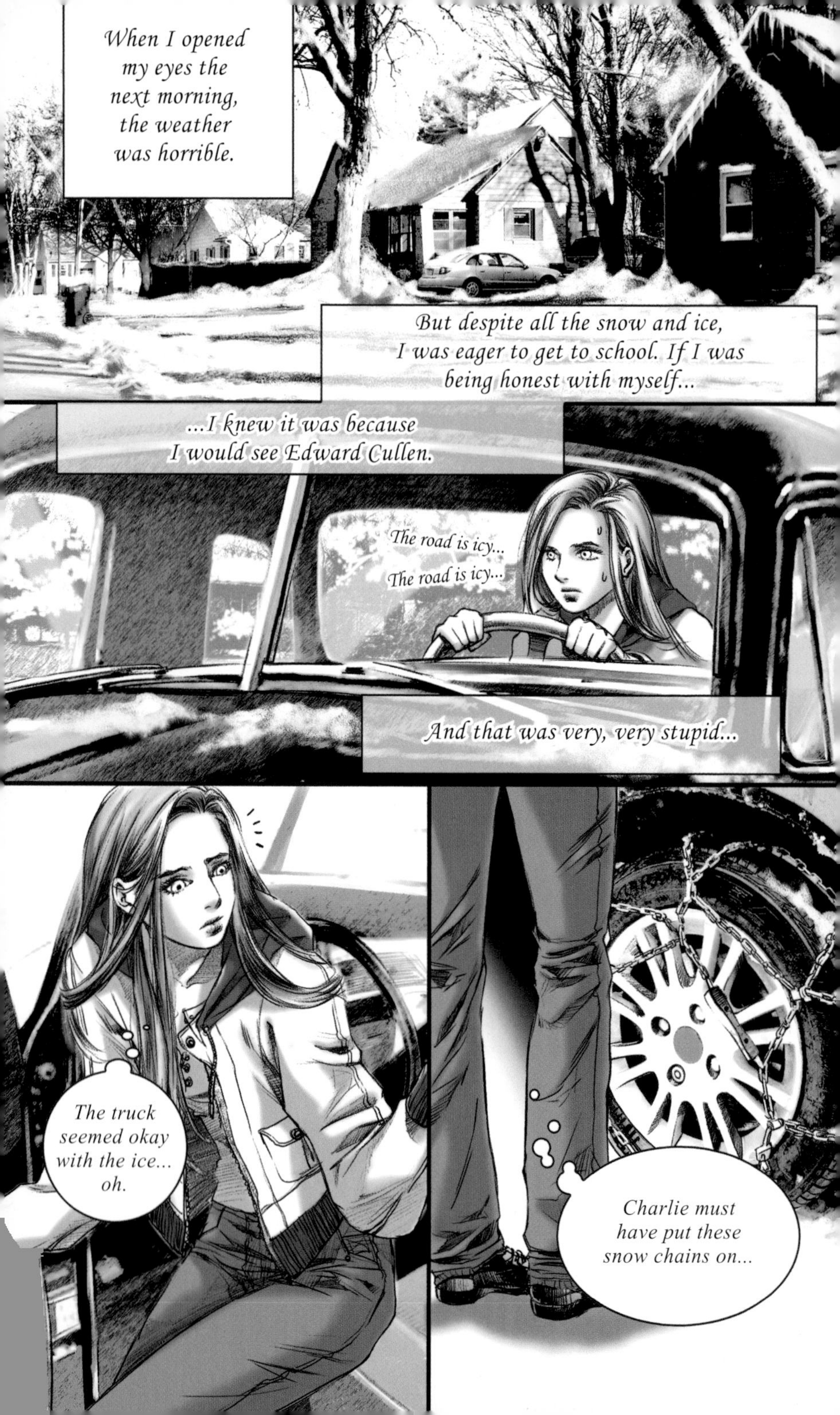

When I opened my eyes the next morning, the weather was horrible.
But despite all the snow and ice, I was eager to get to school. If I was being honest with myself...
...I knew it was because I would see Edward Cullen.
The road is icy...
The road is icy...
And that was very, very stupid...
The truck seemed okay with the ice... oh.
Charlie must have put these snow chains on...

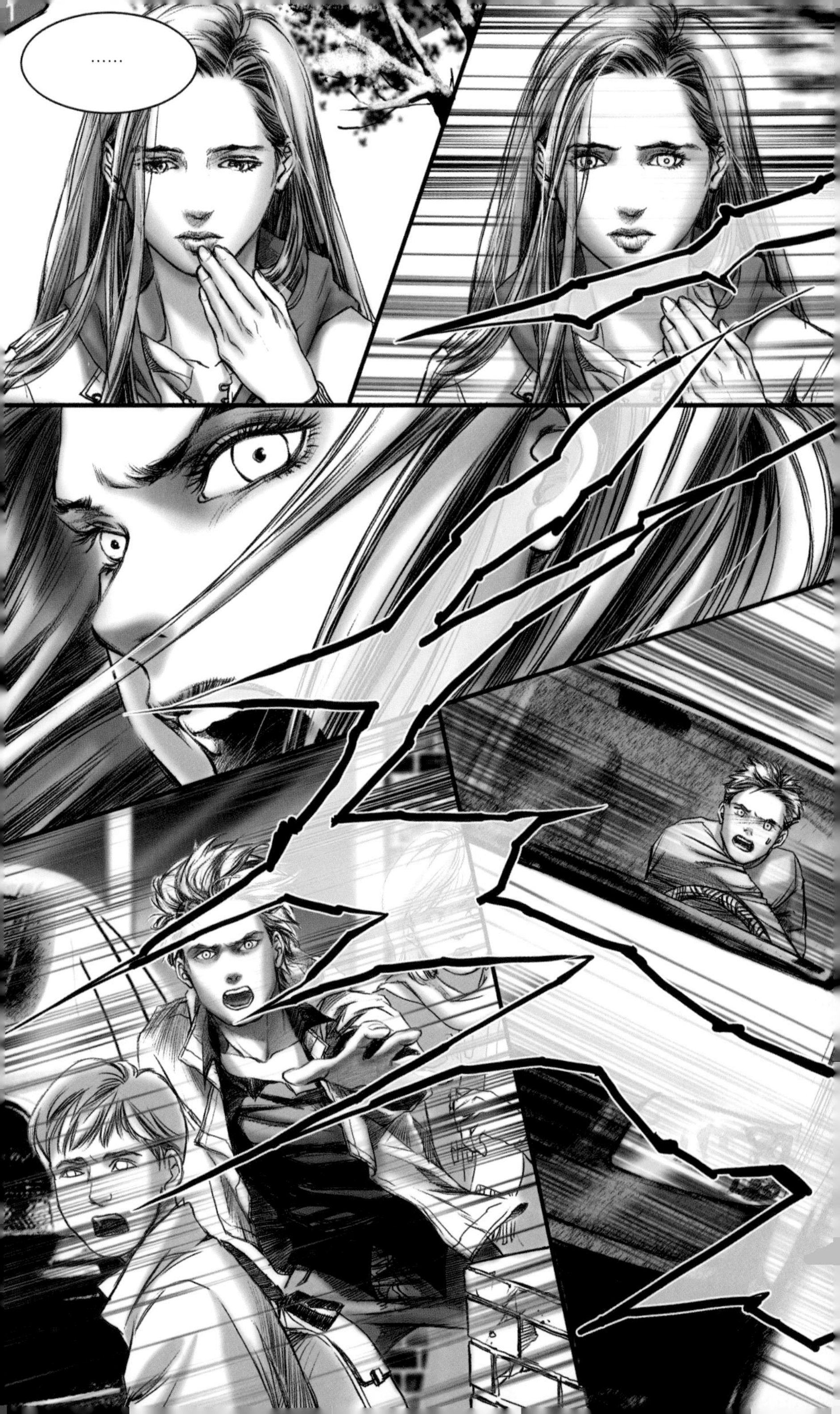
......

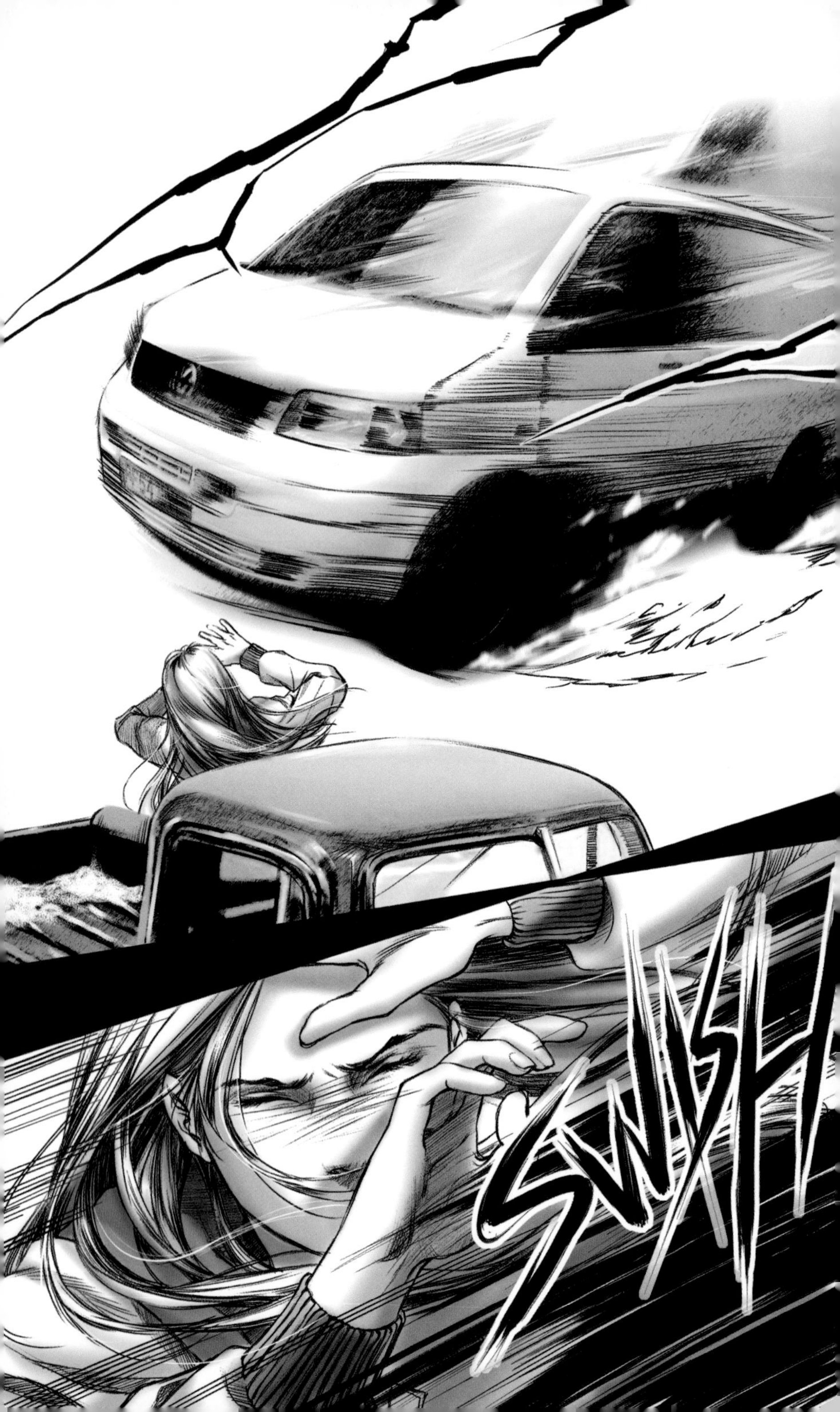
SWISH

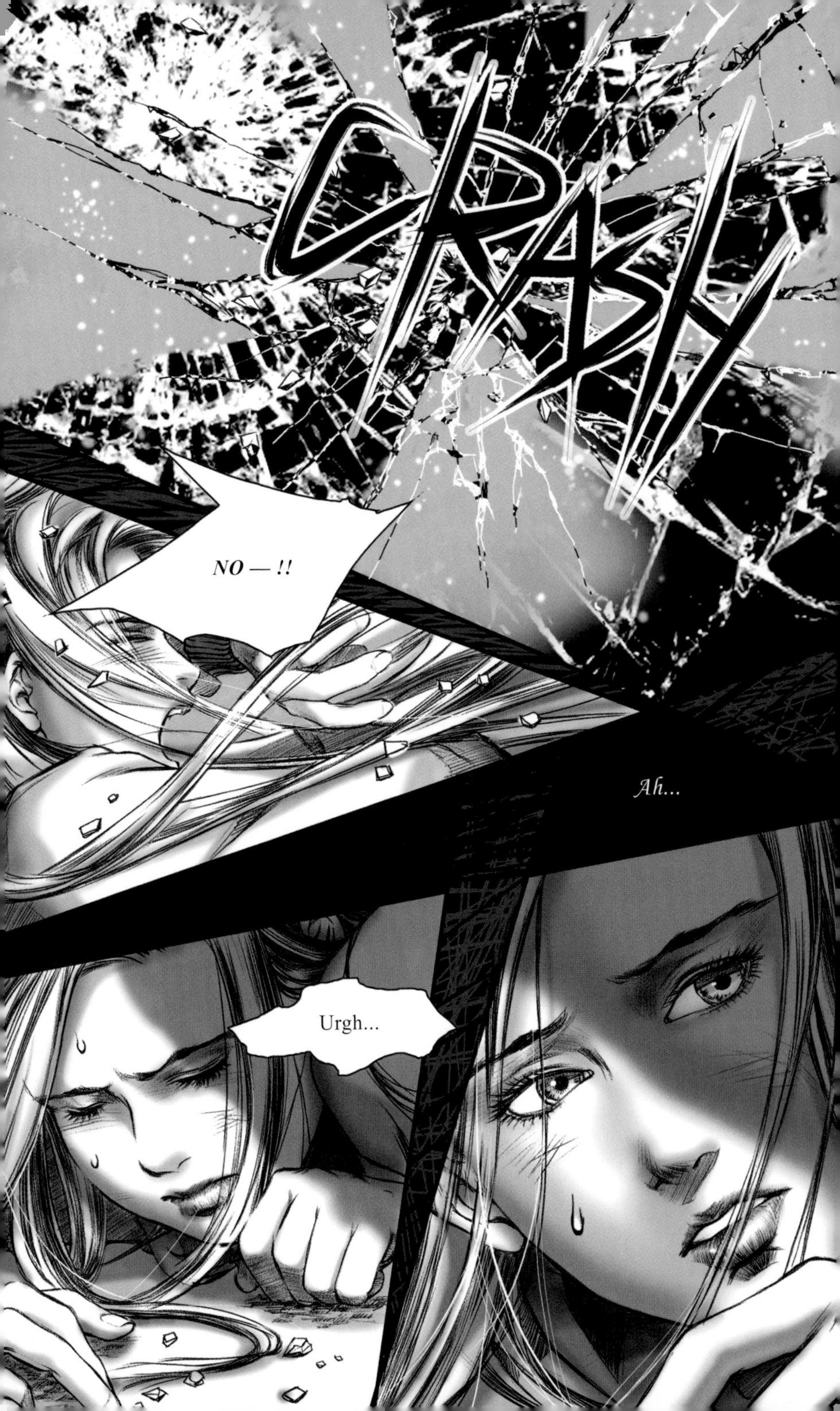
CRASH
NO — !!
Ah...
Urgh...

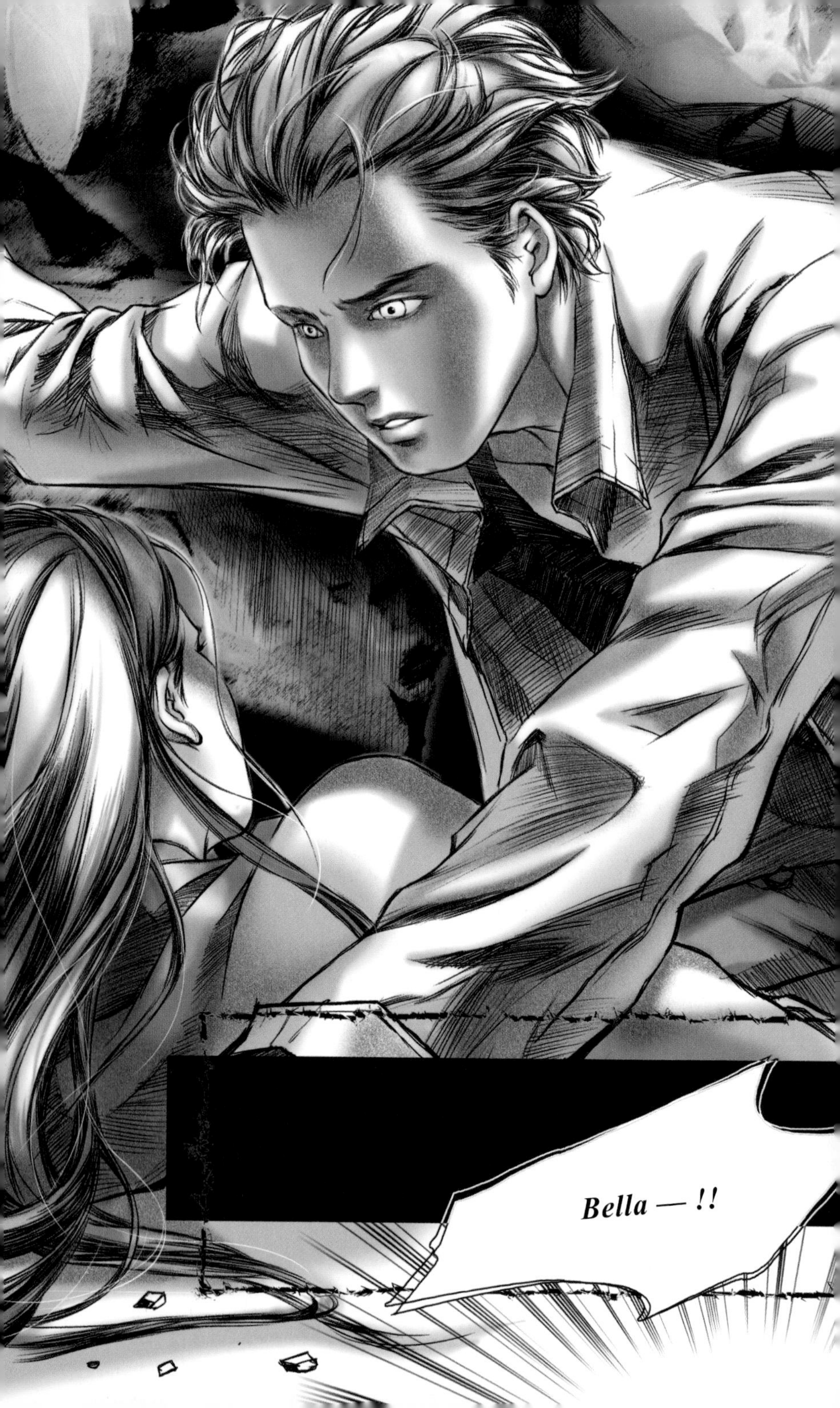
Bella — !!

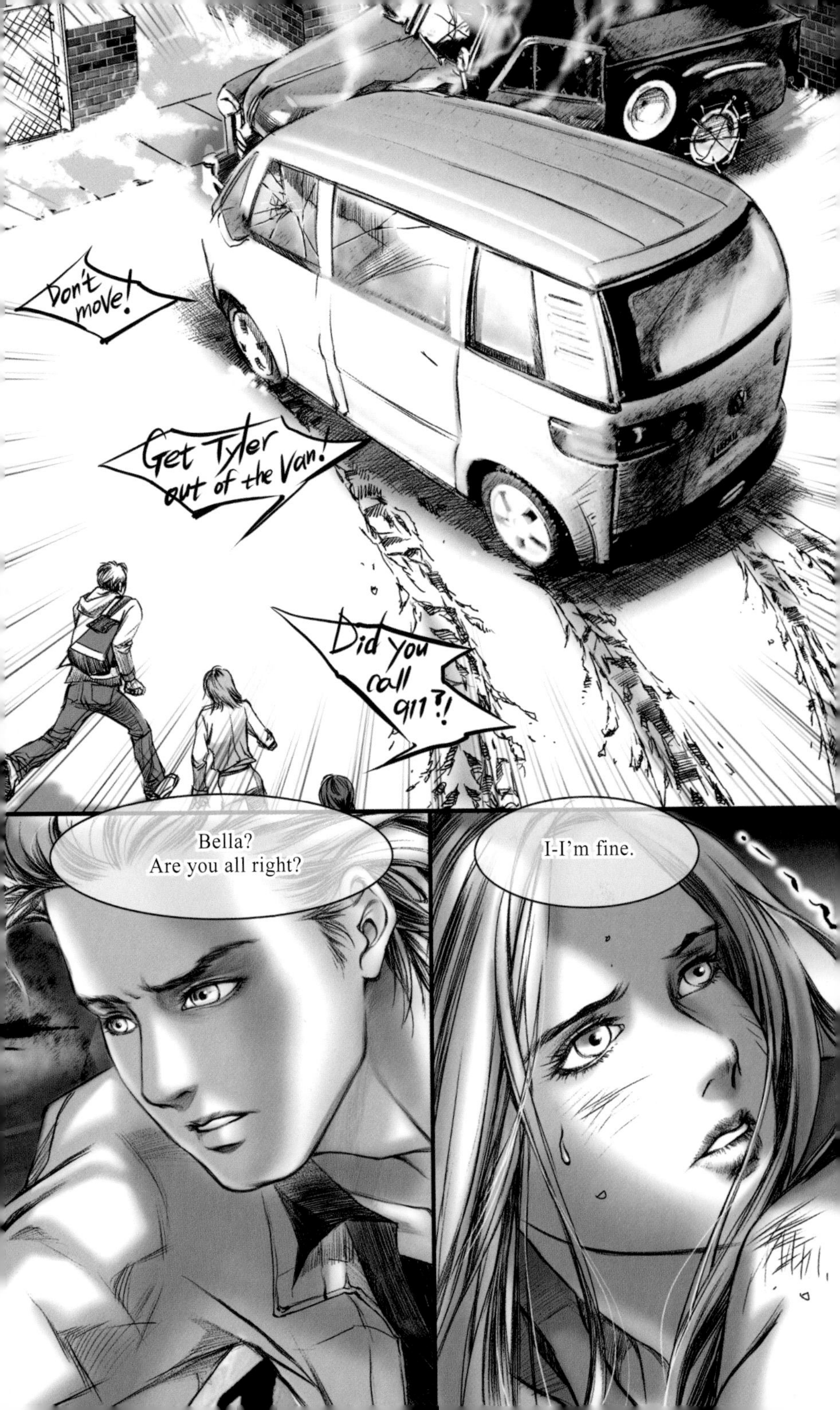
Don't move!
Get Tyler out of the Van!
Did you call 911?!
Bella? Are you all right?
I-I'm fine.

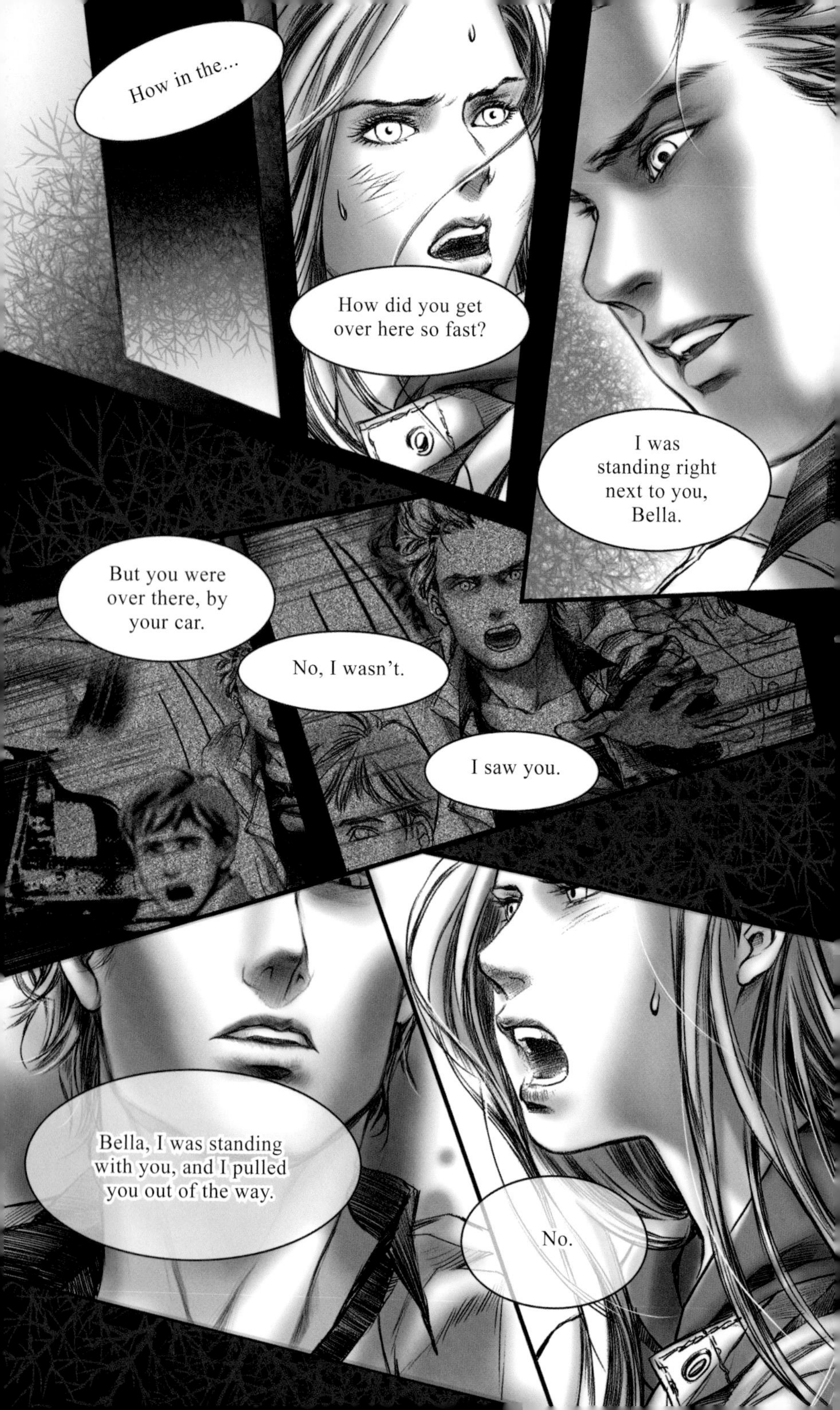
How in the...
How did you get over here so fast?
I was standing right next to you, Bella.
But you were over there, by your car.
No, I wasn't.
I saw you.
Bella, I was standing with you, and I pulled you out of the way.
No.

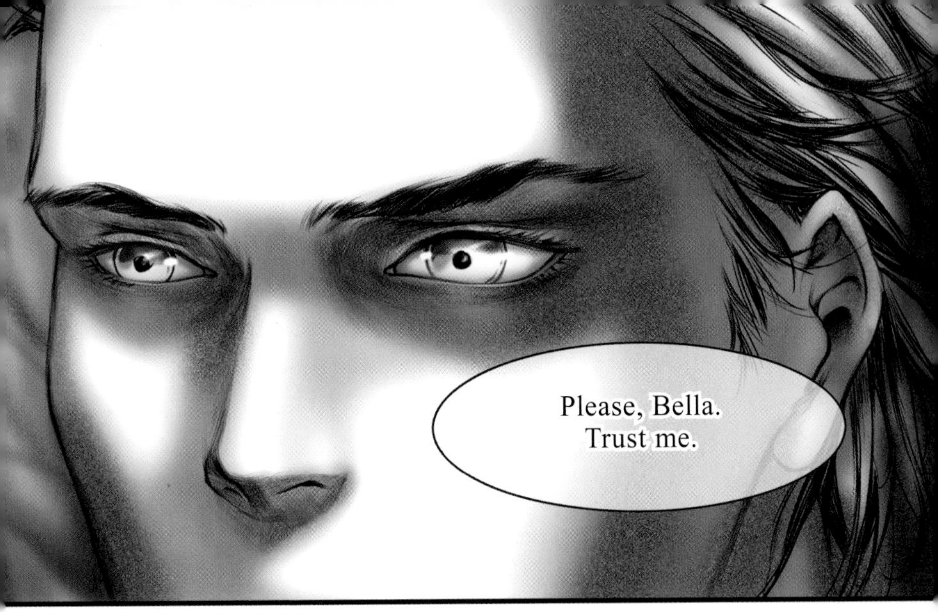
Please, Bella.
Trust me.

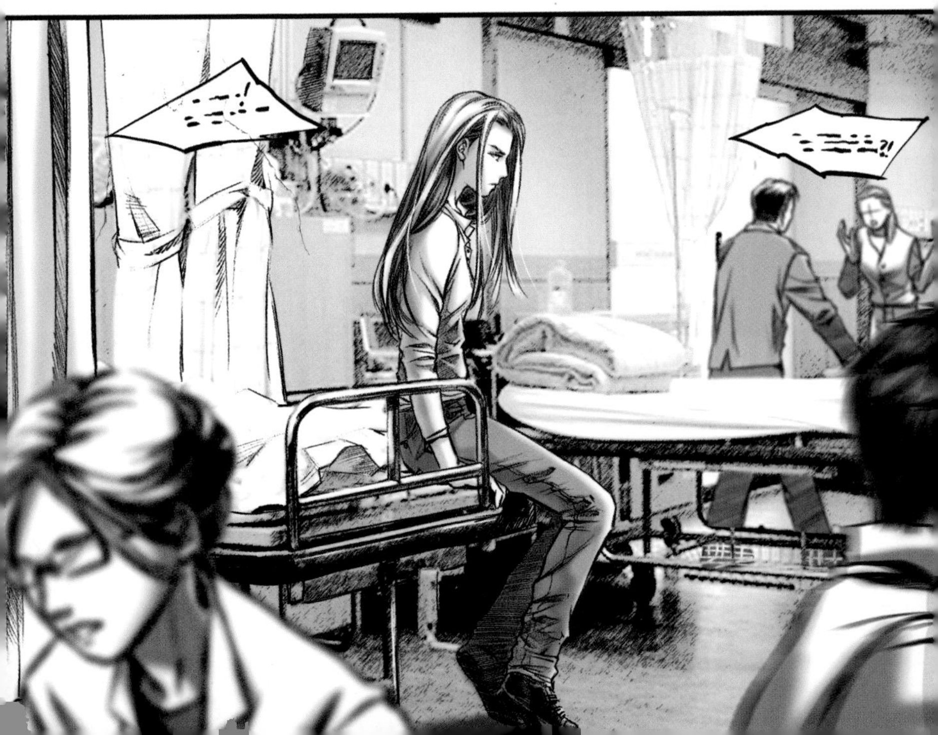

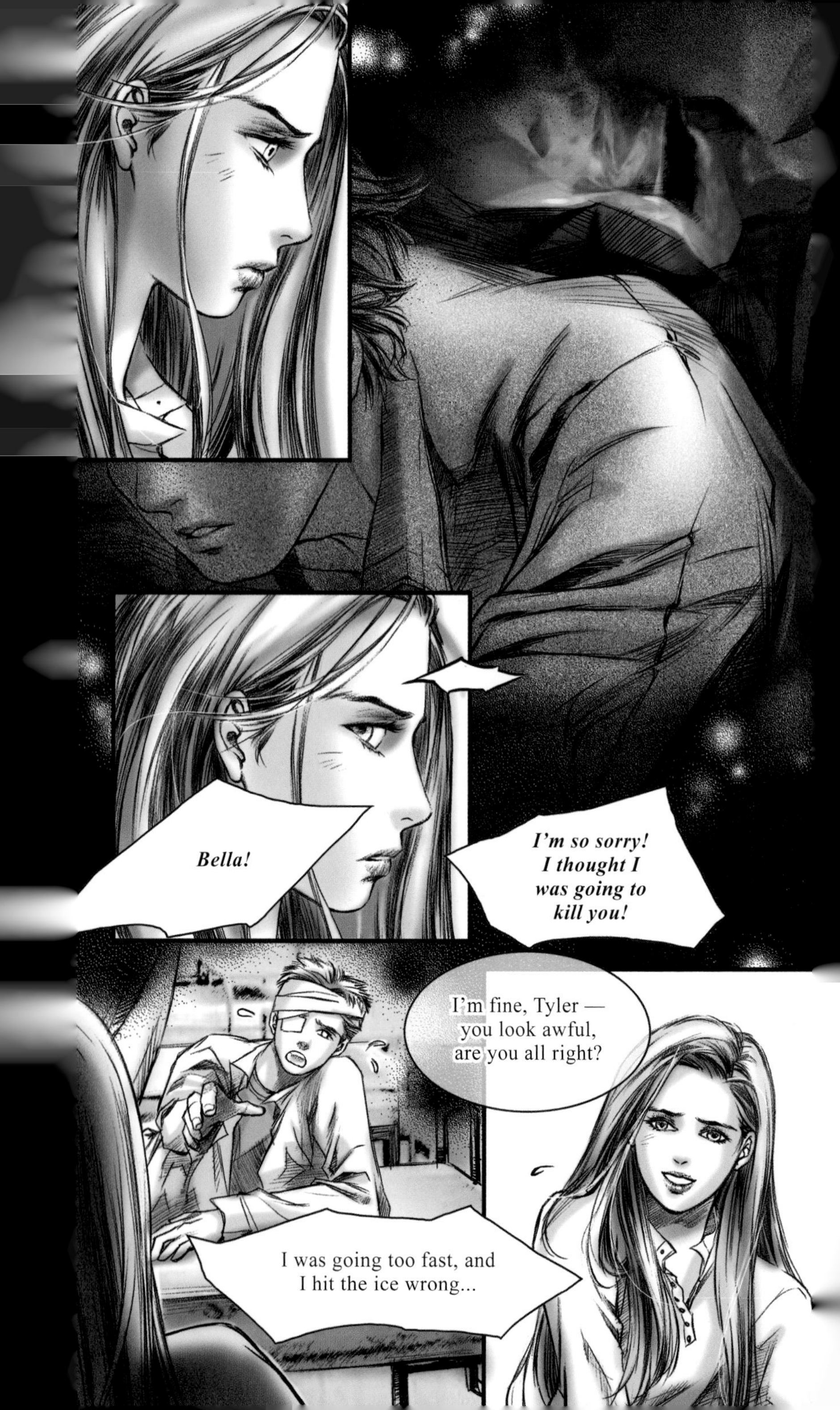
Bella!
I'm so sorry! I thought I was going to kill you!
I'm fine, Tyler — you look awful, are you all right?
I was going too fast, and I hit the ice wrong...

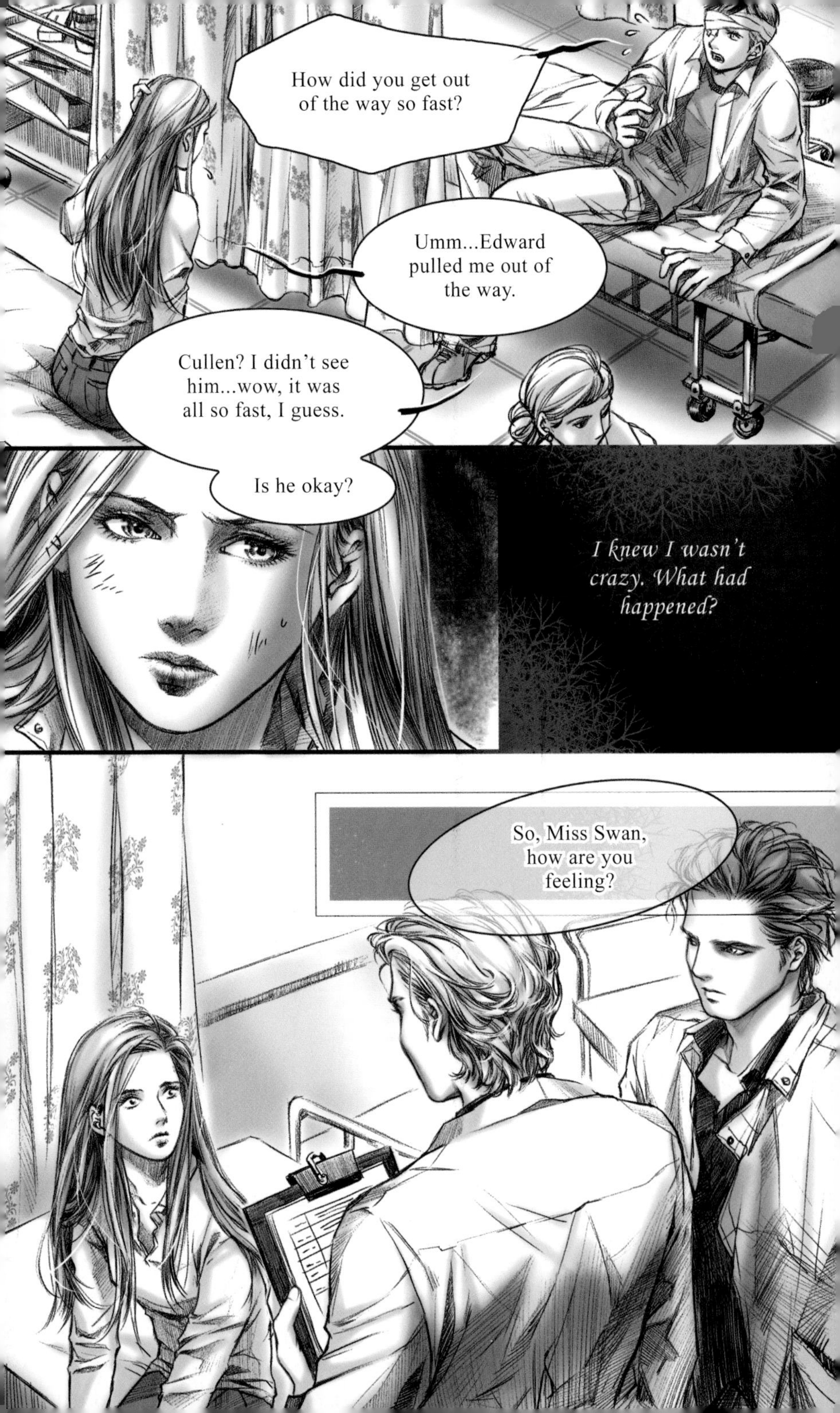
How did you get out of the way so fast?
Umm...Edward pulled me out of the way.
Cullen? I didn't see him...wow, it was all so fast, I guess.
Is he okay?
I knew I wasn't crazy. What had happened?
So, Miss Swan, how are you feeling?

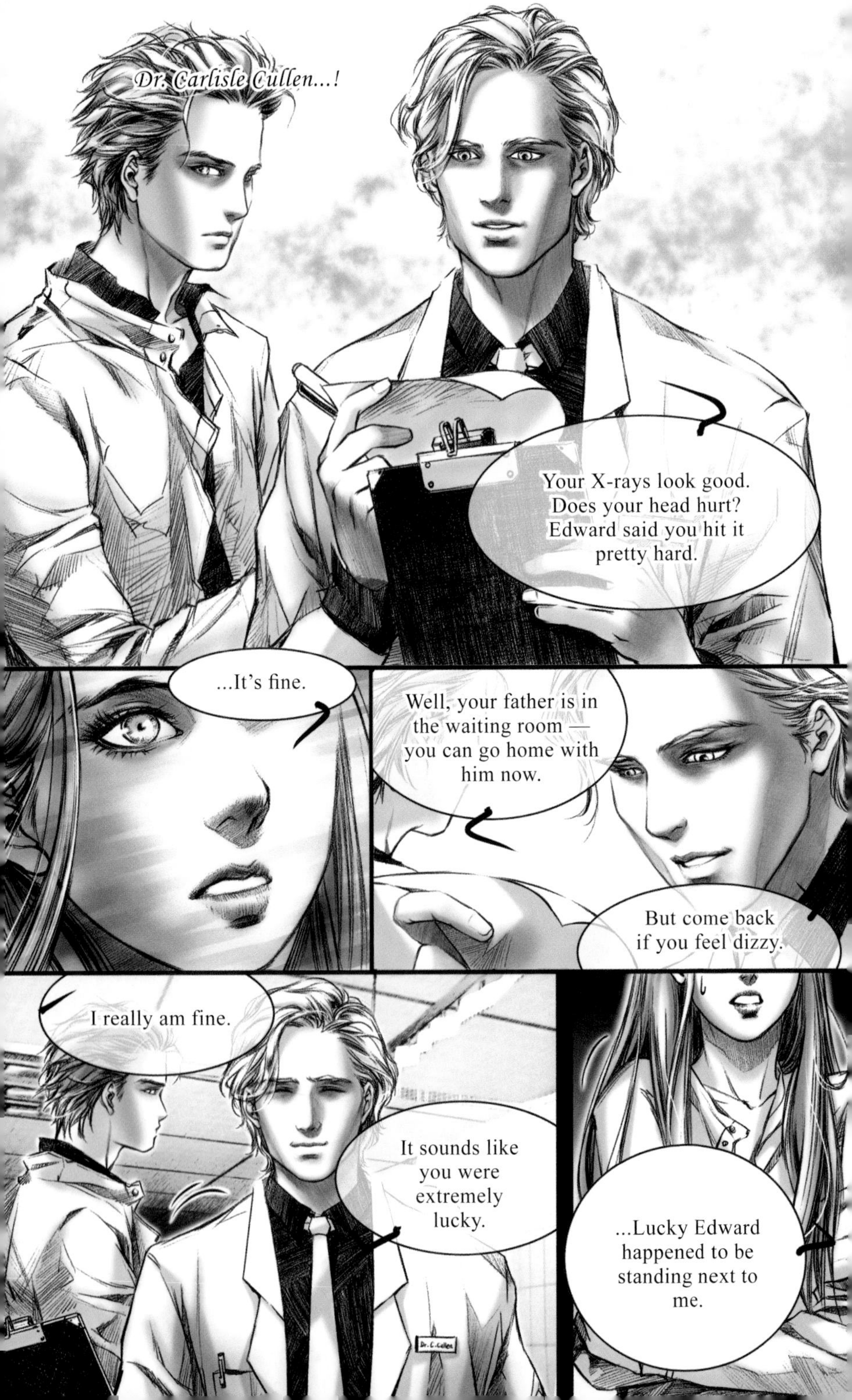
Dr. Carlisle Cullen...!
Your X-rays look good. Does your head hurt? Edward said you hit it pretty hard.
...It's fine.
Well, your father is in the waiting room — you can go home with him now.
But come back if you feel dizzy.
I really am fine.
It sounds like you were extremely lucky.
...Lucky Edward happened to be standing next to me.
Dr. C. Cullen

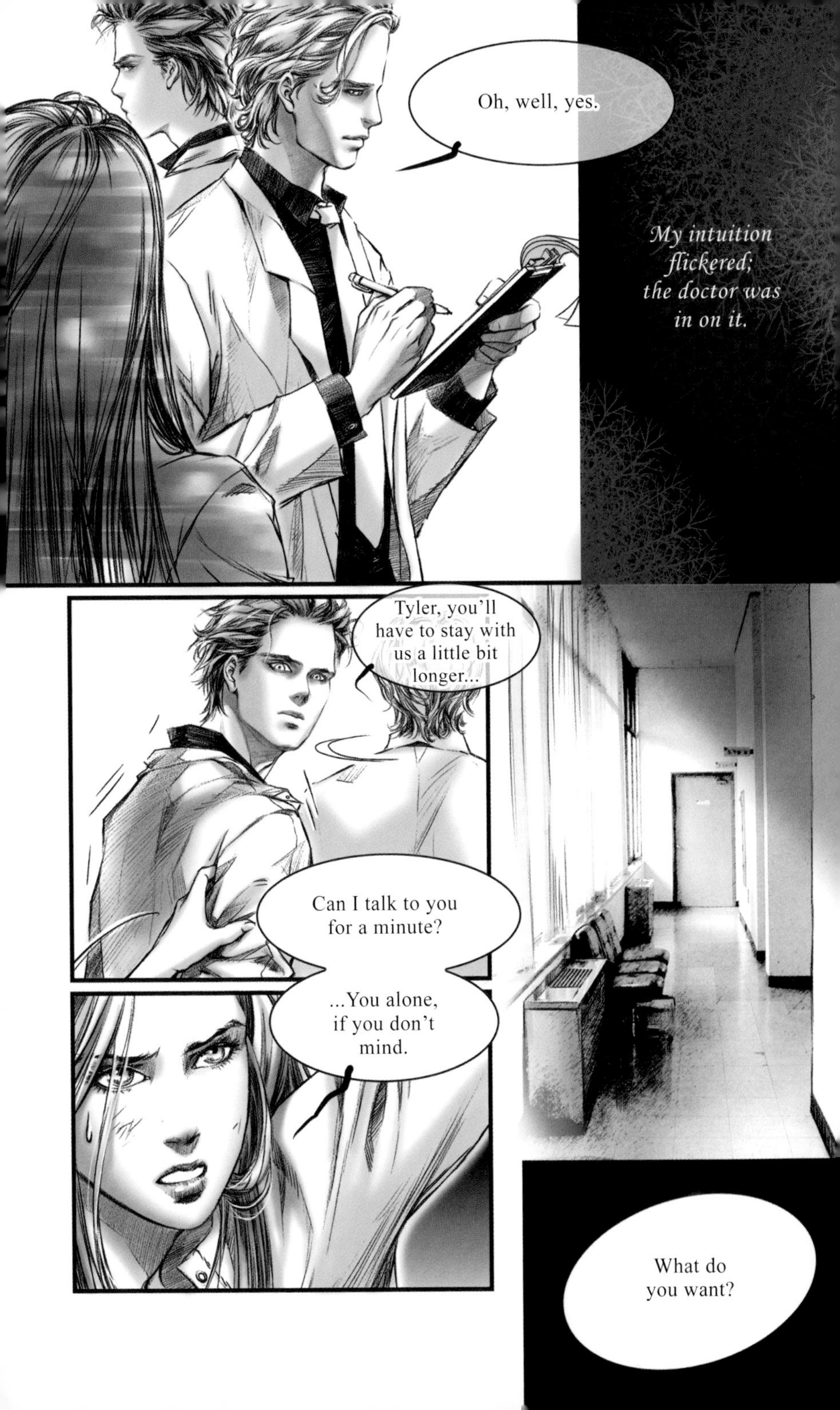
Oh, well, yes.
My intuition flickered; the doctor was in on it.
Tyler, you'll have to stay with us a little bit longer...
Can I talk to you for a minute?
...You alone, if you don't mind.
What do you want?

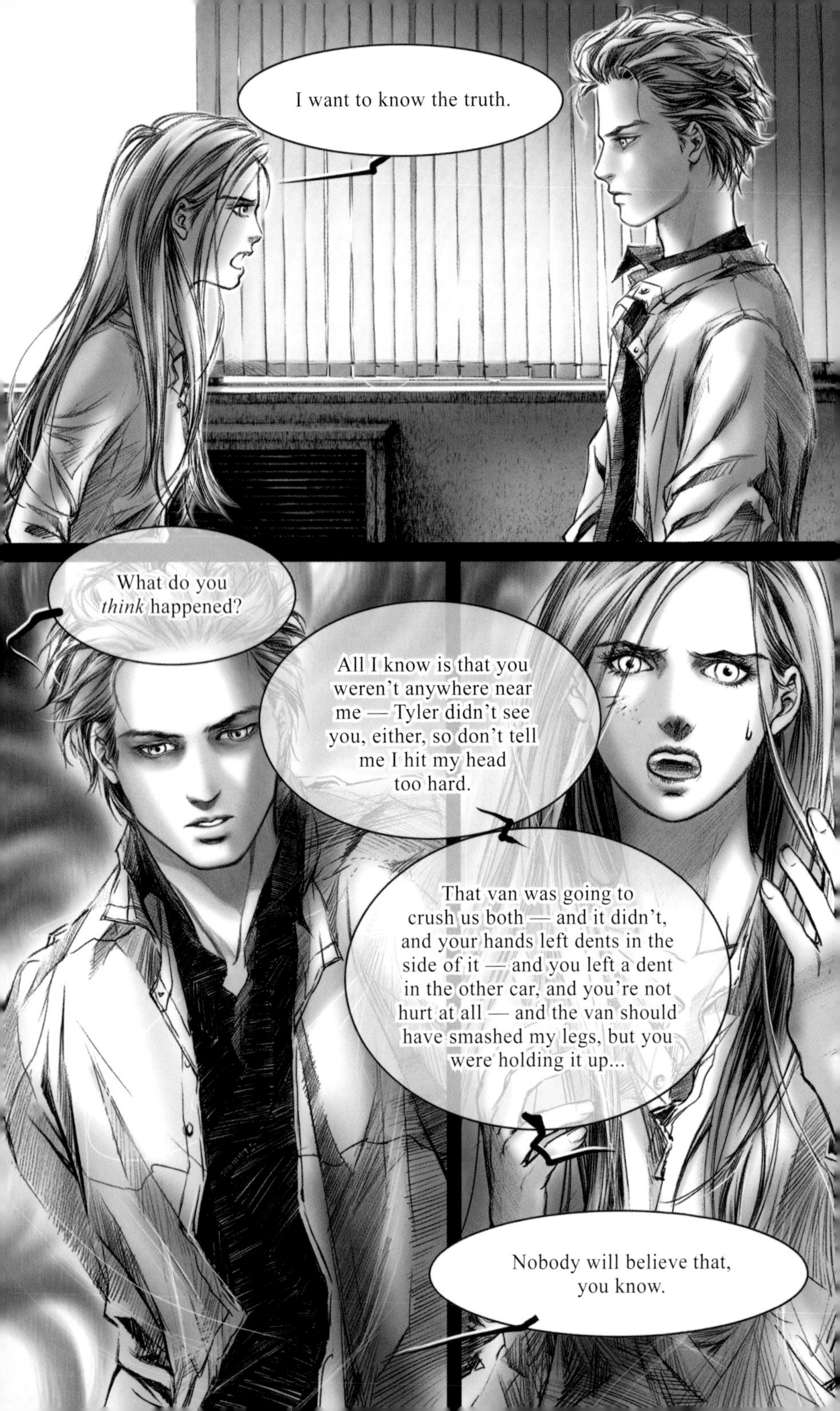
I want to know the truth.
What do you *think* happened?
All I know is that you weren't anywhere near me — Tyler didn't see you, either, so don't tell me I hit my head too hard.
That van was going to crush us both — and it didn't, and your hands left dents in the side of it — and you left a dent in the other car, and you're not hurt at all — and the van should have smashed my legs, but you were holding it up...
Nobody will believe that, you know.

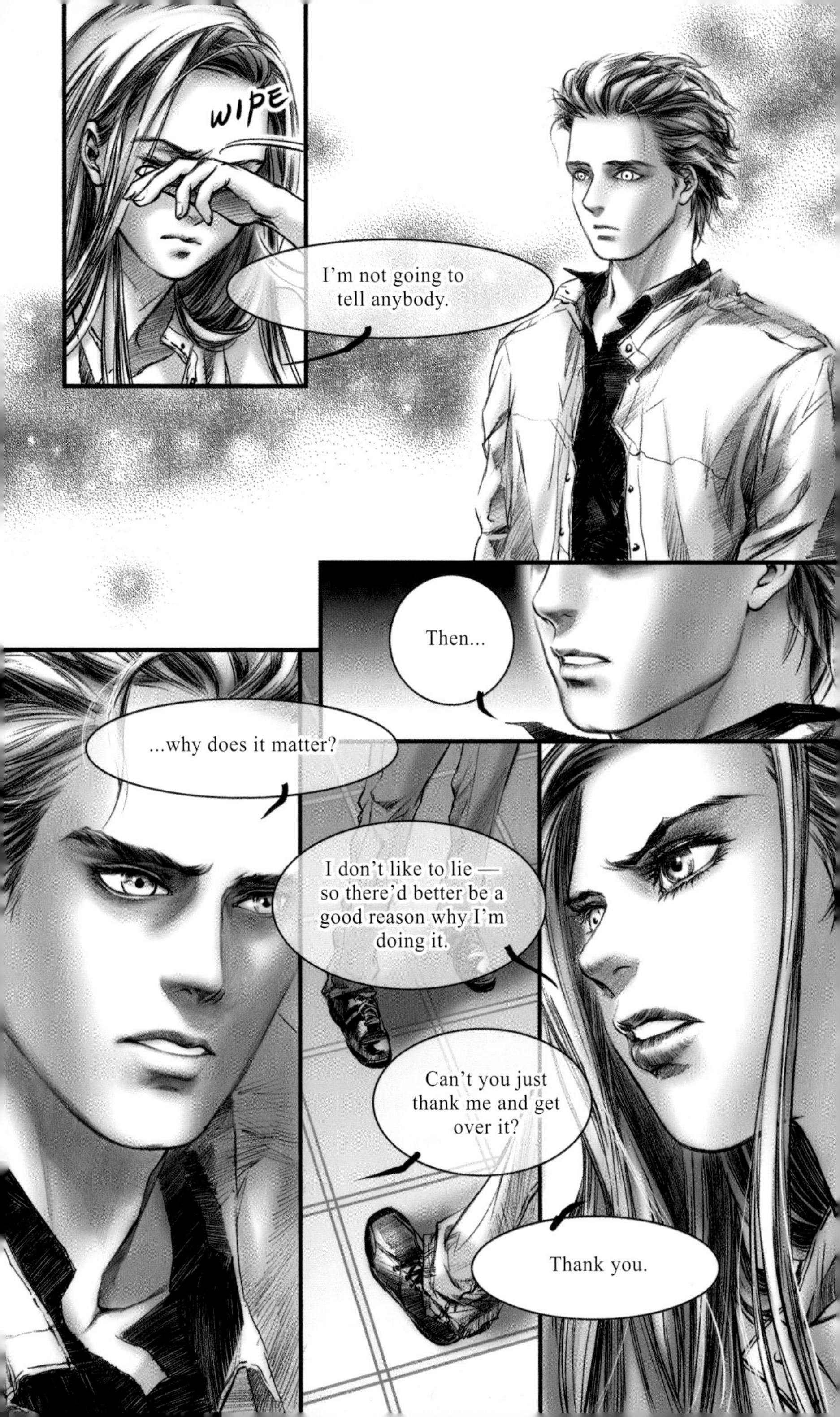
WIPE
I'm not going to tell anybody.
Then...
...why does it matter?
I don't like to lie — so there'd better be a good reason why I'm doing it.
Can't you just thank me and get over it?
Thank you.

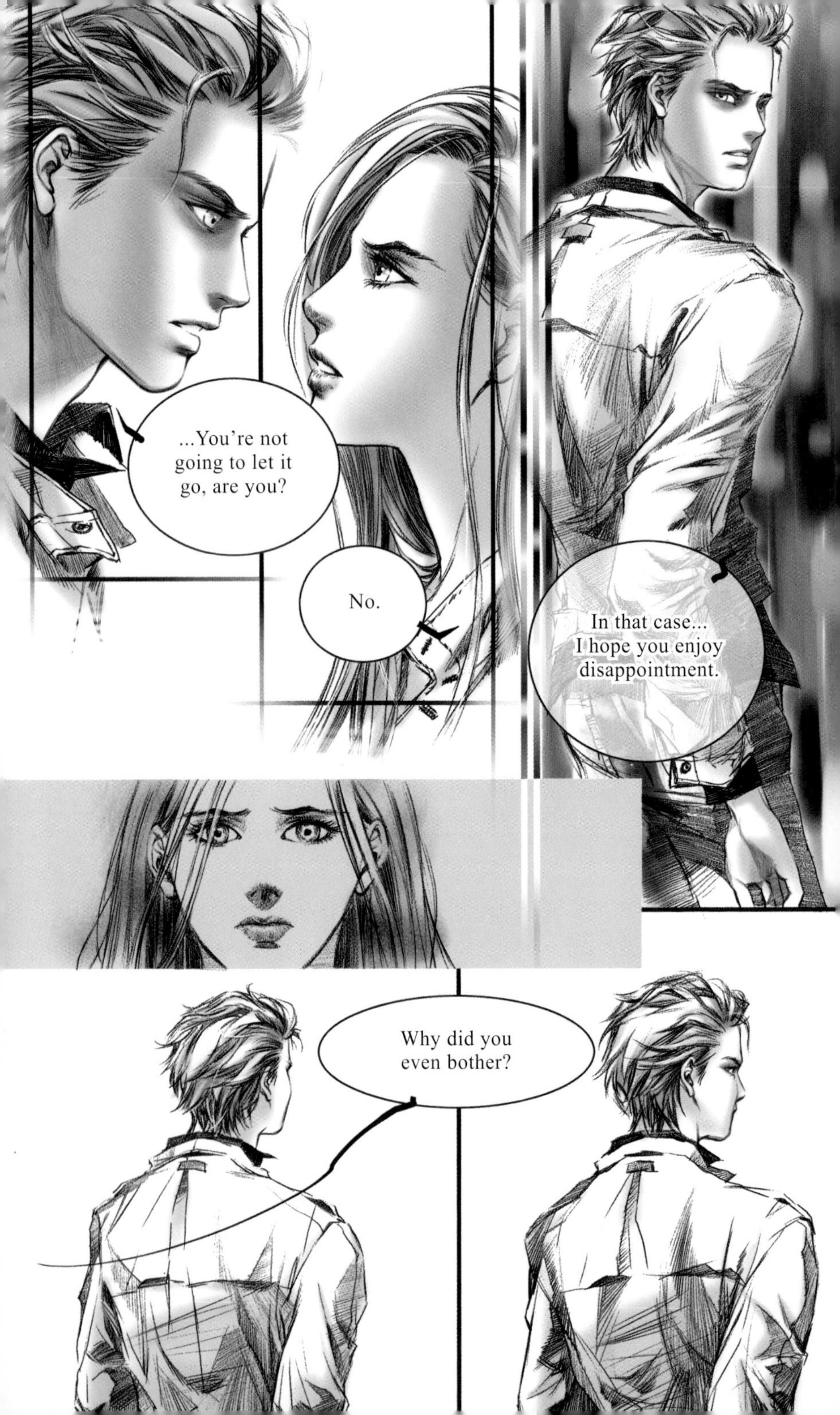
...You're not going to let it go, are you?
No.
In that case... I hope you enjoy disappointment.
Why did you even bother?

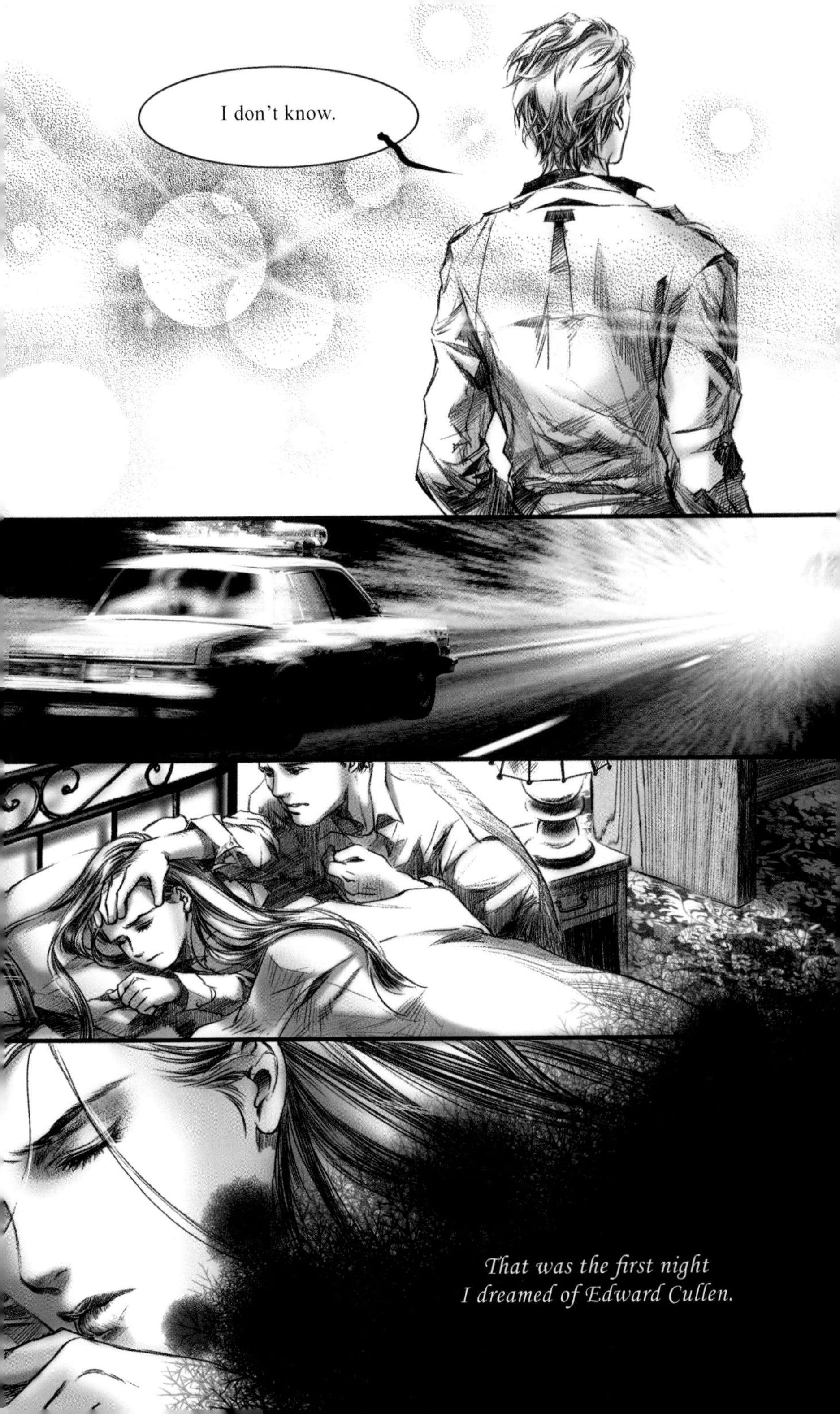
I don't know.
That was the first night
I dreamed of Edward Cullen.

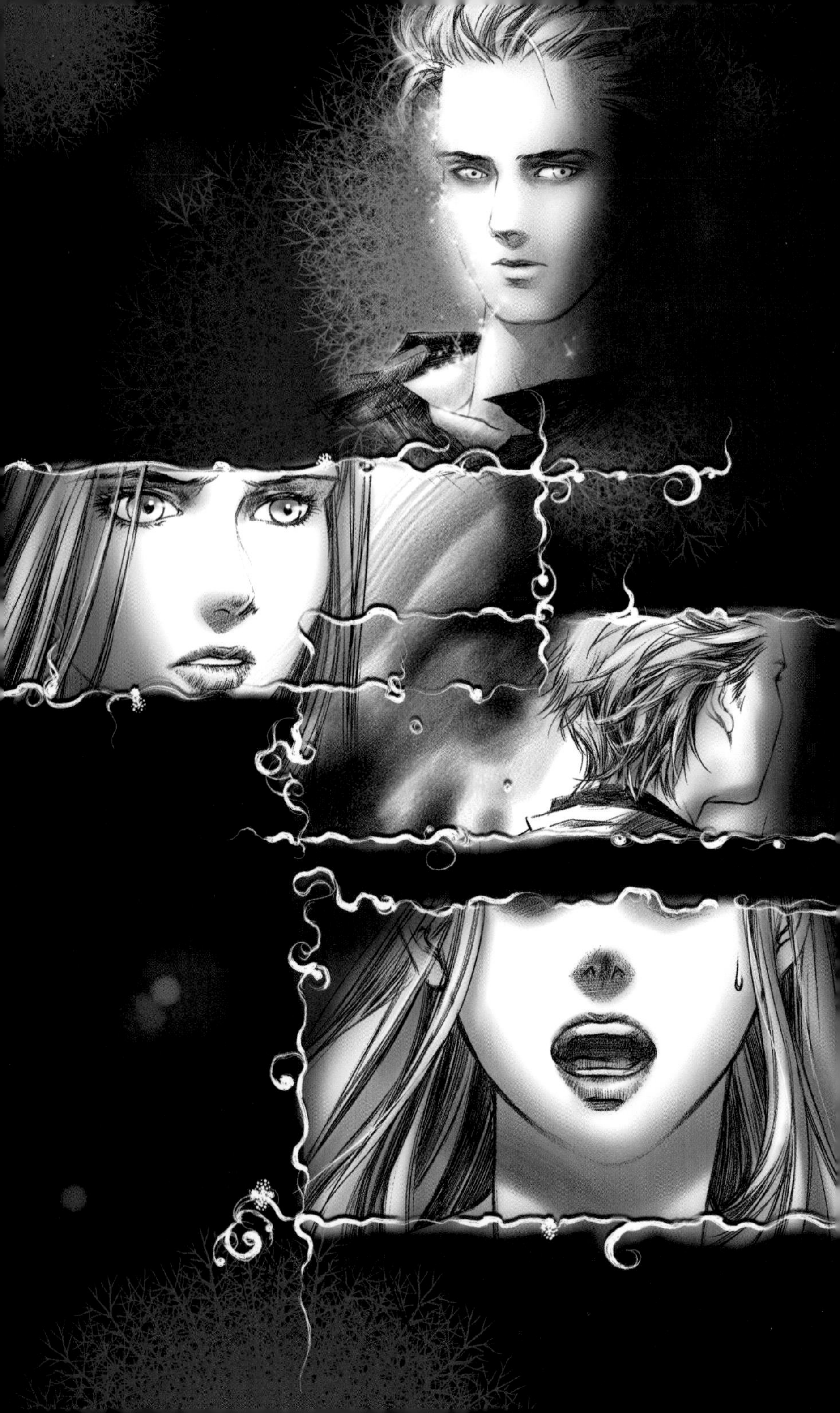

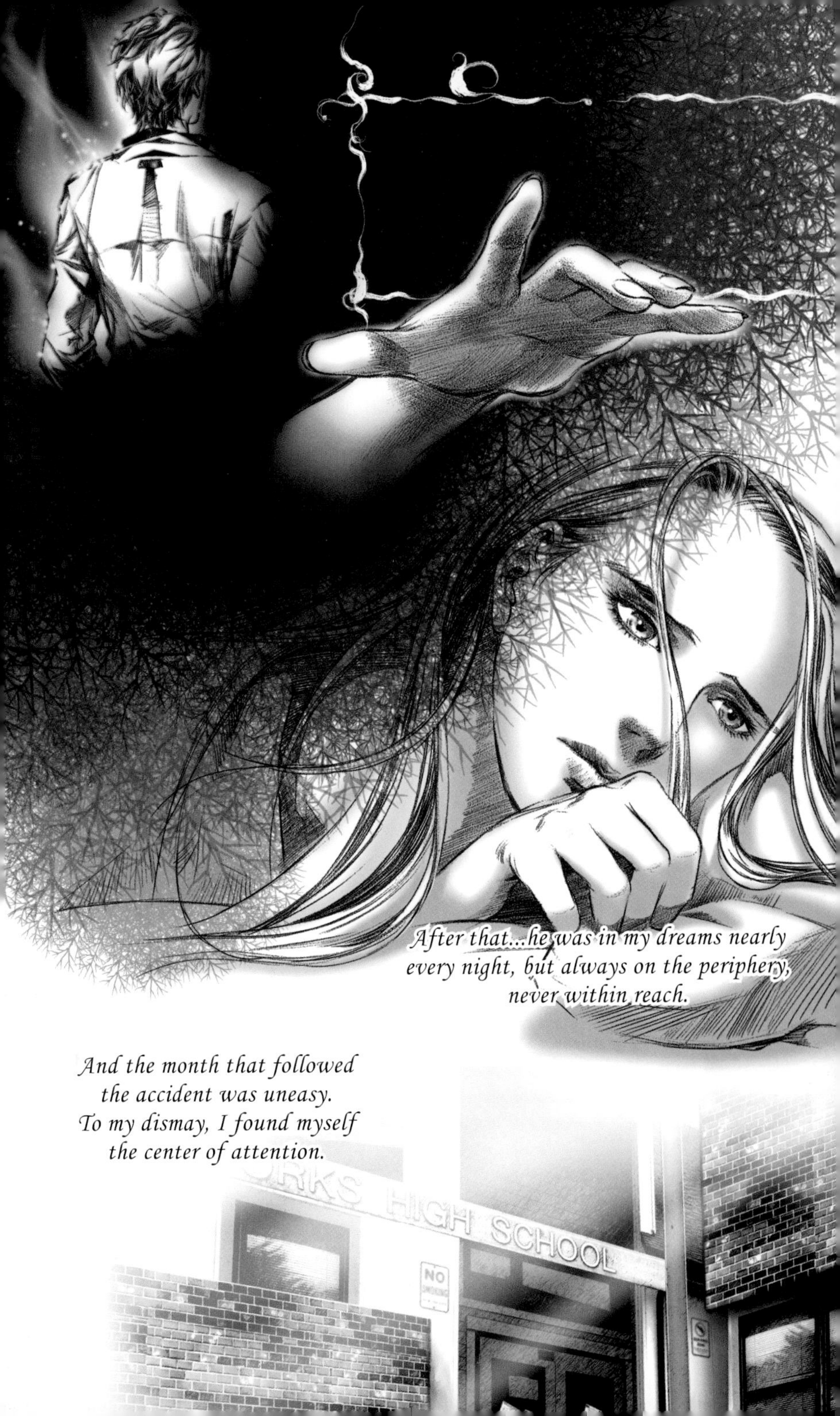
After that...he was in my dreams nearly every night, but always on the periphery, never within reach.
And the month that followed the accident was uneasy. To my dismay, I found myself the center of attention.
HIGH SCHOOL
NO

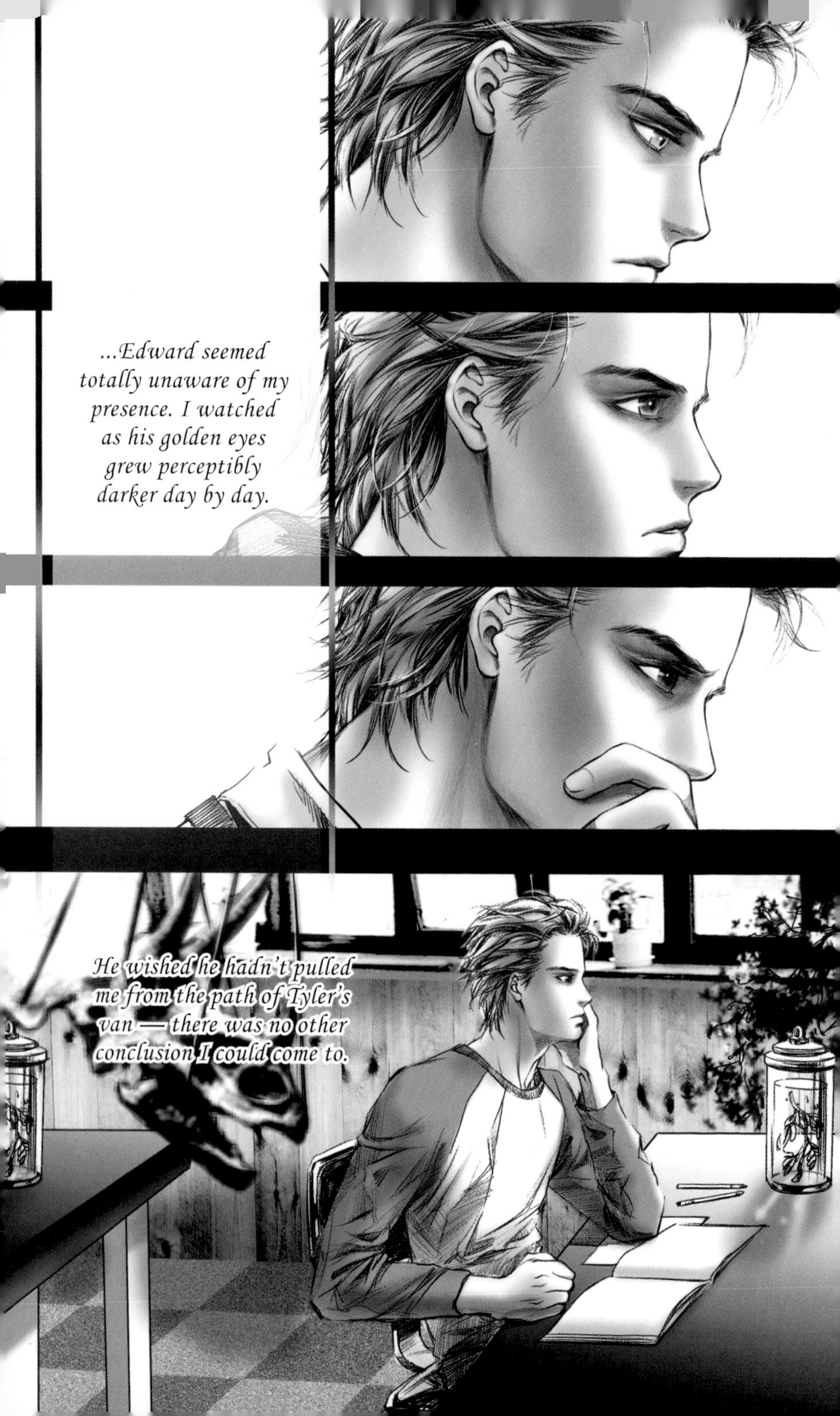
...Edward seemed totally unaware of my presence. I watched as his golden eyes grew perceptibly darker day by day.
He wished he hadn't pulled me from the path of Tyler's van — there was no other conclusion I could come to.

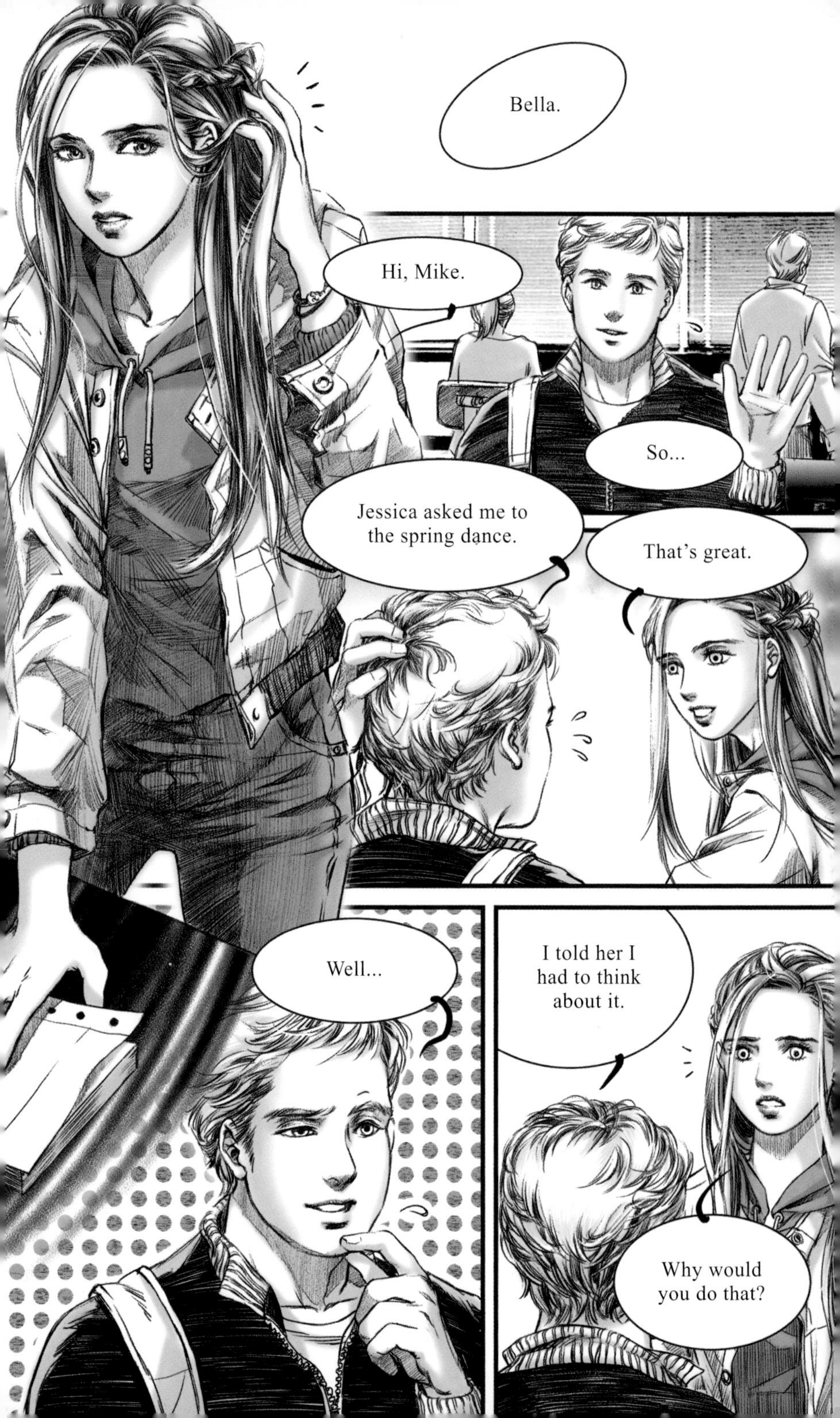
Bella.
Hi, Mike.
So...
Jessica asked me to the spring dance.
That's great.
Well...
I told her I had to think about it.
Why would you do that?

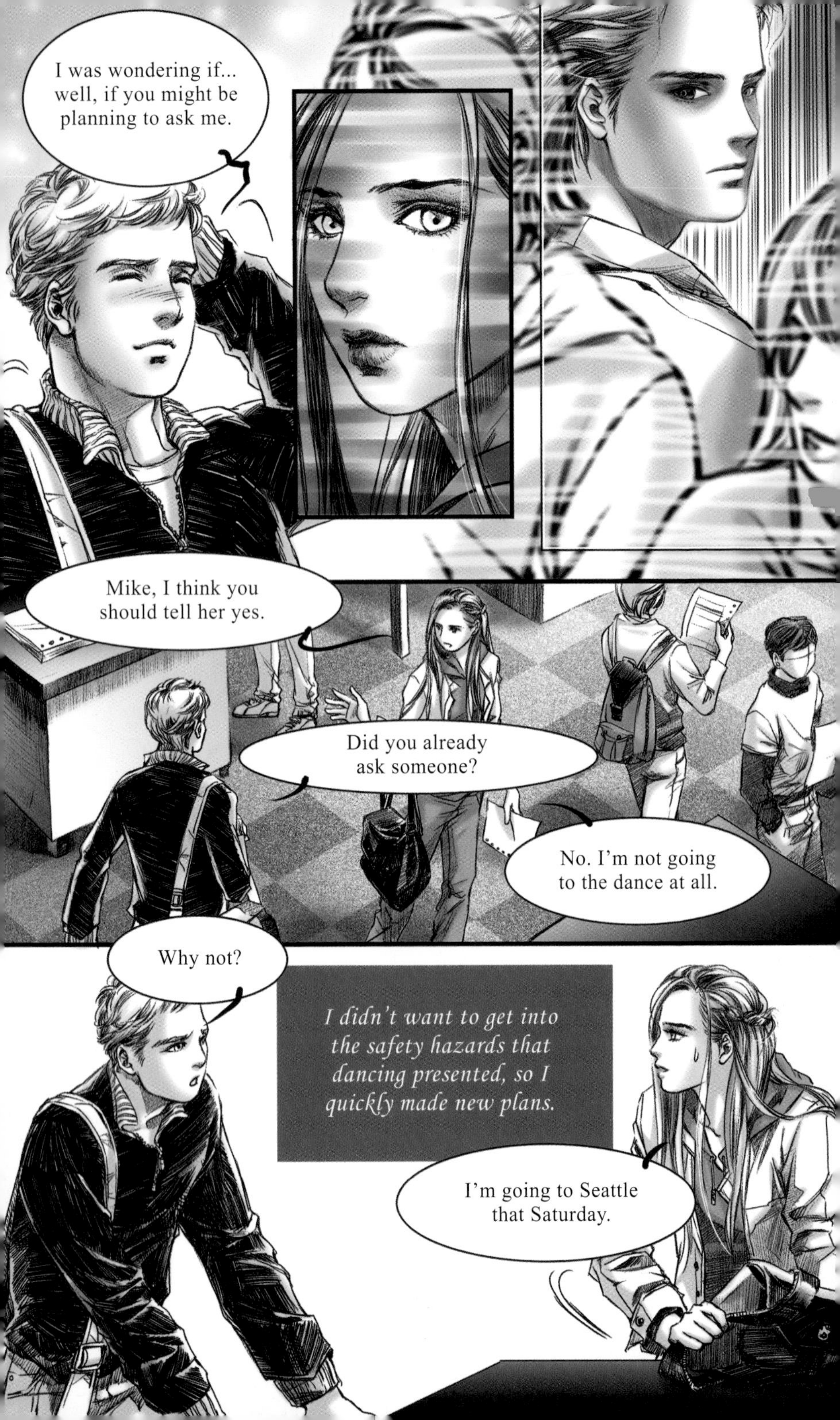
I was wondering if... well, if you might be planning to ask me.
Mike, I think you should tell her yes.
Did you already ask someone?
No. I'm not going to the dance at all.
Why not?
I didn't want to get into the safety hazards that dancing presented, so I quickly made new plans.
I'm going to Seattle that Saturday.

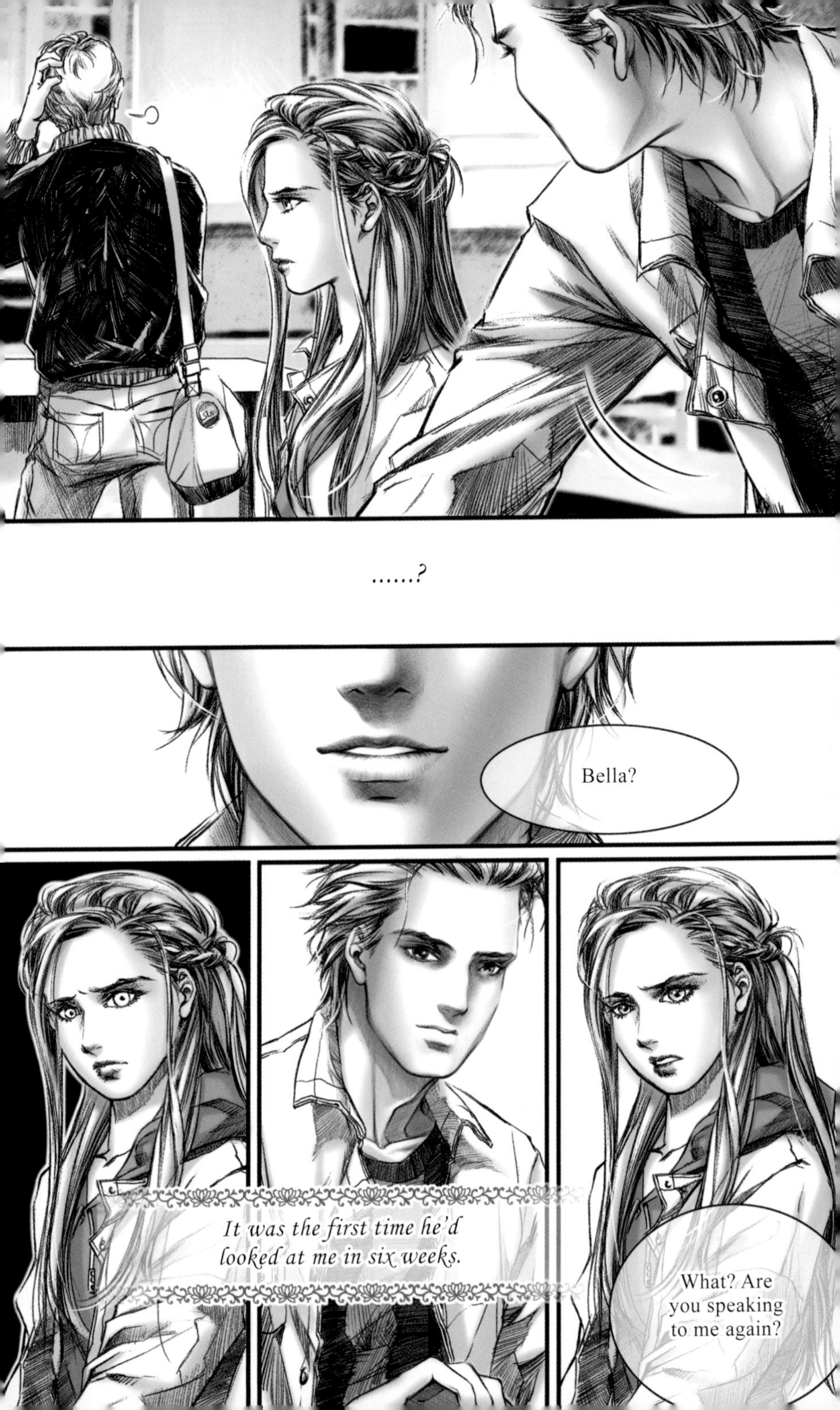
......?
Bella?
It was the first time he'd looked at me in six weeks.
What? Are you speaking to me again?

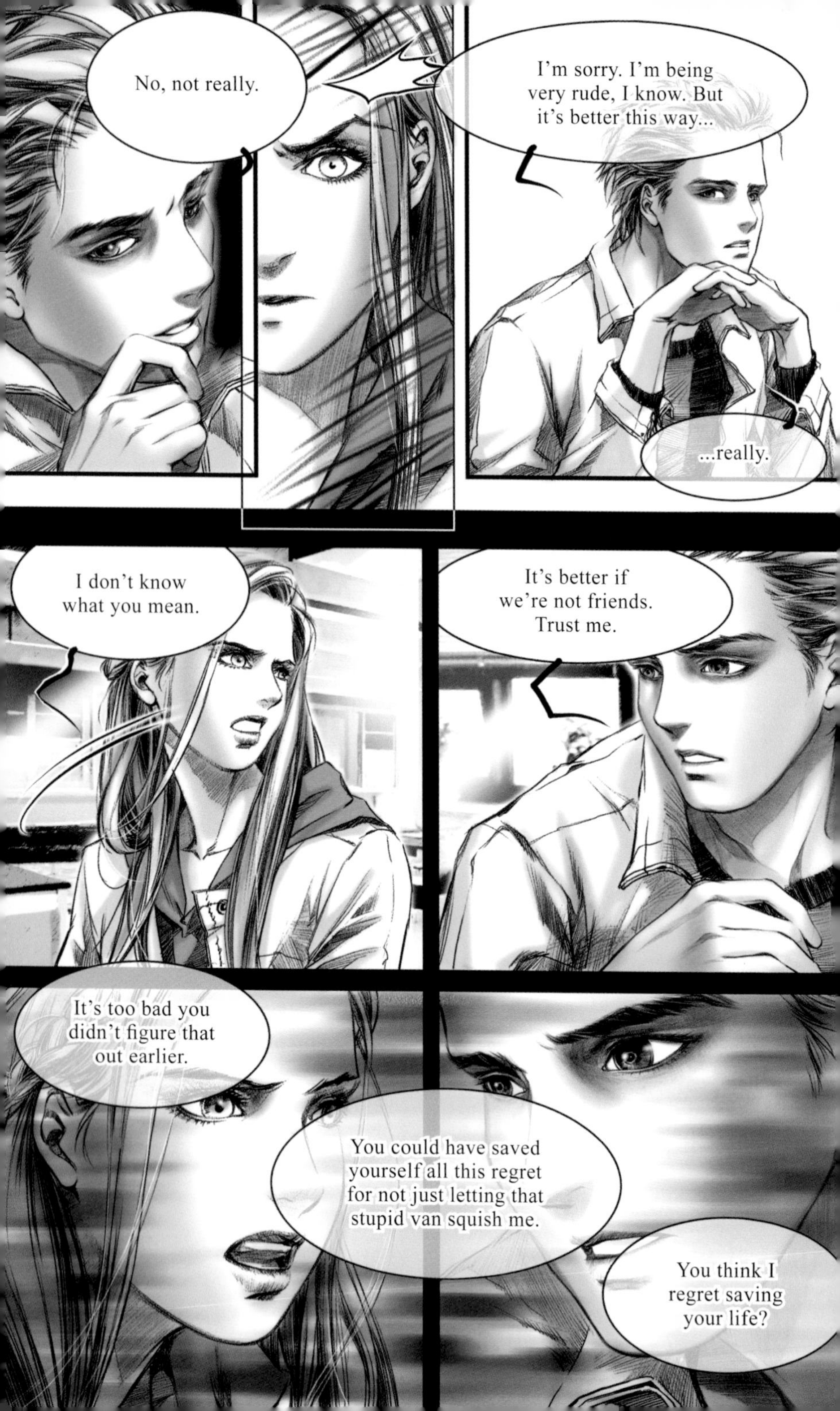
No, not really.
I'm sorry. I'm being very rude, I know. But it's better this way...
...really.
I don't know what you mean.
It's better if we're not friends. Trust me.
It's too bad you didn't figure that out earlier.
You could have saved yourself all this regret for not just letting that stupid van squish me.
You think I regret saving your life?

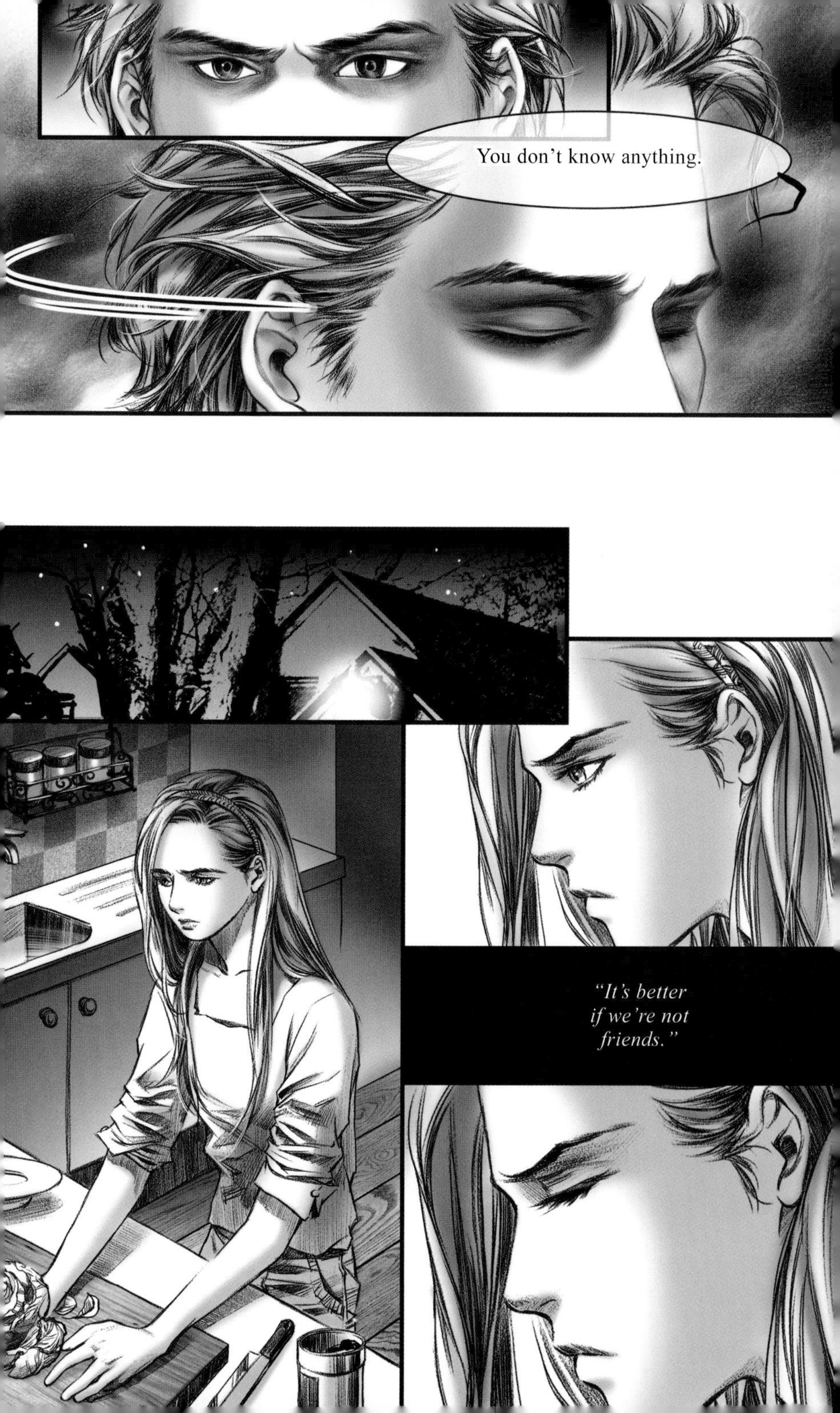
You don't know anything.
"It's better if we're not friends."

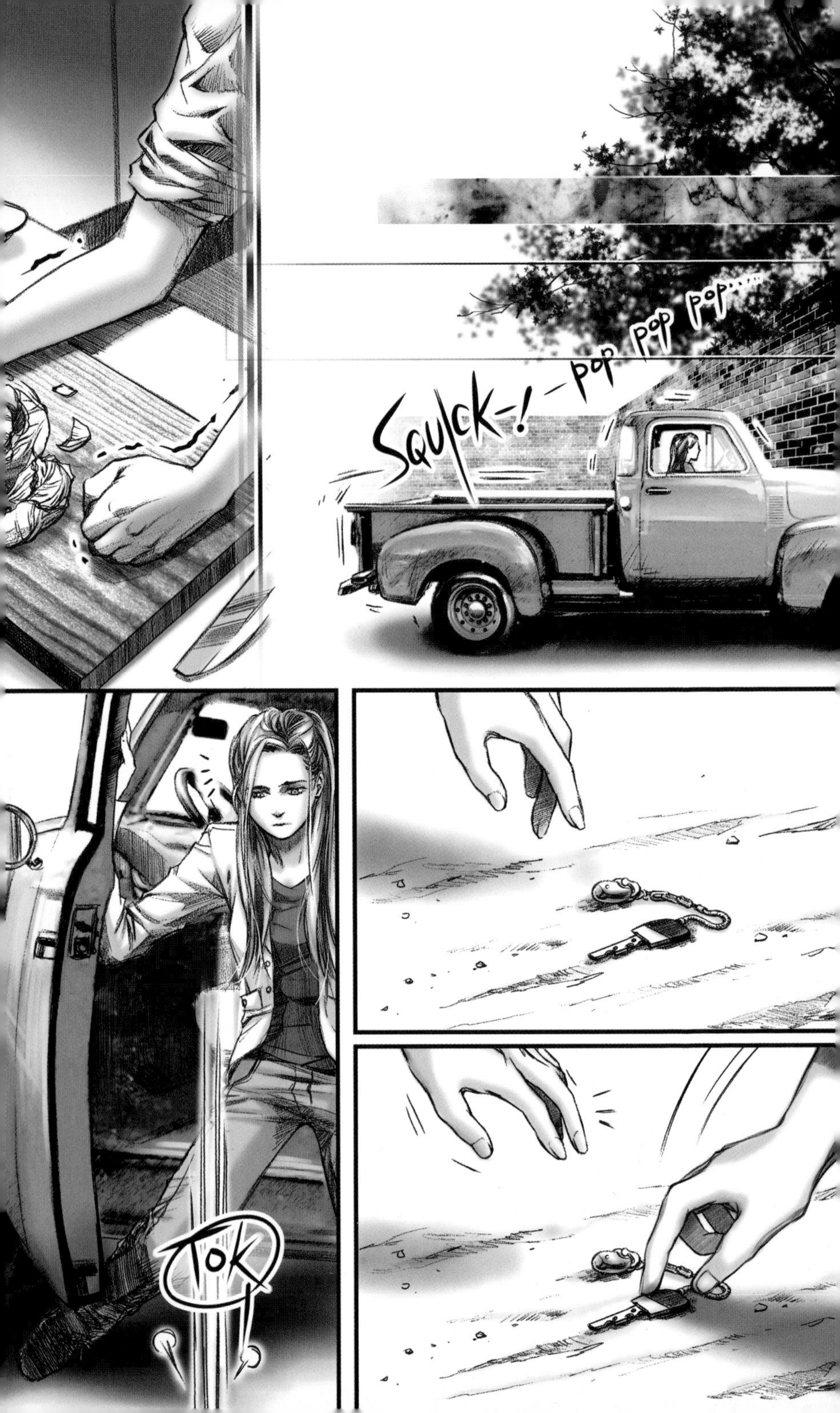
SQUICK--!
--pop
pop pop pop......
TOK

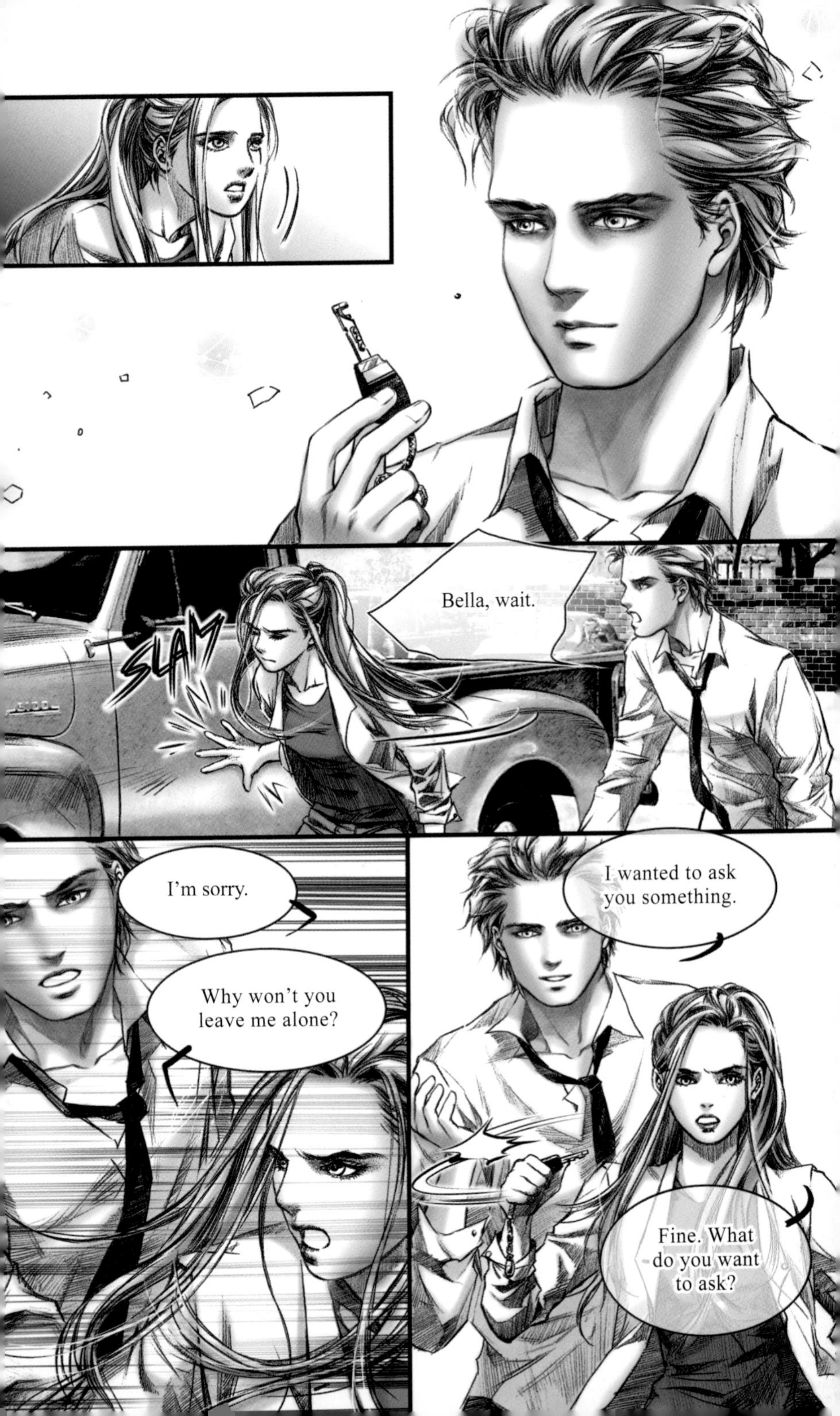
SLAM
Bella, wait.
I'm sorry.
Why won't you leave me alone?
I wanted to ask you something.
Fine. What do you want to ask?

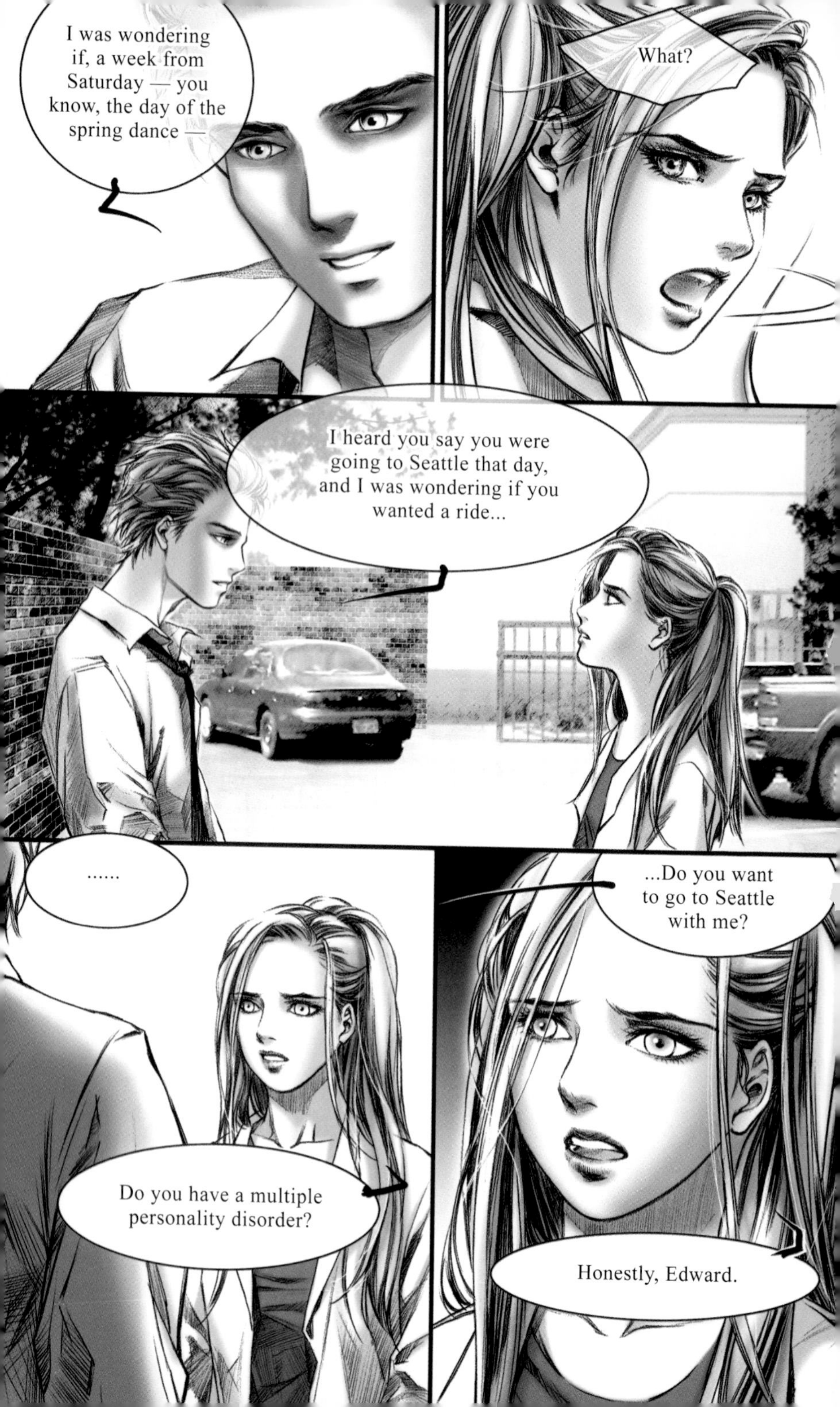

I was wondering if, a week from Saturday — you know, the day of the spring dance —
What?
I heard you say you were going to Seattle that day, and I was wondering if you wanted a ride...
......
...Do you want to go to Seattle with me?
Do you have a multiple personality disorder?
Honestly, Edward.

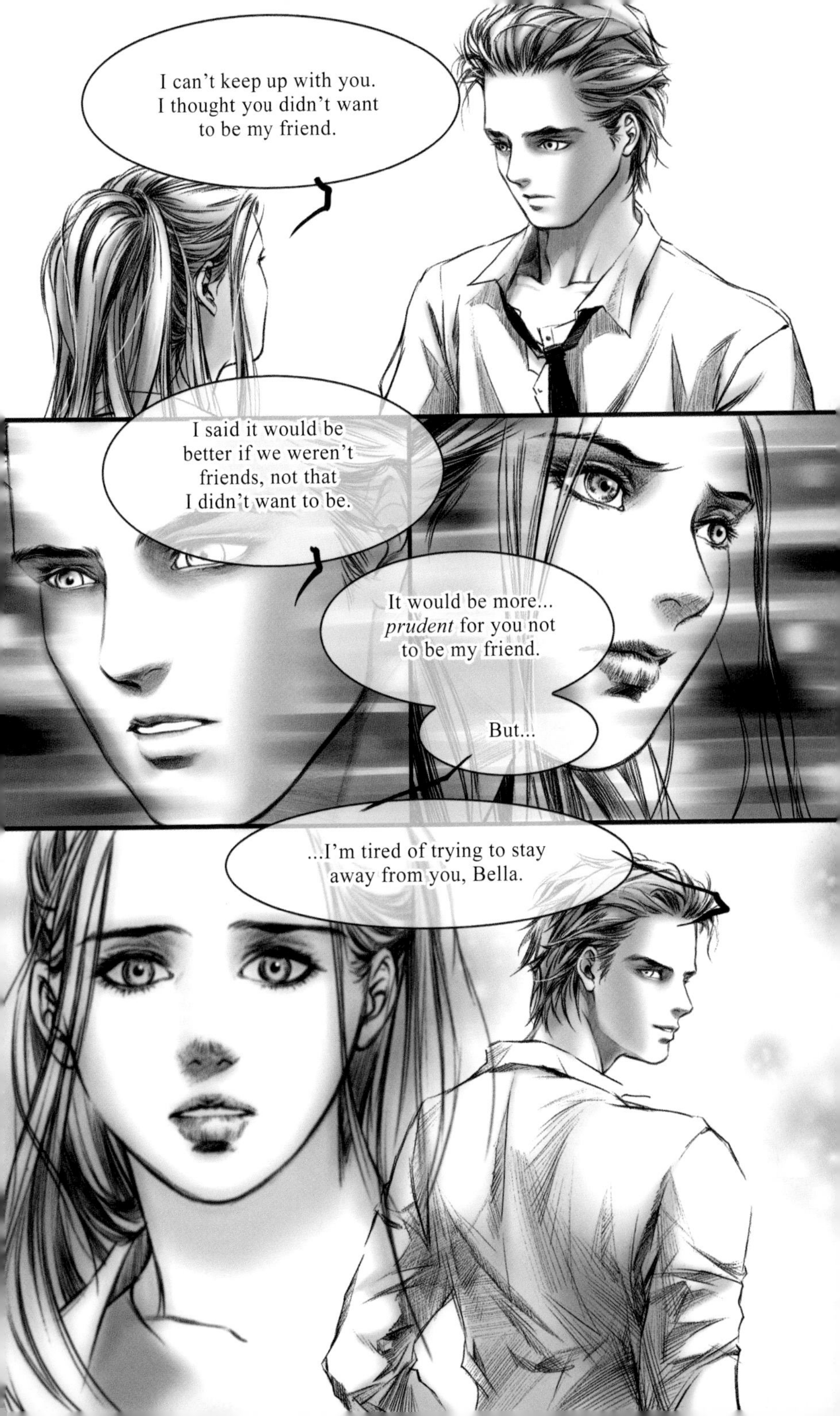
I can't keep up with you. I thought you didn't want to be my friend.
I said it would be better if we weren't friends, not that I didn't want to be.
It would be more... *prudent* for you not to be my friend.
But...
...I'm tired of trying to stay away from you, Bella.

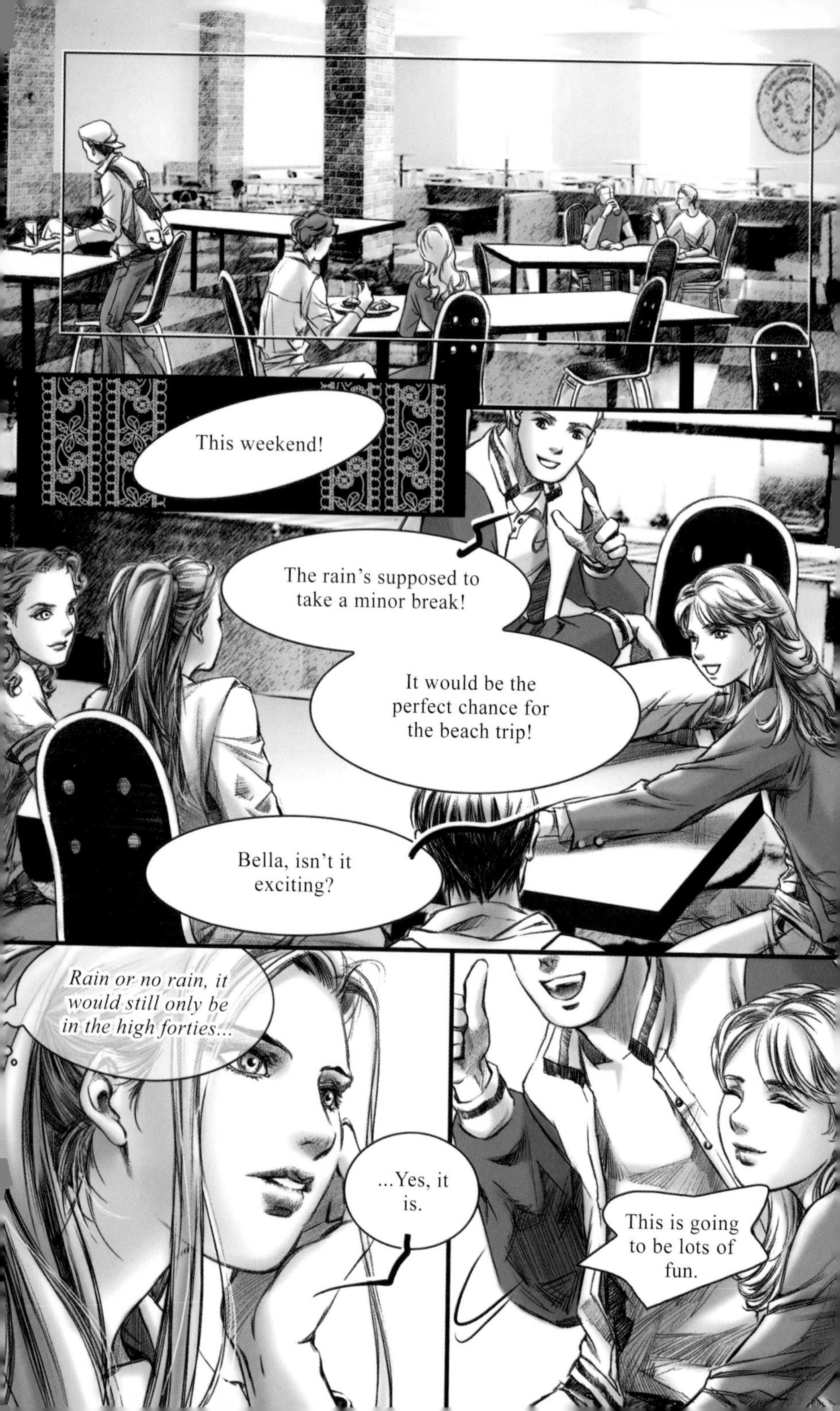
This weekend!
The rain's supposed to take a minor break!
It would be the perfect chance for the beach trip!
Bella, isn't it exciting?
Rain or no rain, it would still only be in the high forties...
...Yes, it is.
This is going to be lots of fun.

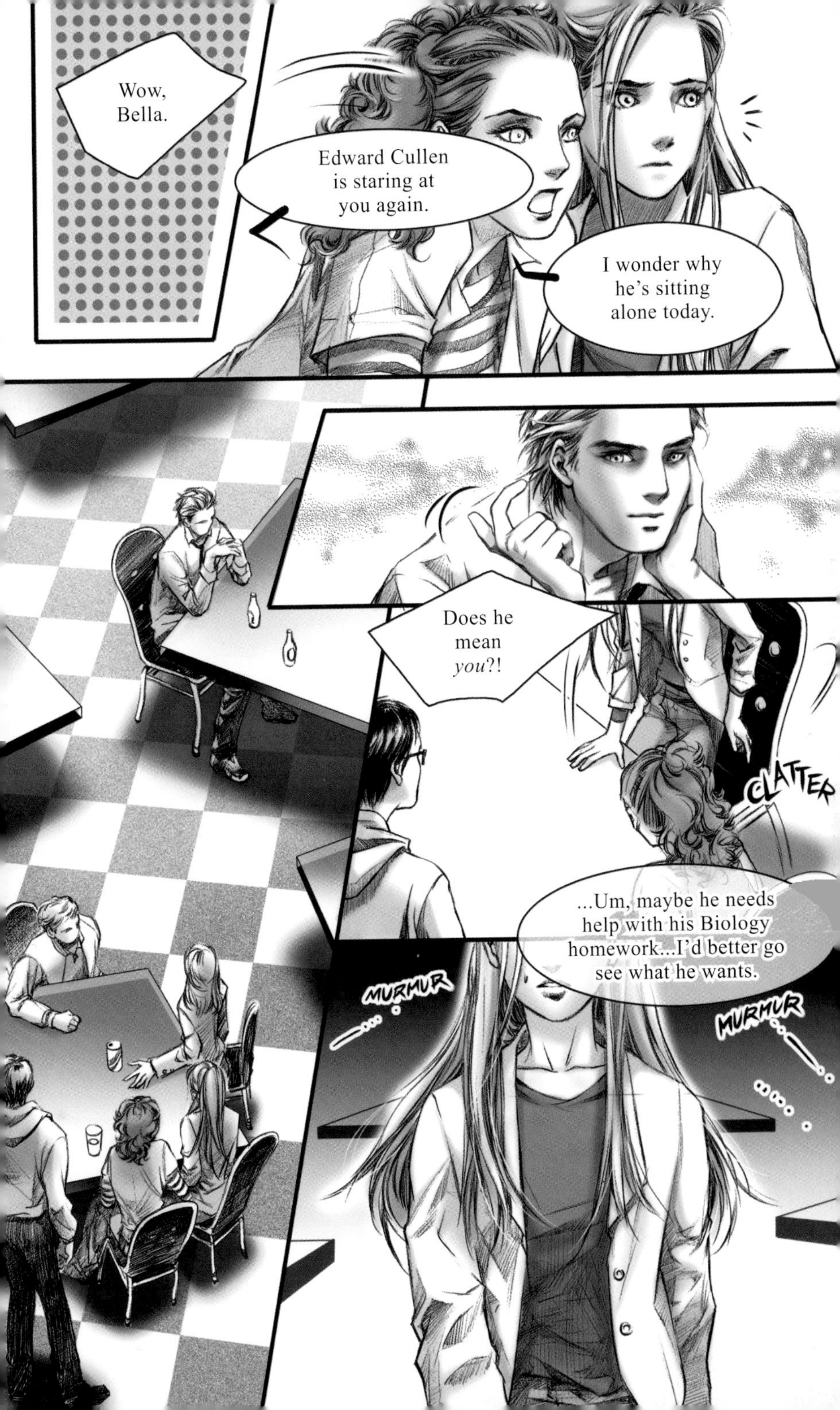
Wow, Bella.
Edward Cullen is staring at you again.
I wonder why he's sitting alone today.
Does he mean *you*?!
CLATTER
...Um, maybe he needs help with his Biology homework...I'd better go see what he wants.
MURMUR
MURMUR

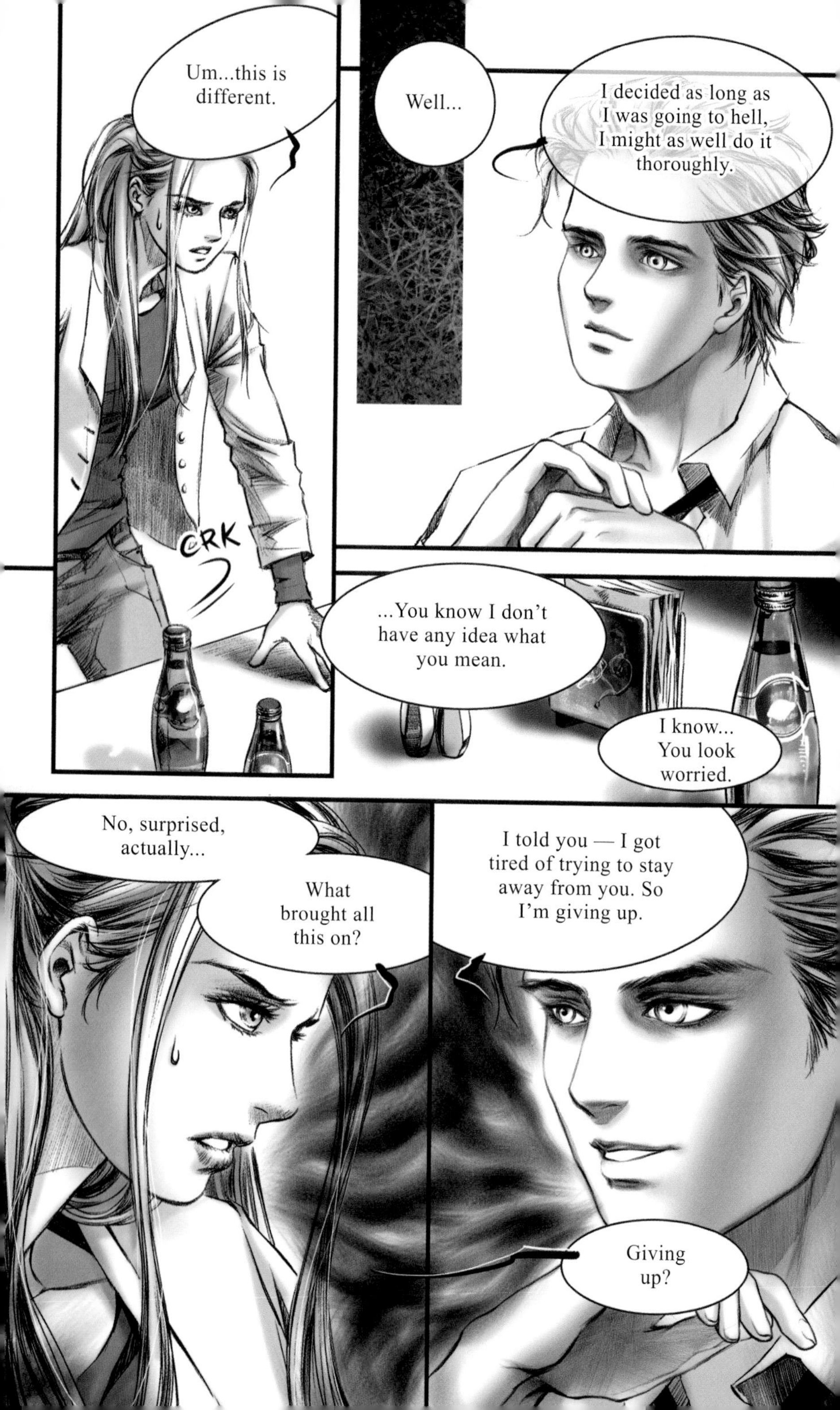
Um...this is different.
Well...
I decided as long as I was going to hell, I might as well do it thoroughly.
CRK
...You know I don't have any idea what you mean.
I know... You look worried.
No, surprised, actually...
What brought all this on?
I told you — I got tired of trying to stay away from you. So I'm giving up.
Giving up?

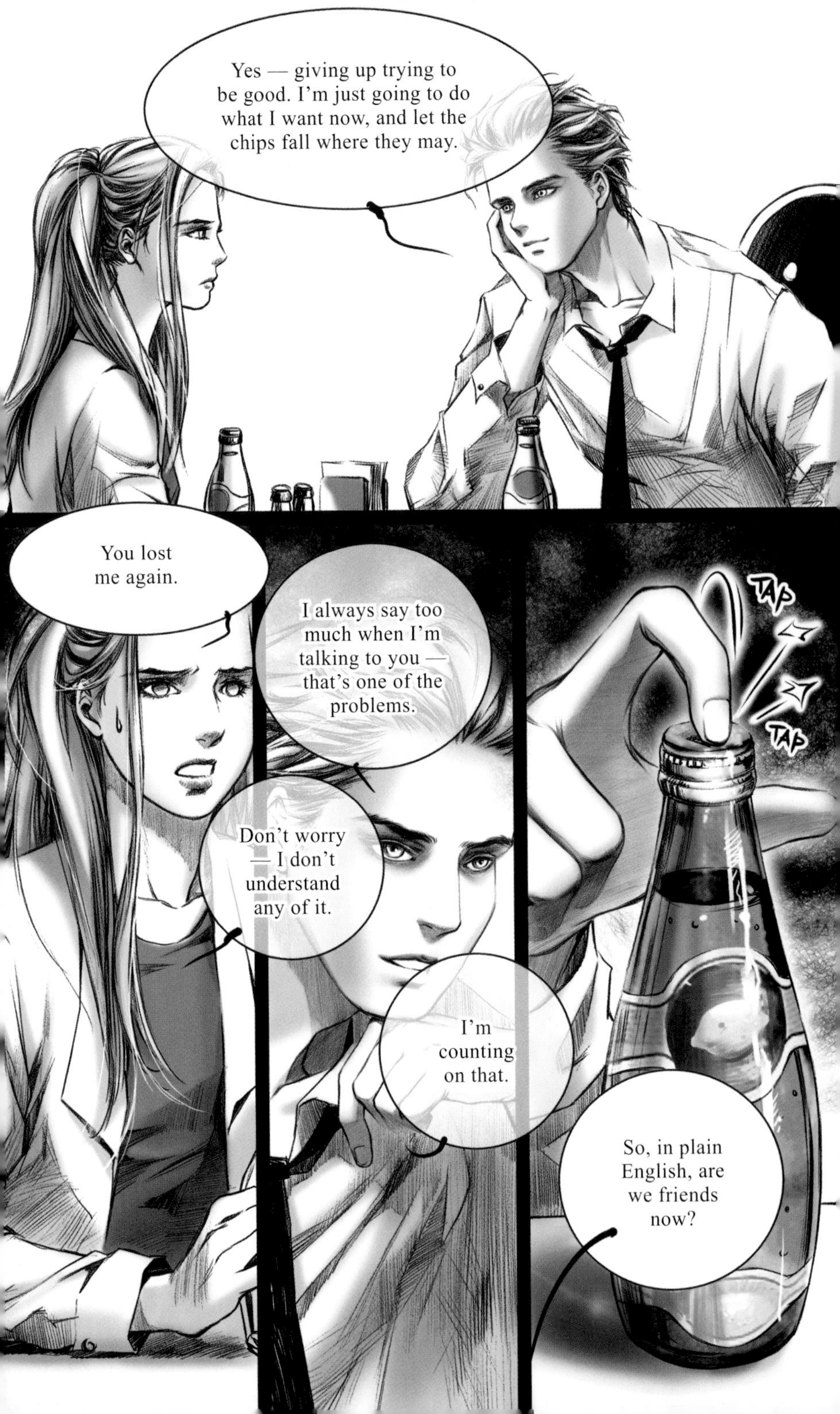
Yes — giving up trying to be good. I'm just going to do what I want now, and let the chips fall where they may.
You lost me again.
I always say too much when I'm talking to you — that's one of the problems.
Don't worry — I don't understand any of it.
I'm counting on that.
TAP
TAP
So, in plain English, are we friends now?

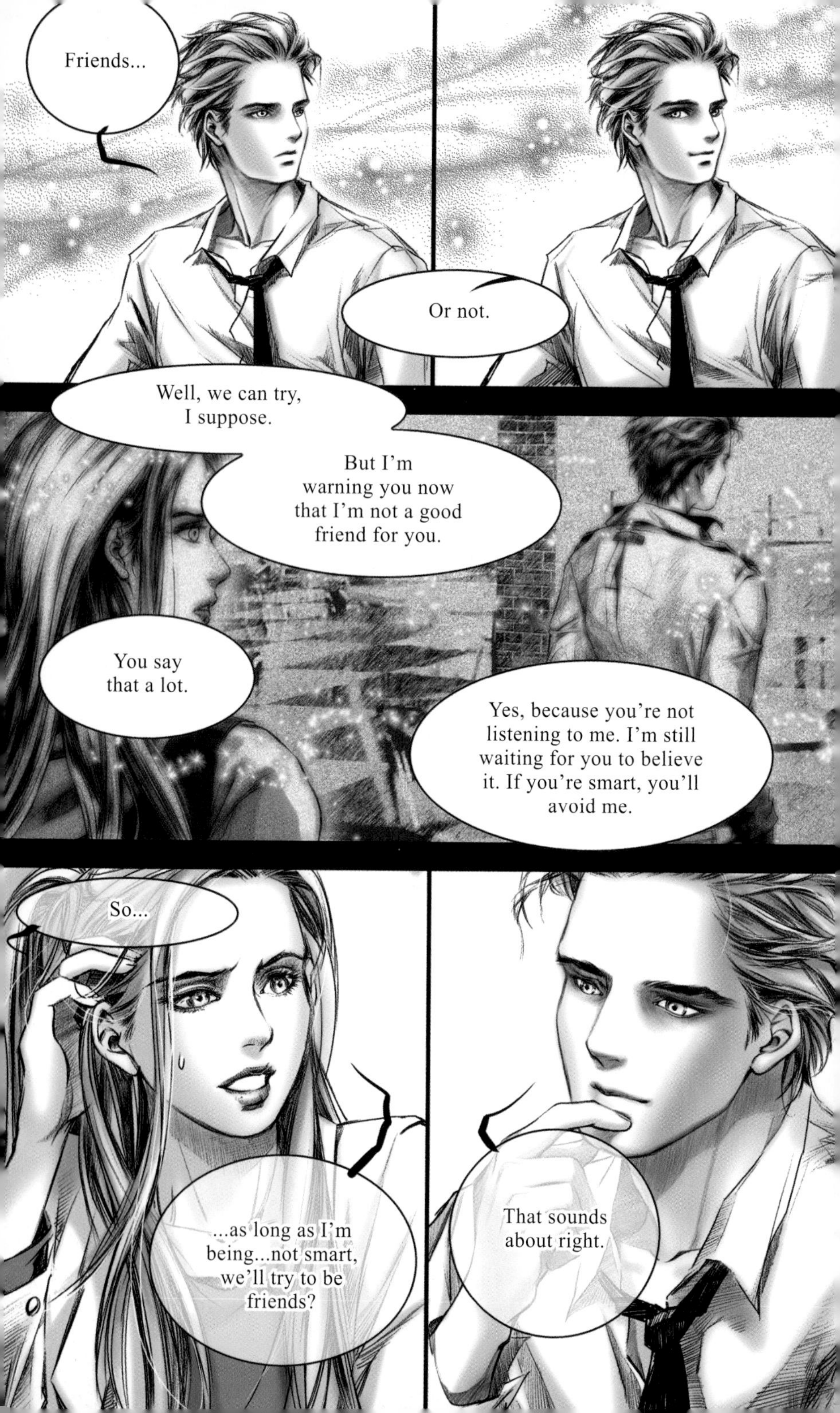
Friends...
Or not.
Well, we can try, I suppose.
But I'm warning you now that I'm not a good friend for you.
You say that a lot.
Yes, because you're not listening to me. I'm still waiting for you to believe it. If you're smart, you'll avoid me.
So...
...as long as I'm being...not smart, we'll try to be friends?
That sounds about right.

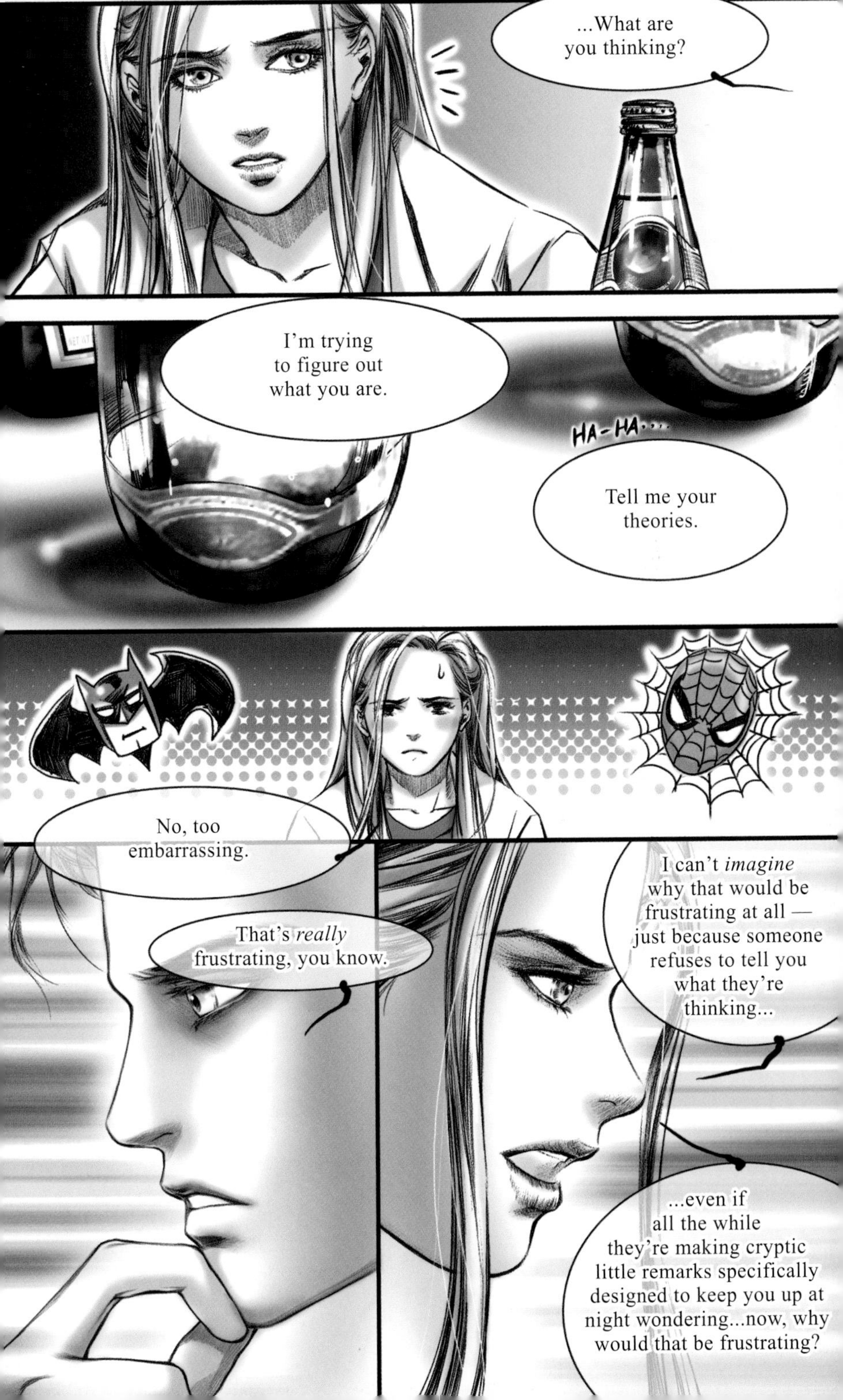
...What are you thinking?
I'm trying to figure out what you are.
HA-HA...
Tell me your theories.
No, too embarrassing.
That's *really* frustrating, you know.
I can't *imagine* why that would be frustrating at all — just because someone refuses to tell you what they're thinking...
...even if all the while they're making cryptic little remarks specifically designed to keep you up at night wondering...now, why would that be frustrating?

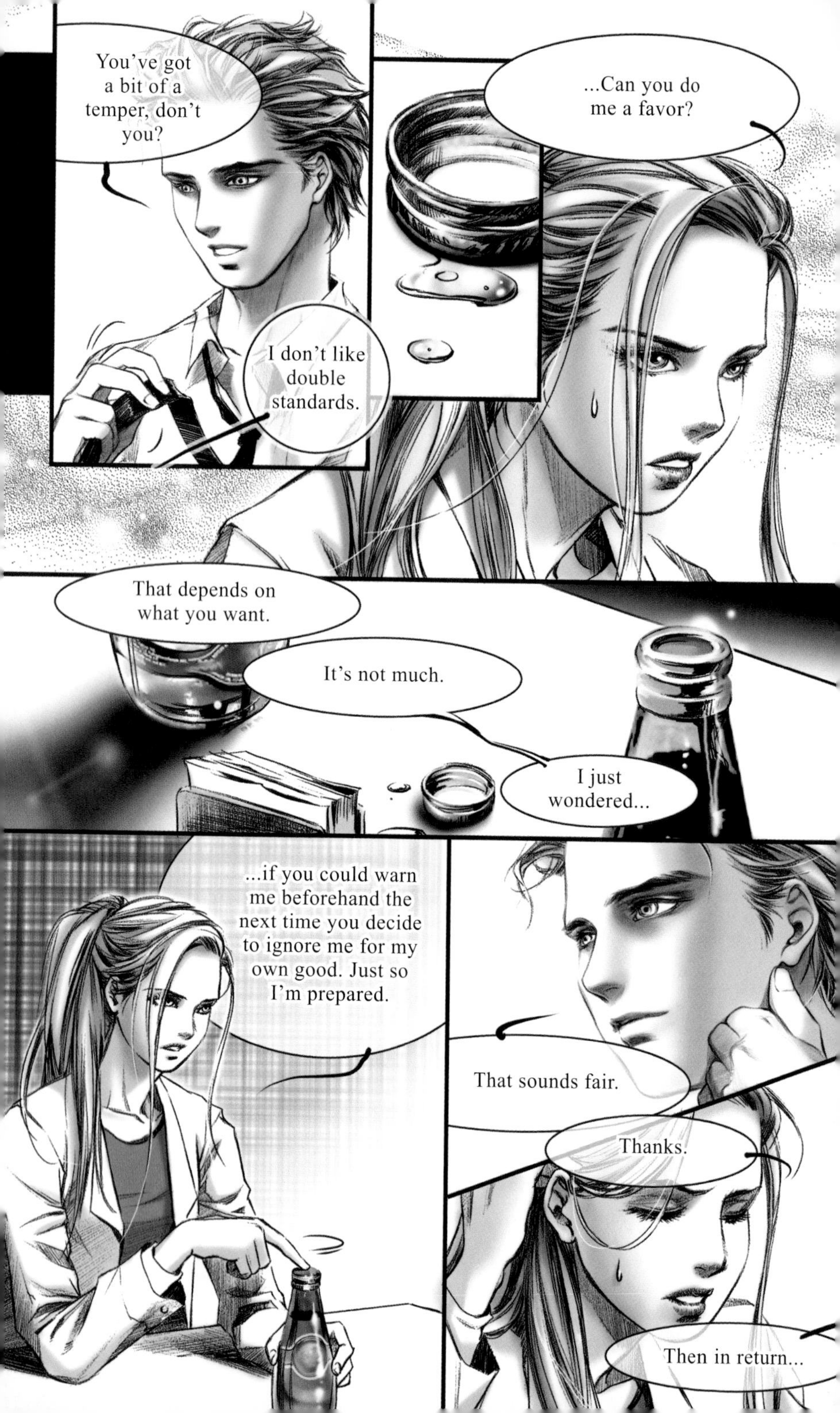
You've got a bit of a temper, don't you?
I don't like double standards.
...Can you do me a favor?
That depends on what you want.
It's not much.
I just wondered...
...if you could warn me beforehand the next time you decide to ignore me for my own good. Just so I'm prepared.
That sounds fair.
Thanks.
Then in return...

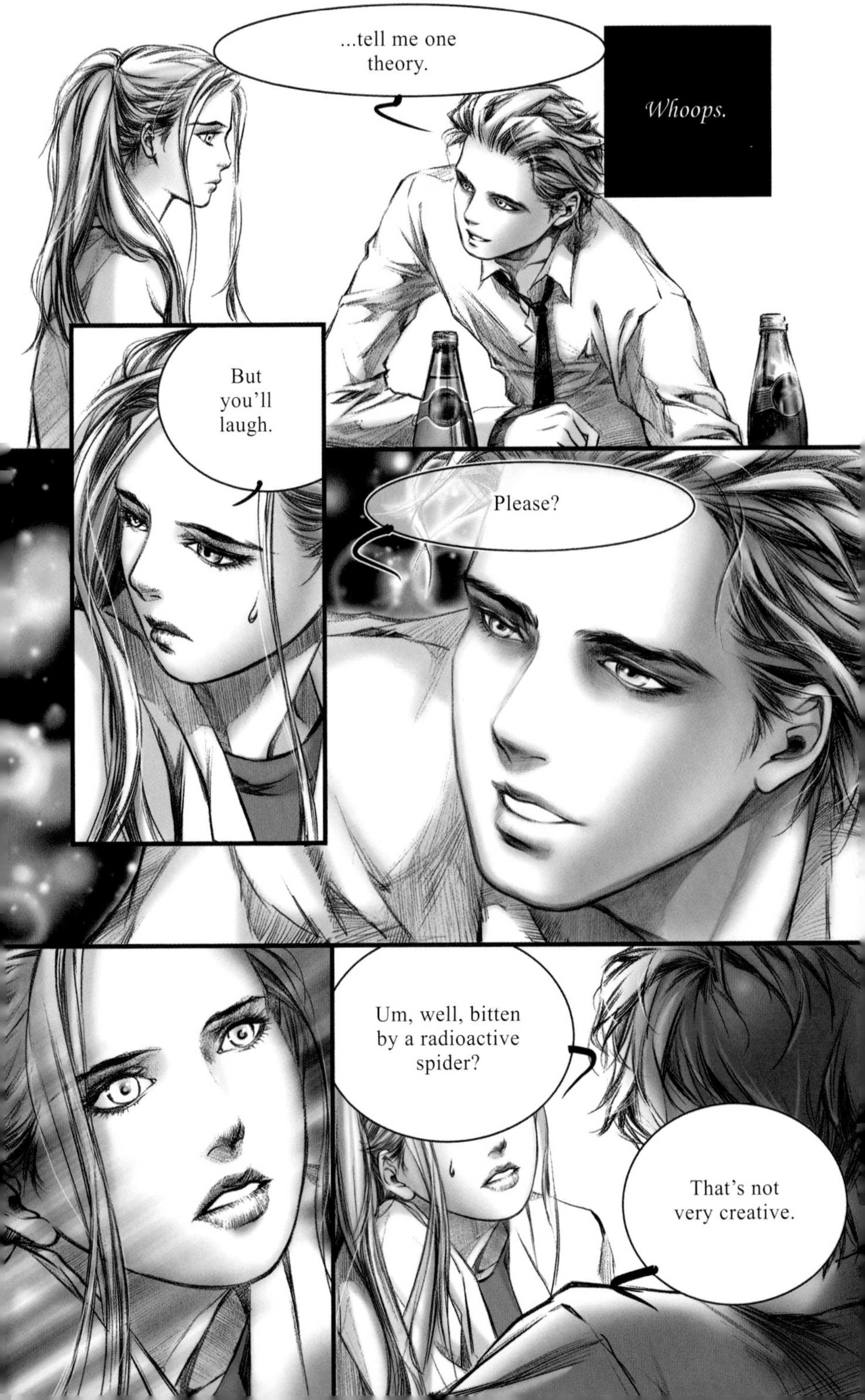
...tell me one theory.
Whoops.
But you'll laugh.
Please?
Um, well, bitten by a radioactive spider?
That's not very creative.

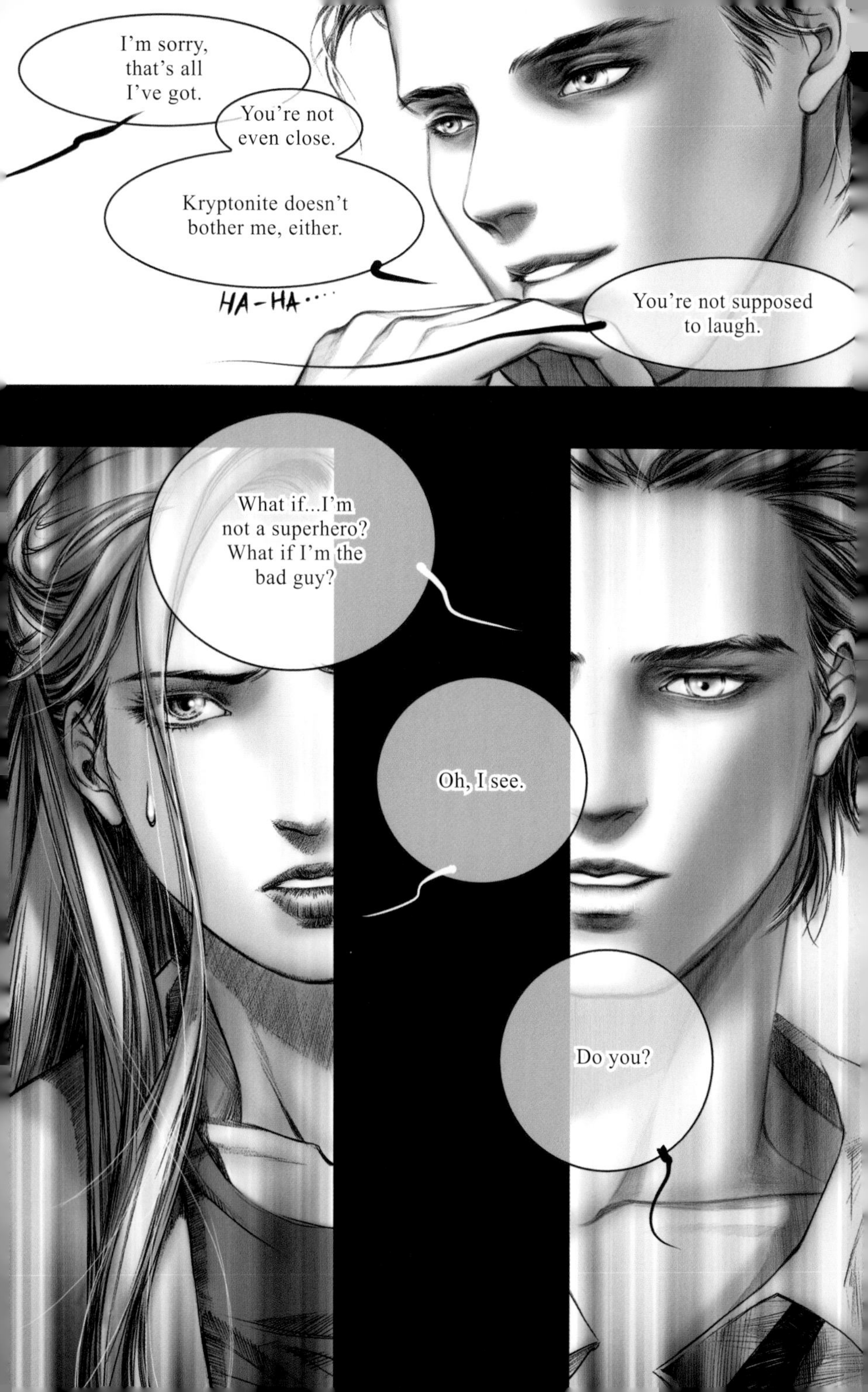

I'm sorry, that's all I've got.
You're not even close.
Kryptonite doesn't bother me, either.
HA-HA....
You're not supposed to laugh.
What if...I'm not a superhero? What if I'm the bad guy?
Oh, I see.
Do you?

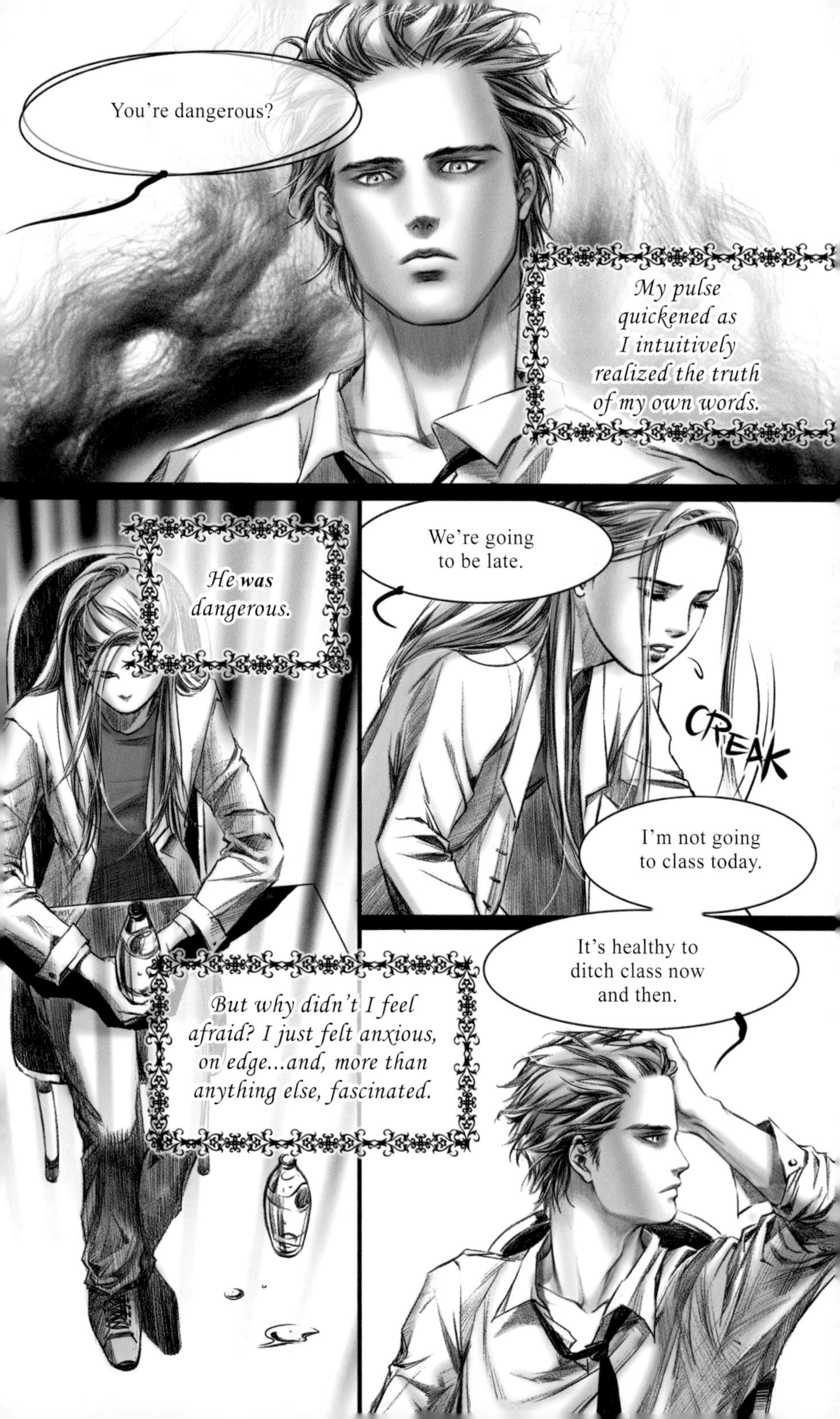
You're dangerous?
My pulse quickened as I intuitively realized the truth of my own words.
He was dangerous.
We're going to be late.
CREAK
I'm not going to class today.
It's healthy to ditch class now and then.
But why didn't I feel afraid? I just felt anxious, on edge...and, more than anything else, fascinated.

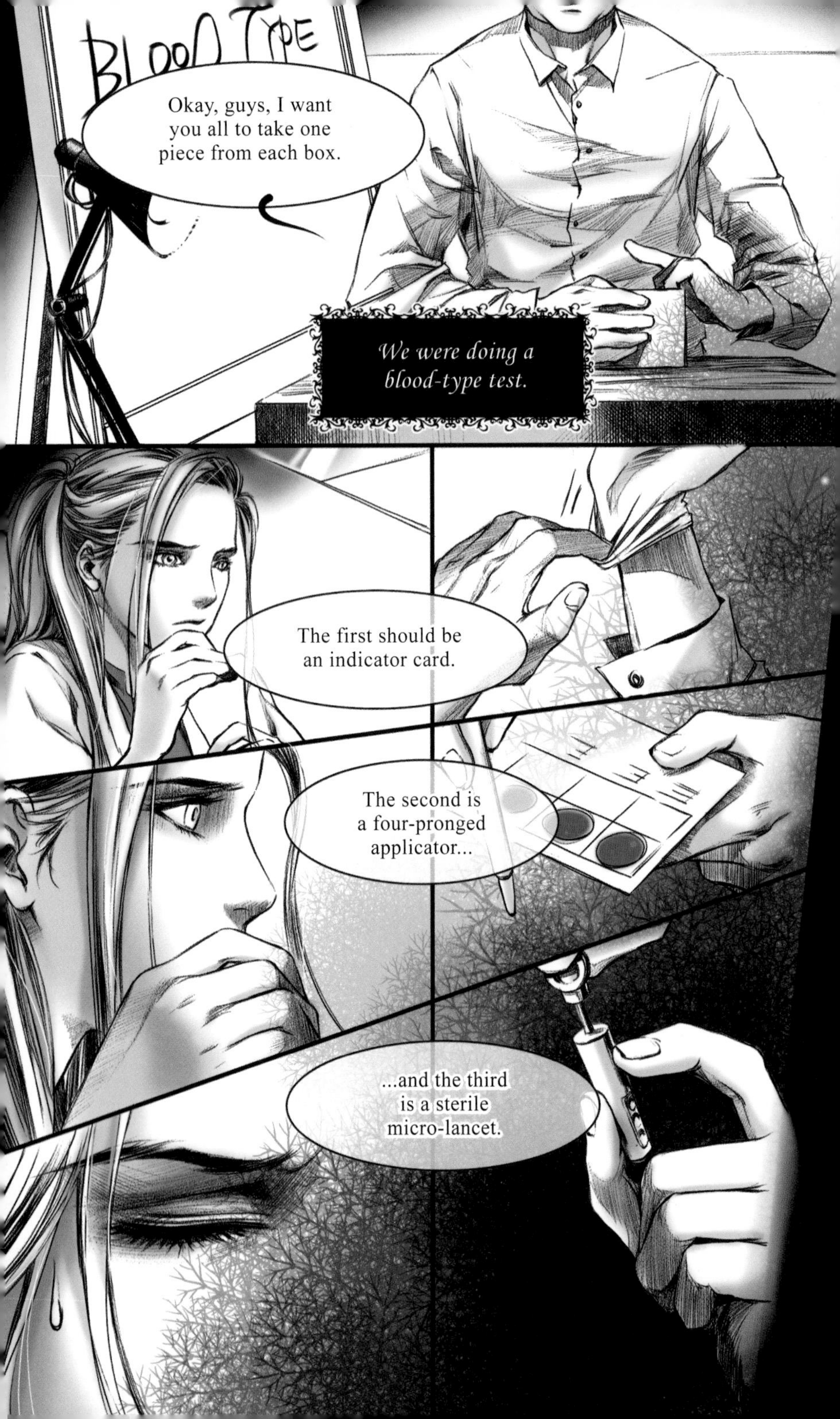
BLOOD TYPE
Okay, guys, I want you all to take one piece from each box.
We were doing a blood-type test.
The first should be an indicator card.
The second is a four-pronged applicator...
...and the third is a sterile micro-lancet.

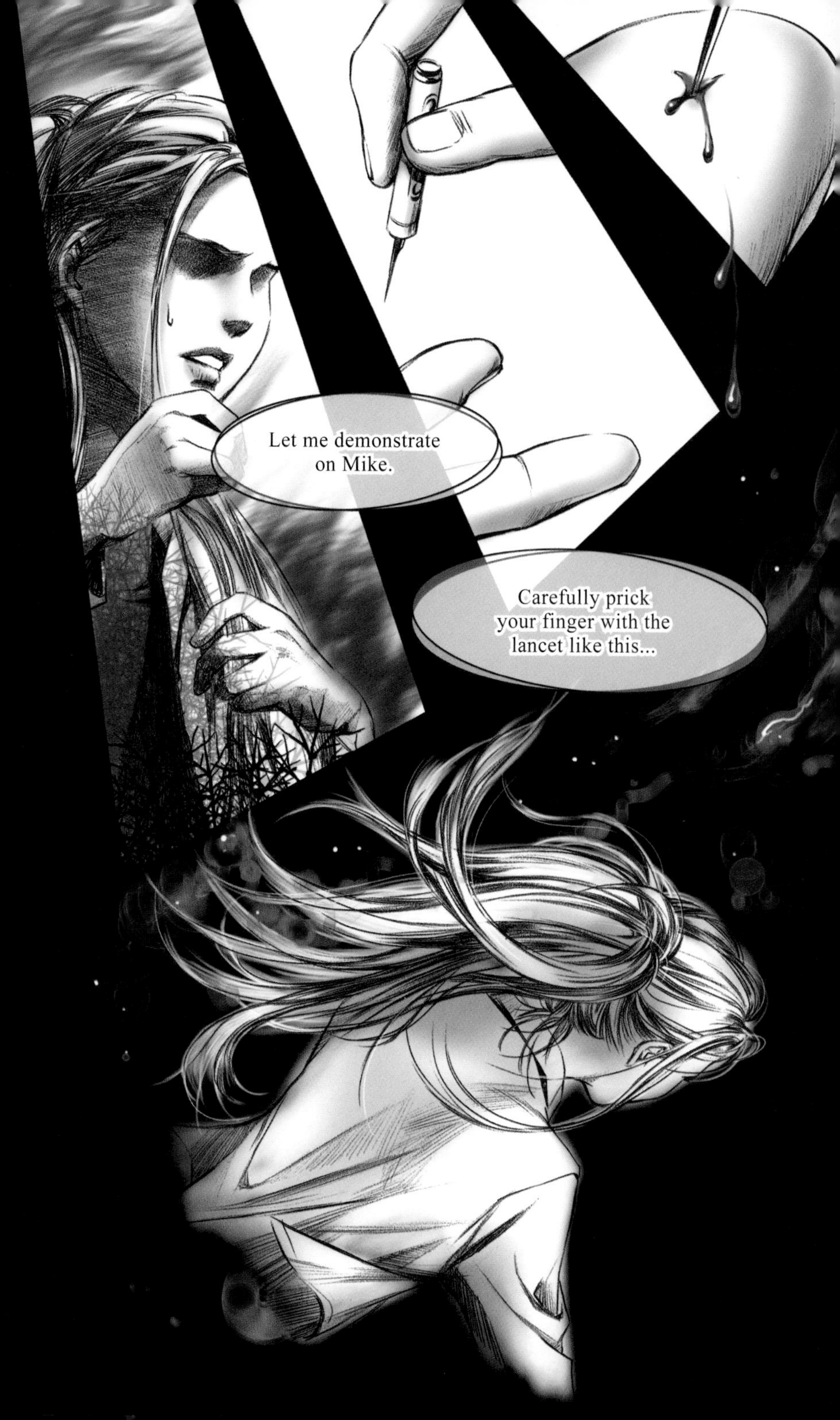
Let me demonstrate on Mike.
Carefully prick your finger with the lancet like this...

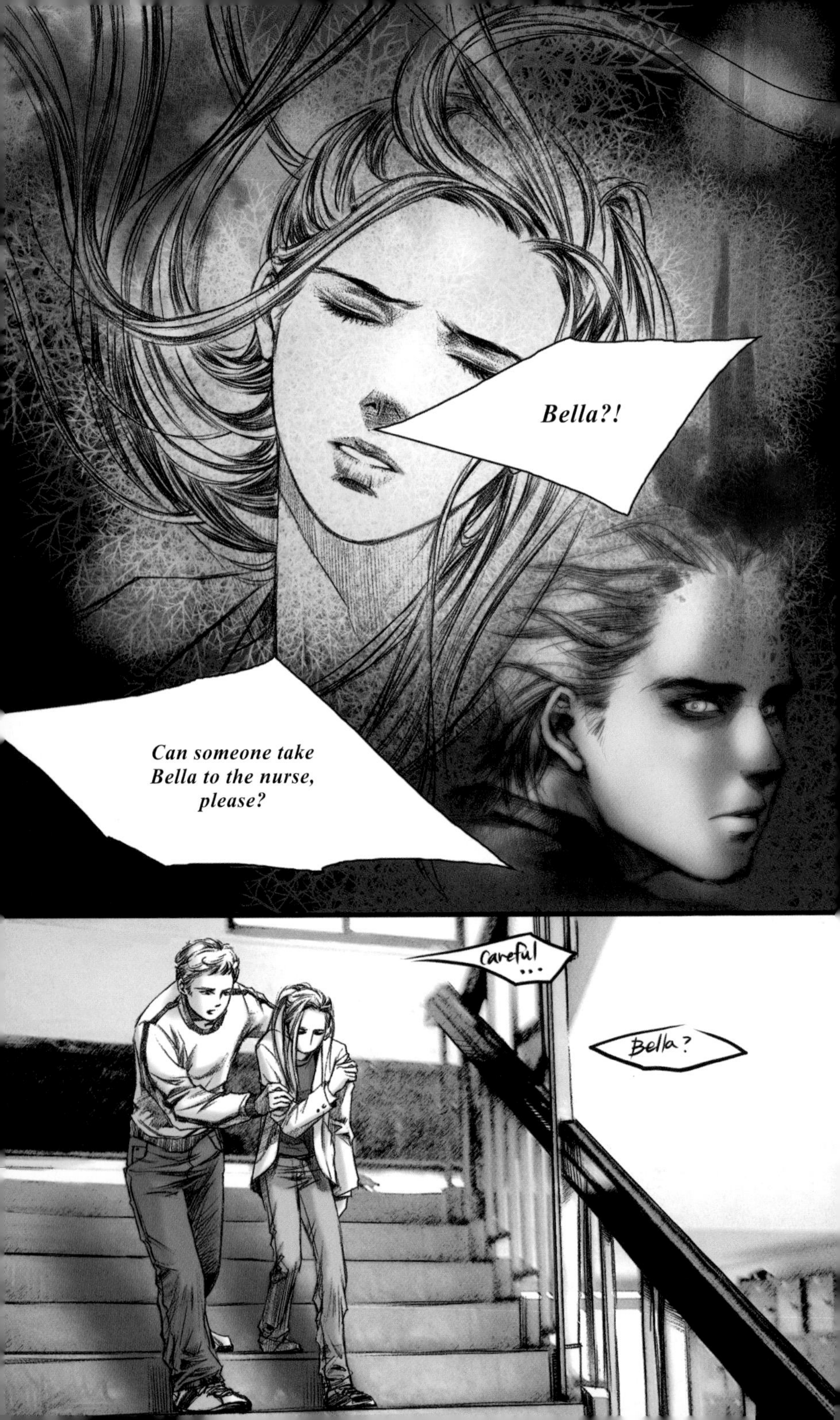
Bella?!
Can someone take Bella to the nurse, please?
Careful...
Bella?

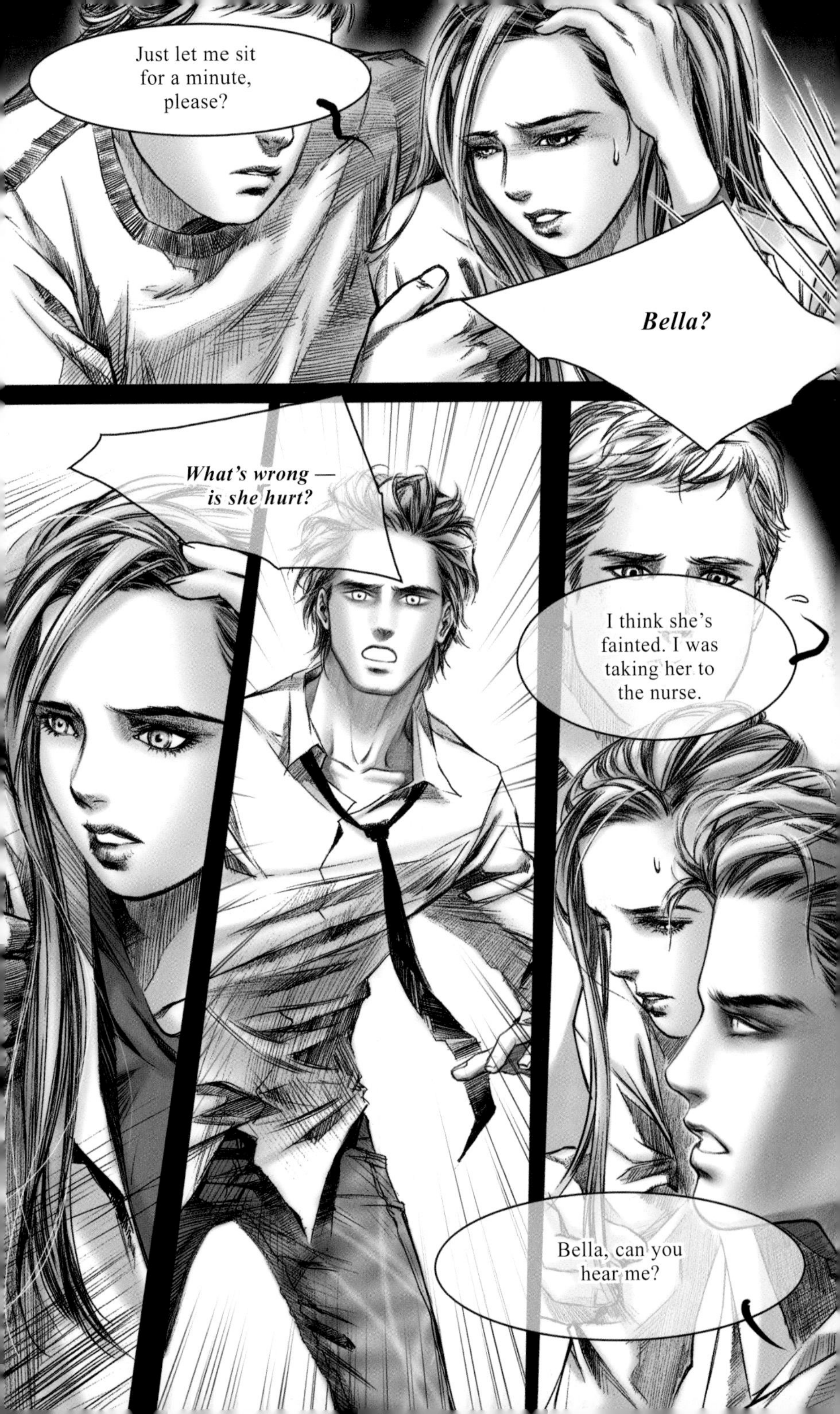

Just let me sit for a minute, please?
Bella?
What's wrong — is she hurt?
I think she's fainted. I was taking her to the nurse.
Bella, can you hear me?

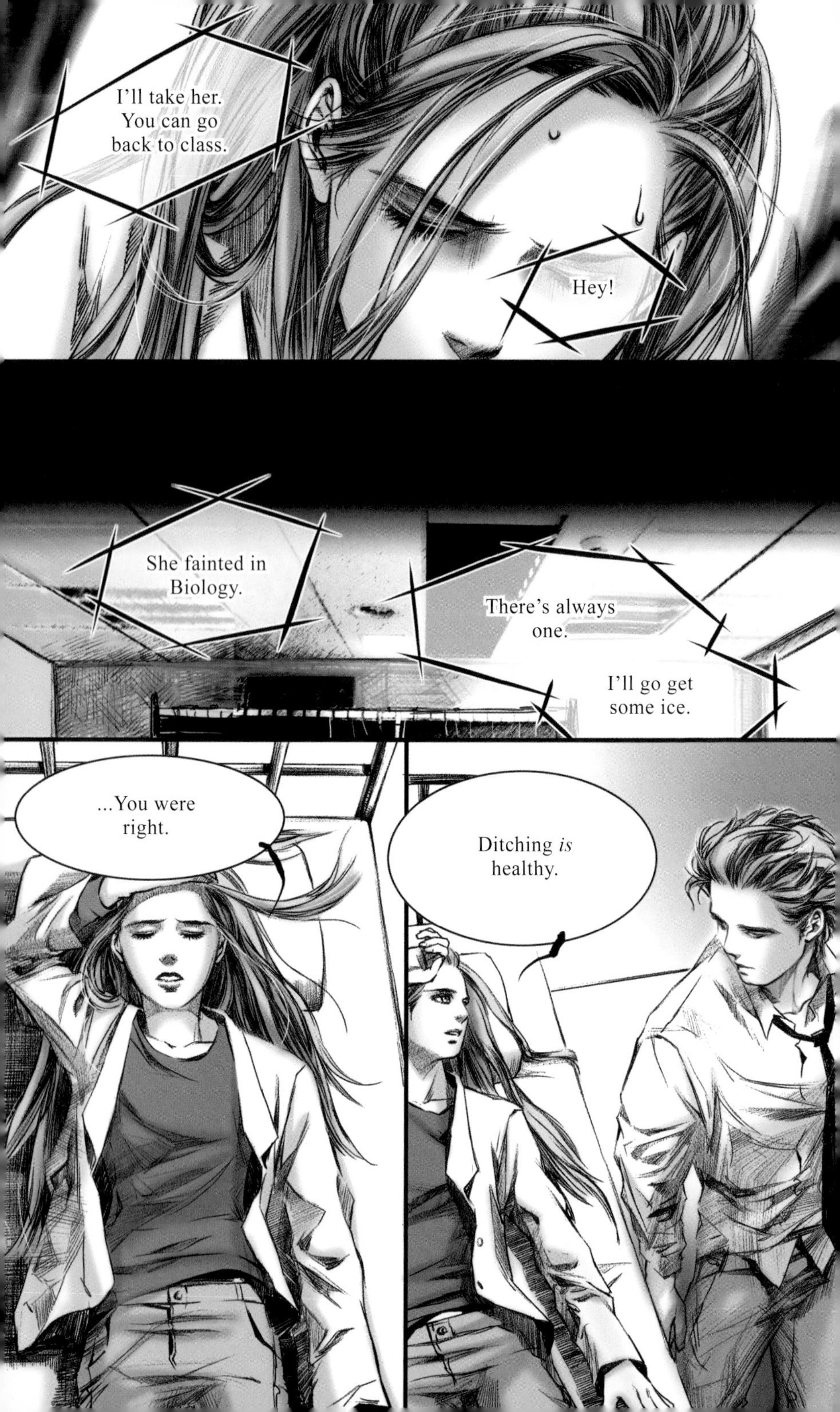
I'll take her. You can go back to class.
Hey!
She fainted in Biology.
There's always one.
I'll go get some ice.
...You were right.
Ditching *is* healthy.

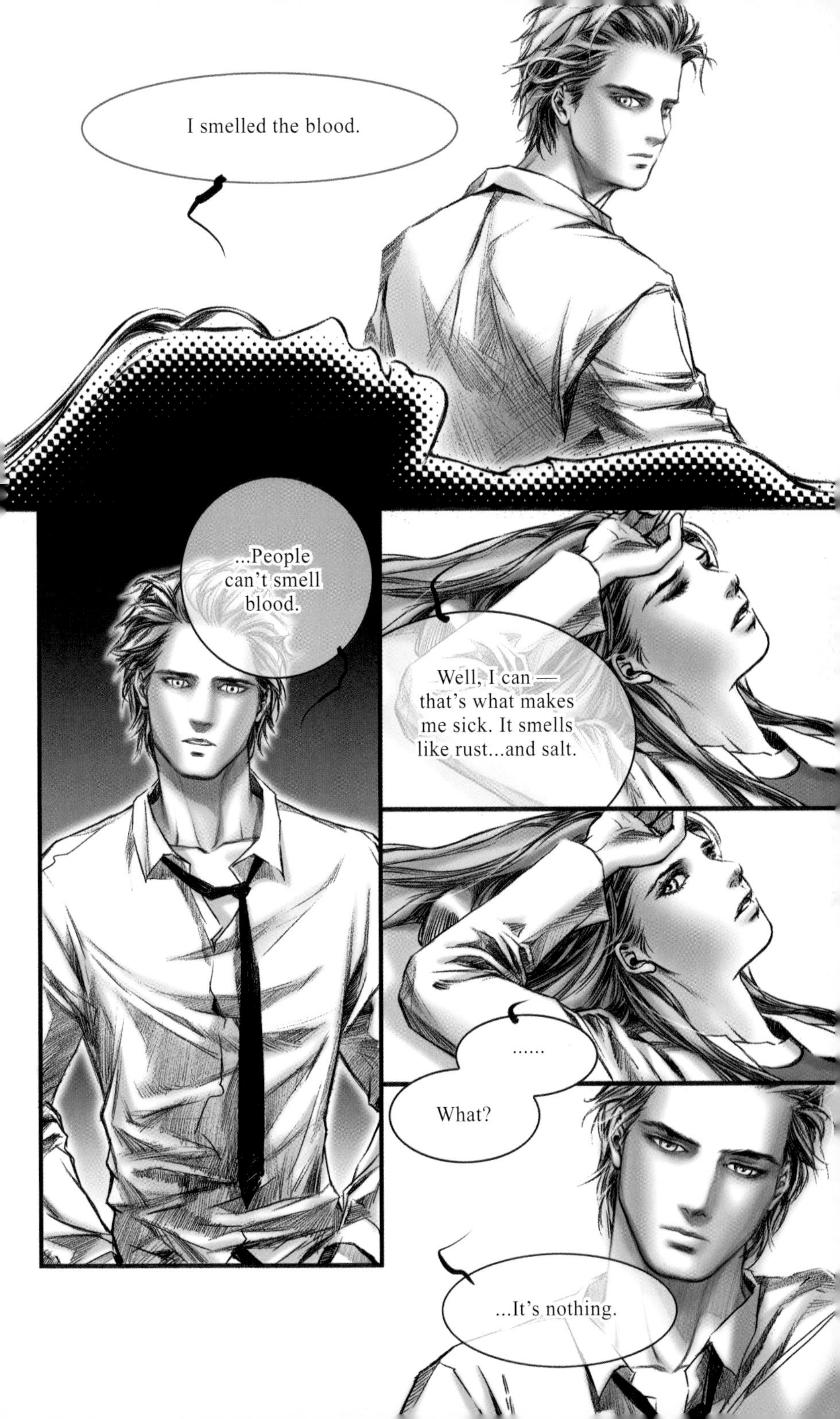
I smelled the blood.
...People can't smell blood.
Well, I can — that's what makes me sick. It smells like rust...and salt.
......
What?
...It's nothing.

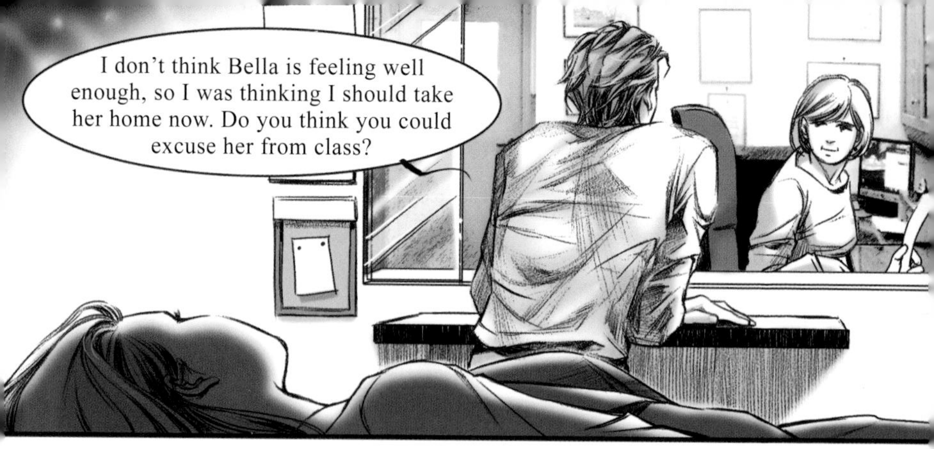
I don't think Bella is feeling well enough, so I was thinking I should take her home now. Do you think you could excuse her from class?

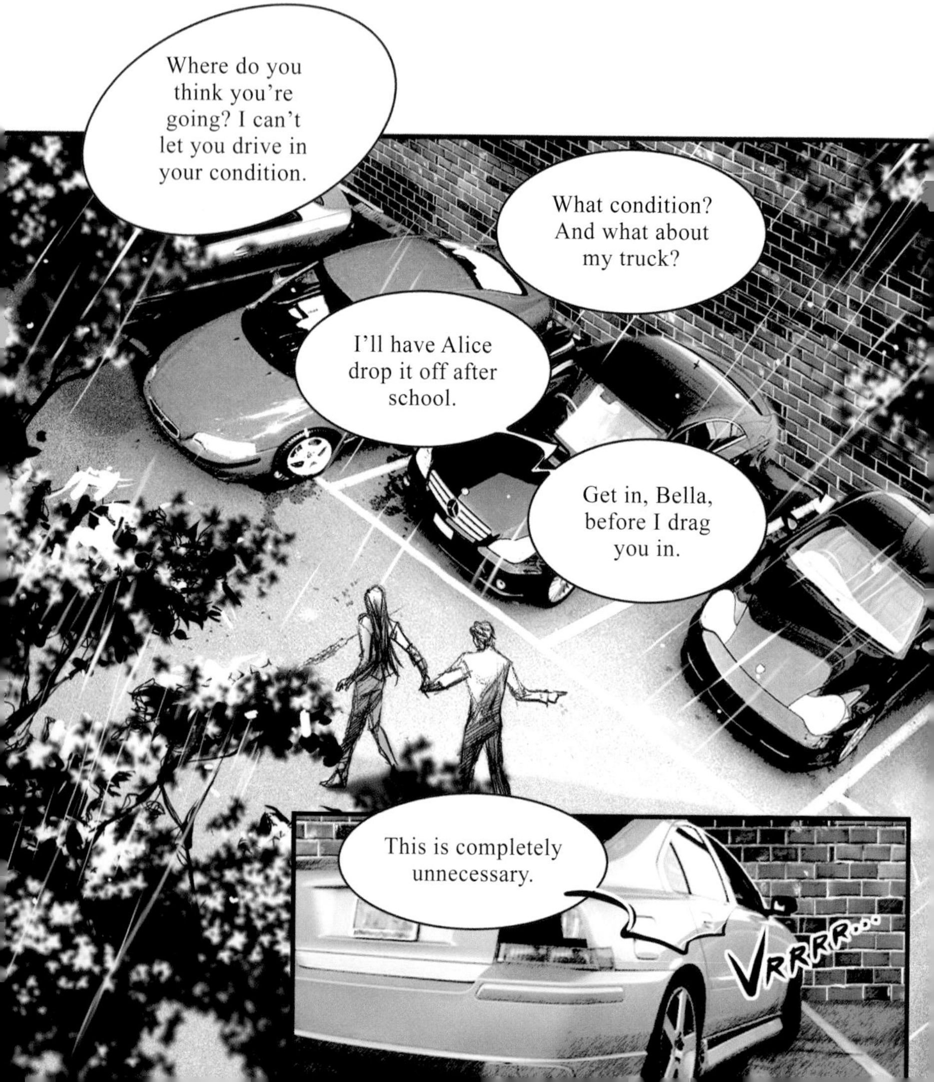
Where do you think you're going? I can't let you drive in your condition.
What condition? And what about my truck?
I'll have Alice drop it off after school.
Get in, Bella, before I drag you in.
This is completely unnecessary.
VRRRR...

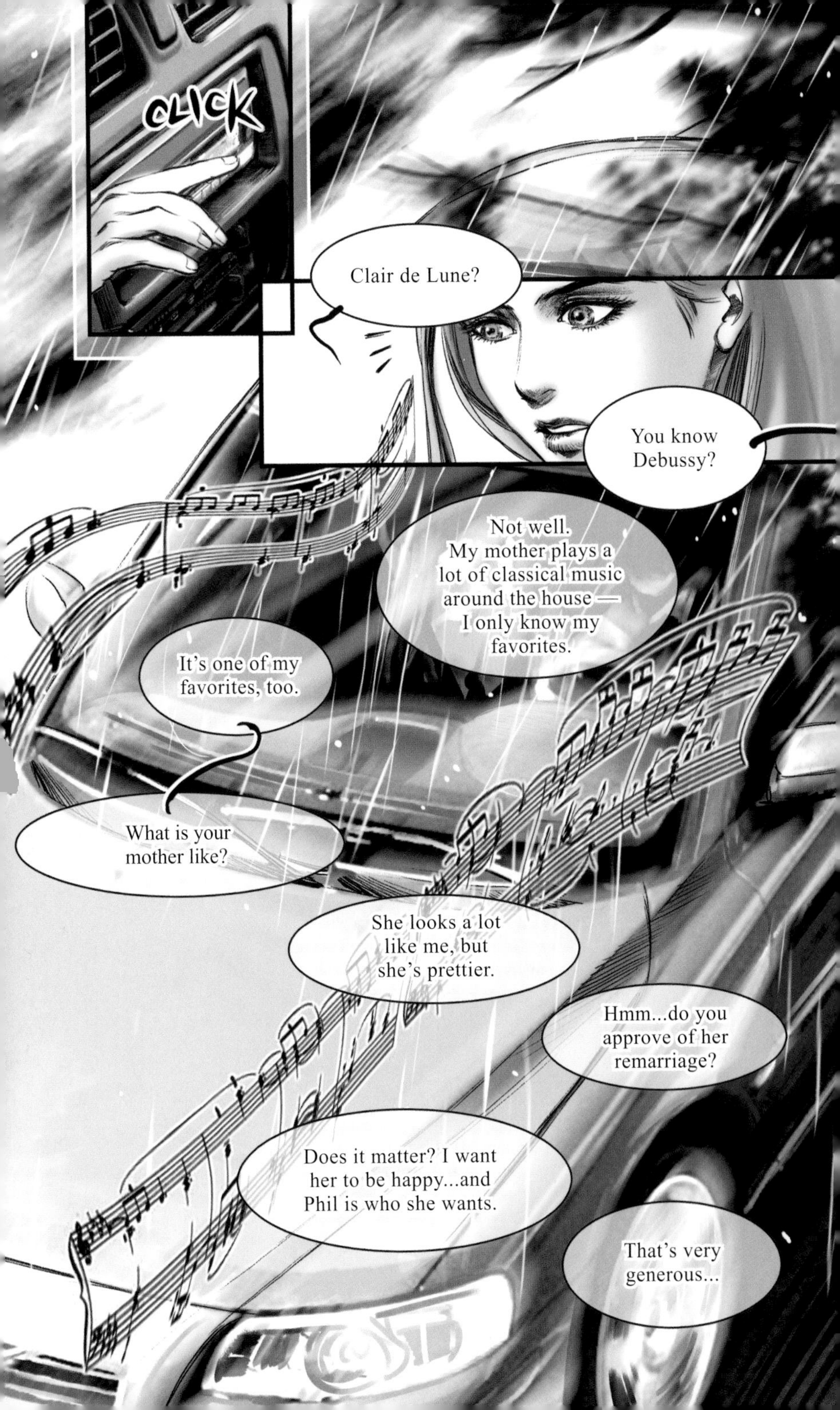
CLICK
Clair de Lune?
You know Debussy?
Not well. My mother plays a lot of classical music around the house — I only know my favorites.
It's one of my favorites, too.
What is your mother like?
She looks a lot like me, but she's prettier.
Hmm...do you approve of her remarriage?
Does it matter? I want her to be happy...and Phil is who she wants.
That's very generous...

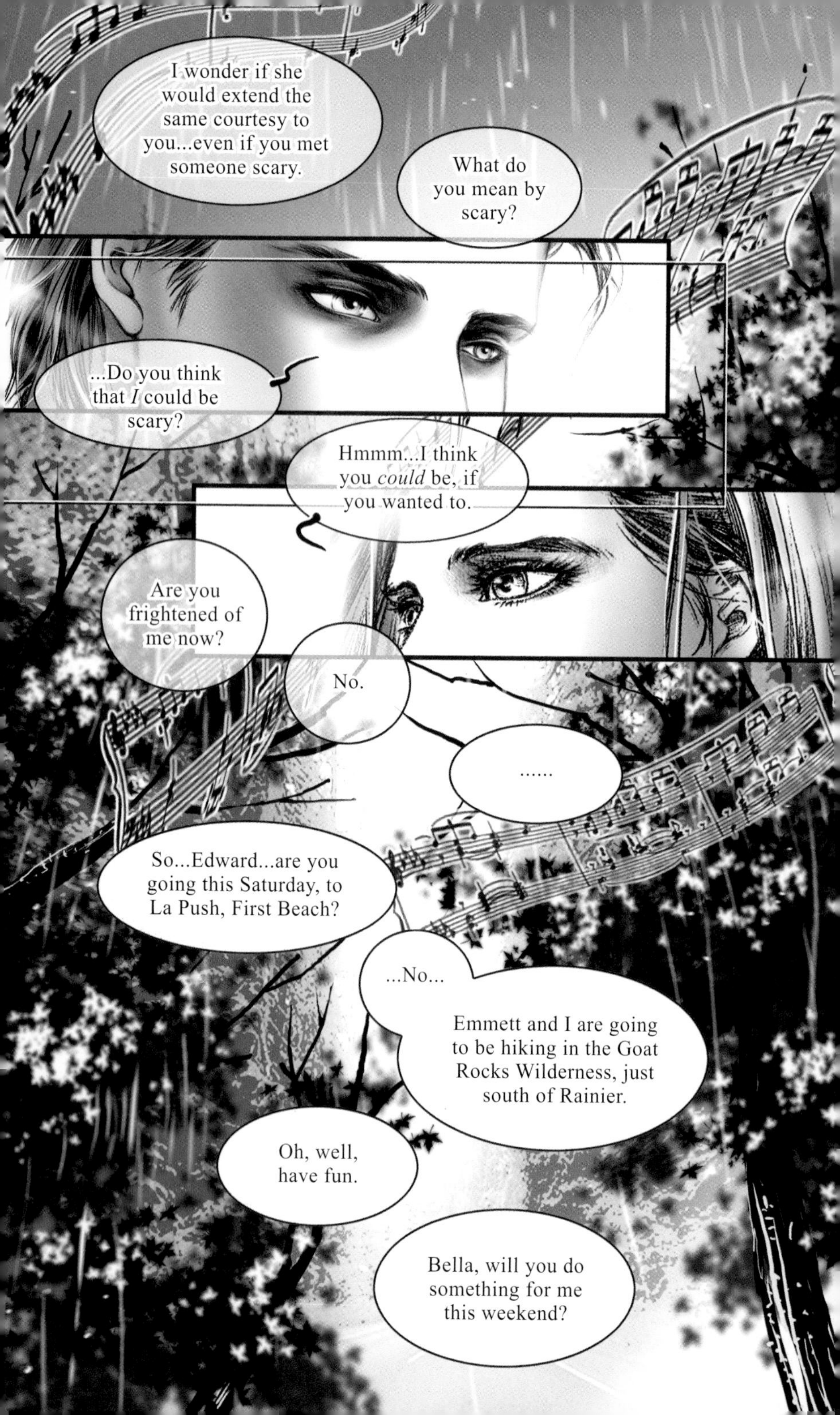
I wonder if she would extend the same courtesy to you...even if you met someone scary.
What do you mean by scary?
...Do you think that *I* could be scary?
Hmmm...I think you *could* be, if you wanted to.
Are you frightened of me now?
No.
......
So...Edward...are you going this Saturday, to La Push, First Beach?
...No...
Emmett and I are going to be hiking in the Goat Rocks Wilderness, just south of Rainier.
Oh, well, have fun.
Bella, will you do something for me this weekend?

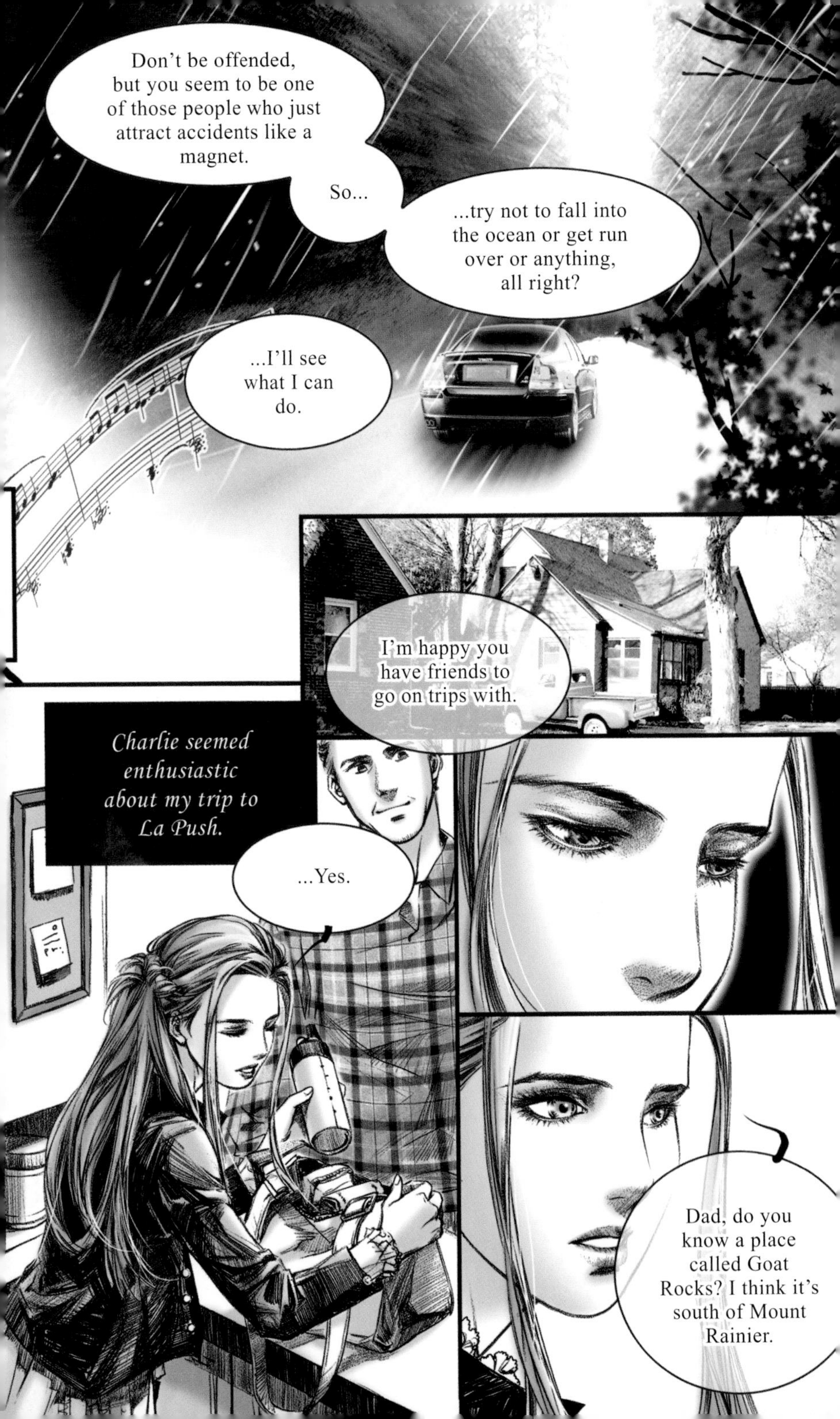
Don't be offended, but you seem to be one of those people who just attract accidents like a magnet.
So...
...try not to fall into the ocean or get run over or anything, all right?
...I'll see what I can do.
I'm happy you have friends to go on trips with.
Charlie seemed enthusiastic about my trip to La Push.
...Yes.
Dad, do you know a place called Goat Rocks? I think it's south of Mount Rainier.

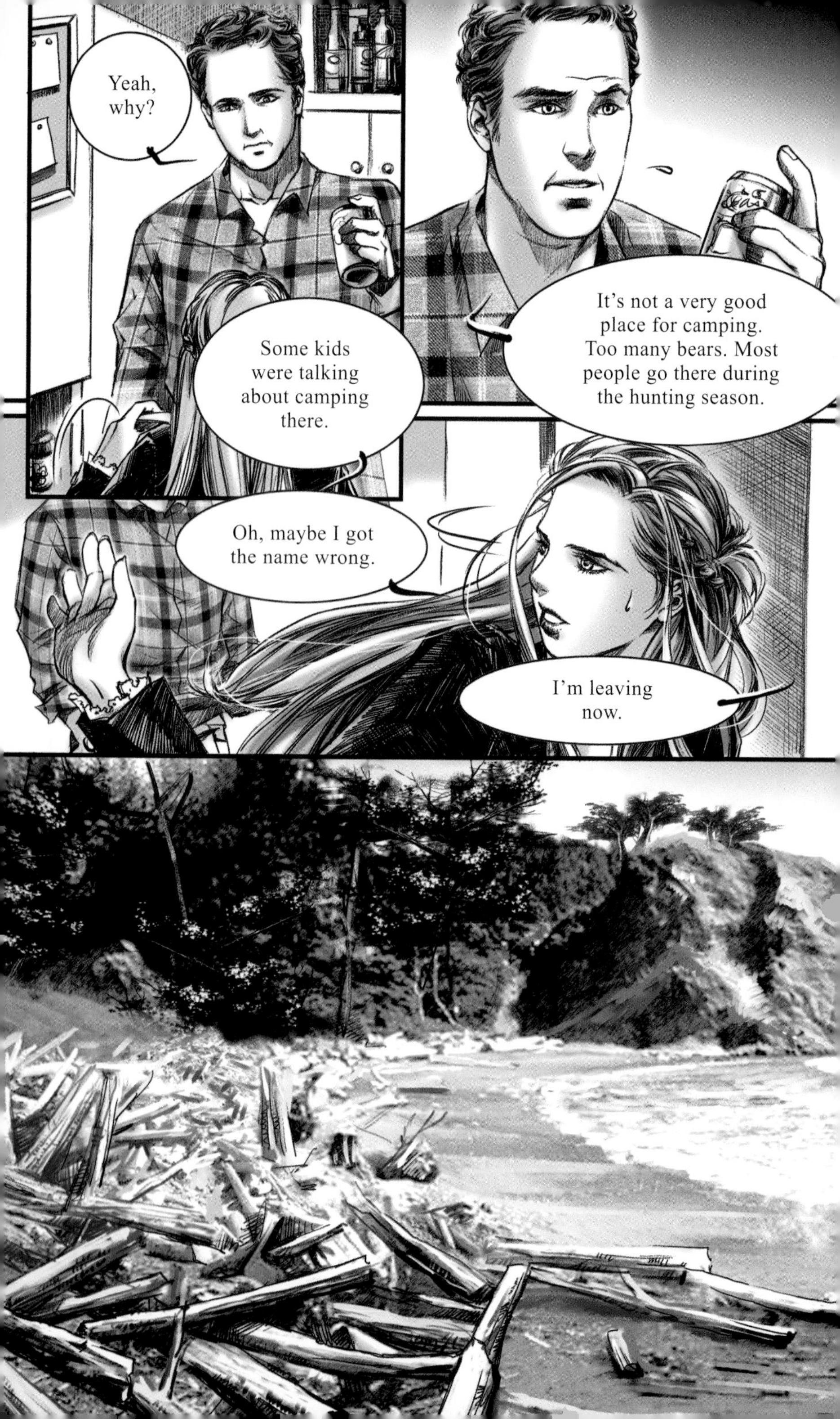
Yeah, why?
Some kids were talking about camping there.
It's not a very good place for camping. Too many bears. Most people go there during the hunting season.
Oh, maybe I got the name wrong.
I'm leaving now.

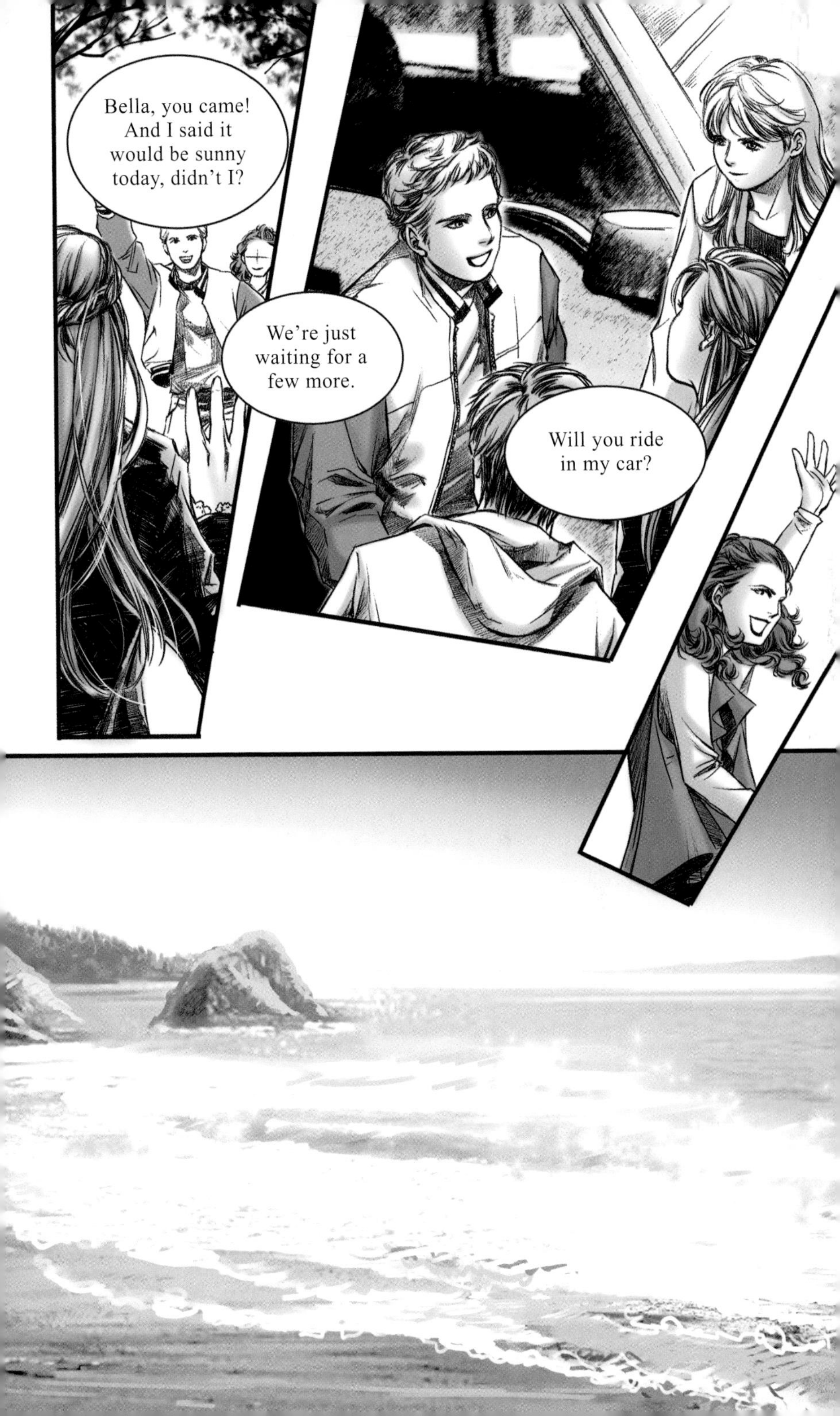
Bella, you came! And I said it would be sunny today, didn't I?
We're just waiting for a few more.
Will you ride in my car?

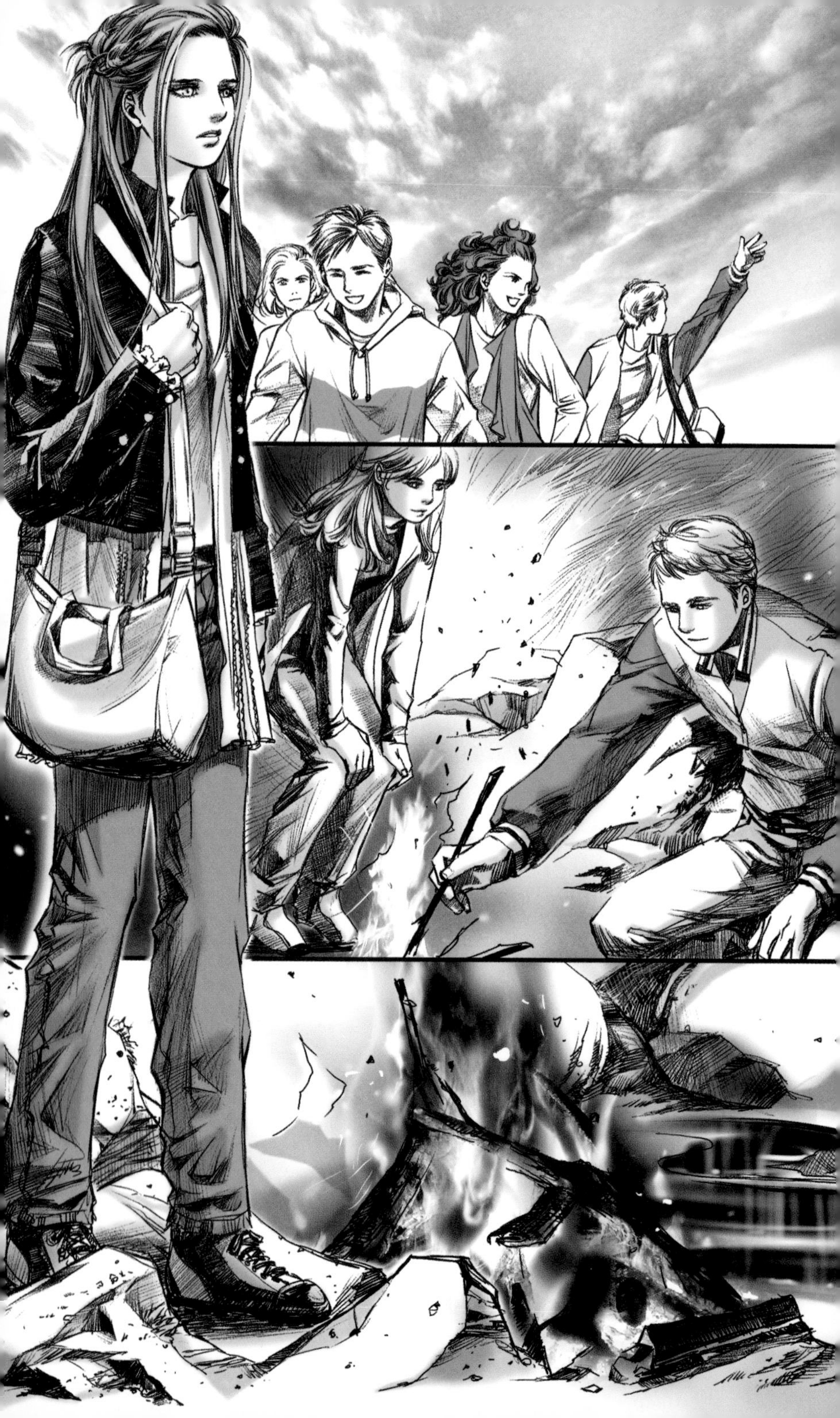

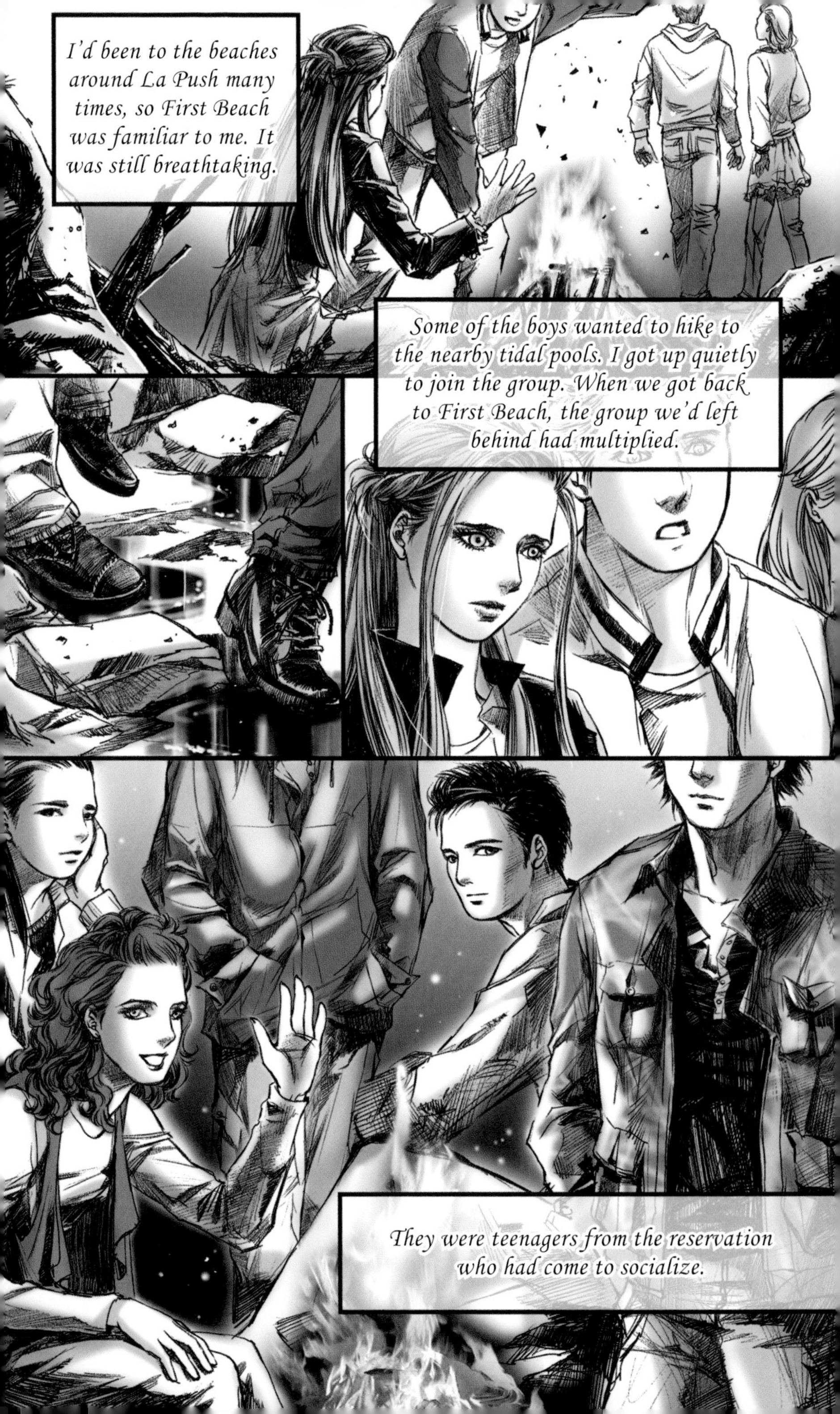
I'd been to the beaches around La Push many times, so First Beach was familiar to me. It was still breathtaking.
Some of the boys wanted to hike to the nearby tidal pools. I got up quietly to join the group. When we got back to First Beach, the group we'd left behind had multiplied.
They were teenagers from the reservation who had come to socialize.

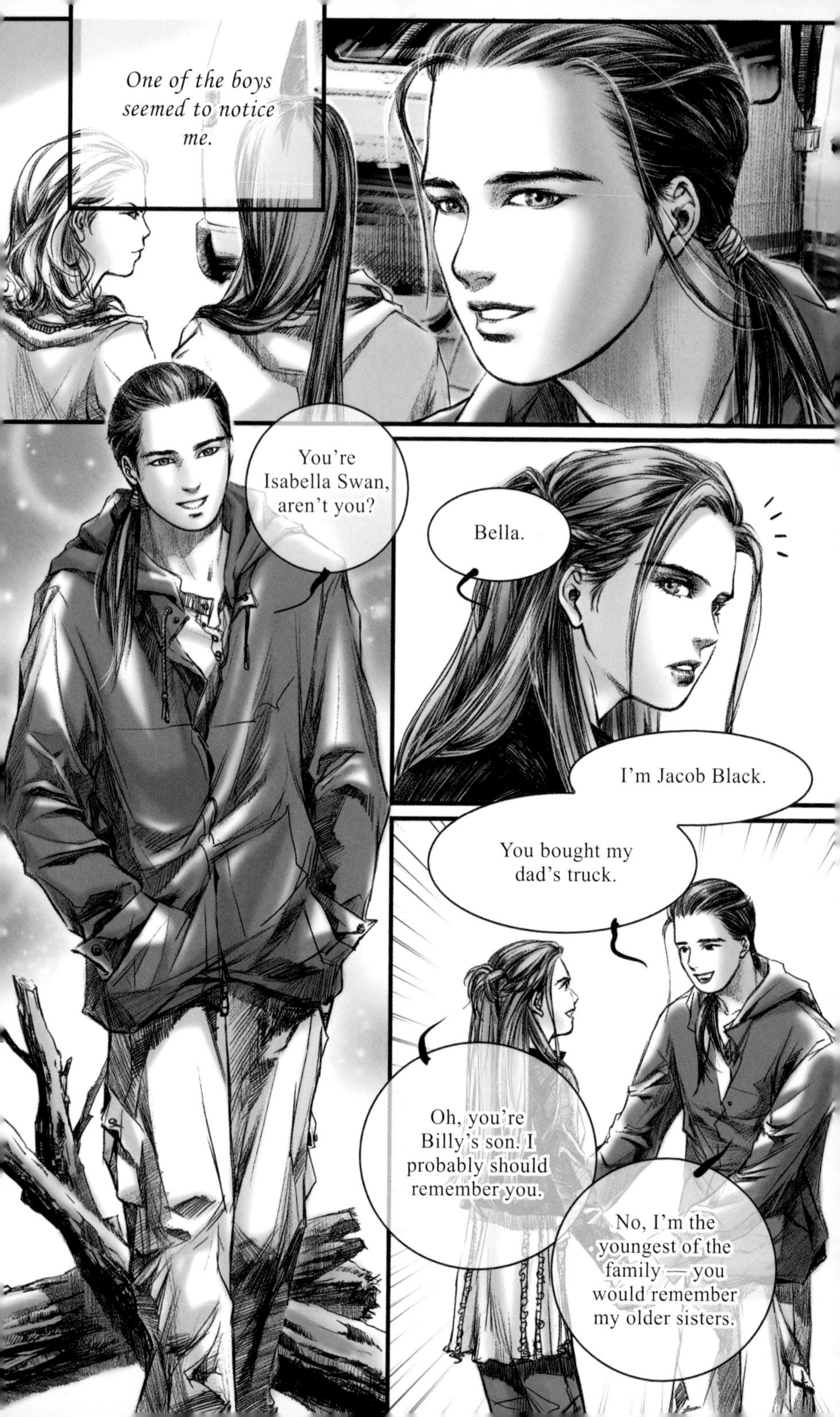
One of the boys seemed to notice me.
You're Isabella Swan, aren't you?
Bella.
I'm Jacob Black.
You bought my dad's truck.
Oh, you're Billy's son. I probably should remember you.
No, I'm the youngest of the family — you would remember my older sisters.

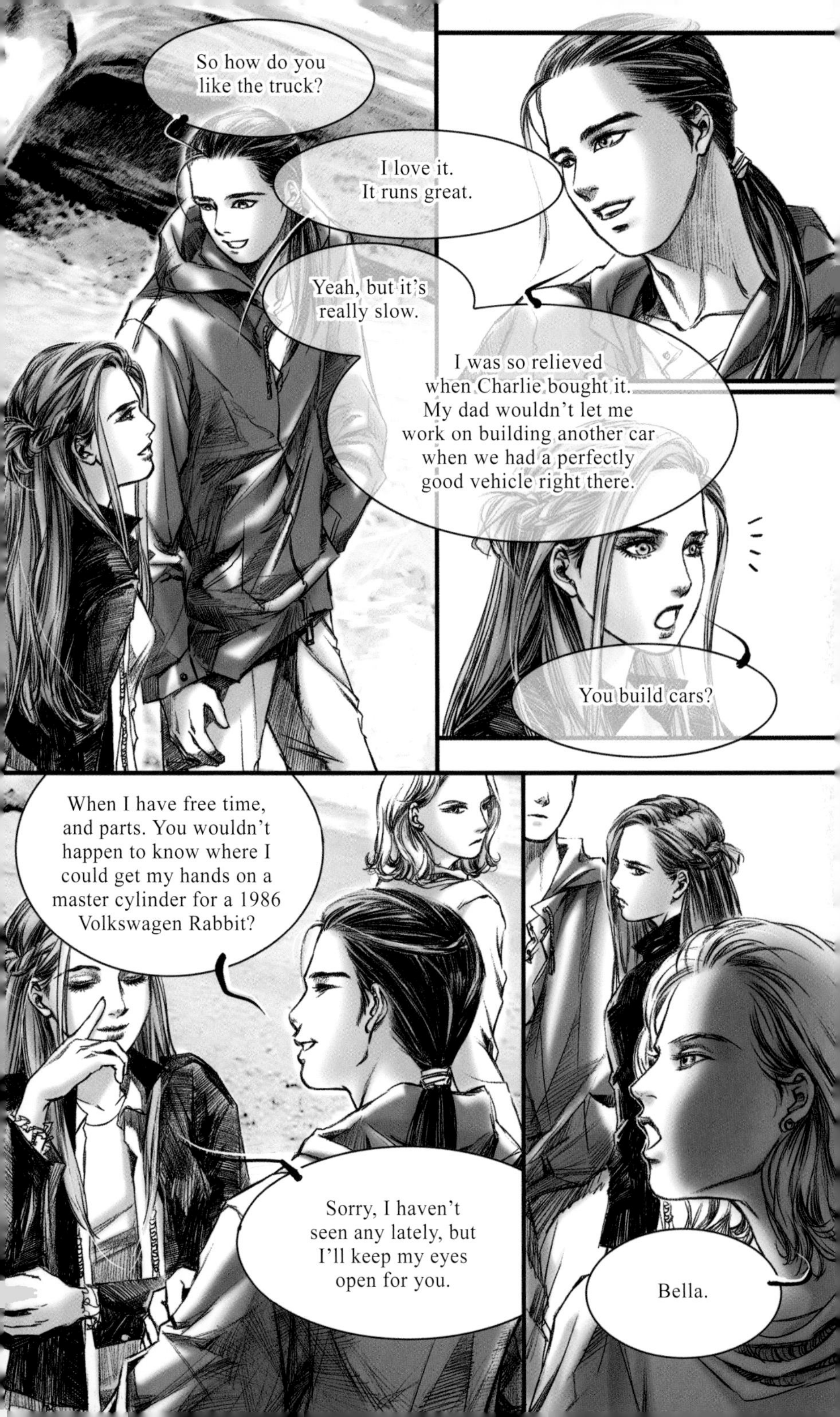
So how do you like the truck?
I love it. It runs great.
Yeah, but it's really slow.
I was so relieved when Charlie bought it. My dad wouldn't let me work on building another car when we had a perfectly good vehicle right there.
You build cars?
When I have free time, and parts. You wouldn't happen to know where I could get my hands on a master cylinder for a 1986 Volkswagen Rabbit?
Sorry, I haven't seen any lately, but I'll keep my eyes open for you.
Bella.

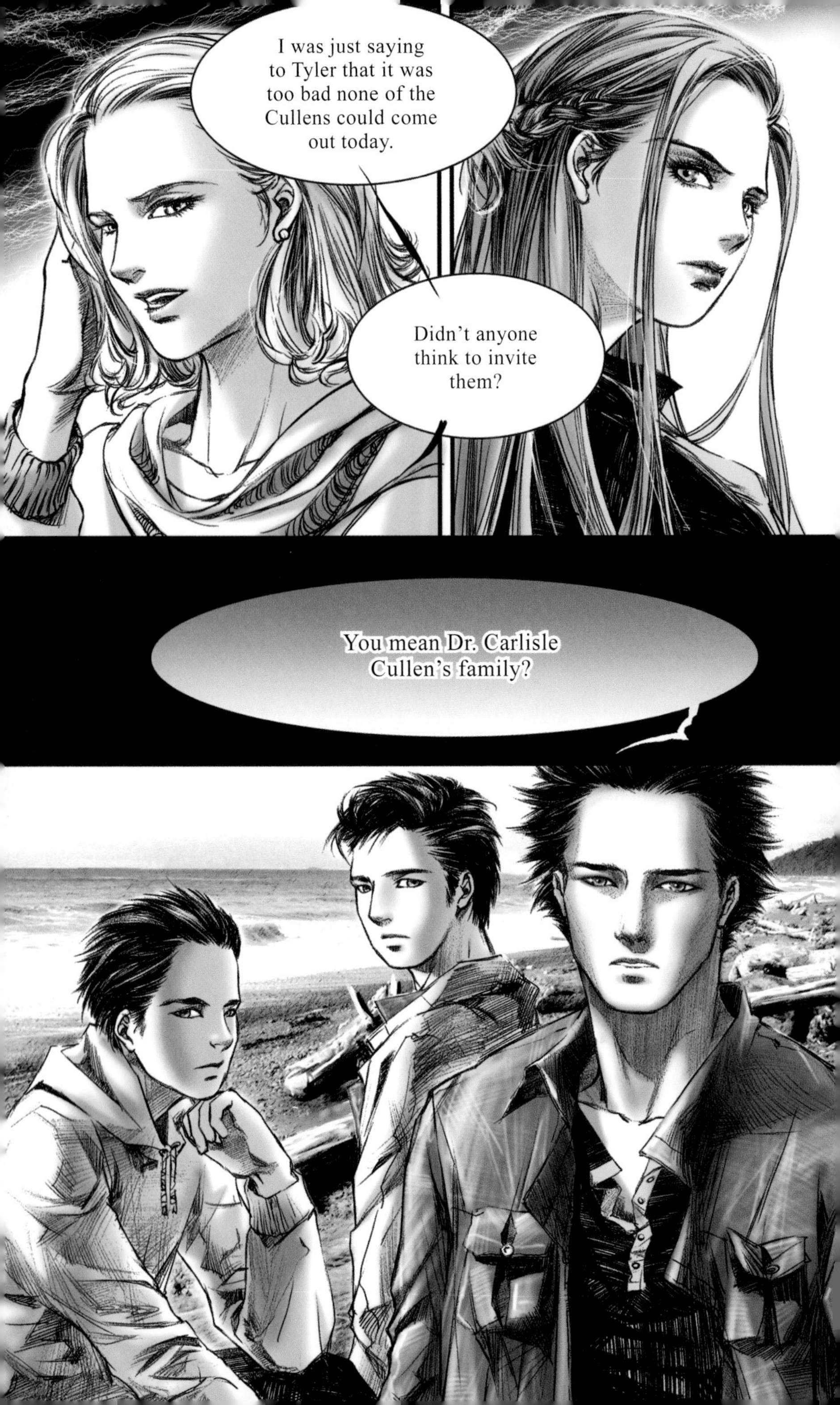

I was just saying to Tyler that it was too bad none of the Cullens could come out today.
Didn't anyone think to invite them?
You mean Dr. Carlisle Cullen's family?

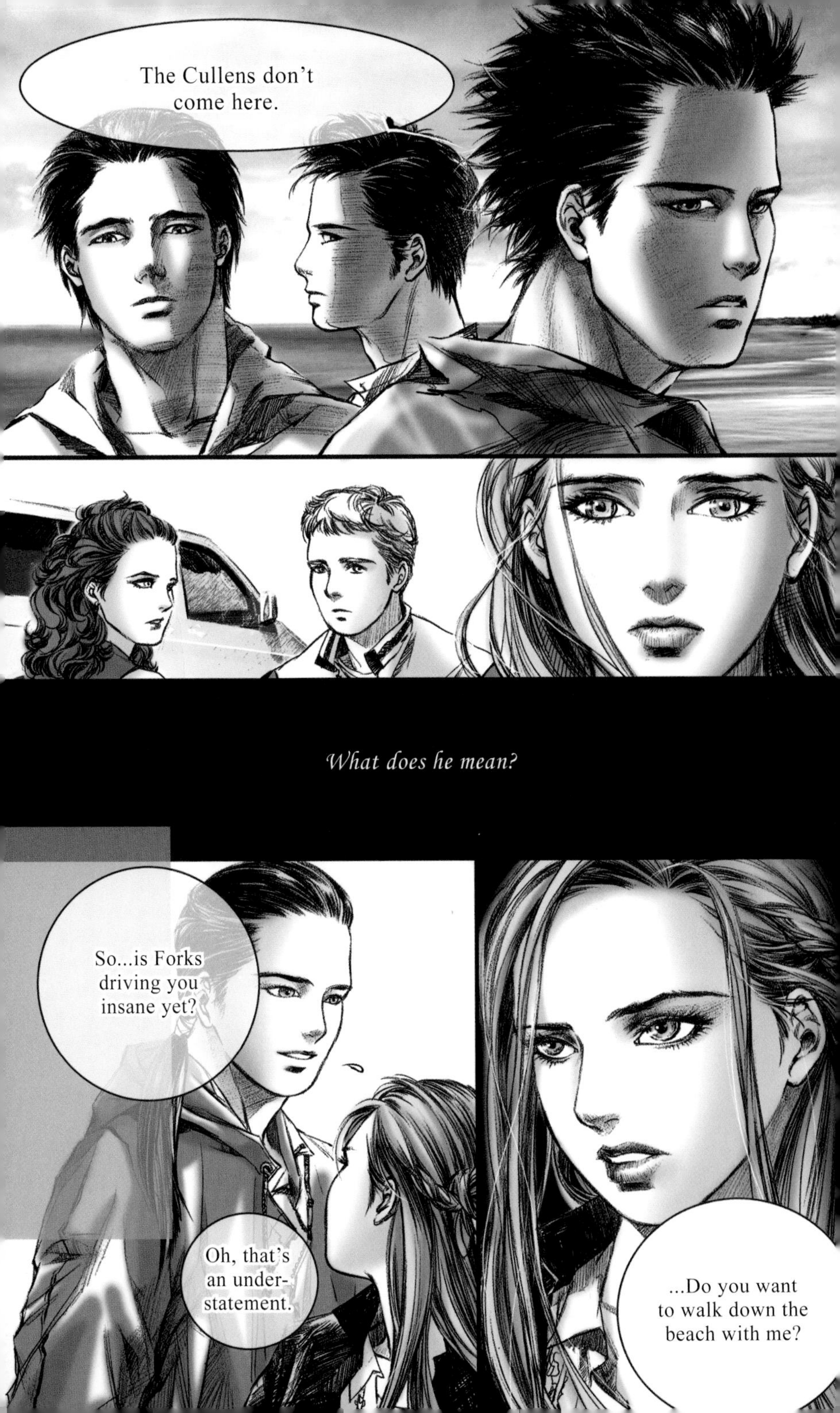
The Cullens don't come here.
What does he mean?
So...is Forks driving you insane yet?
Oh, that's an understatement.
...Do you want to walk down the beach with me?

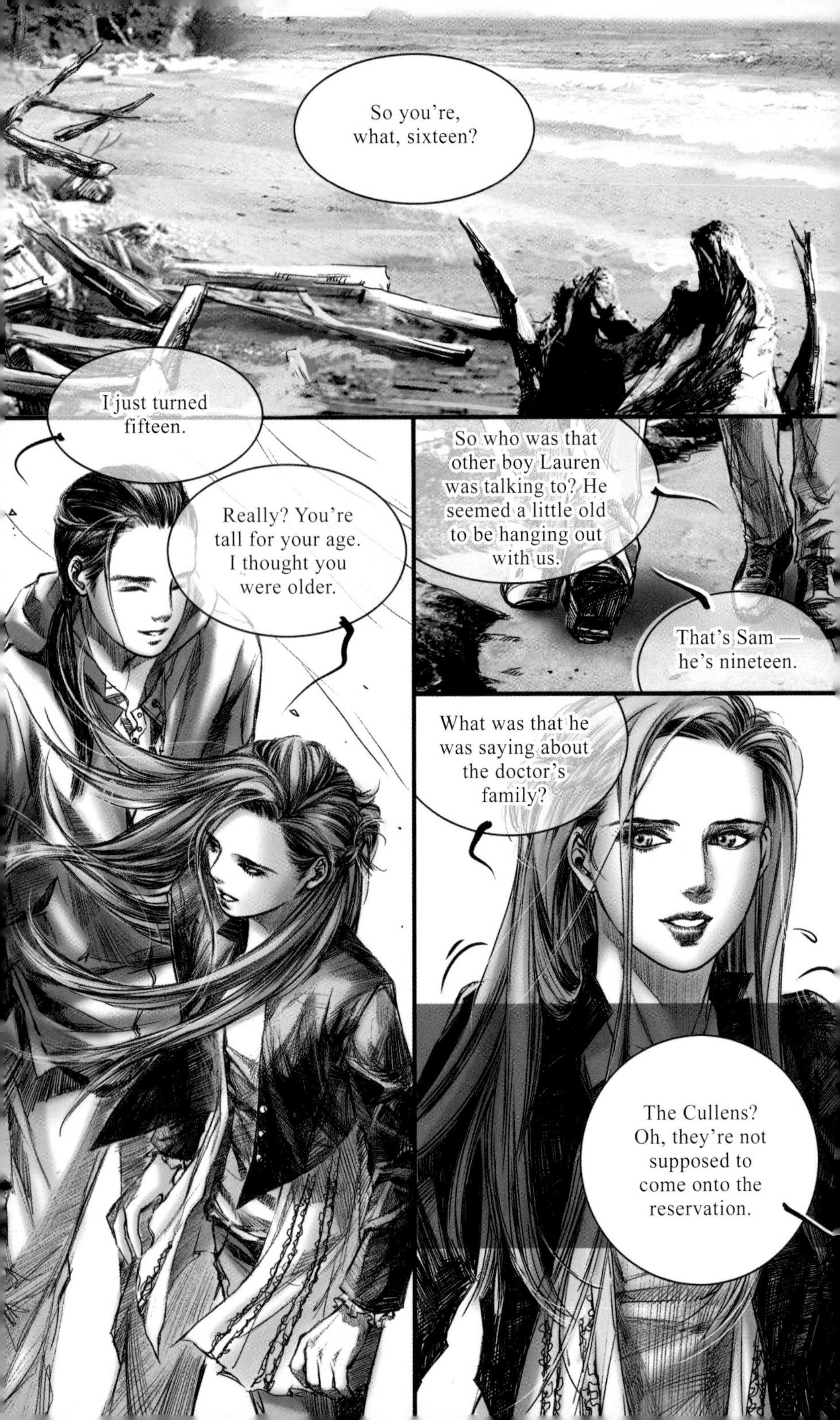
So you're, what, sixteen?
I just turned fifteen.
Really? You're tall for your age. I thought you were older.
So who was that other boy Lauren was talking to? He seemed a little old to be hanging out with us.
That's Sam — he's nineteen.
What was that he was saying about the doctor's family?
The Cullens? Oh, they're not supposed to come onto the reservation.

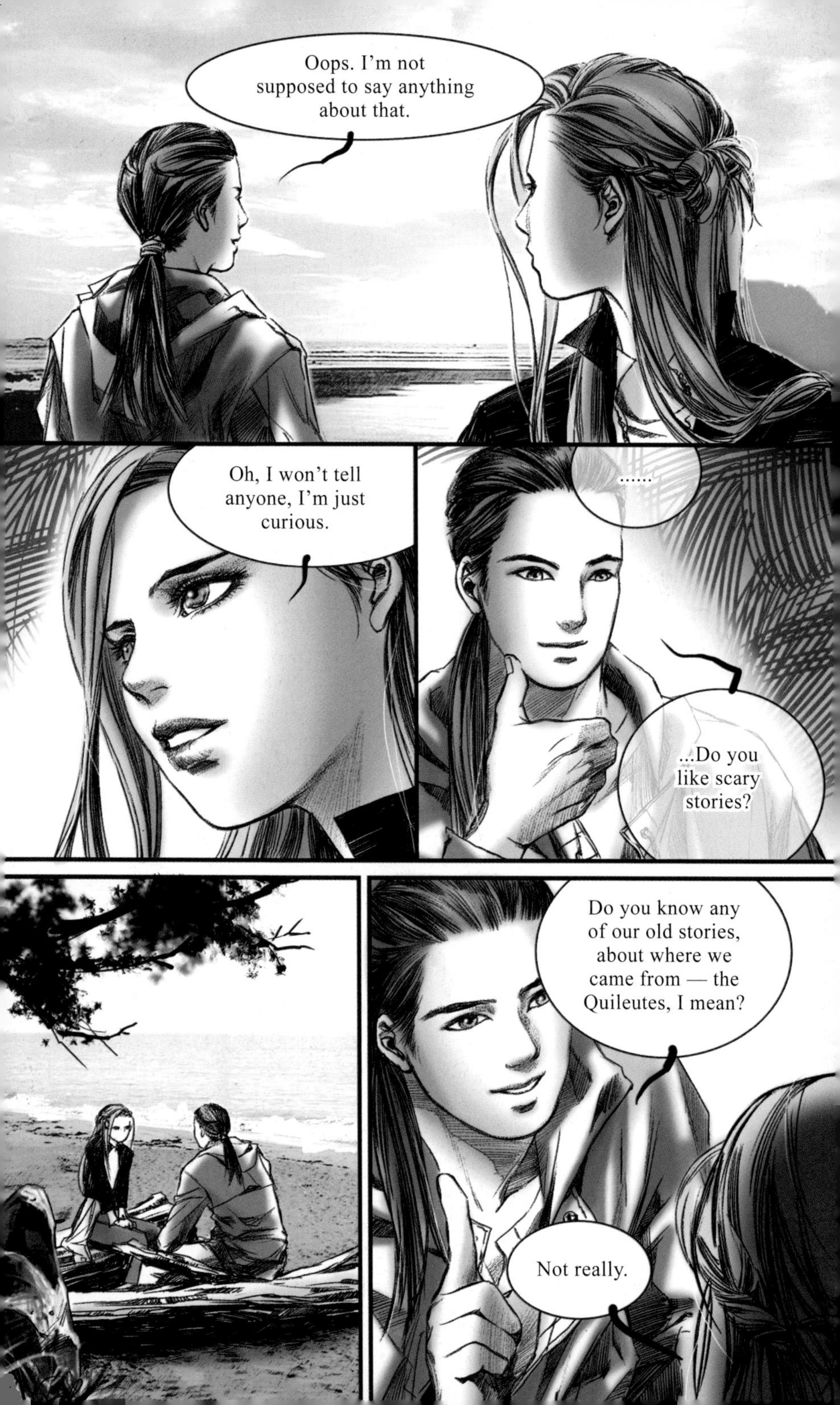
Oops. I'm not supposed to say anything about that.
Oh, I won't tell anyone, I'm just curious.
......
...Do you like scary stories?
Do you know any of our old stories, about where we came from — the Quileutes, I mean?
Not really.

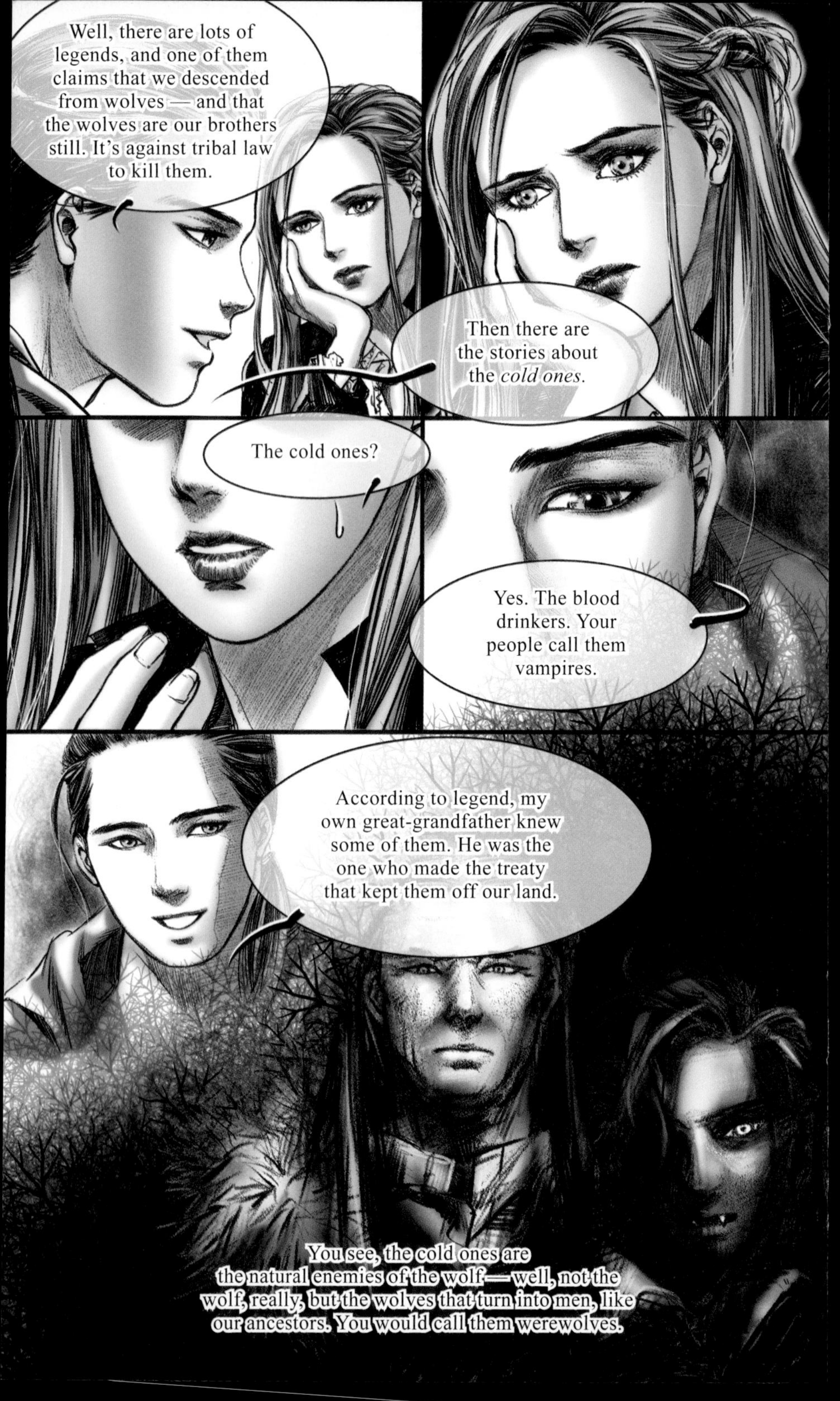
Well, there are lots of legends, and one of them claims that we descended from wolves — and that the wolves are our brothers still. It's against tribal law to kill them.
Then there are the stories about the *cold ones.*
The cold ones?
Yes. The blood drinkers. Your people call them vampires.
According to legend, my own great-grandfather knew some of them. He was the one who made the treaty that kept them off our land.
You see, the cold ones are the natural enemies of the wolf — well, not the wolf, really, but the wolves that turn into men, like our ancestors. You would call them werewolves.

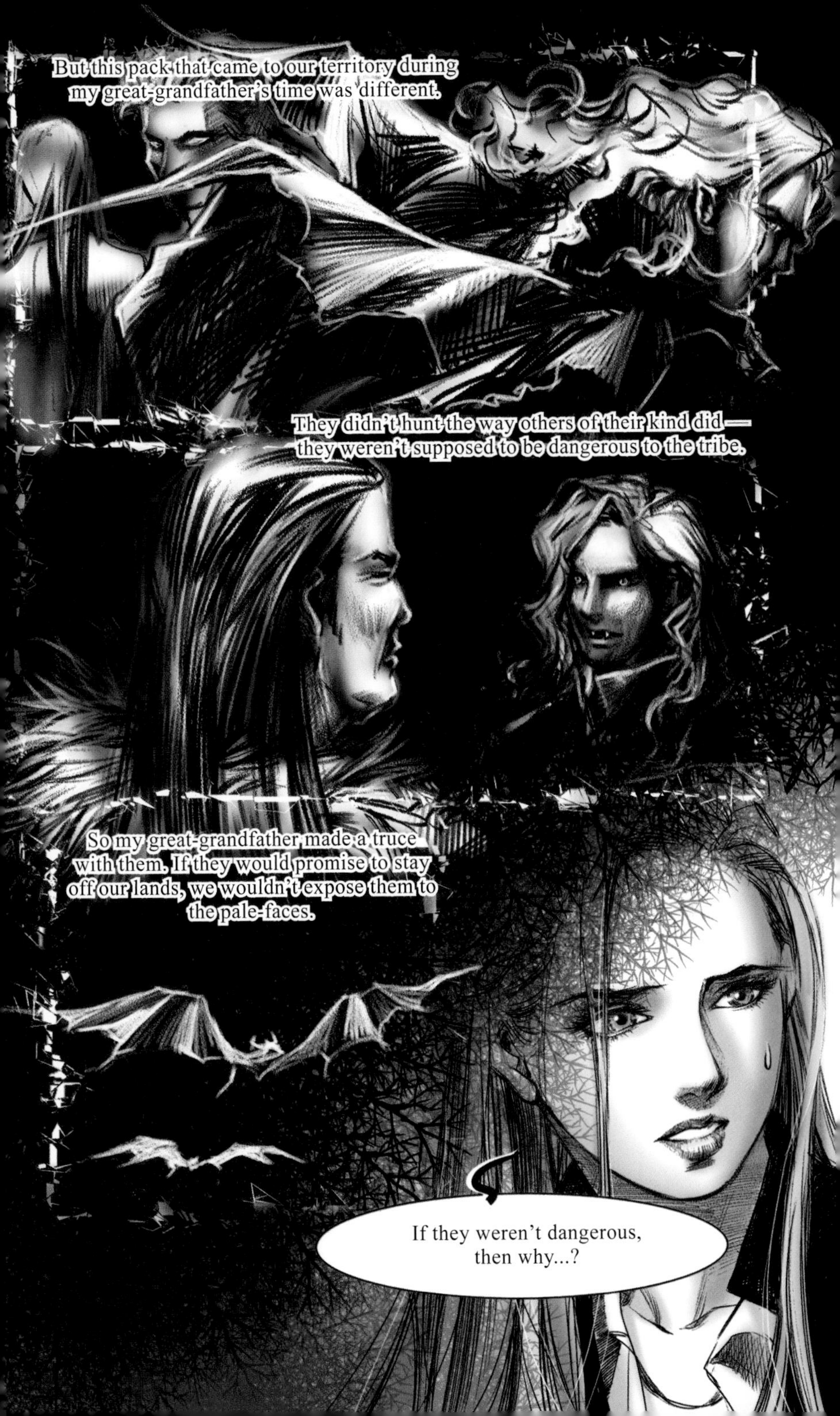
But this pack that came to our territory during my great-grandfather's time was different.
They didn't hunt the way others of their kind did— they weren't supposed to be dangerous to the tribe.
So my great-grandfather made a truce with them. If they would promise to stay off our lands, we wouldn't expose them to the pale-faces.
If they weren't dangerous, then why...?

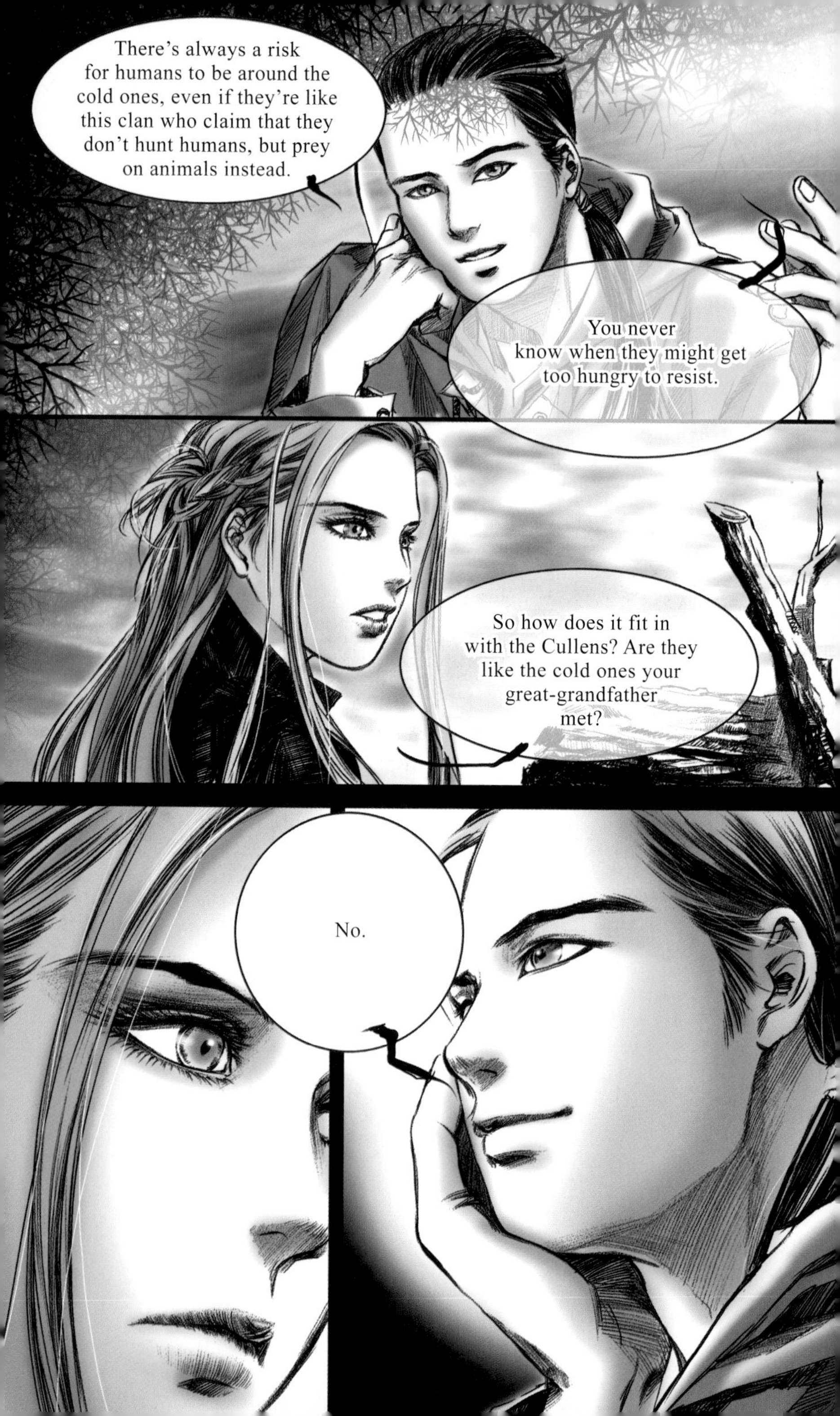
There's always a risk for humans to be around the cold ones, even if they're like this clan who claim that they don't hunt humans, but prey on animals instead.
You never know when they might get too hungry to resist.
So how does it fit in with the Cullens? Are they like the cold ones your great-grandfather met?
No.

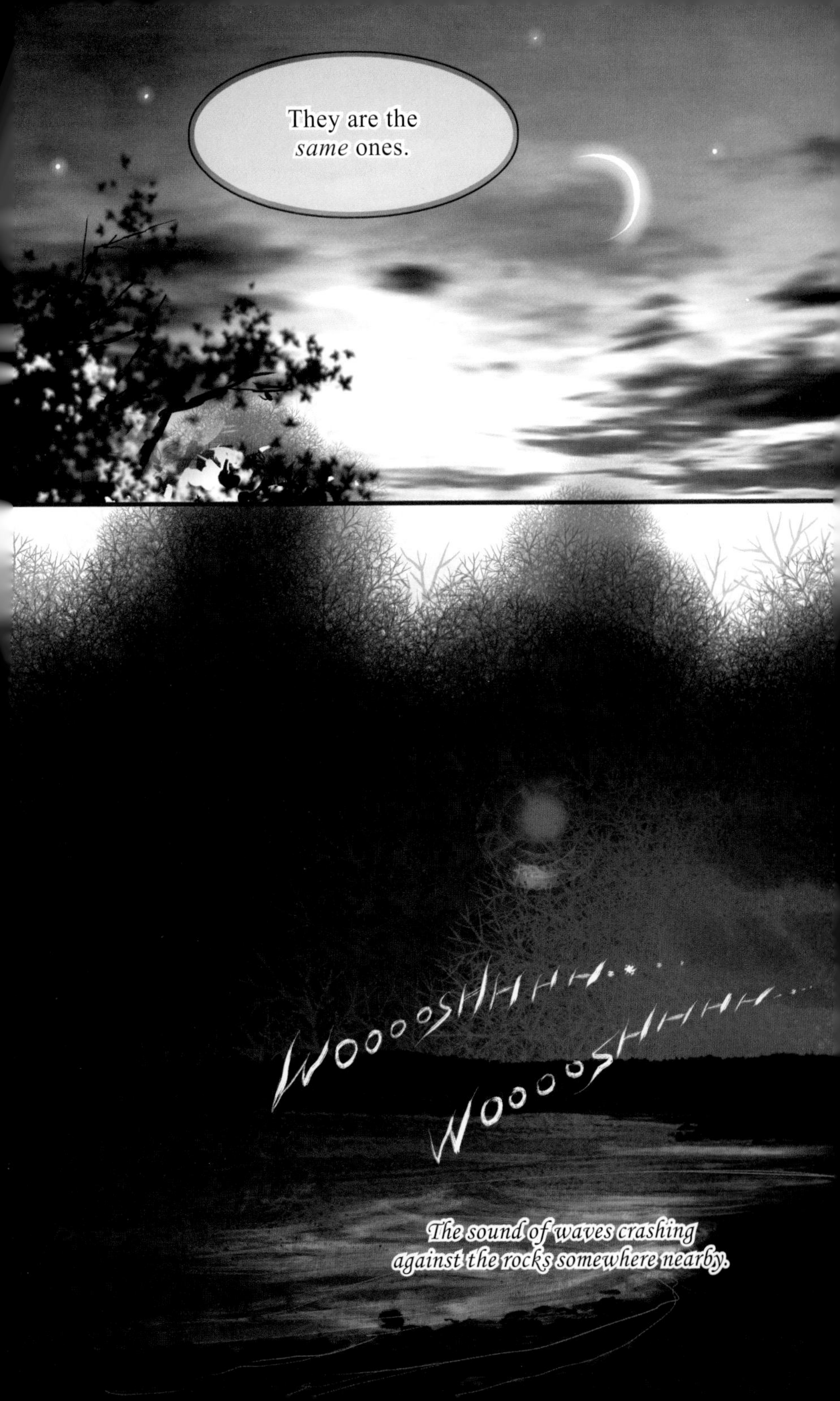
They are the *same* ones.
WOOOOSHHHHH...
WOOOOSHHHHH...
The sound of waves crashing against the rocks somewhere nearby.

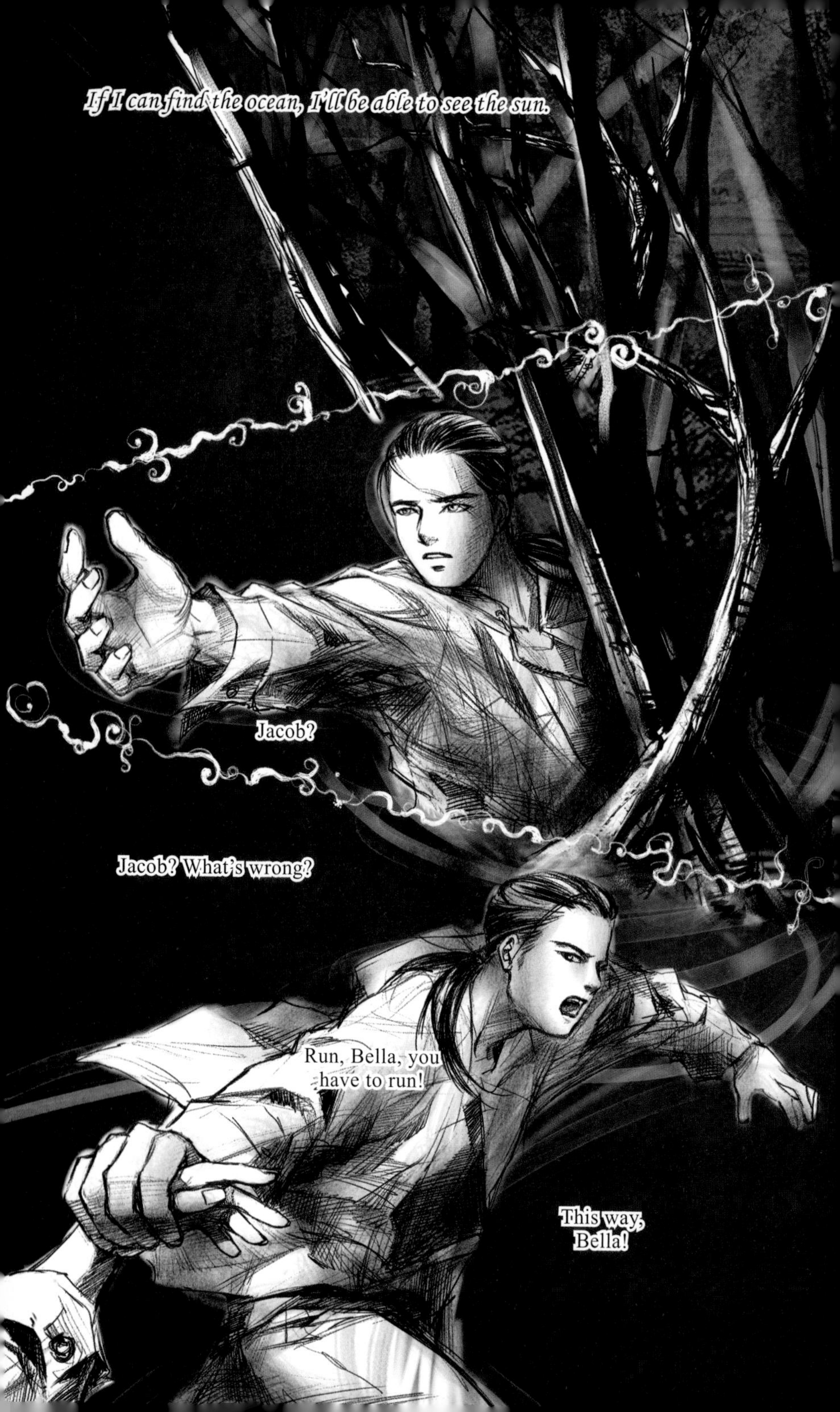
If I can find the ocean, I'll be able to see the sun.
Jacob?
Jacob? What's wrong?
Run, Bella, you have to run!
This way, Bella!

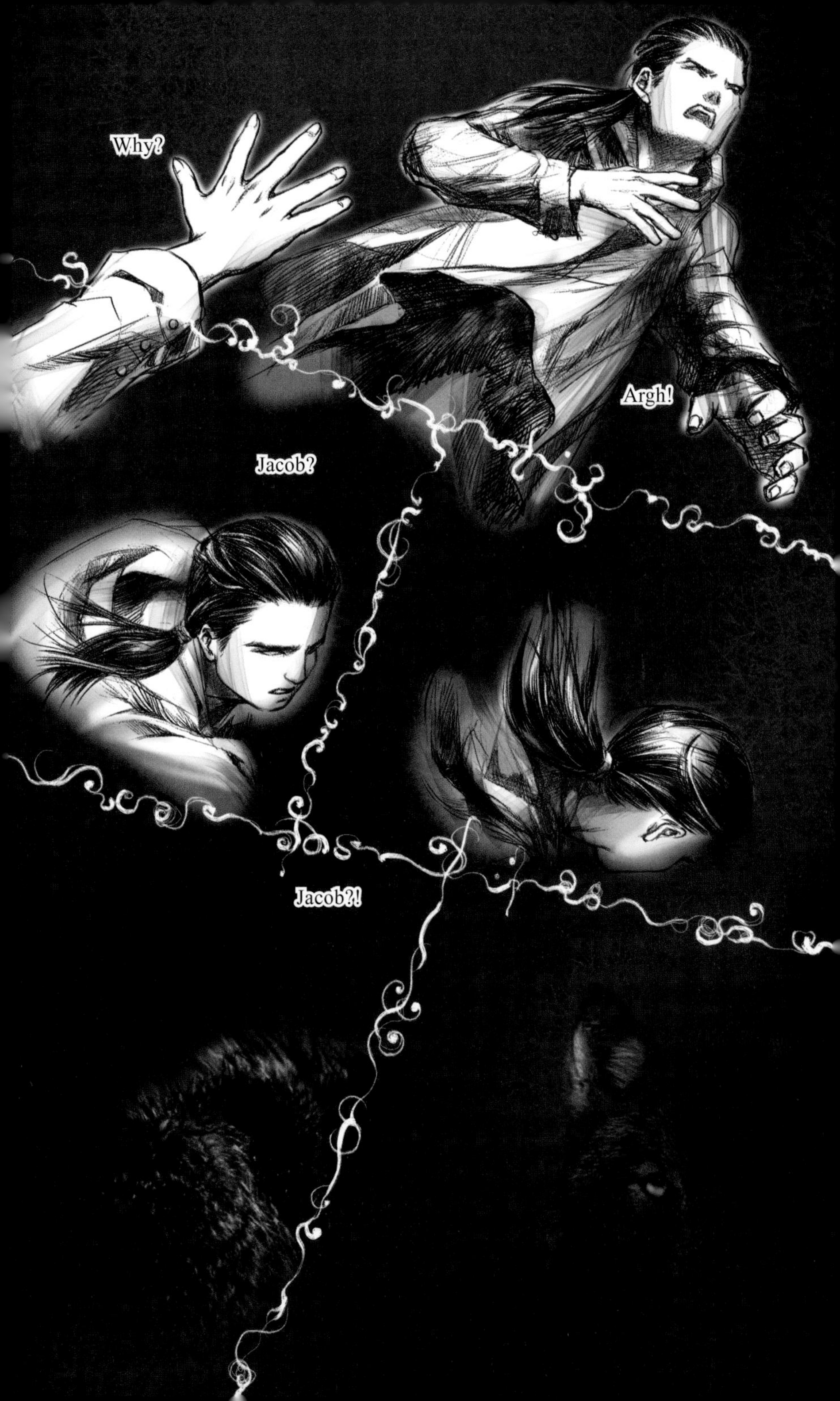
Why?
Argh!
Jacob?
Jacob?!

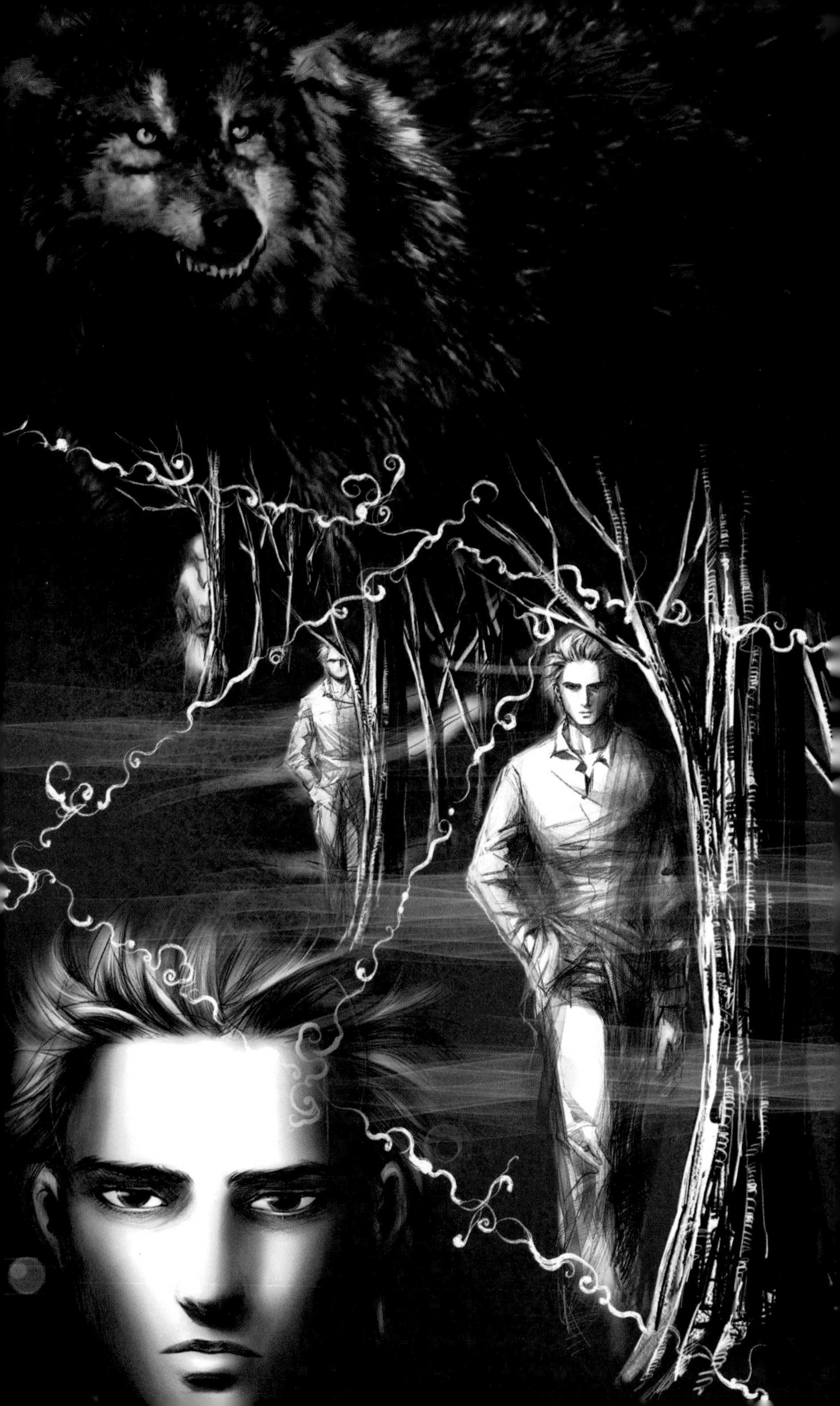

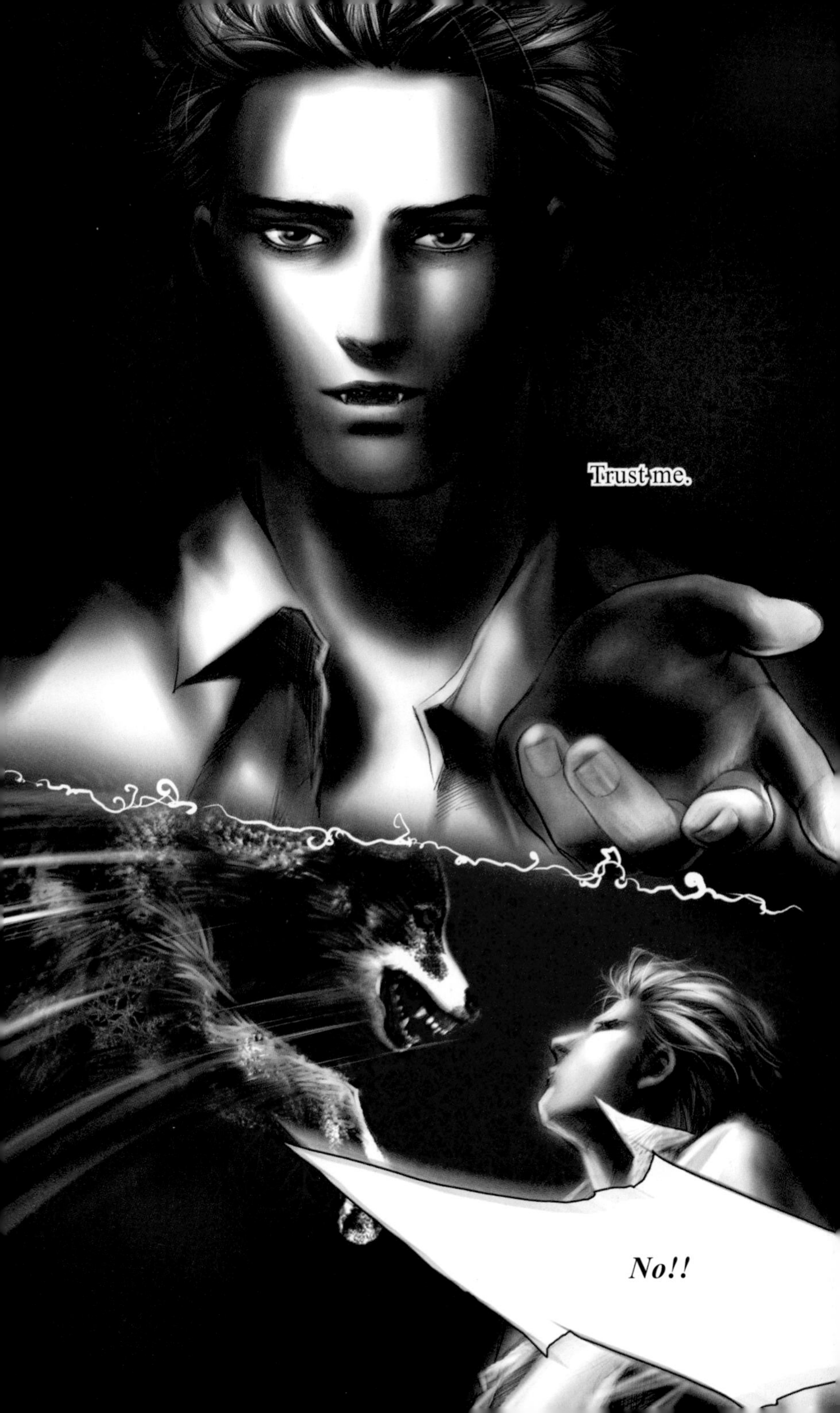
Trust me.
No!!

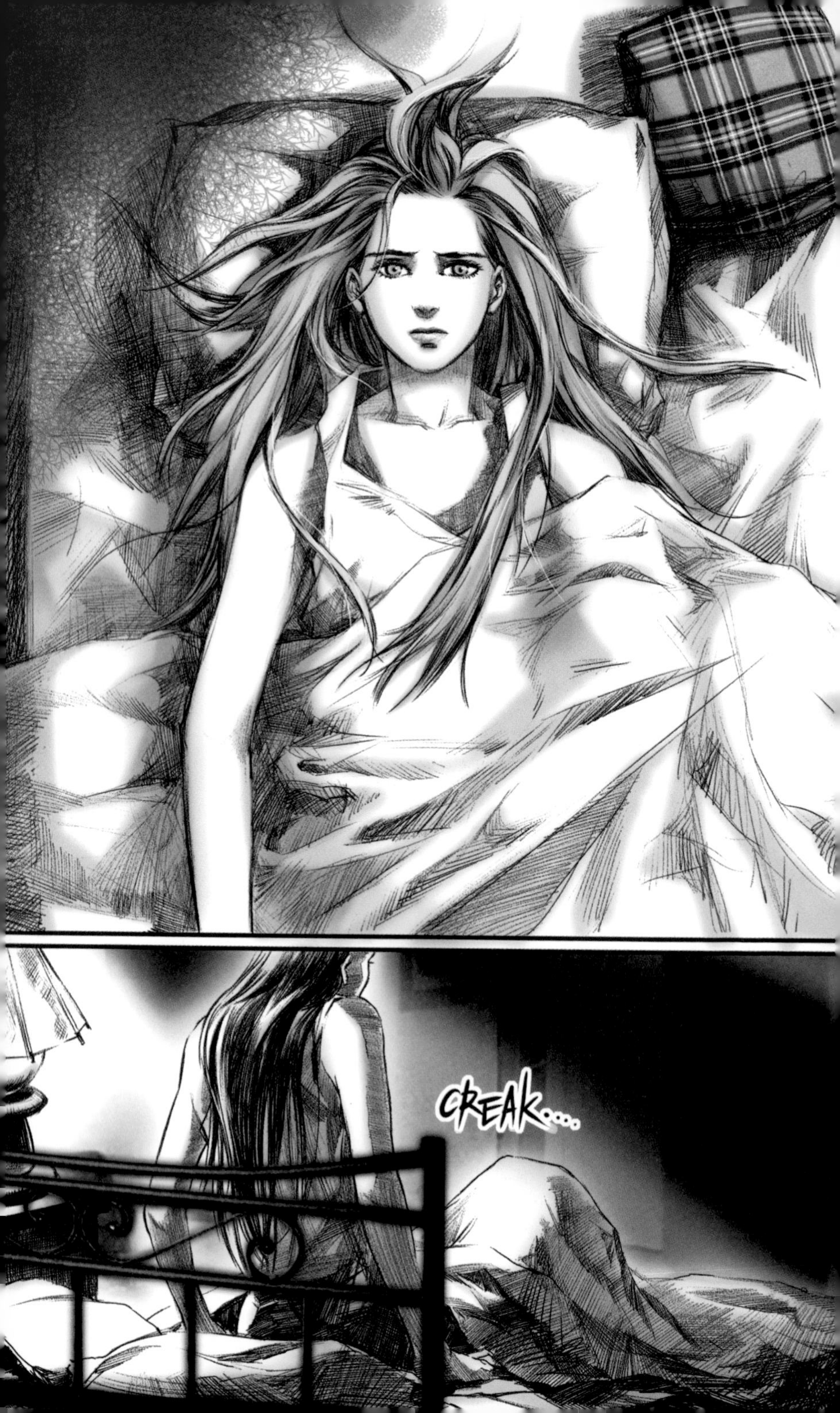
CREAK....

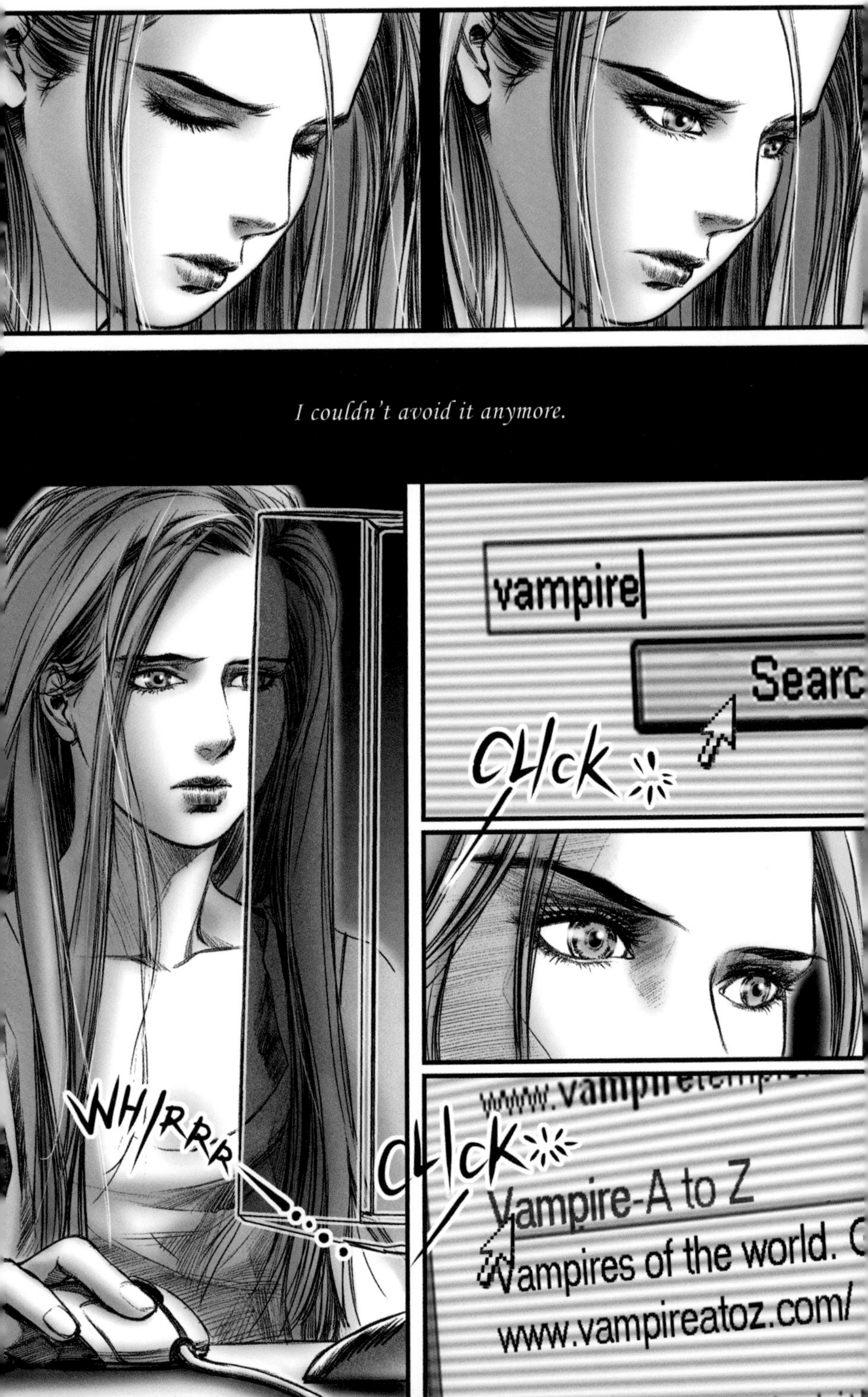
I couldn't avoid it anymore.
vampire
Searc
CLICK
WHIRRR
CLICK
www.vampiretemp
Vampire-A to Z
Vampires of the world.
www.vampireatoz.com/

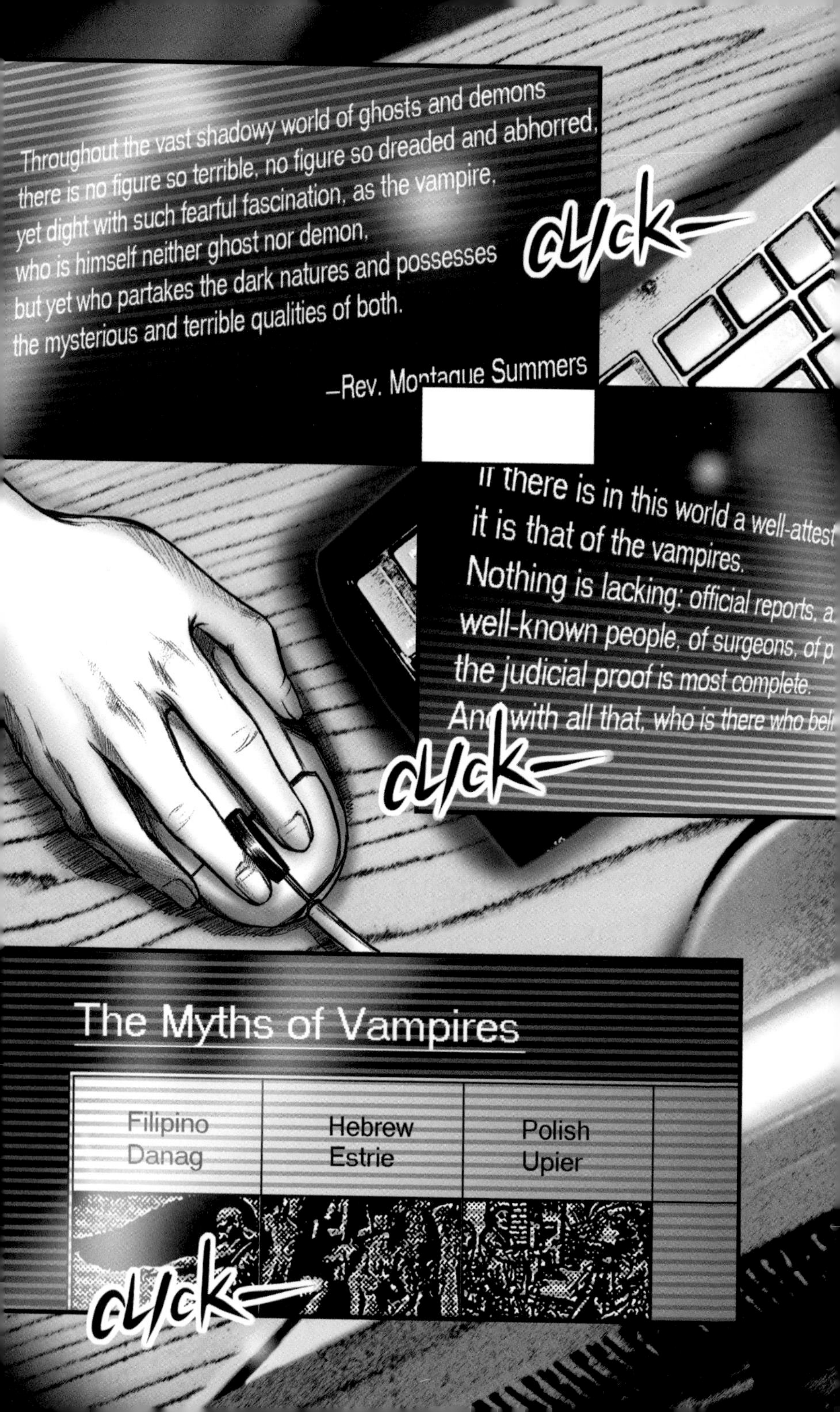
Throughout the vast shadowy world of ghosts and demons
there is no figure so terrible, no figure so dreaded and abhorred,
yet dight with such fearful fascination, as the vampire,
who is himself neither ghost nor demon,
but yet who partakes the dark natures and possesses
the mysterious and terrible qualities of both.
–Rev. Montague Summers
CLICK
If there is in this world a well-attest
it is that of the vampires.
Nothing is lacking: official reports, a
well-known people, of surgeons, of p
the judicial proof is most complete.
And with all that, who is there who bel
CLICK
The Myths of Vampires
Filipino
Danag
Hebrew
Estrie
Polish
Upier
CLICK

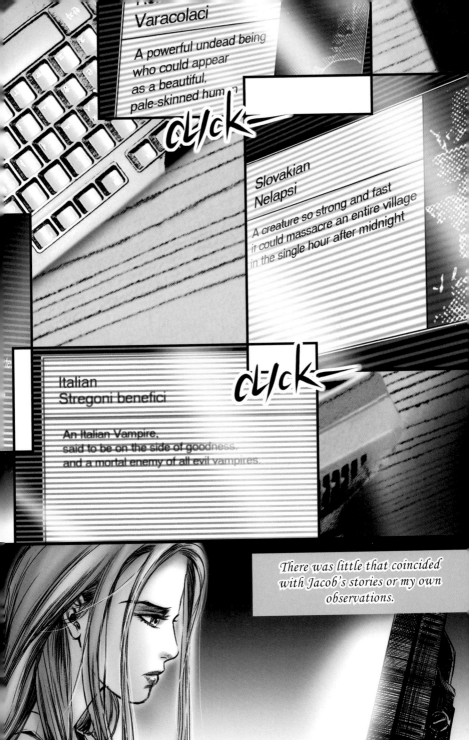

Varacolaci

A powerful undead being
who could appear
as a beautiful,
pale-skinned human

CLICK

Slovakian
Nelapsi

A creature so strong and fast
it could massacre an entire village
in the single hour after midnight

CLICK

Italian
Stregoni benefici

An Italian Vampire,
said to be on the side of goodness,
and a mortal enemy of all evil vampires.

*There was little that coincided
with Jacob's stories or my own
observations.*

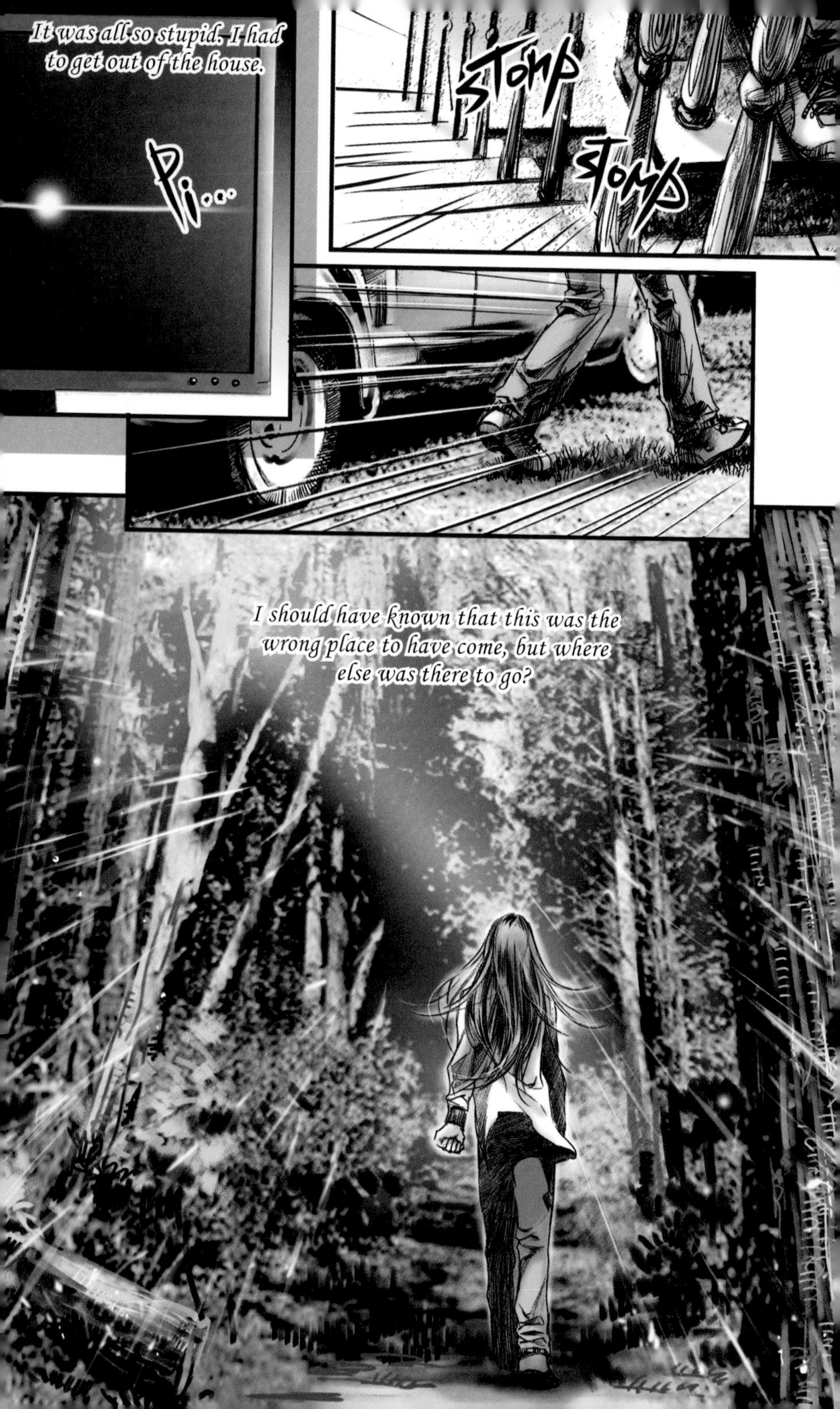
It was all so stupid. I had to get out of the house.
Pi...
STOMP
STOMP
I should have known that this was the wrong place to have come, but where else was there to go?

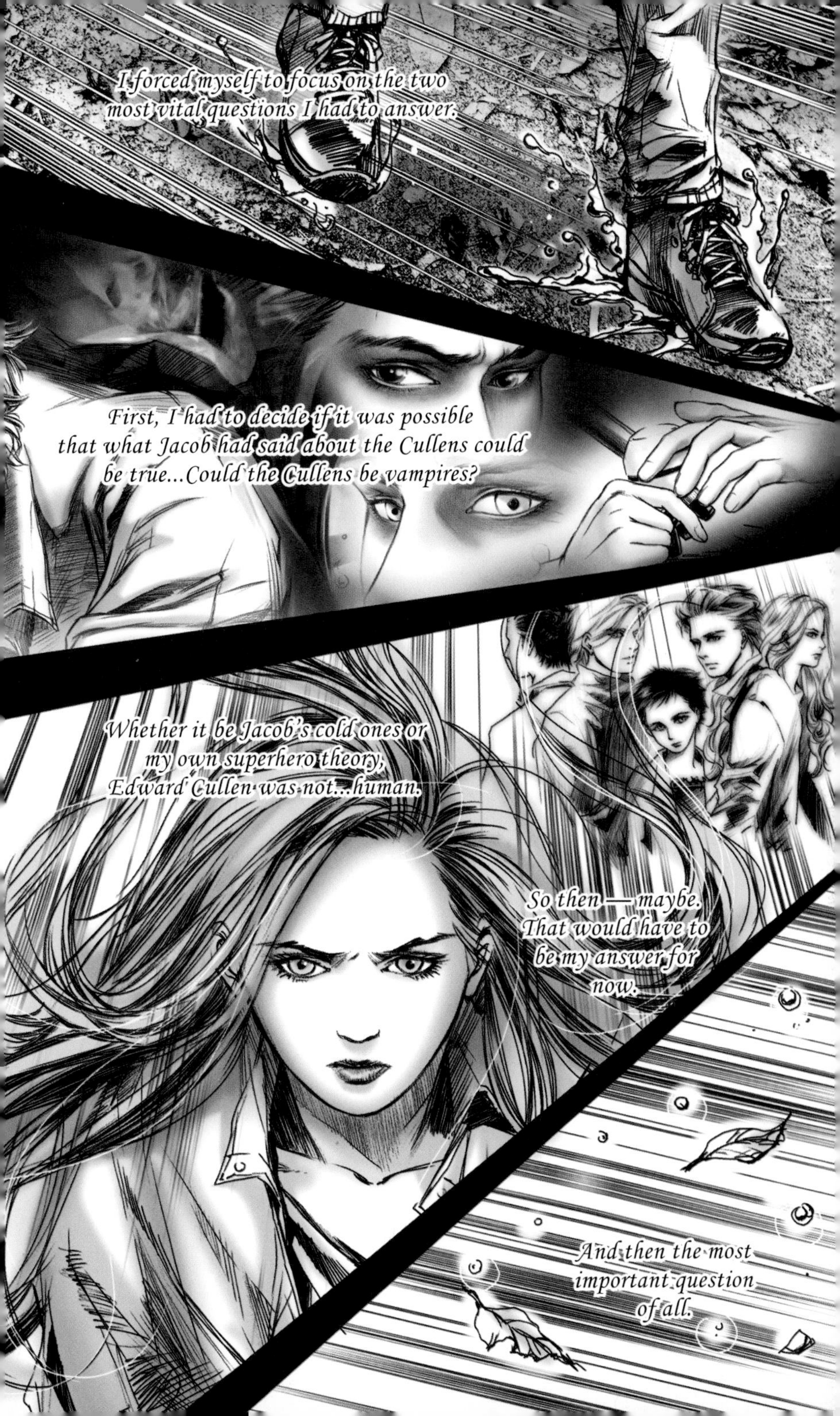
I forced myself to focus on the two most vital questions I had to answer.
First, I had to decide if it was possible that what Jacob had said about the Cullens could be true...Could the Cullens be vampires?
Whether it be Jacob's cold ones or my own superhero theory, Edward Cullen was not...human.
So then — maybe. That would have to be my answer for now.
And then the most important question of all.

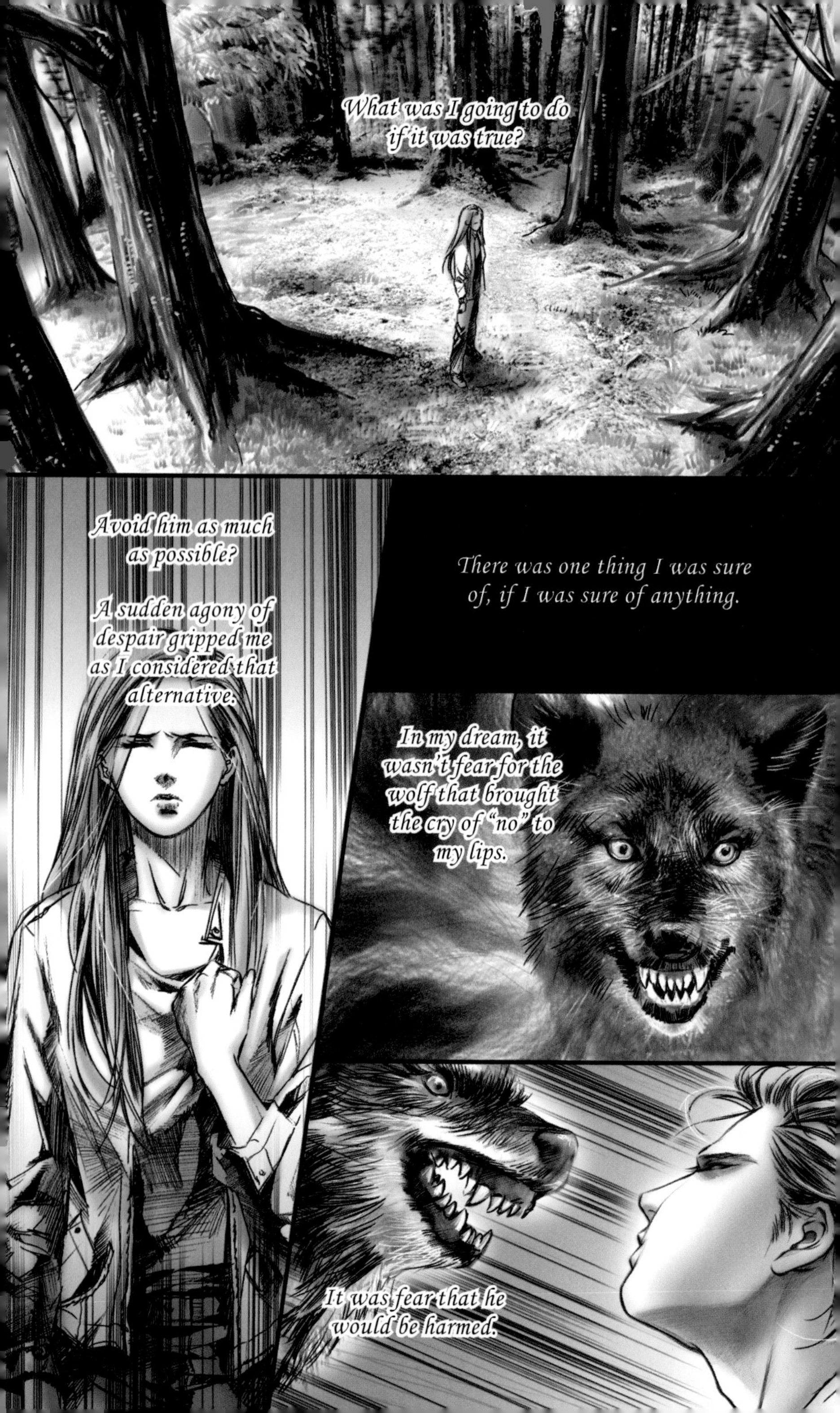
What was I going to do if it was true?
Avoid him as much as possible?
A sudden agony of despair gripped me as I considered that alternative.
There was one thing I was sure of, if I was sure of anything.
In my dream, it wasn't fear for the wolf that brought the cry of "no" to my lips.
It was fear that he would be harmed.

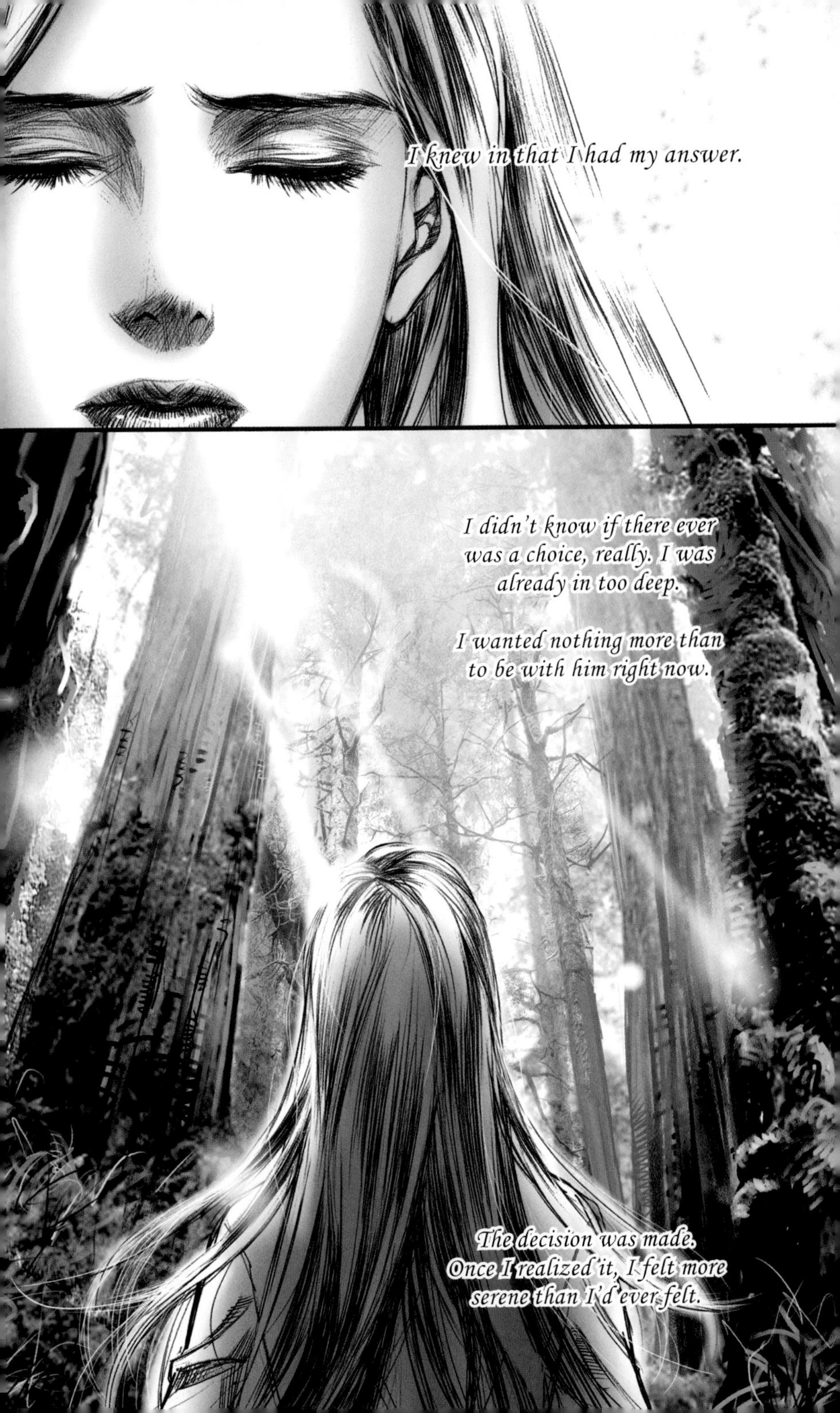
I knew in that I had my answer.
I didn't know if there ever was a choice, really. I was already in too deep.
I wanted nothing more than to be with him right now.
The decision was made. Once I realized it, I felt more serene than I'd ever felt.

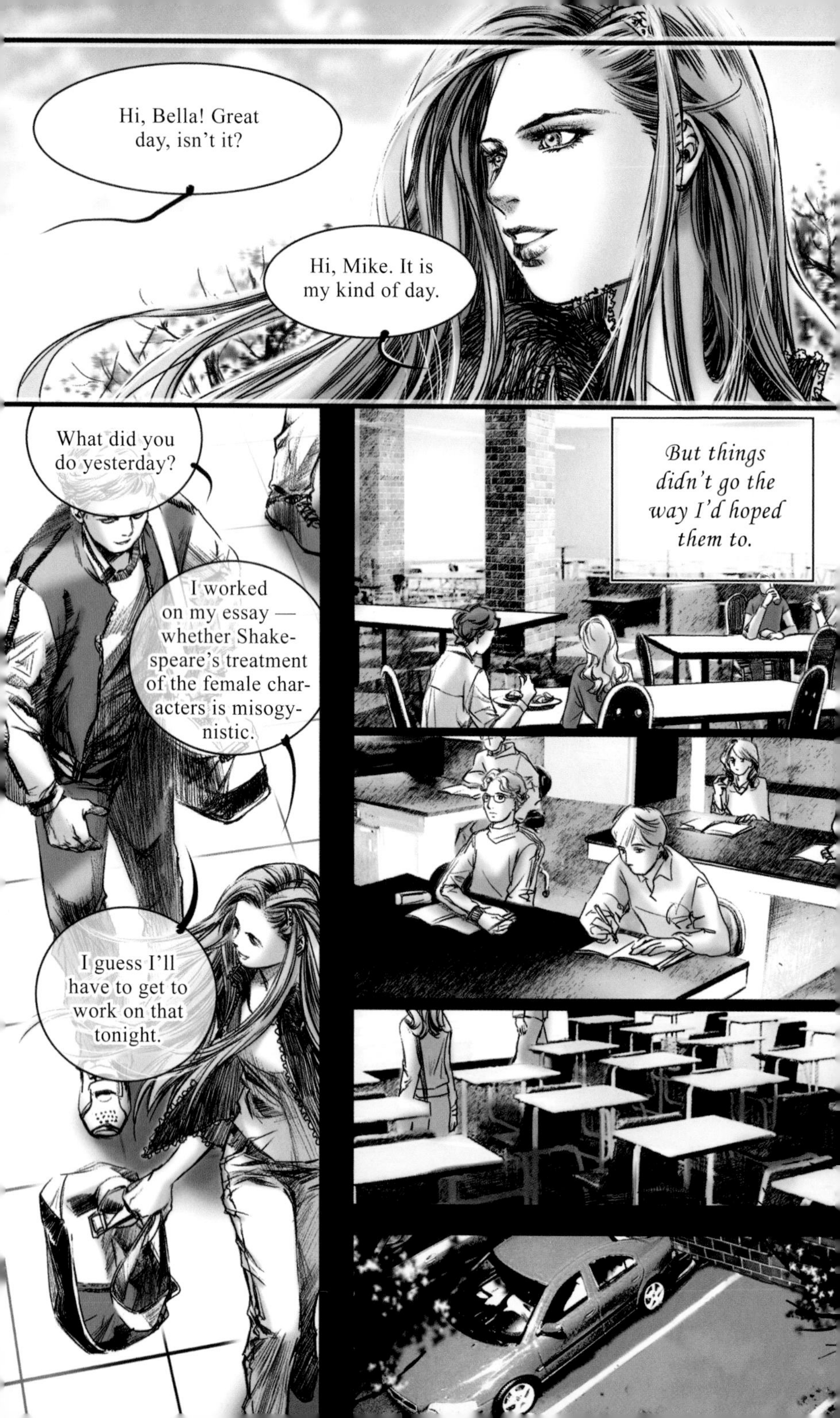
Hi, Bella! Great day, isn't it?
Hi, Mike. It is my kind of day.
What did you do yesterday?
I worked on my essay — whether Shakespeare's treatment of the female characters is misogynistic.
I guess I'll have to get to work on that tonight.
But things didn't go the way I'd hoped them to.

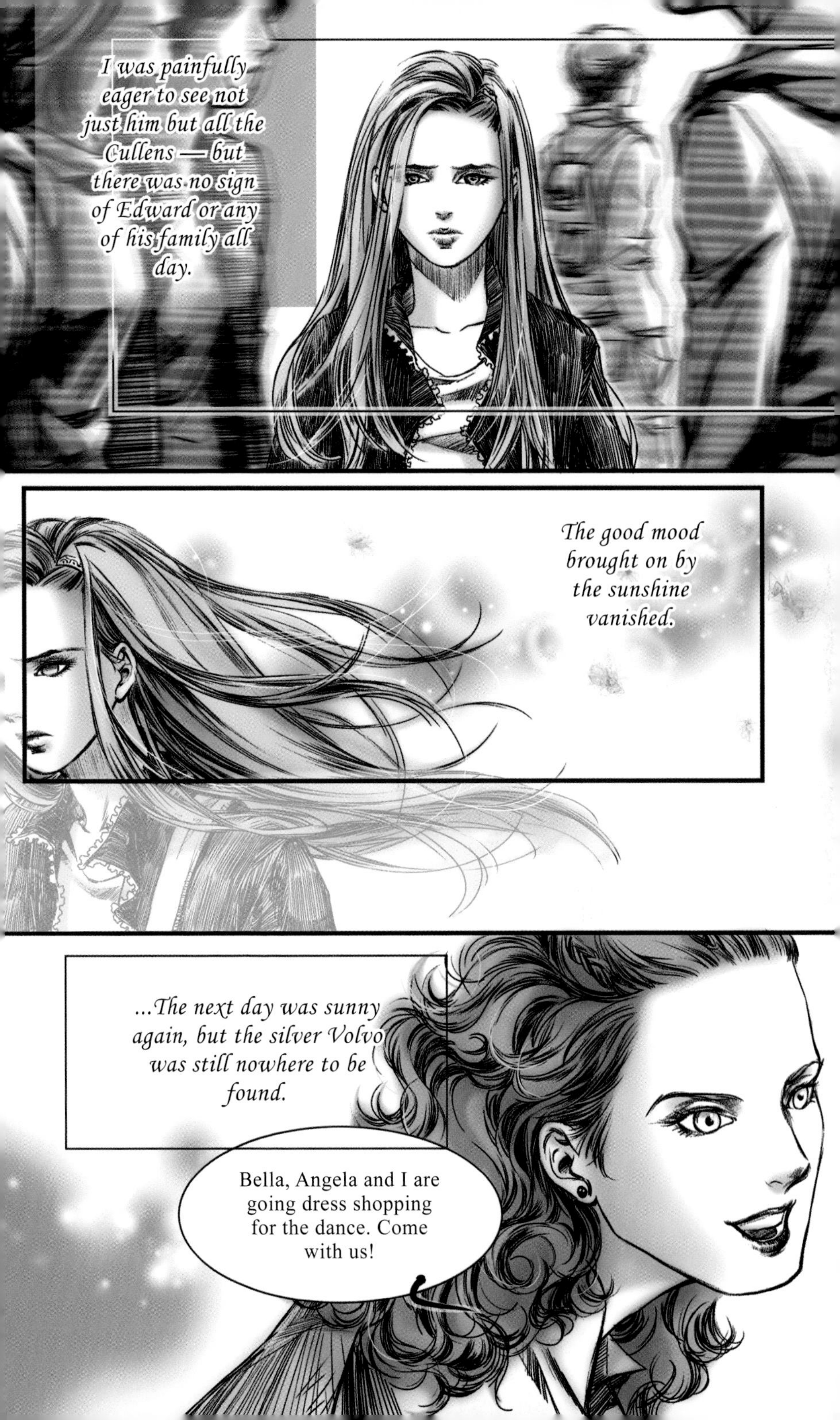
I was painfully eager to see not just him but all the Cullens — but there was no sign of Edward or any of his family all day.
The good mood brought on by the sunshine vanished.
...The next day was sunny again, but the silver Volvo was still nowhere to be found.
Bella, Angela and I are going dress shopping for the dance. Come with us!

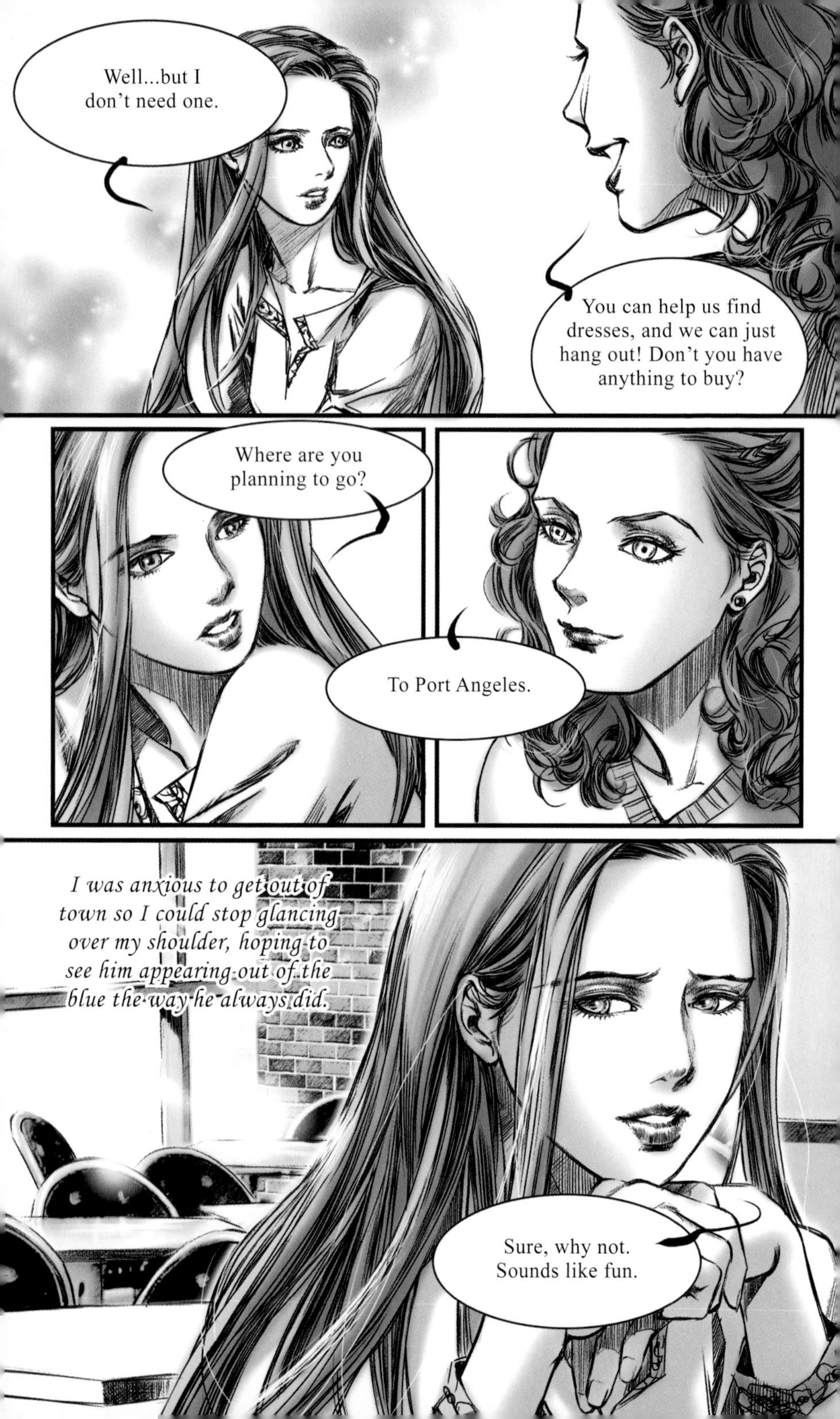
Well...but I don't need one.
You can help us find dresses, and we can just hang out! Don't you have anything to buy?
Where are you planning to go?
To Port Angeles.
I was anxious to get out of town so I could stop glancing over my shoulder, hoping to see him appearing out of the blue the way he always did.
Sure, why not. Sounds like fun.

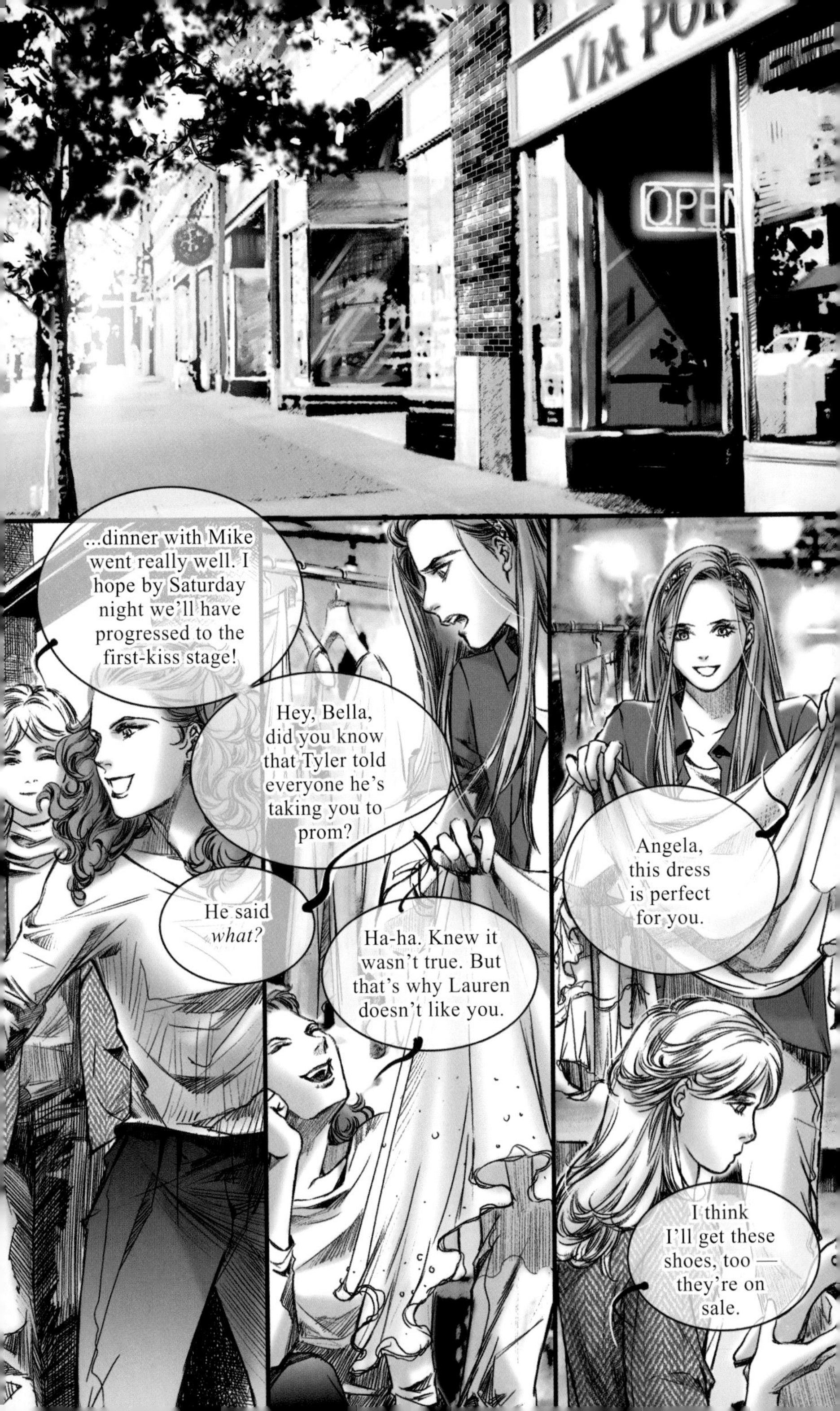
VIA PO
OPEN
...dinner with Mike went really well. I hope by Saturday night we'll have progressed to the first-kiss stage!
Hey, Bella, did you know that Tyler told everyone he's taking you to prom?
He said *what?*
Ha-ha. Knew it wasn't true. But that's why Lauren doesn't like you.
Angela, this dress is perfect for you.
I think I'll get these shoes, too — they're on sale.

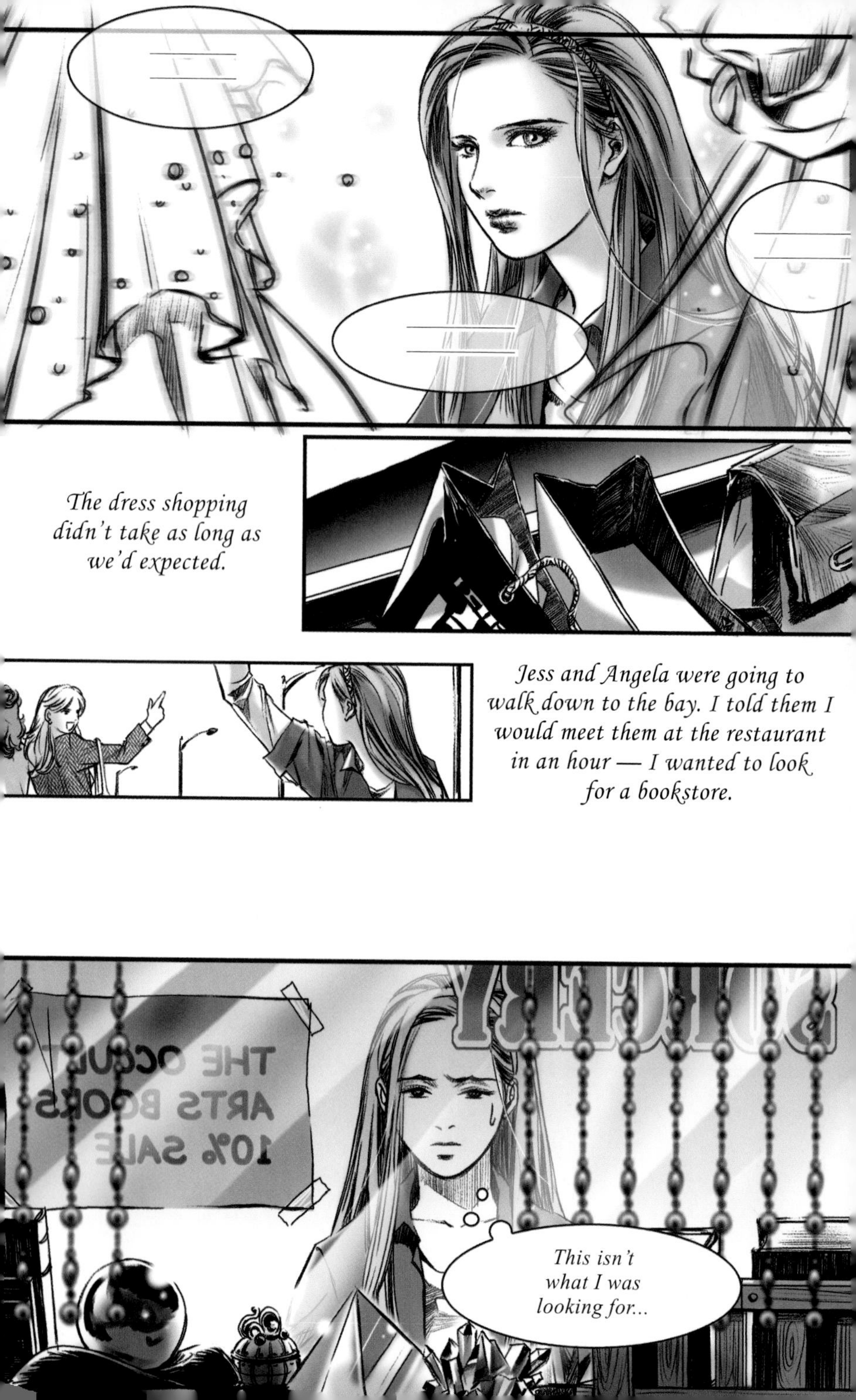
The dress shopping didn't take as long as we'd expected.
Jess and Angela were going to walk down to the bay. I told them I would meet them at the restaurant in an hour — I wanted to look for a bookstore.
This isn't what I was looking for...

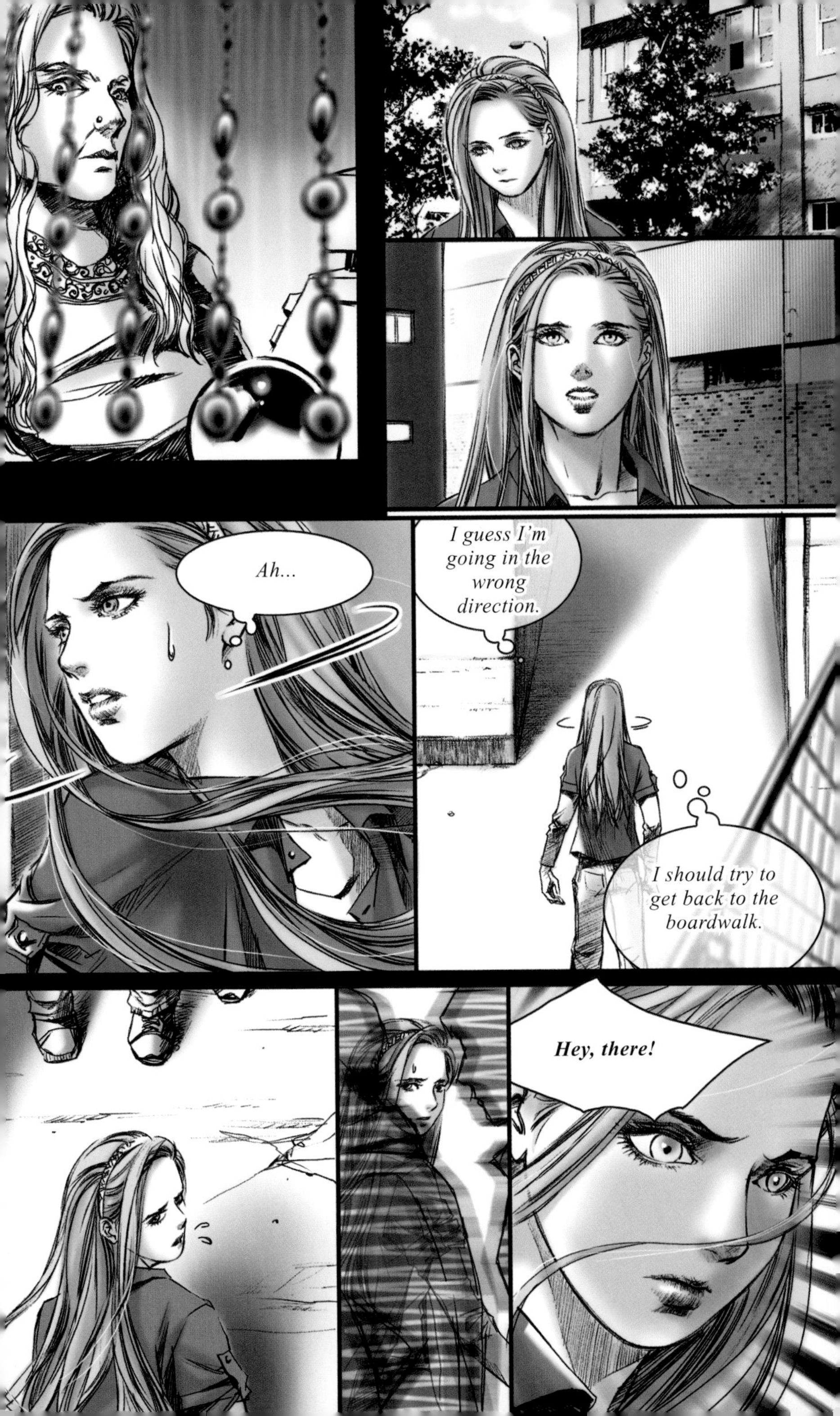
Ah...
I guess I'm going in the wrong direction.
I should try to get back to the boardwalk.
Hey, there!

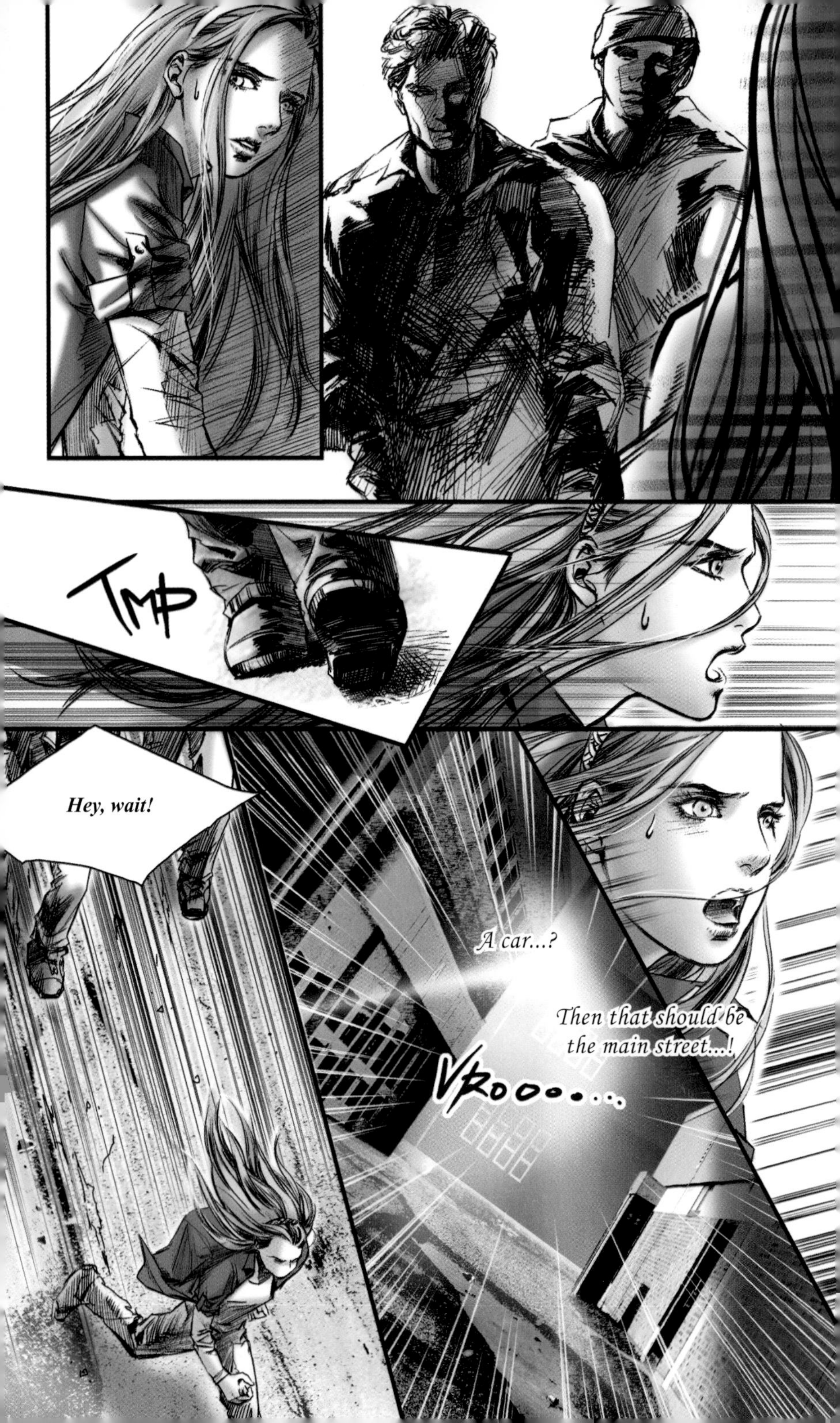
TMP
Hey, wait!
A car...?
Then that should be the main street...!
VROOOo...

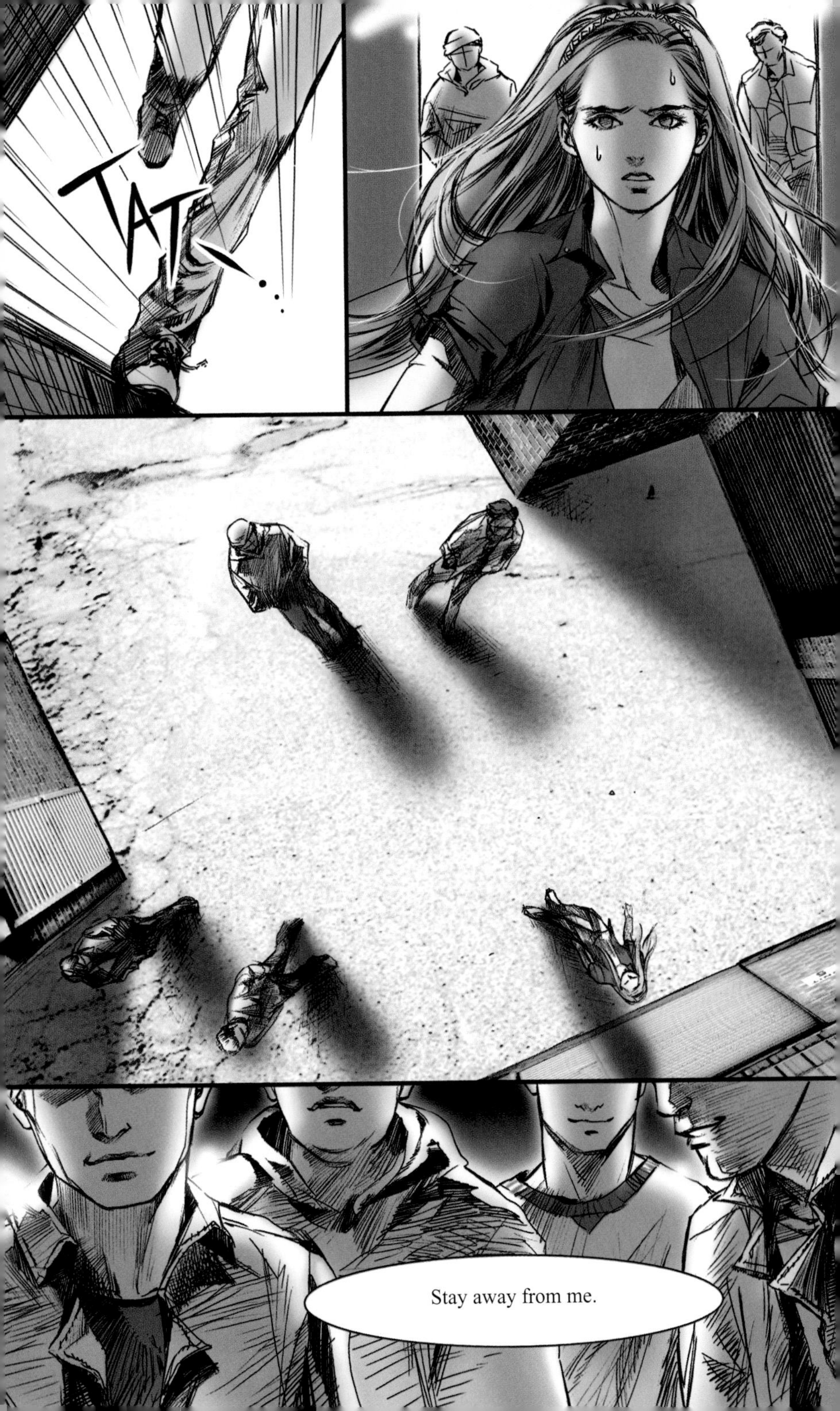
TAT...
Stay away from me.

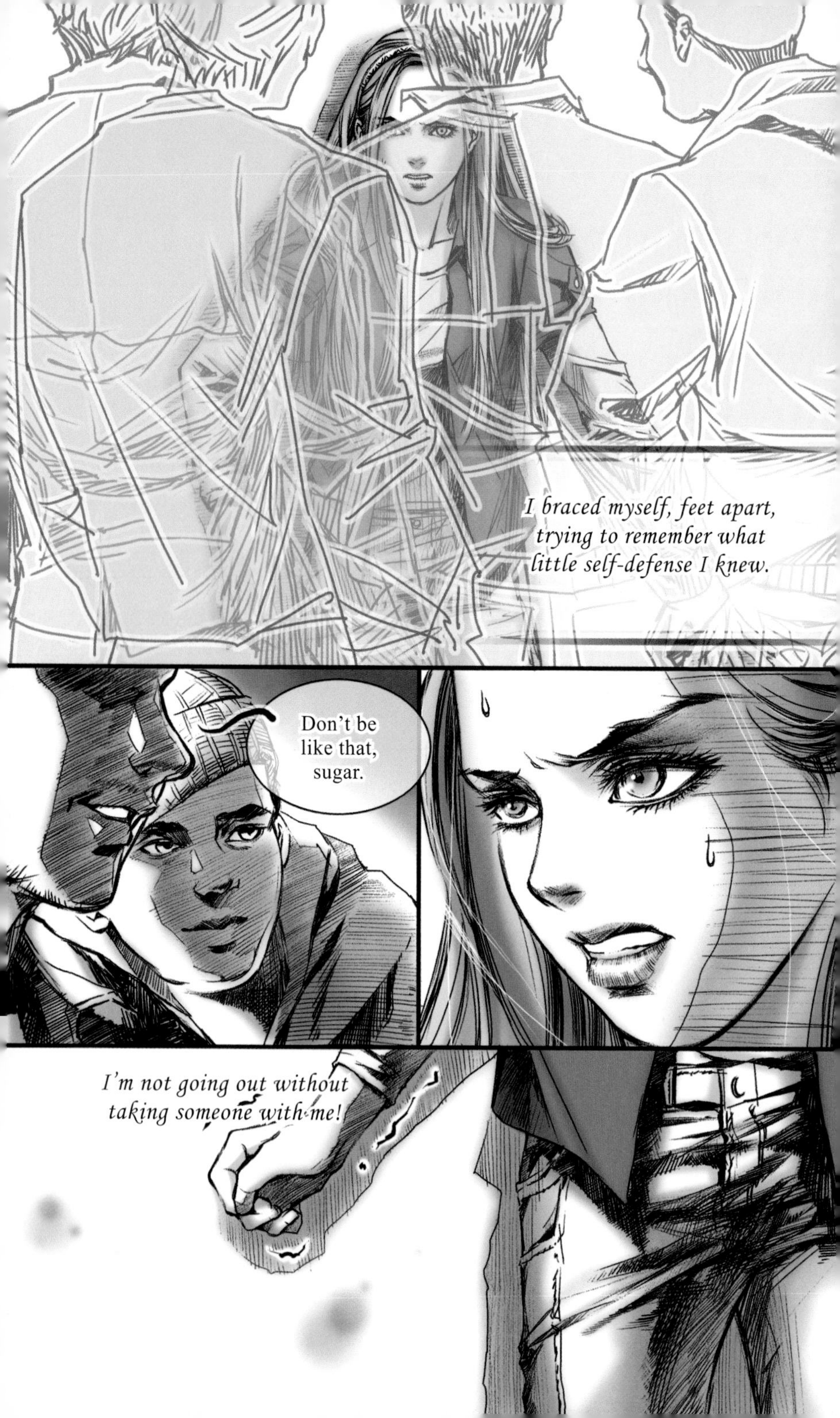
I braced myself, feet apart,
trying to remember what
little self-defense I knew.
Don't be like that, sugar.
I'm not going out without taking someone with me!

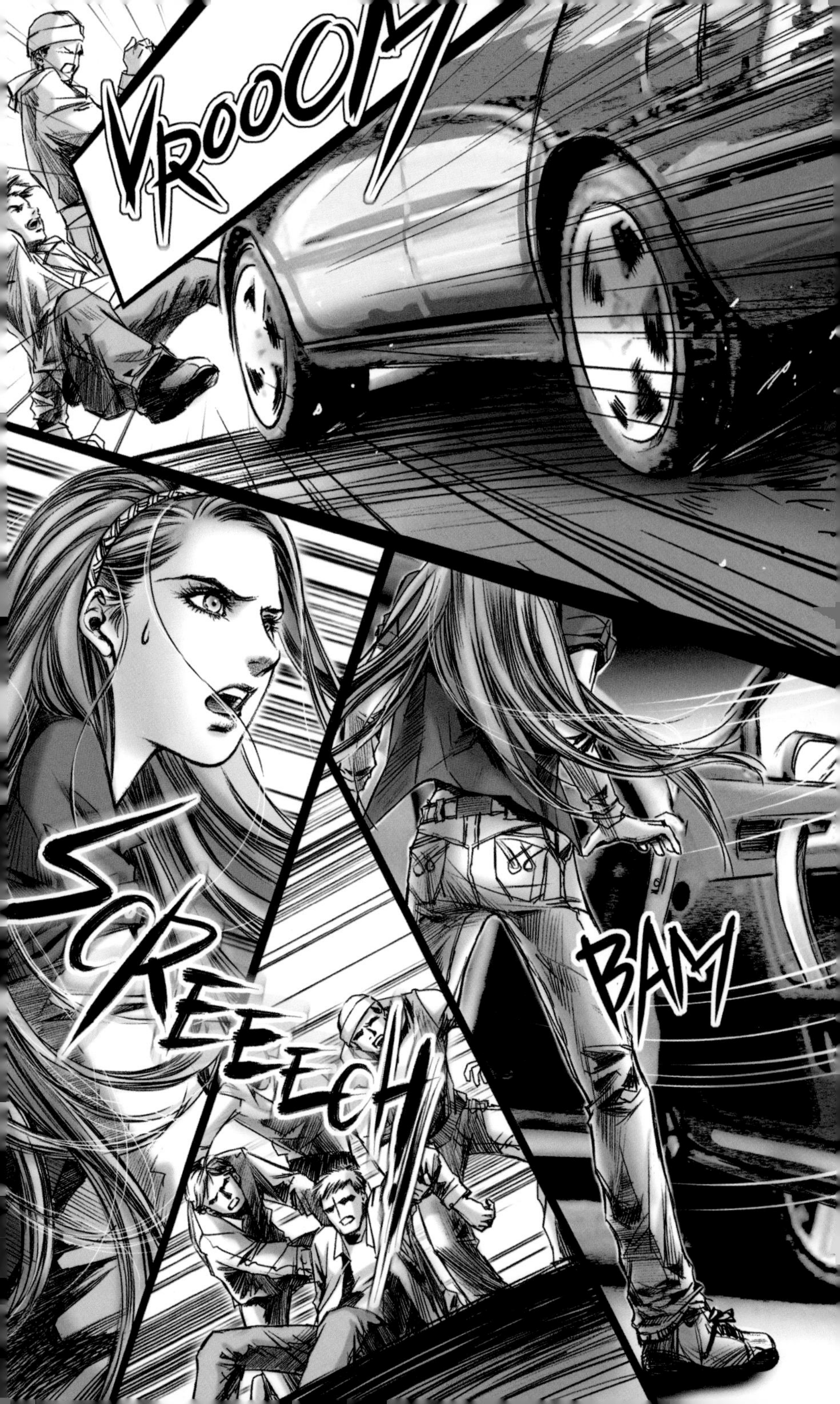
VROOOOM
SCREEECH
BAM

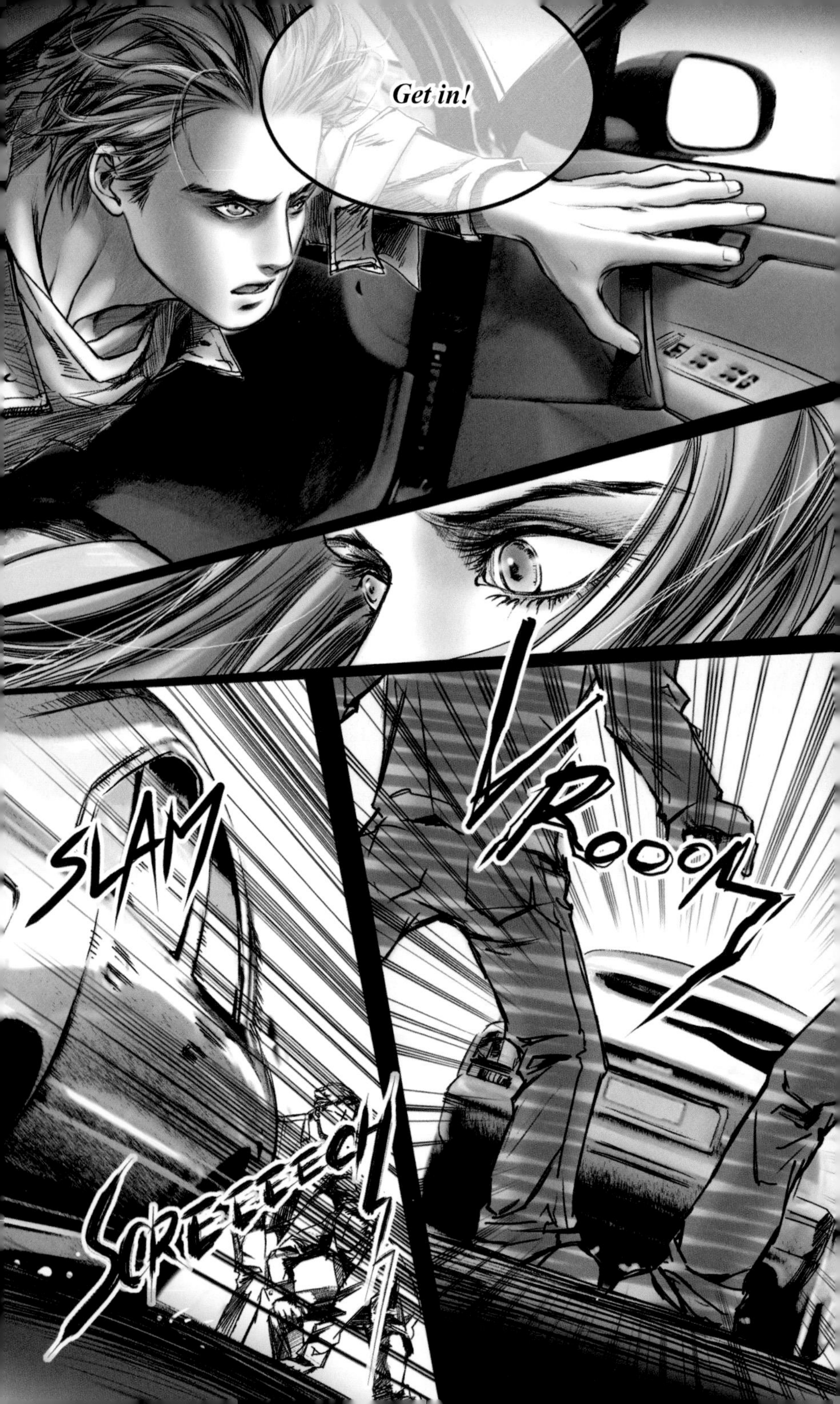
Get in!
SLAM
VROOOM
SCREEEECH

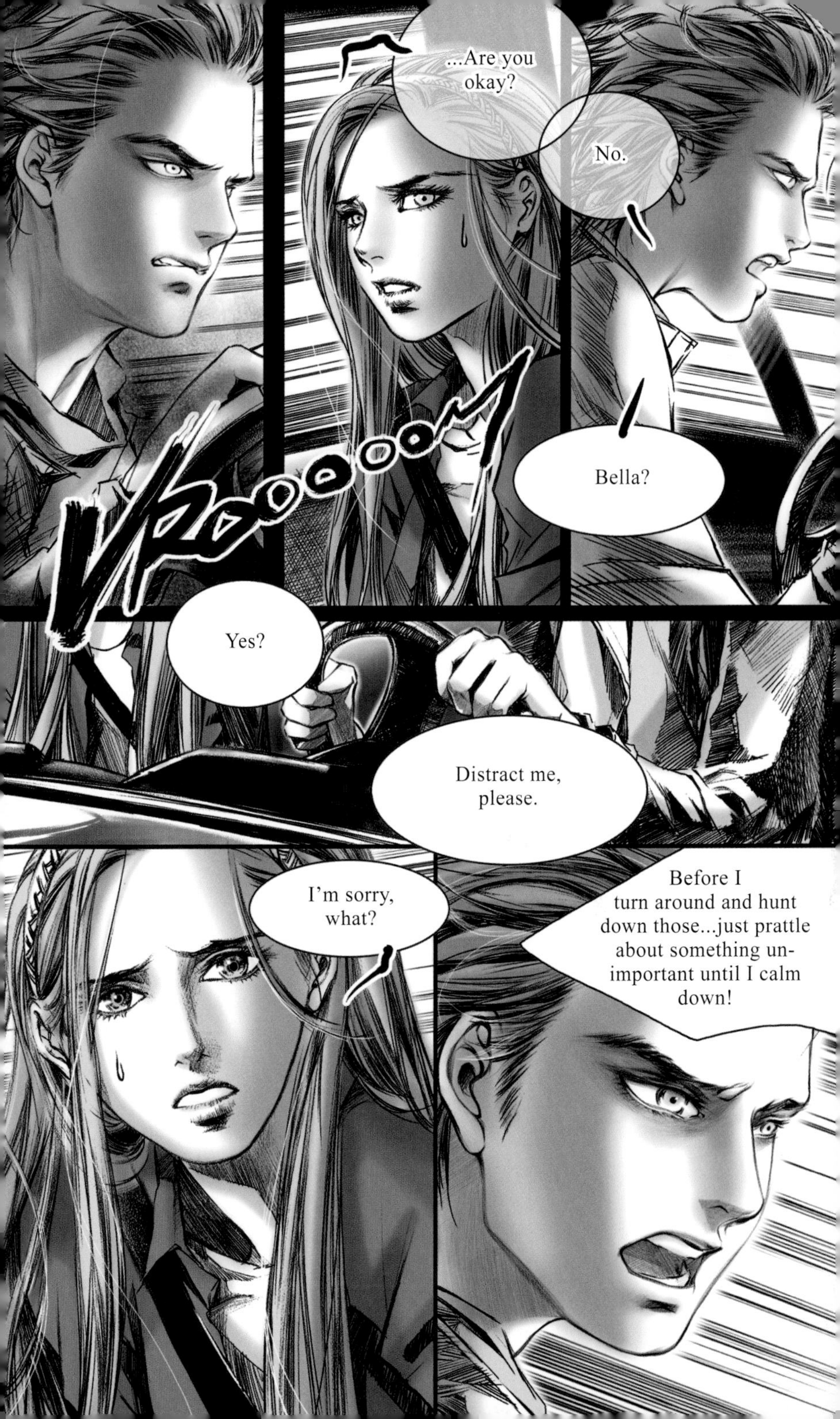
VROOOOOOM
...Are you okay?
No.
Bella?
Yes?
Distract me, please.
I'm sorry, what?
Before I turn around and hunt down those...just prattle about something un-important until I calm down!

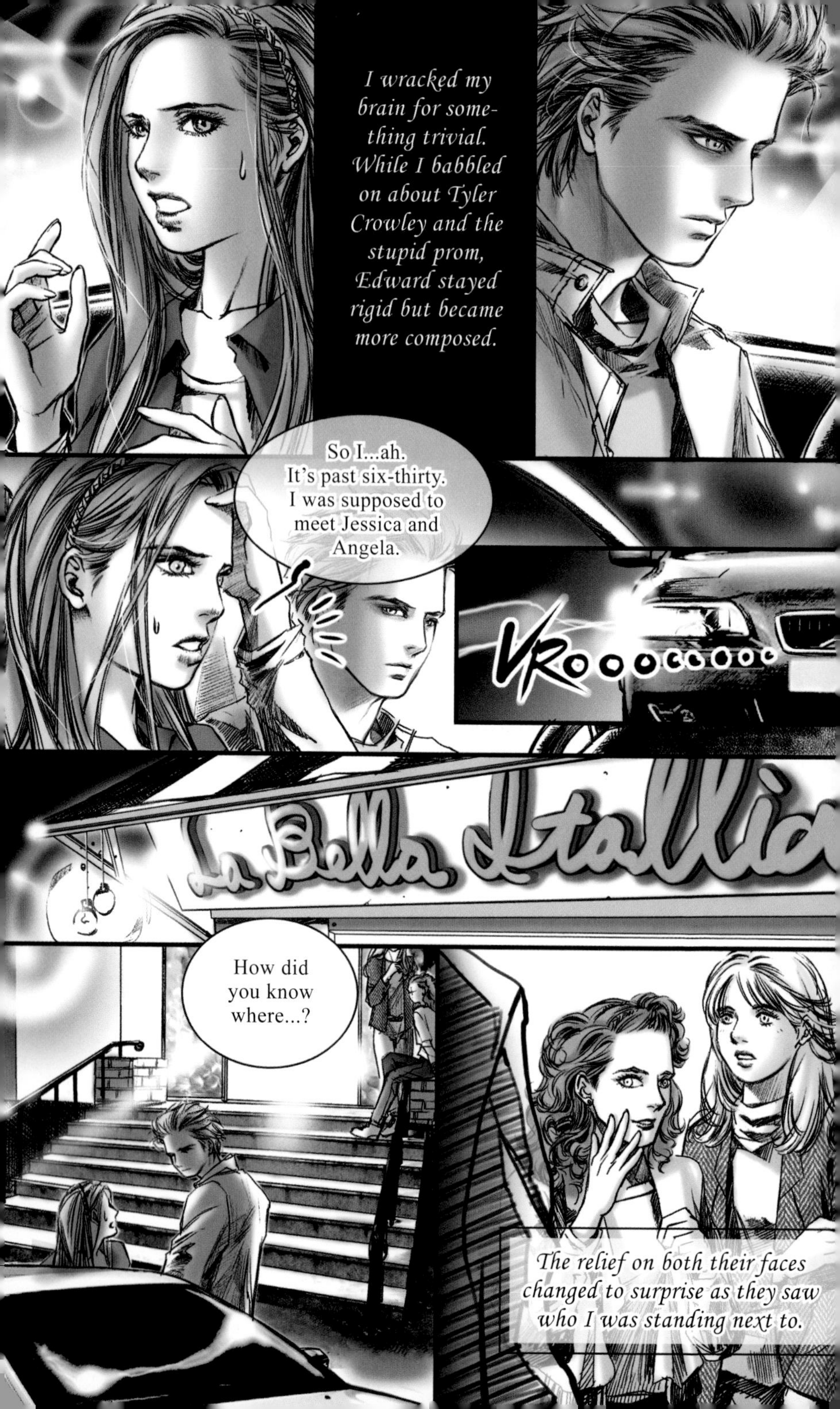
I wracked my brain for some-thing trivial. While I babbled on about Tyler Crowley and the stupid prom, Edward stayed rigid but became more composed.
So I...ah. It's past six-thirty. I was supposed to meet Jessica and Angela.
VROOOOOOOO
La Bella Italia
How did you know where...?
The relief on both their faces changed to surprise as they saw who I was standing next to.

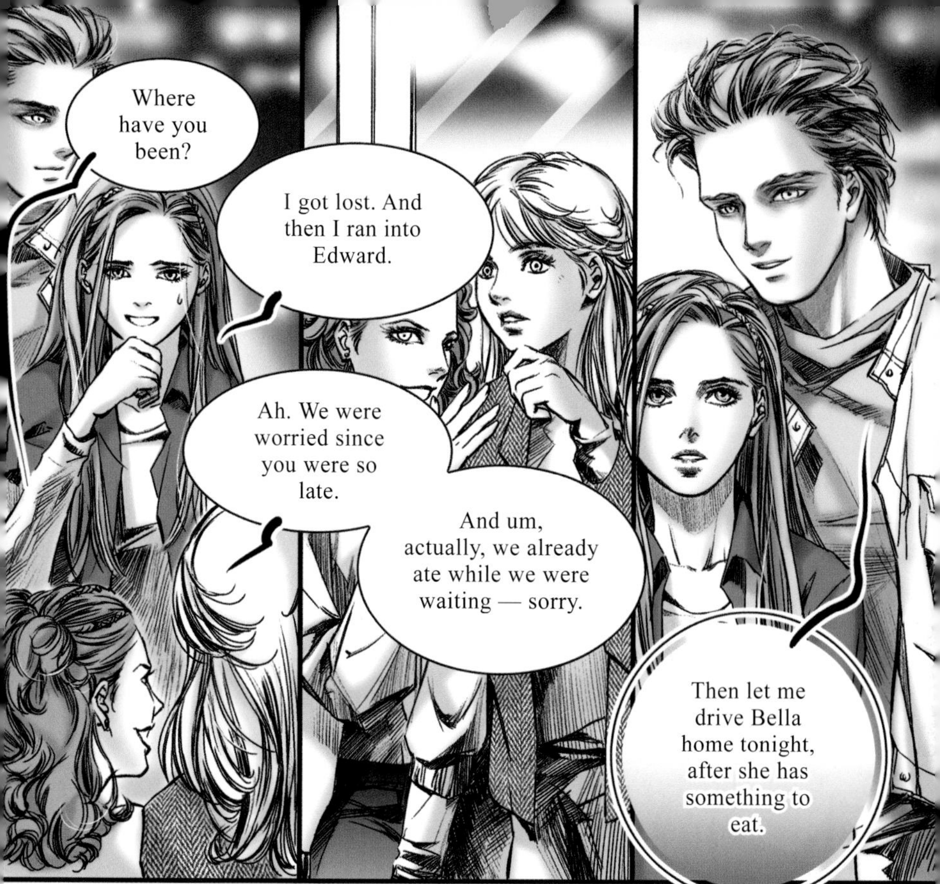
Where have you been?
I got lost. And then I ran into Edward.
Ah. We were worried since you were so late.
And um, actually, we already ate while we were waiting — sorry.
Then let me drive Bella home tonight, after she has something to eat.

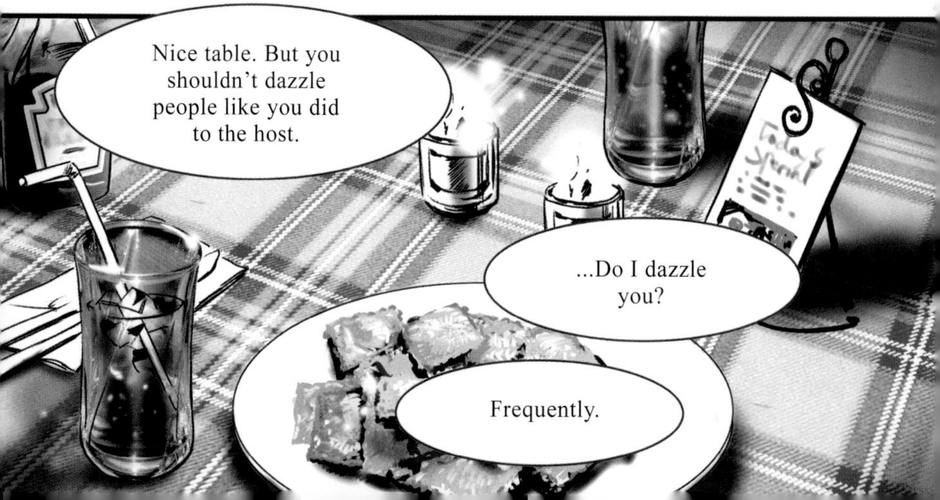
Nice table. But you shouldn't dazzle people like you did to the host.
...Do I dazzle you?
Frequently.

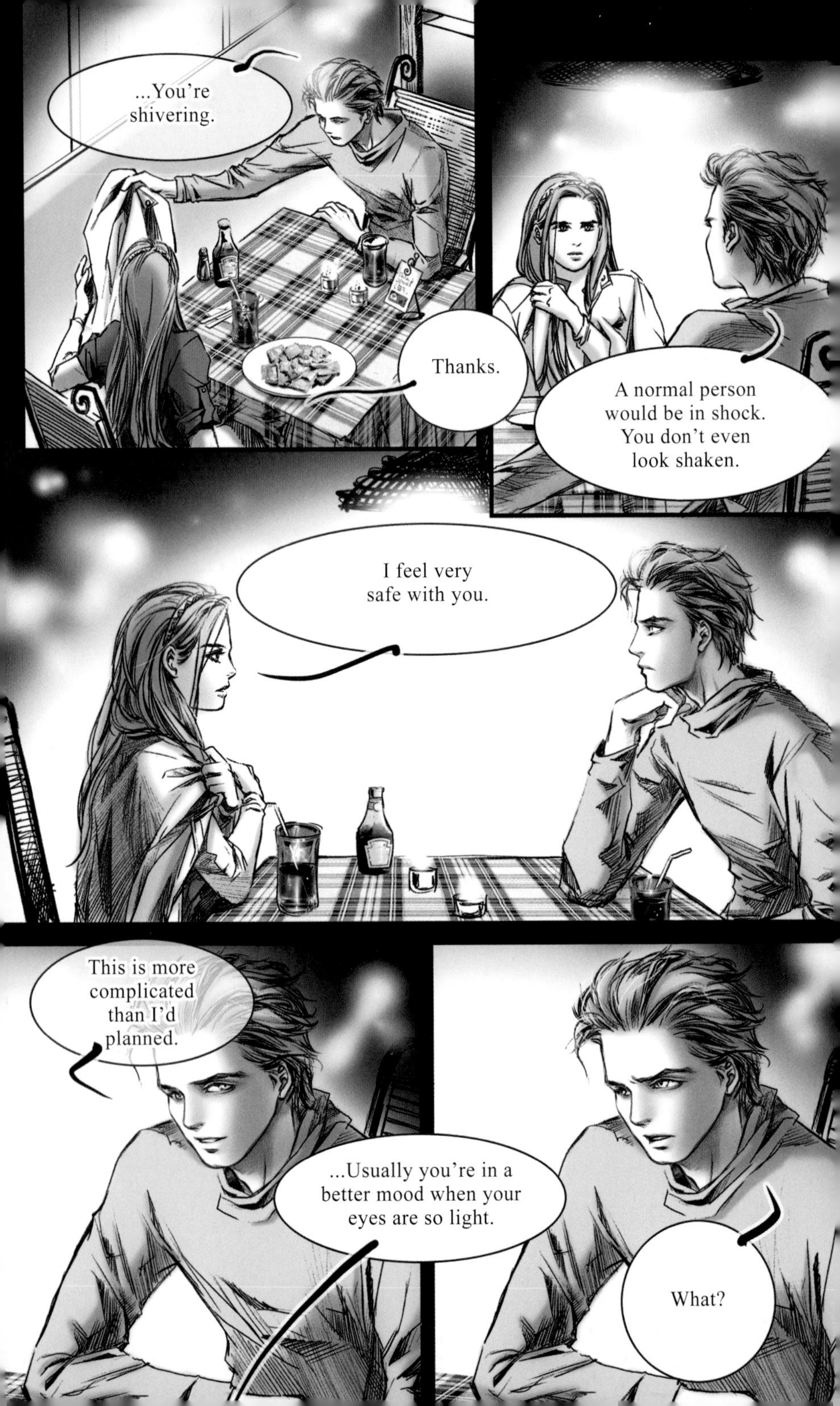
...You're shivering.
Thanks.
A normal person would be in shock. You don't even look shaken.
I feel very safe with you.
This is more complicated than I'd planned.
...Usually you're in a better mood when your eyes are so light.
What?

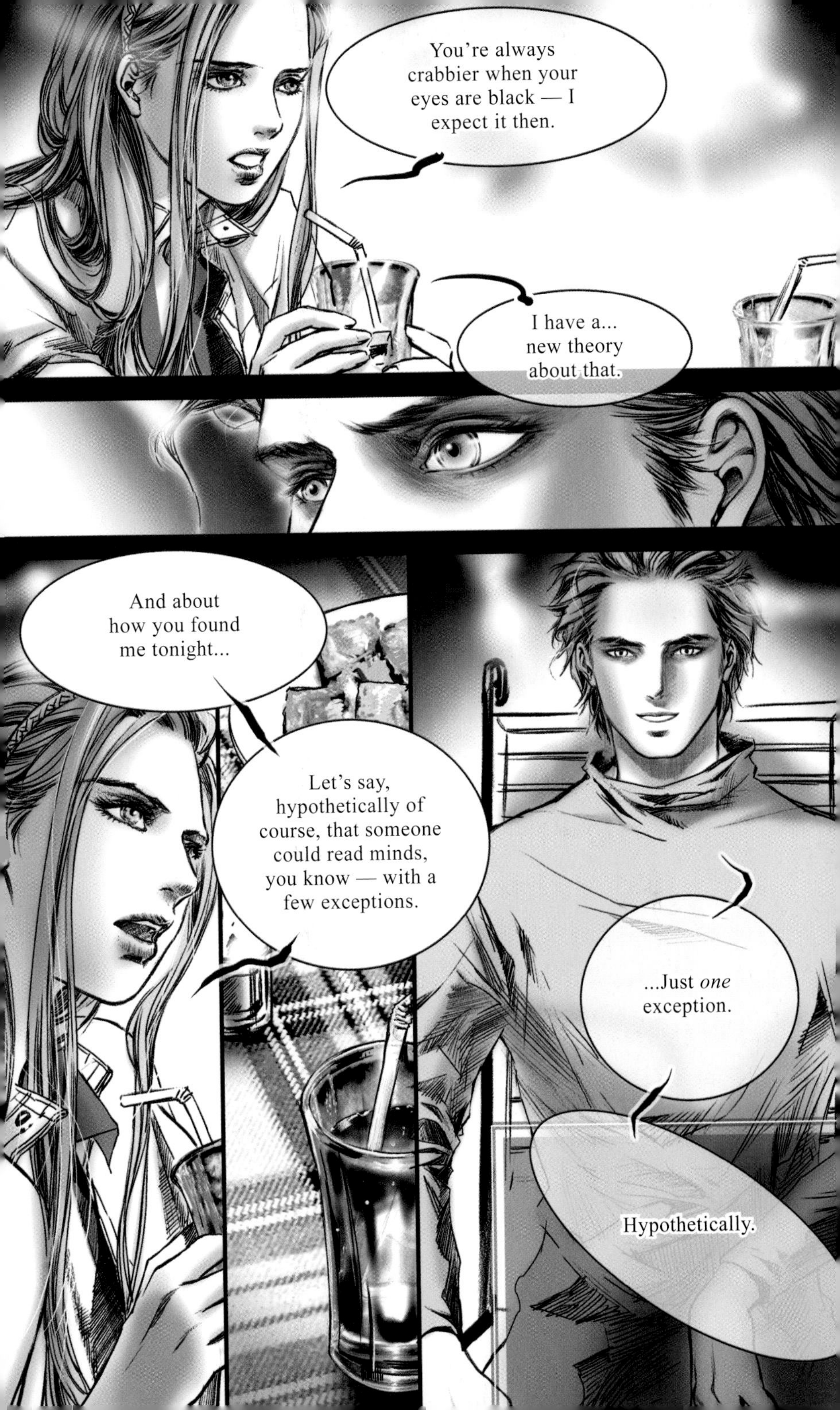
You're always crabbier when your eyes are black — I expect it then.
I have a... new theory about that.
And about how you found me tonight...
Let's say, hypothetically of course, that someone could read minds, you know — with a few exceptions.
...Just *one* exception.
Hypothetically.

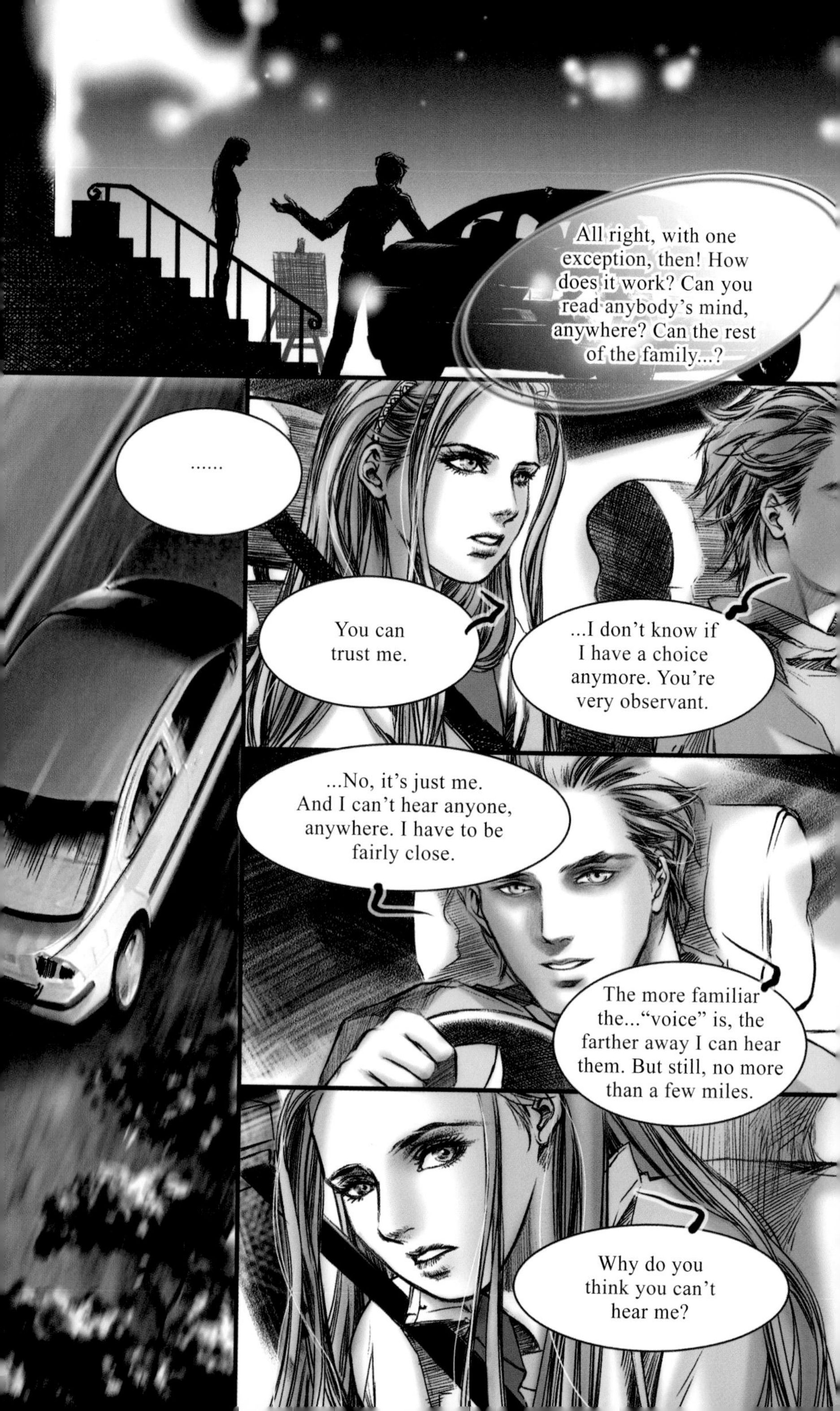
All right, with one exception, then! How does it work? Can you read anybody's mind, anywhere? Can the rest of the family...?
......
You can trust me.
...I don't know if I have a choice anymore. You're very observant.
...No, it's just me. And I can't hear anyone, anywhere. I have to be fairly close.
The more familiar the..."voice" is, the farther away I can hear them. But still, no more than a few miles.
Why do you think you can't hear me?

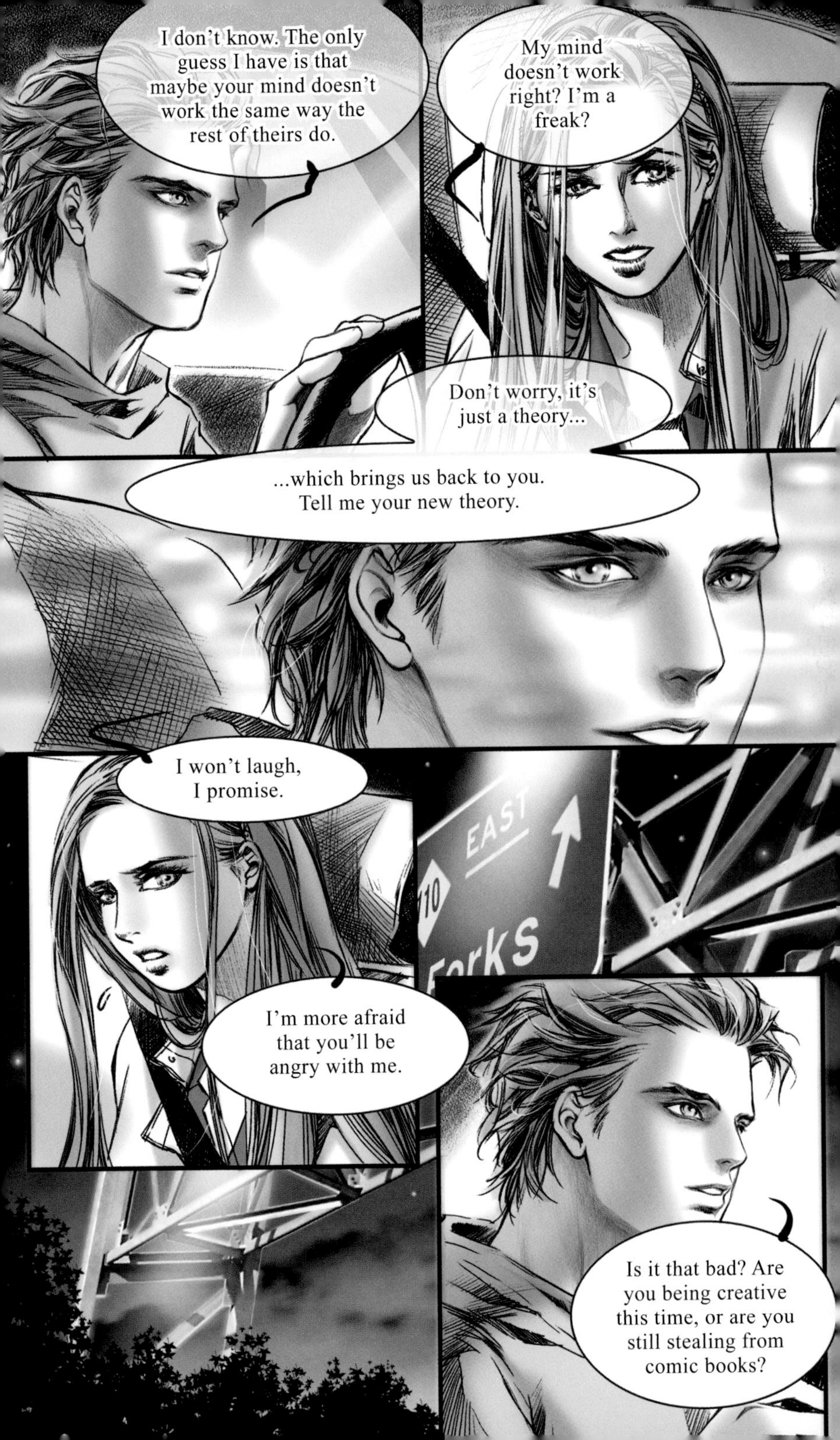
I don't know. The only guess I have is that maybe your mind doesn't work the same way the rest of theirs do.
My mind doesn't work right? I'm a freak?
Don't worry, it's just a theory...
...which brings us back to you. Tell me your new theory.
I won't laugh, I promise.
EAST
110
Forks
I'm more afraid that you'll be angry with me.
Is it that bad? Are you being creative this time, or are you still stealing from comic books?

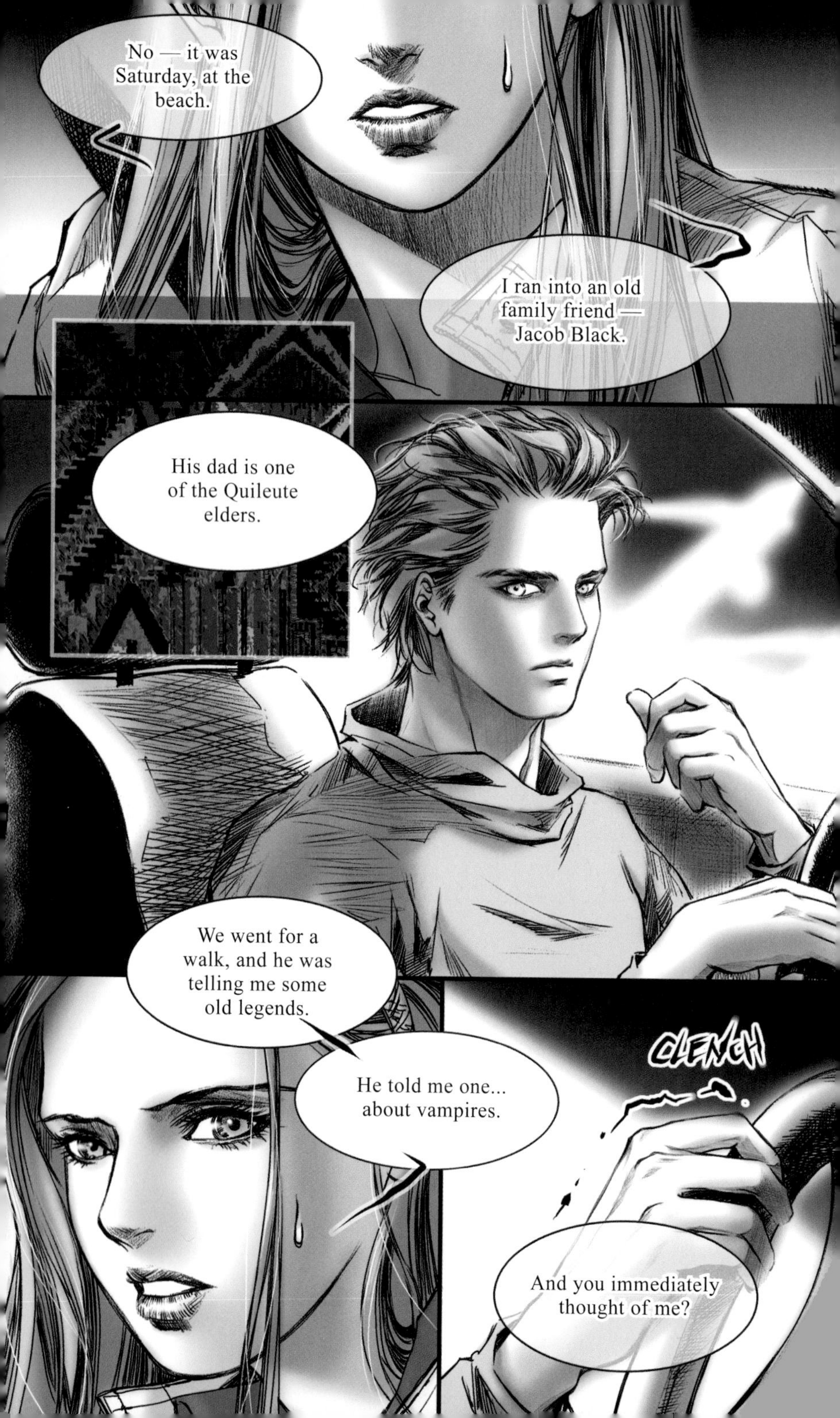
No — it was Saturday, at the beach.
I ran into an old family friend — Jacob Black.
His dad is one of the Quileute elders.
We went for a walk, and he was telling me some old legends.
He told me one... about vampires.
CLENCH
And you immediately thought of me?

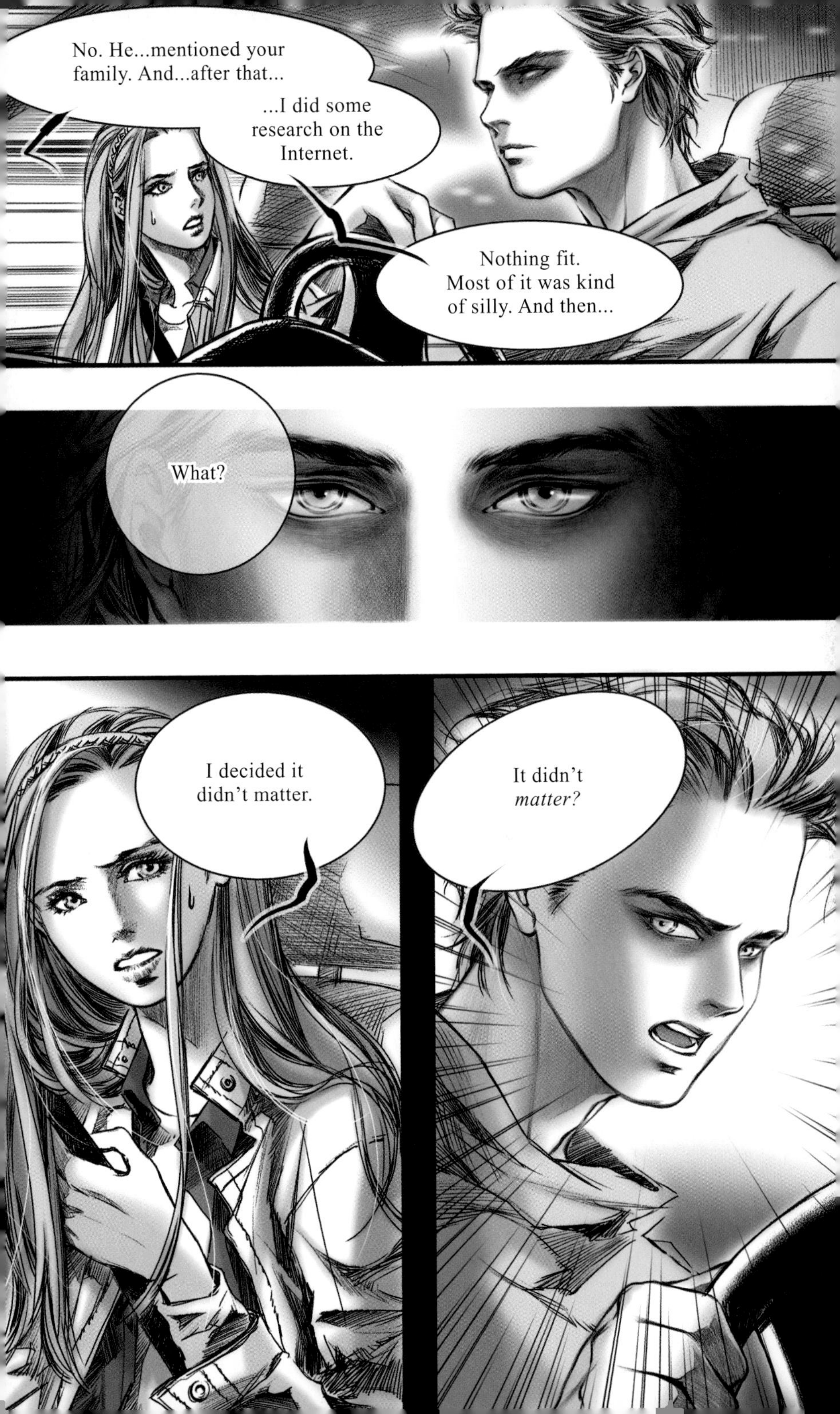
No. He...mentioned your family. And...after that...
...I did some research on the Internet.
Nothing fit. Most of it was kind of silly. And then...
What?
I decided it didn't matter.
It didn't *matter?*

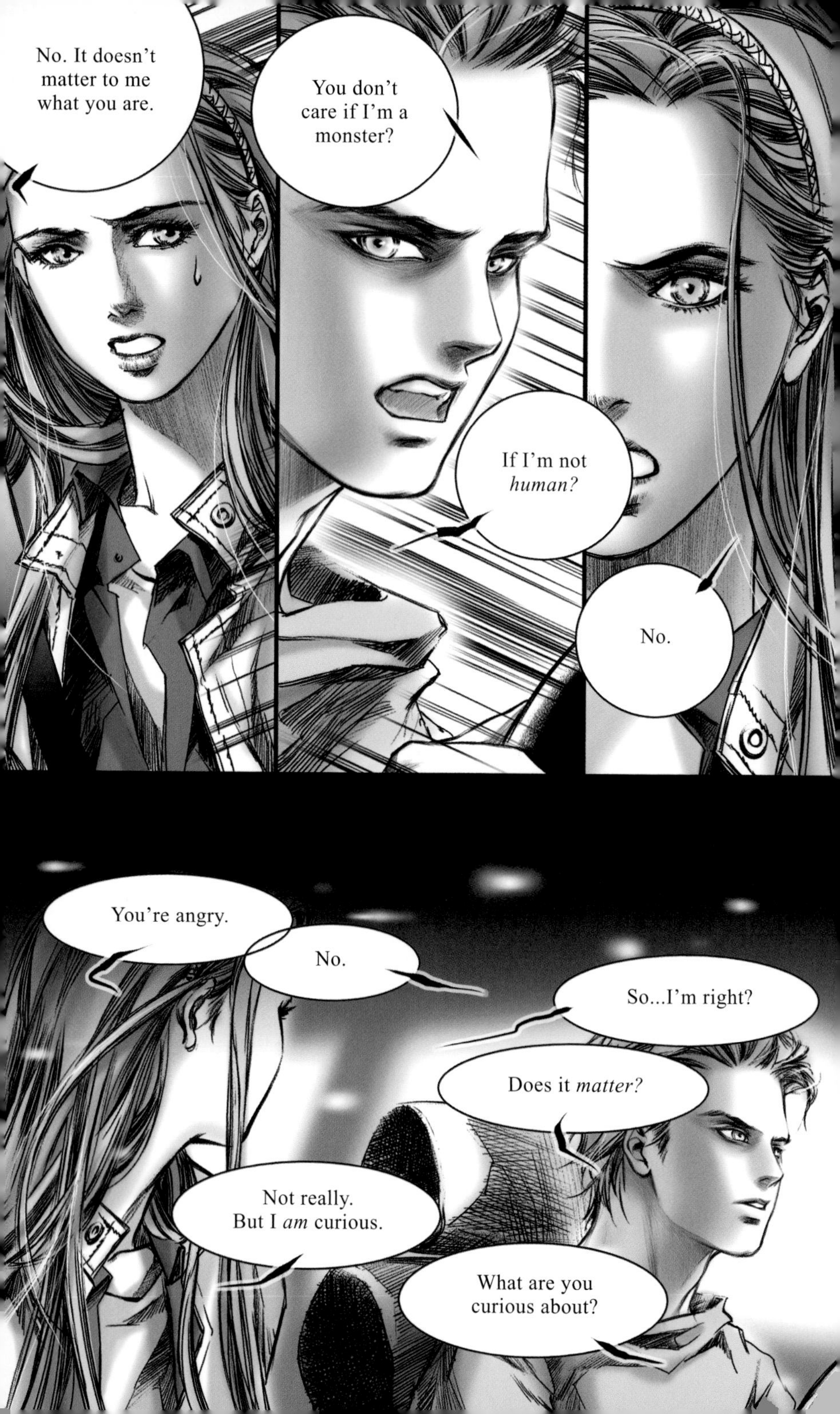
No. It doesn't matter to me what you are.
You don't care if I'm a monster?
If I'm not *human?*
No.
You're angry.
No.
So...I'm right?
Does it *matter?*
Not really. But I *am* curious.
What are you curious about?

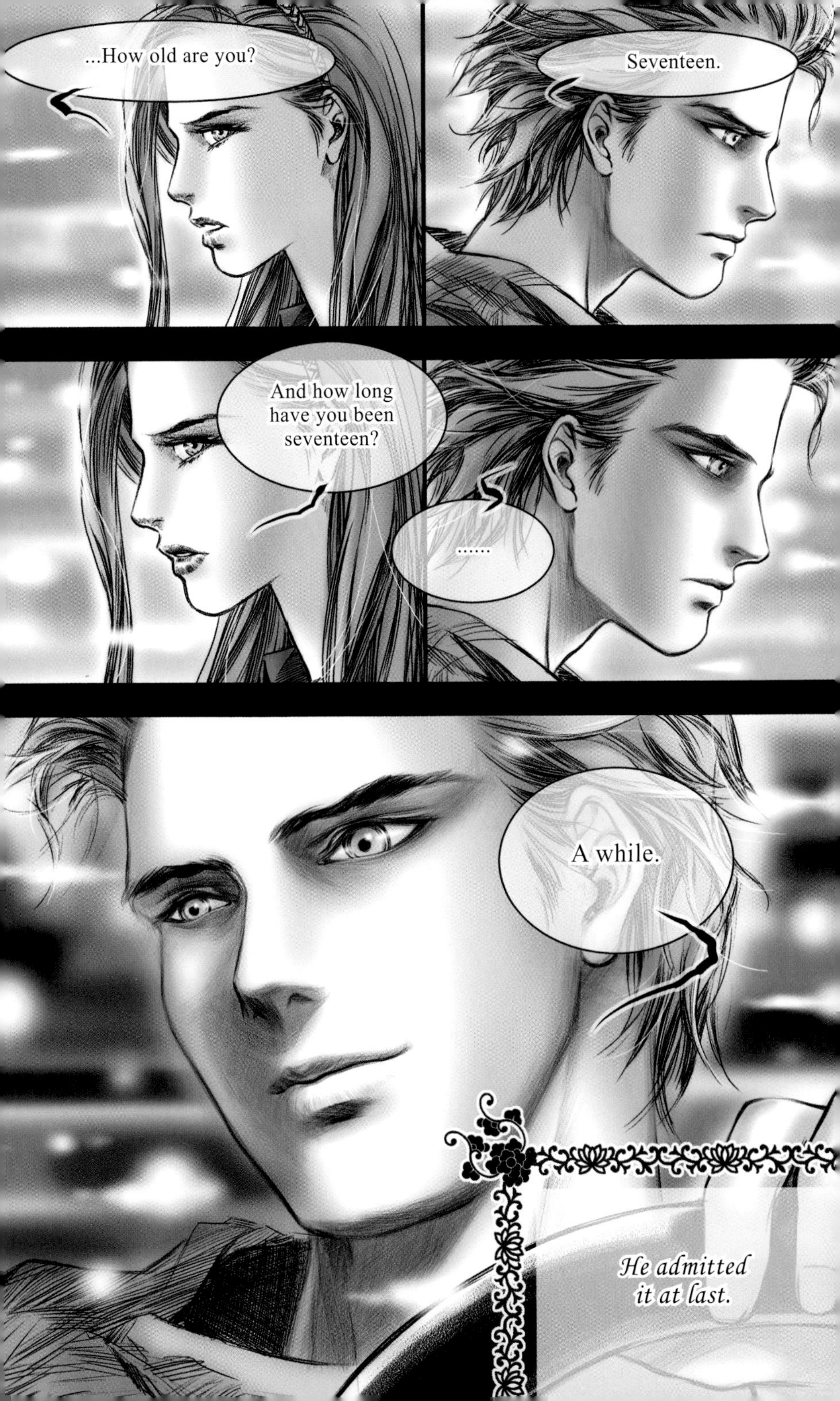
...How old are you?
Seventeen.
And how long have you been seventeen?
......
A while.
He admitted it at last.

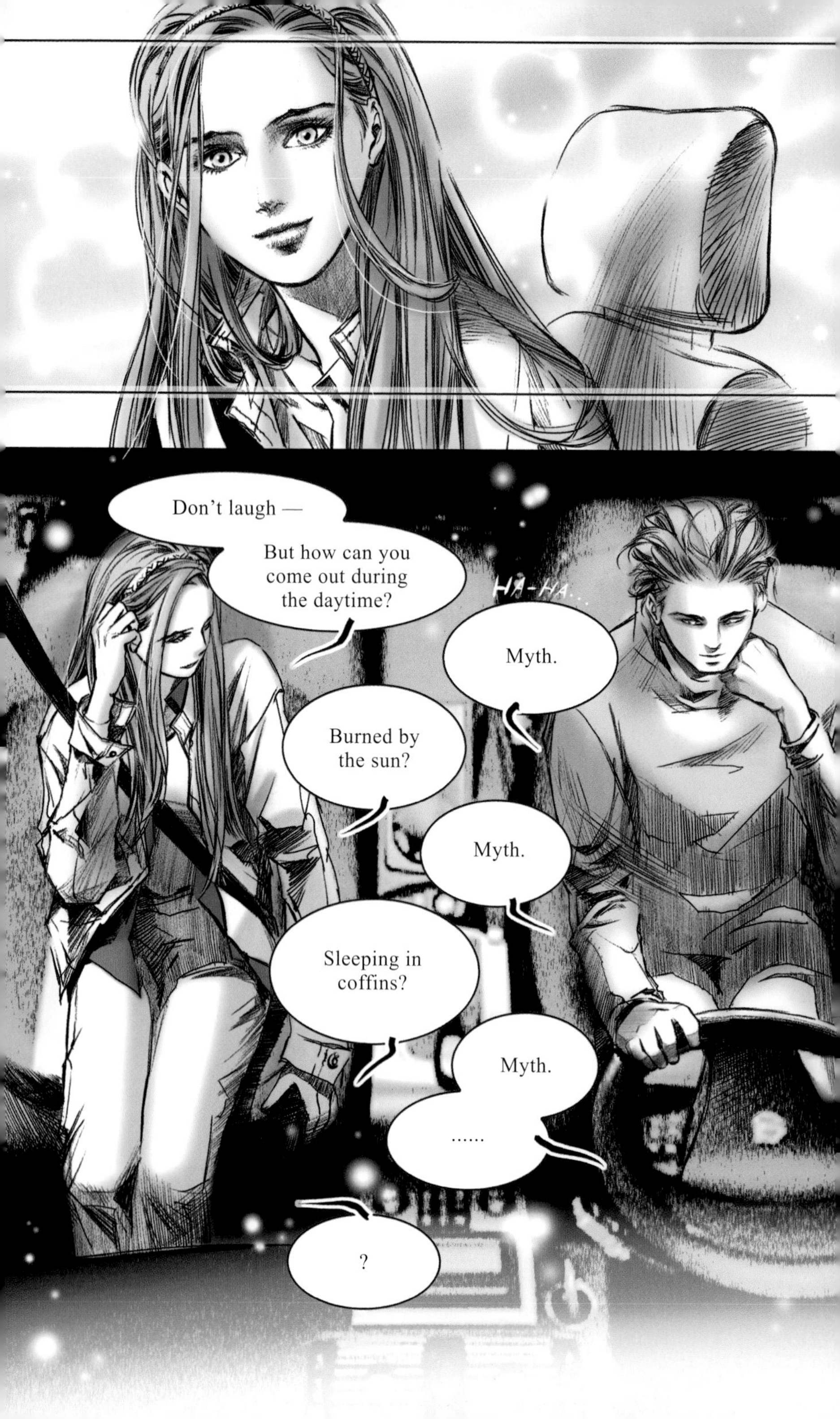
Don't laugh —
But how can you come out during the daytime?
HA-HA...
Myth.
Burned by the sun?
Myth.
Sleeping in coffins?
Myth.
......
?

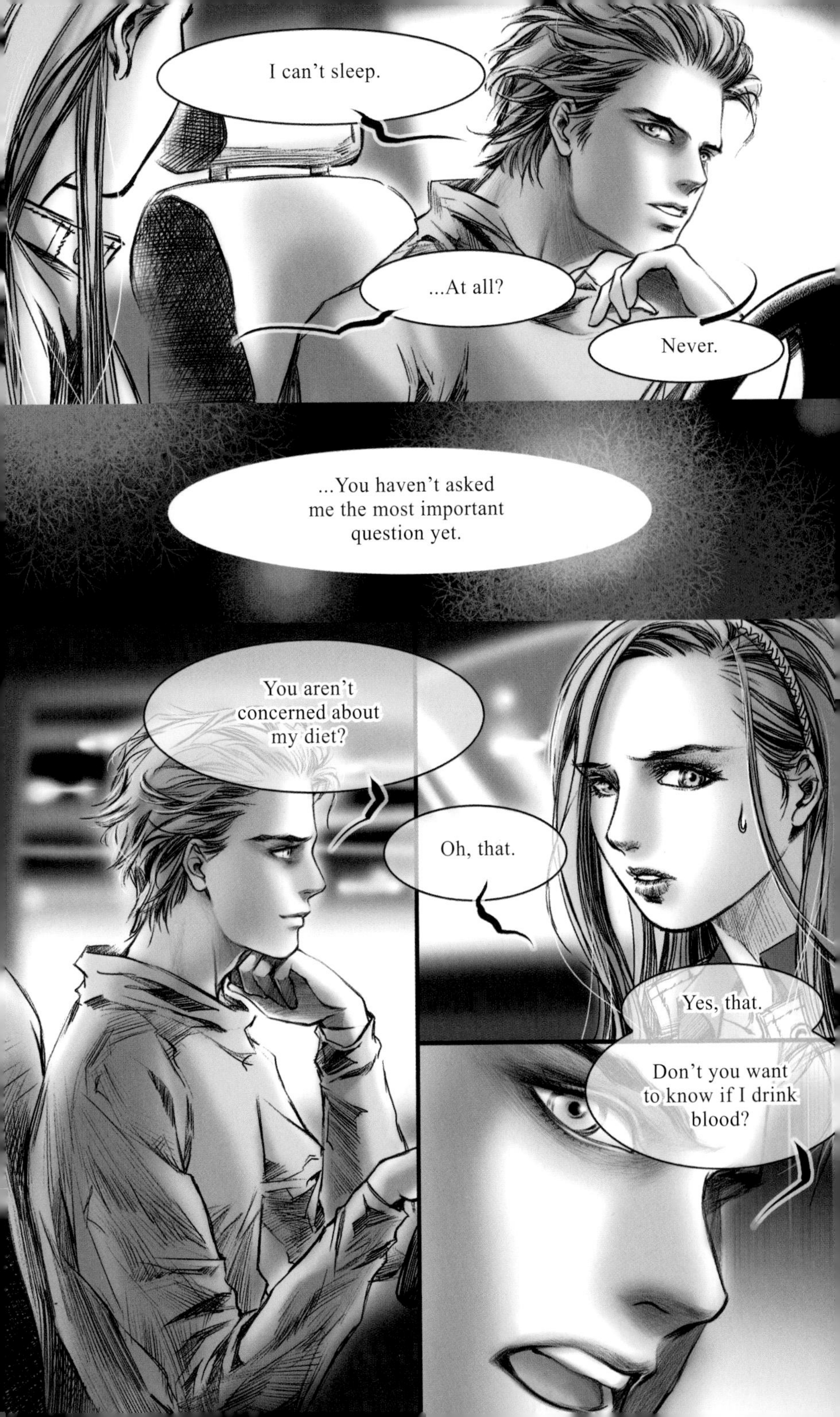
I can't sleep.
...At all?
Never.
...You haven't asked me the most important question yet.
You aren't concerned about my diet?
Oh, that.
Yes, that.
Don't you want to know if I drink blood?

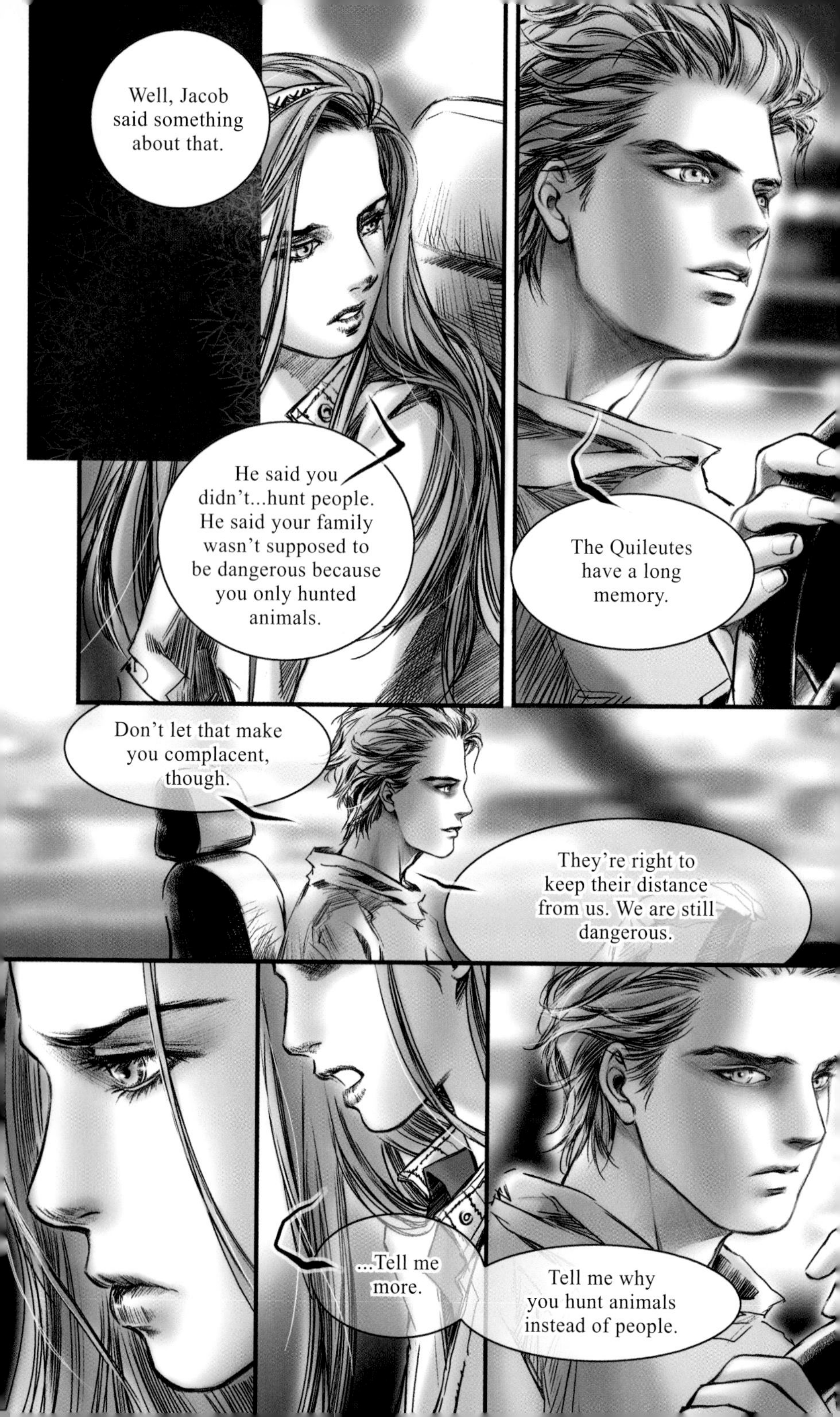
Well, Jacob said something about that.
He said you didn't...hunt people. He said your family wasn't supposed to be dangerous because you only hunted animals.
The Quileutes have a long memory.
Don't let that make you complacent, though.
They're right to keep their distance from us. We are still dangerous.
...Tell me more.
Tell me why you hunt animals instead of people.

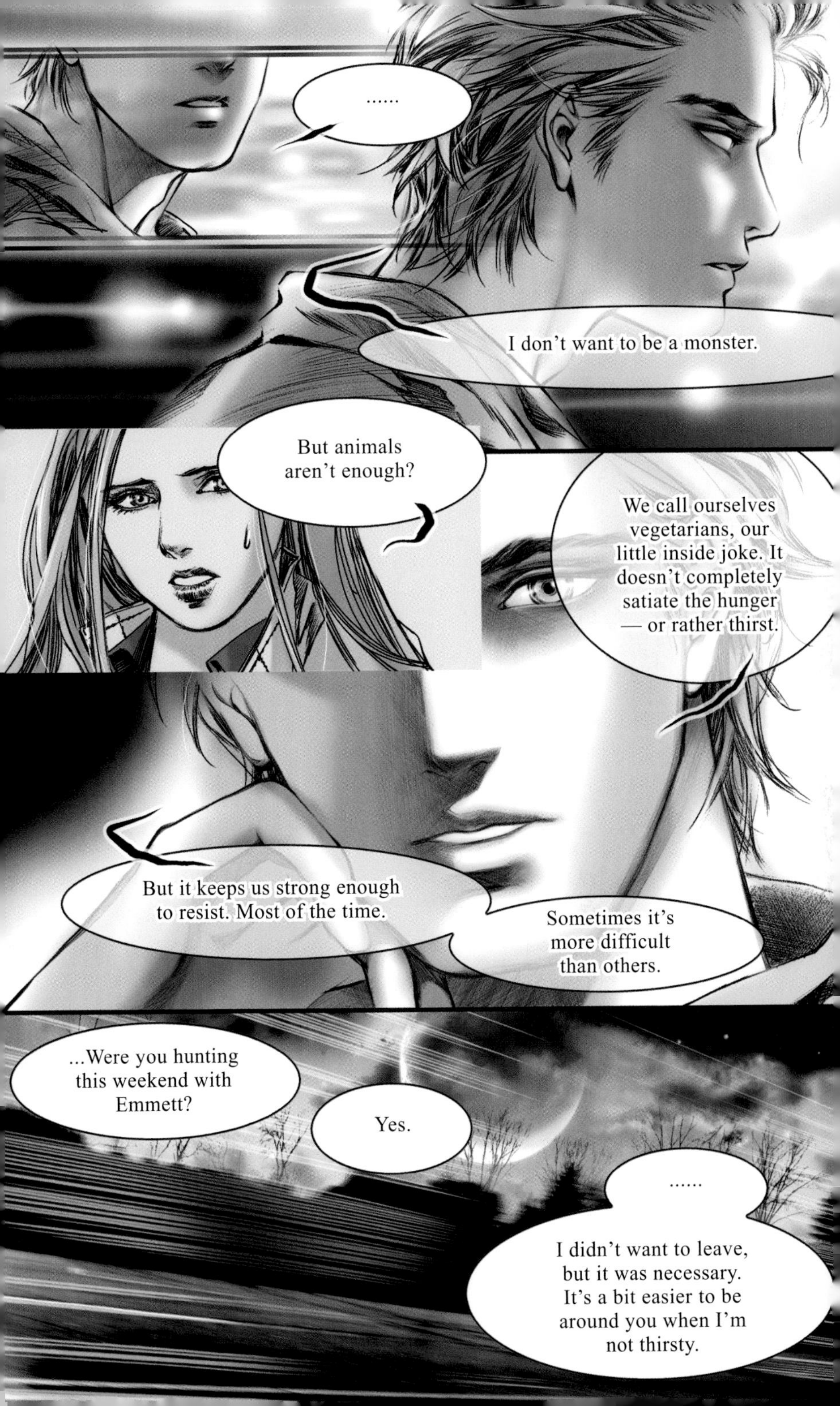
......
I don't want to be a monster.
But animals aren't enough?
We call ourselves vegetarians, our little inside joke. It doesn't completely satiate the hunger — or rather thirst.
But it keeps us strong enough to resist. Most of the time.
Sometimes it's more difficult than others.
...Were you hunting this weekend with Emmett?
Yes.
......
I didn't want to leave, but it was necessary. It's a bit easier to be around you when I'm not thirsty.

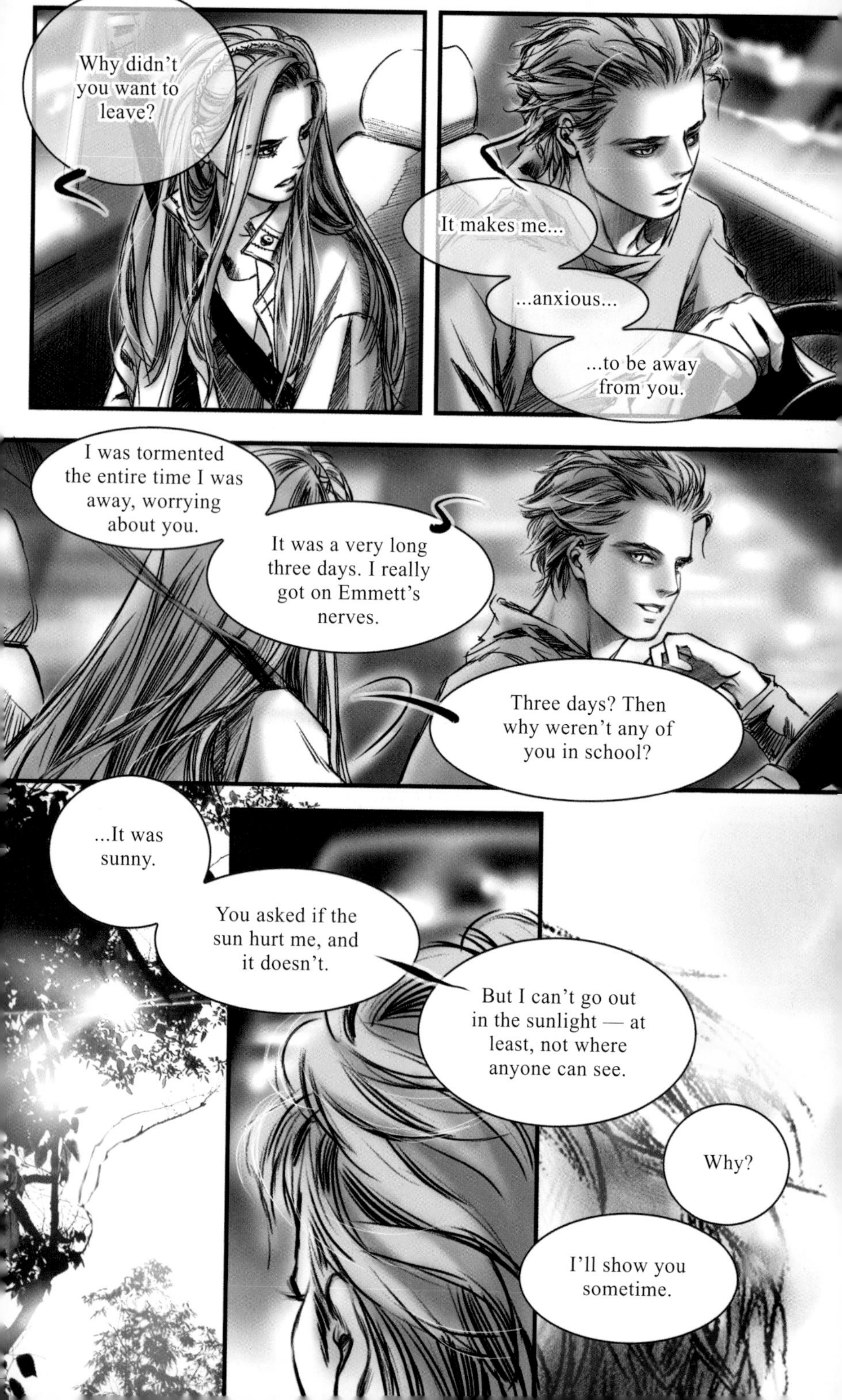
Why didn't you want to leave?
It makes me...
...anxious...
...to be away from you.
I was tormented the entire time I was away, worrying about you.
It was a very long three days. I really got on Emmett's nerves.
Three days? Then why weren't any of you in school?
...It was sunny.
You asked if the sun hurt me, and it doesn't.
But I can't go out in the sunlight — at least, not where anyone can see.
Why?
I'll show you sometime.

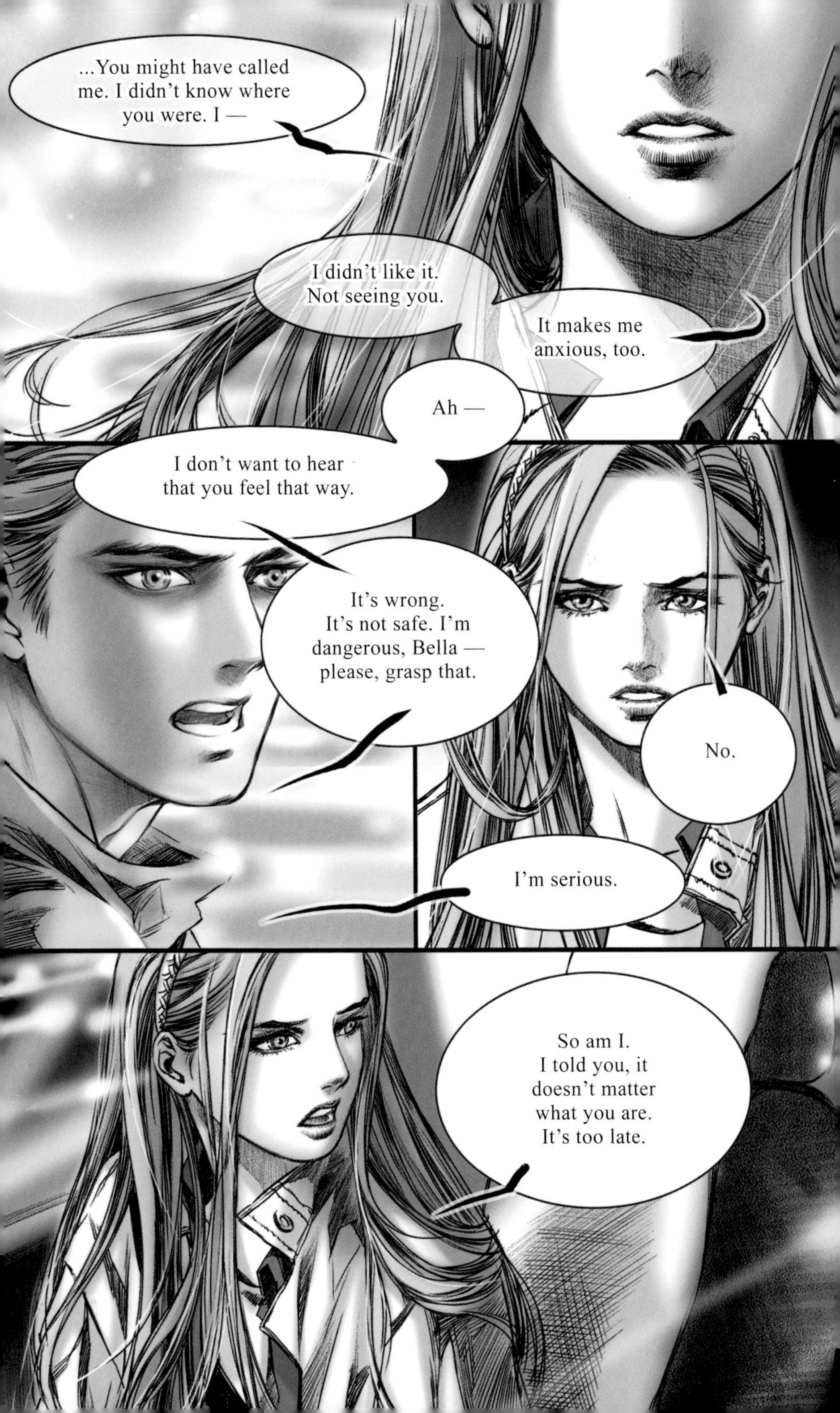
...You might have called me. I didn't know where you were. I —
I didn't like it. Not seeing you.
It makes me anxious, too.
Ah —
I don't want to hear that you feel that way.
It's wrong. It's not safe. I'm dangerous, Bella — please, grasp that.
No.
I'm serious.
So am I. I told you, it doesn't matter what you are. It's too late.

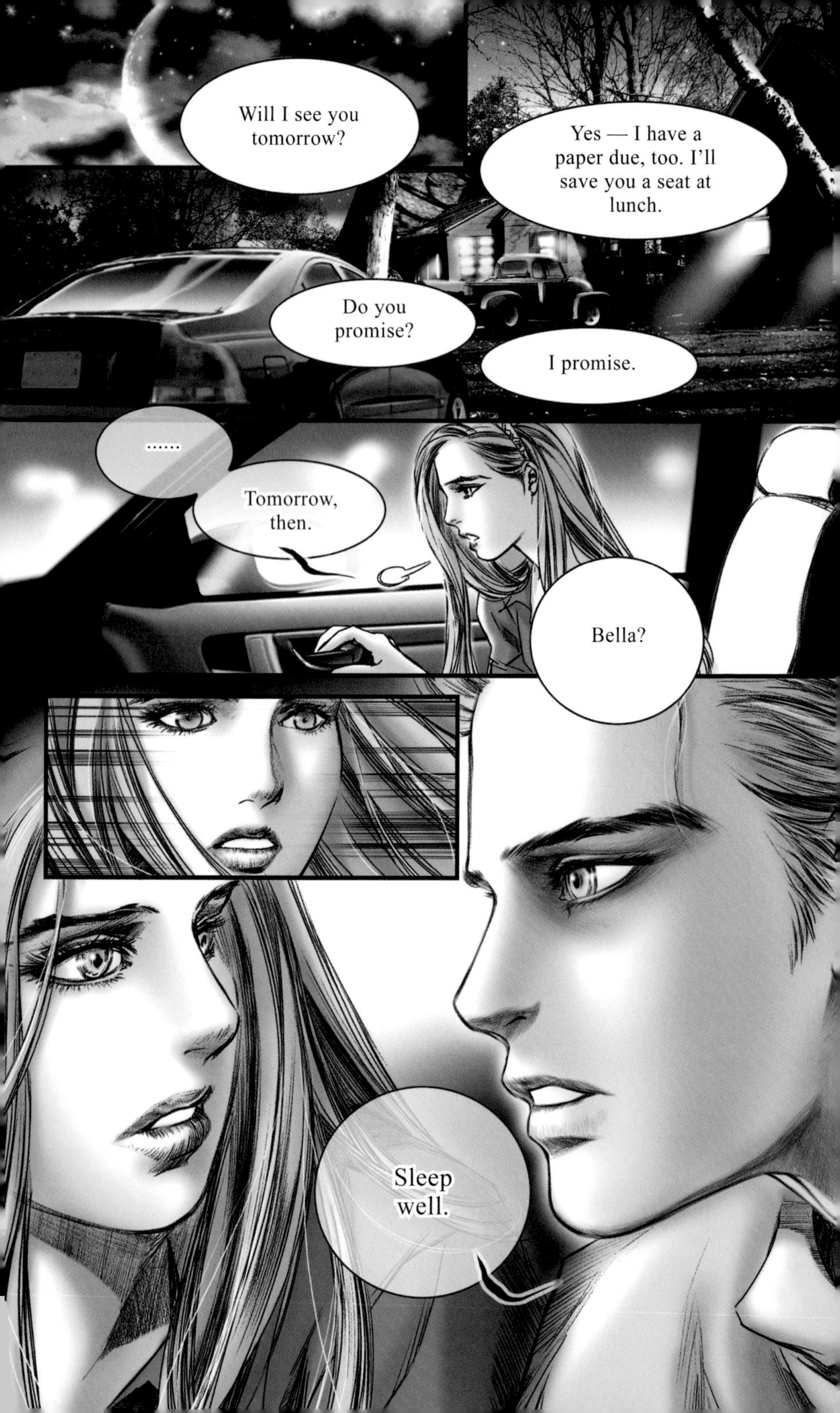
Will I see you tomorrow?
Yes — I have a paper due, too. I'll save you a seat at lunch.
Do you promise?
I promise.
……
Tomorrow, then.
Bella?
Sleep well.

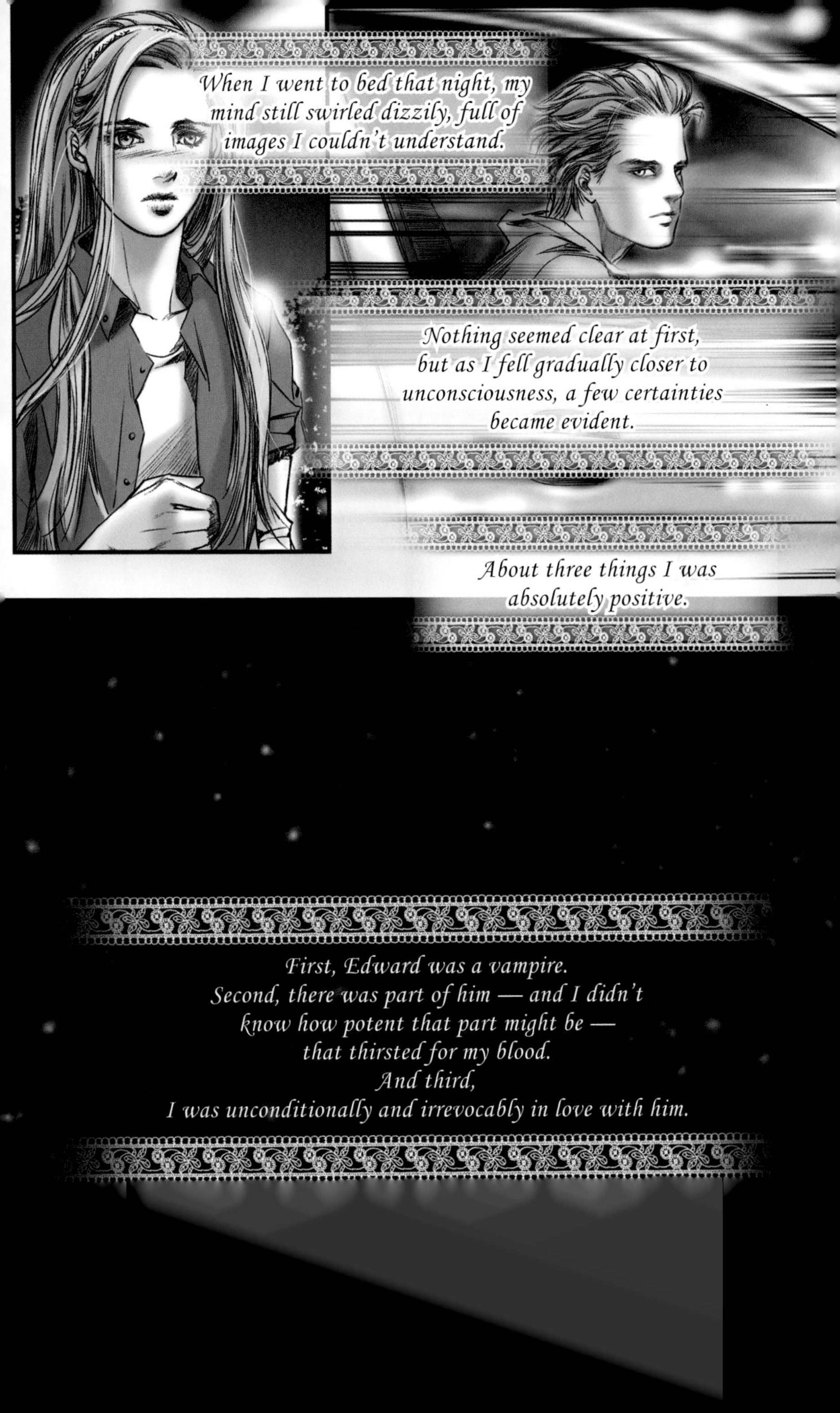
When I went to bed that night, my mind still swirled dizzily, full of images I couldn't understand.
Nothing seemed clear at first, but as I fell gradually closer to unconsciousness, a few certainties became evident.
About three things I was absolutely positive.
First, Edward was a vampire.
Second, there was part of him — and I didn't know how potent that part might be — that thirsted for my blood.
And third,
I was unconditionally and irrevocably in love with him.

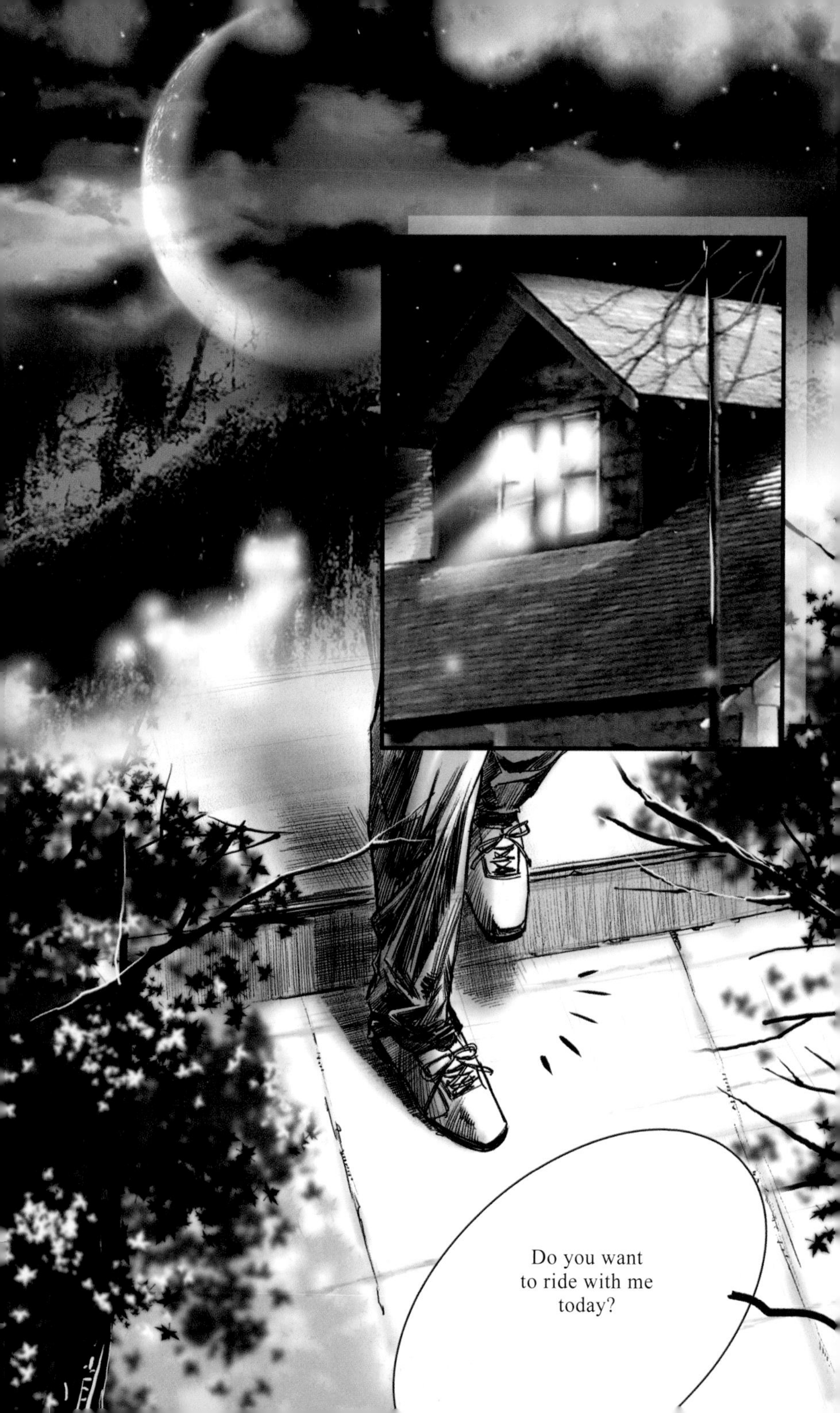
Do you want to ride with me today?

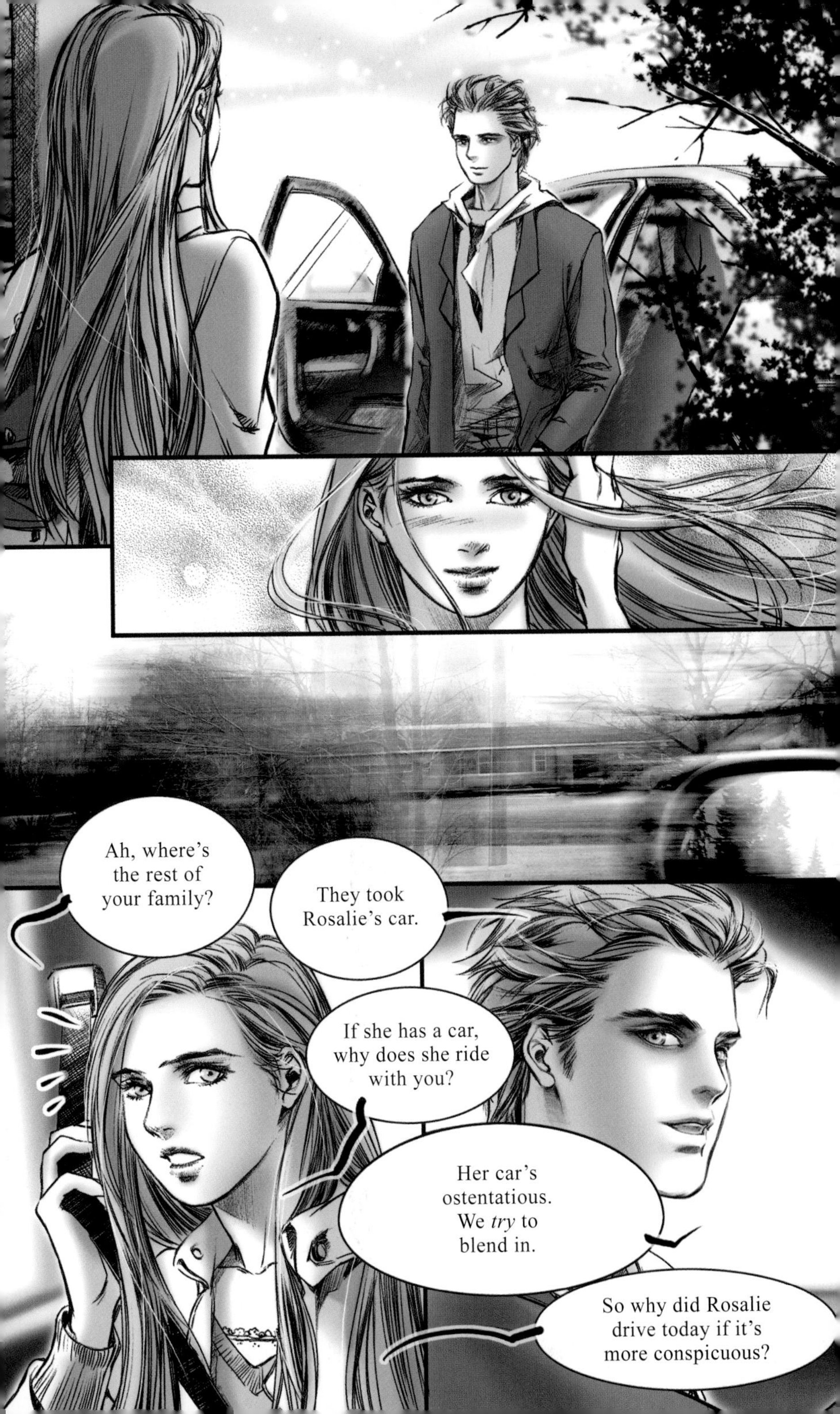

Ah, where's the rest of your family?
They took Rosalie's car.
If she has a car, why does she ride with you?
Her car's ostentatious. We *try* to blend in.
So why did Rosalie drive today if it's more conspicuous?

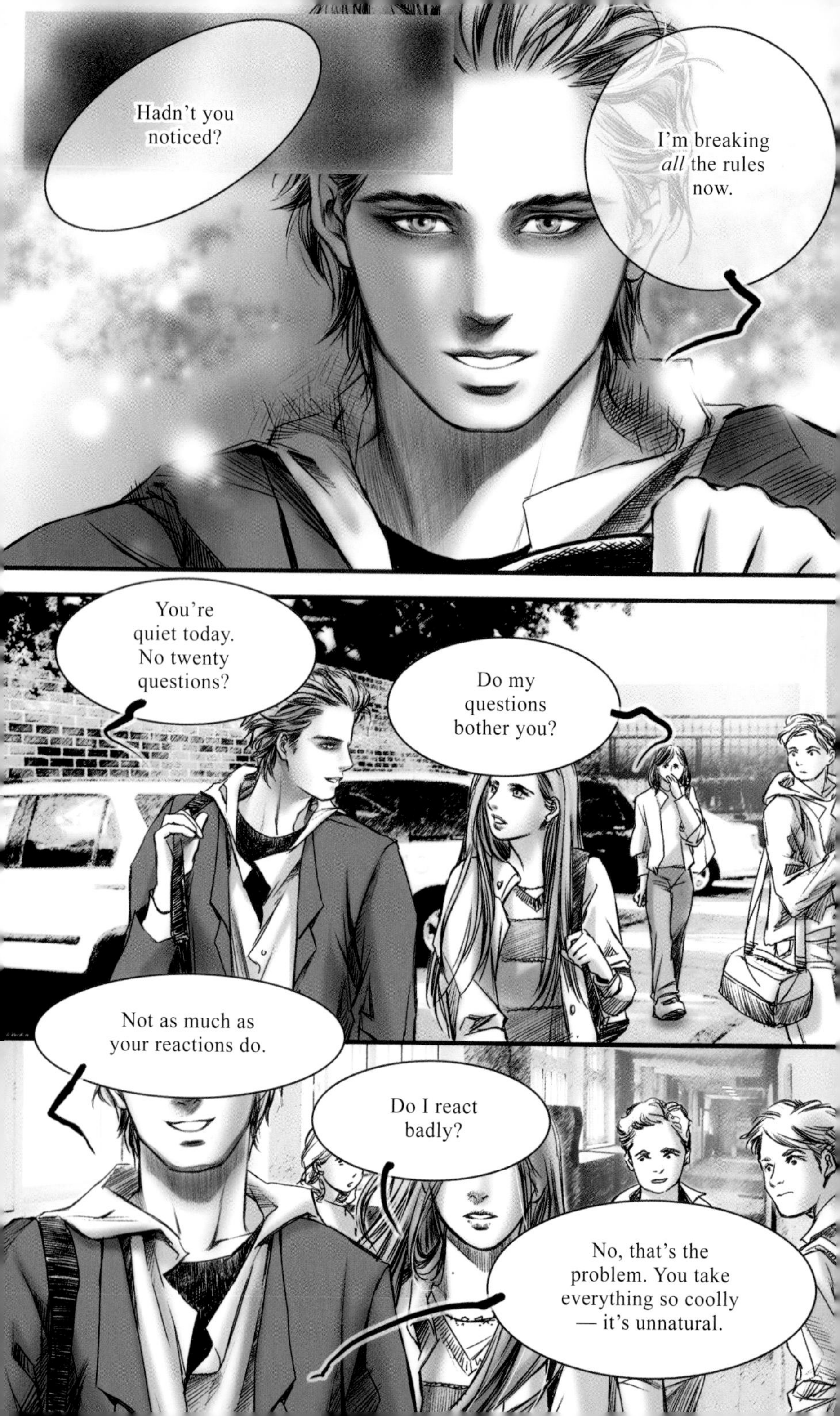
Hadn't you noticed?
I'm breaking *all* the rules now.
You're quiet today. No twenty questions?
Do my questions bother you?
Not as much as your reactions do.
Do I react badly?
No, that's the problem. You take everything so coolly — it's unnatural.

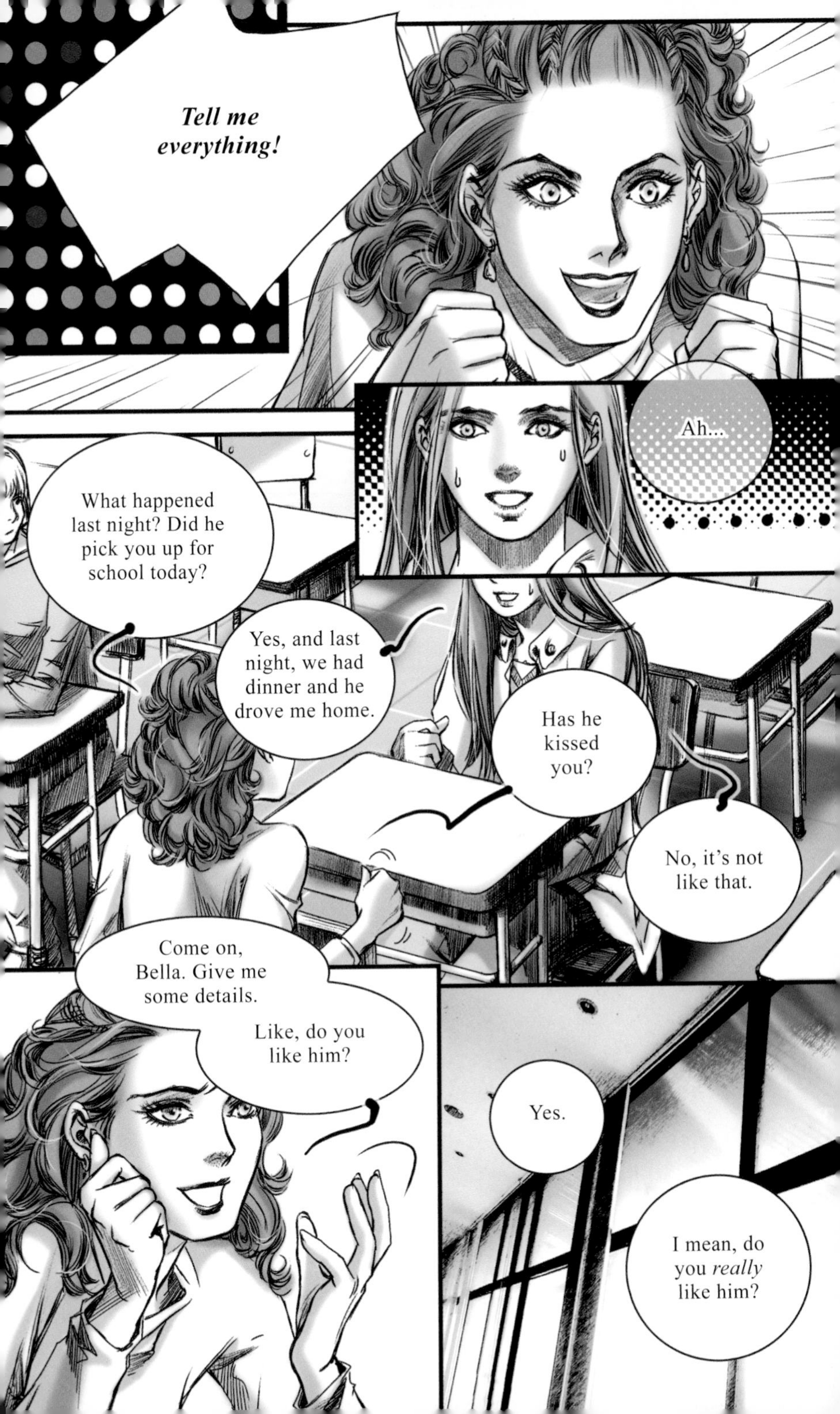
Tell me everything!
Ah...
What happened last night? Did he pick you up for school today?
Yes, and last night, we had dinner and he drove me home.
Has he kissed you?
No, it's not like that.
Come on, Bella. Give me some details.
Like, do you like him?
Yes.
I mean, do you *really* like him?

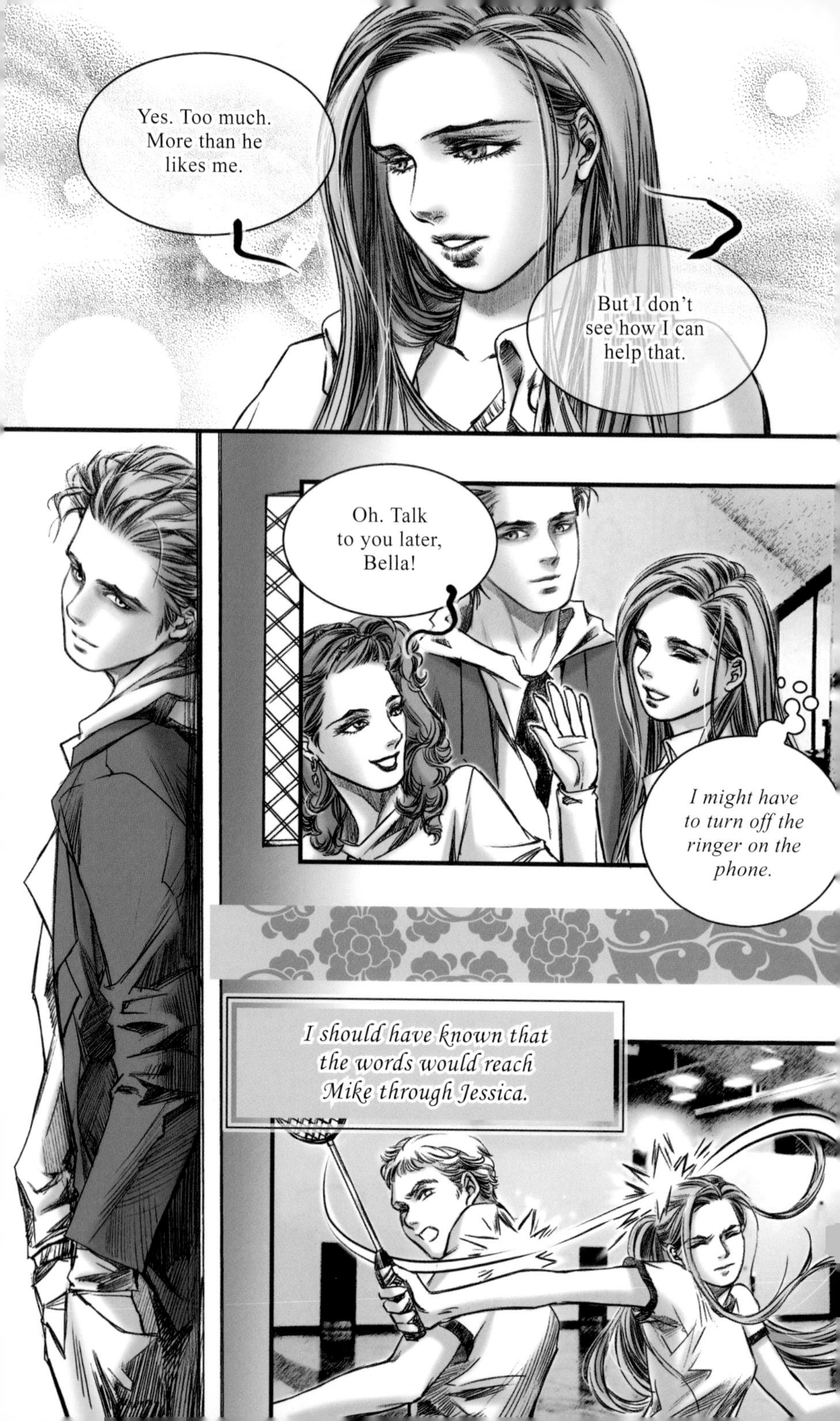
Yes. Too much. More than he likes me.
But I don't see how I can help that.
Oh. Talk to you later, Bella!
I might have to turn off the ringer on the phone.
I should have known that the words would reach Mike through Jessica.

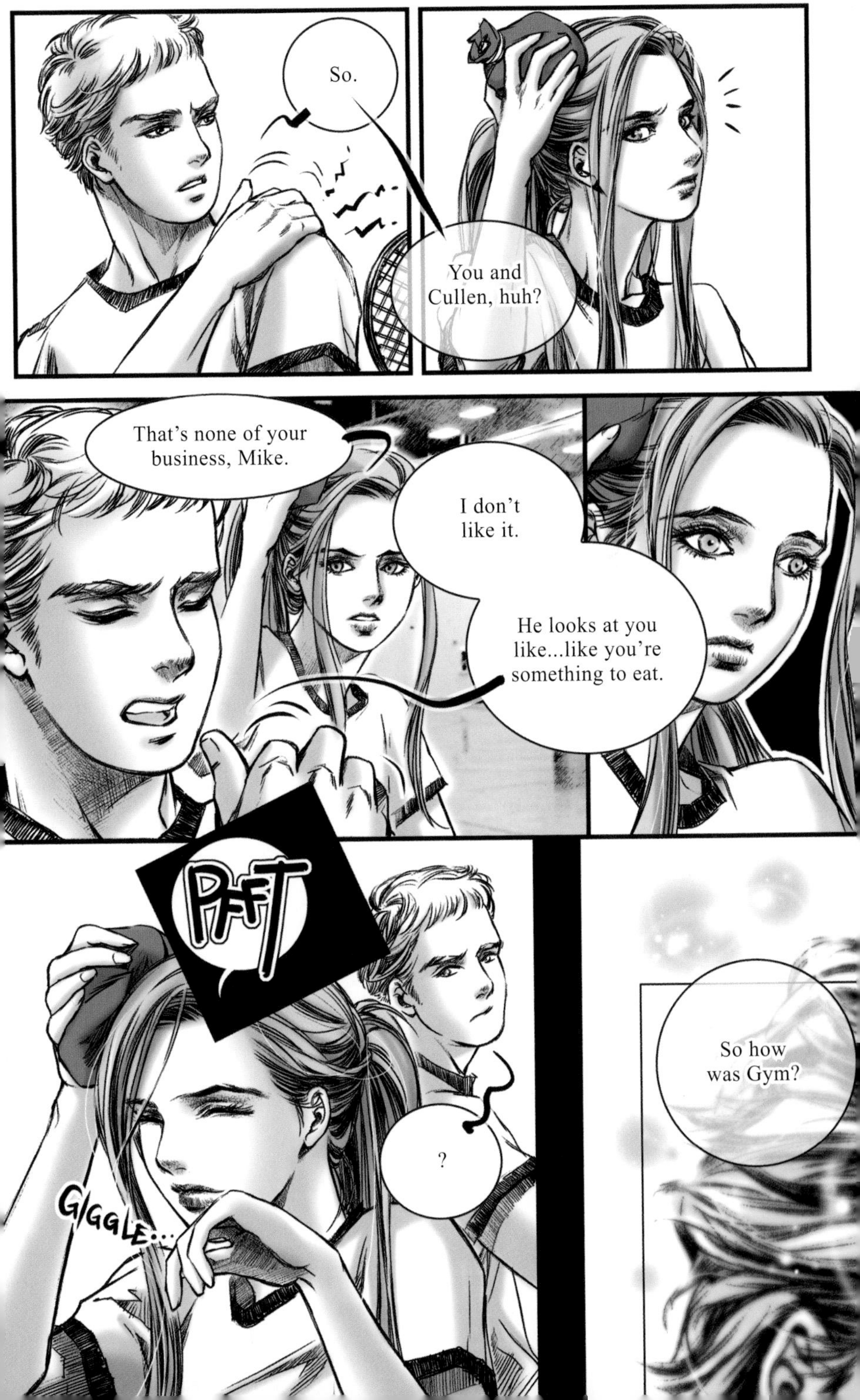
So.
You and Cullen, huh?
That's none of your business, Mike.
I don't like it.
He looks at you like...like you're something to eat.
PFFT
GIGGLE...
?
So how was Gym?

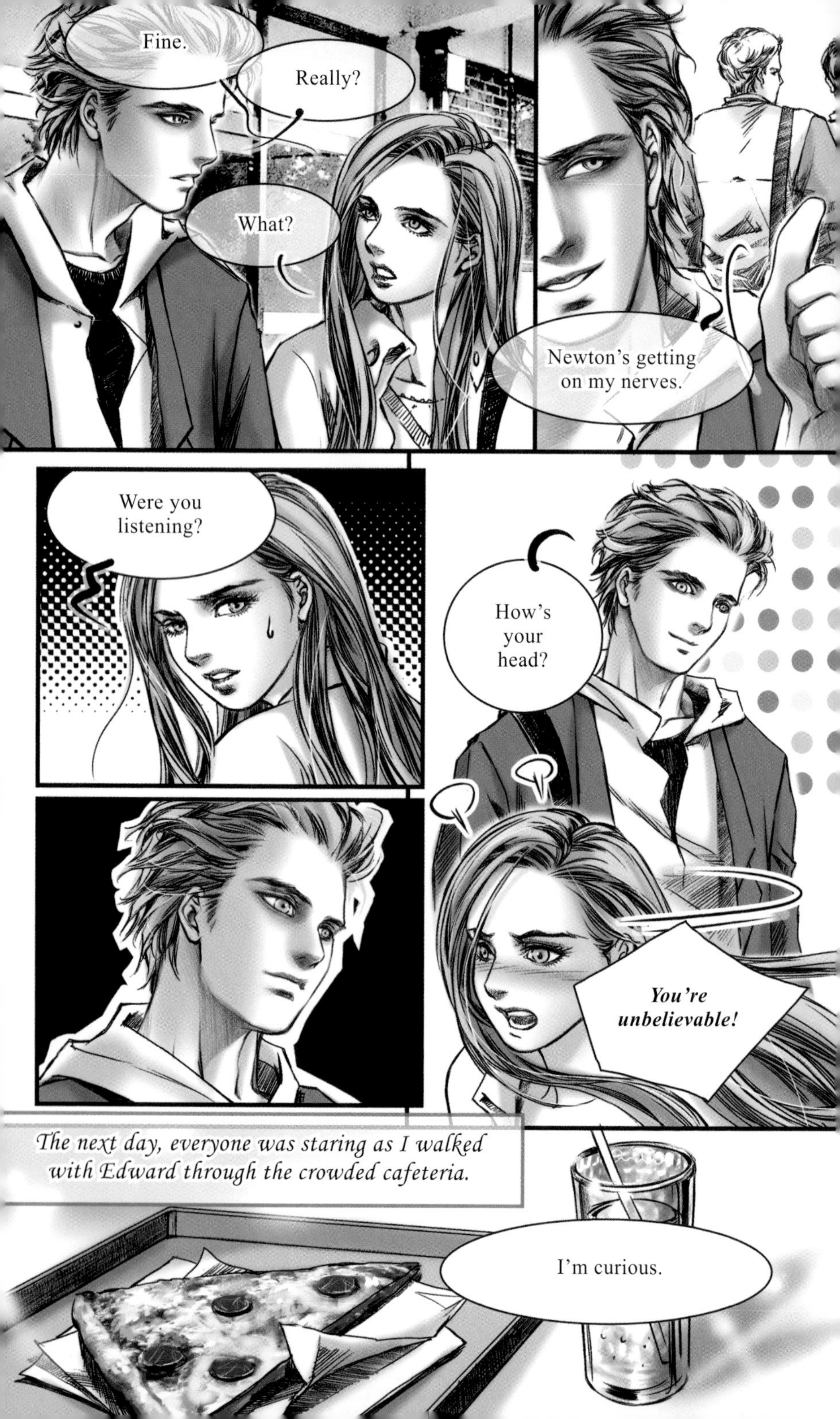
Fine.
Really?
What?
Newton's getting on my nerves.
Were you listening?
How's your head?
You're unbelievable!
The next day, everyone was staring as I walked with Edward through the crowded cafeteria.
I'm curious.

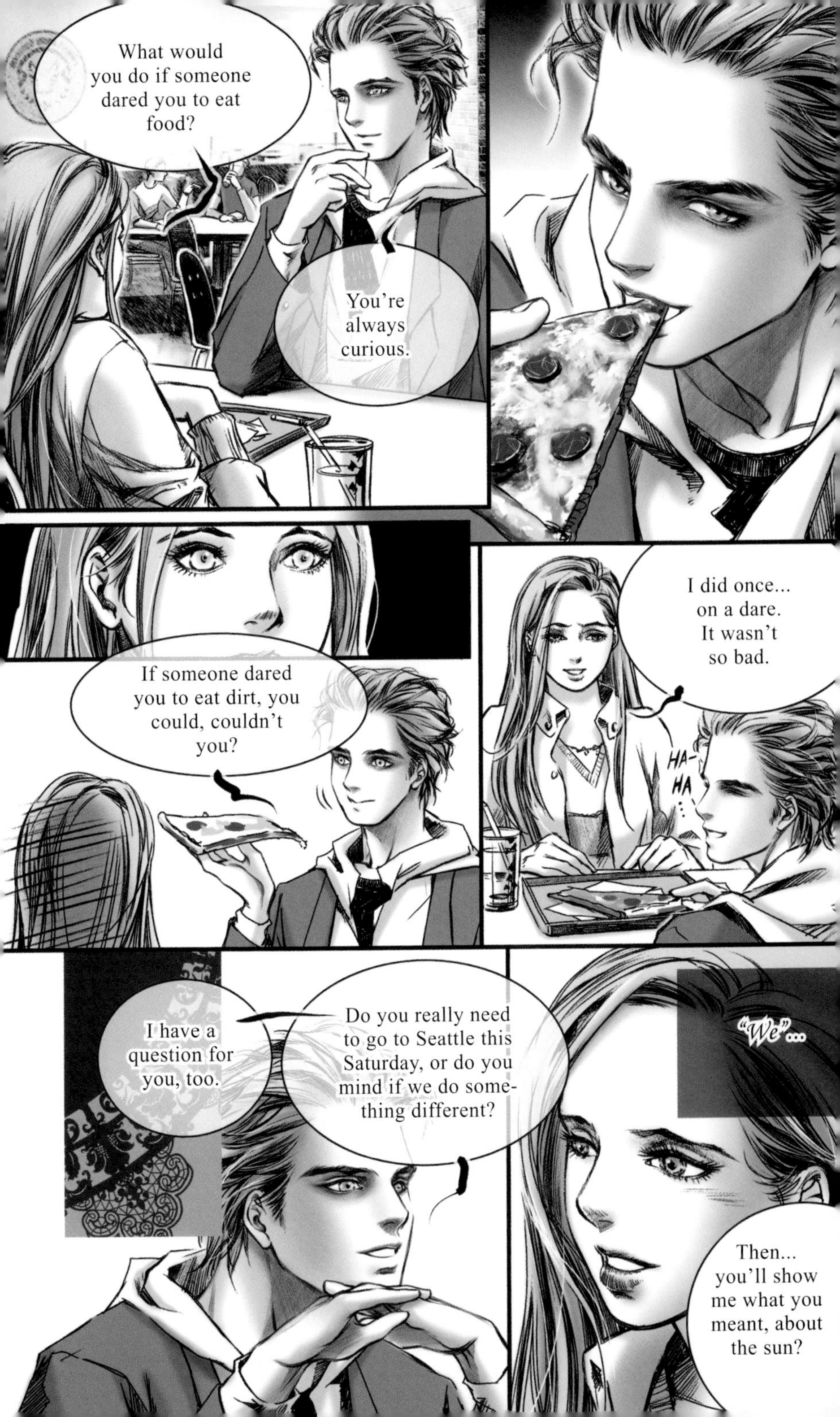
What would you do if someone dared you to eat food?
You're always curious.
If someone dared you to eat dirt, you could, couldn't you?
I did once... on a dare. It wasn't so bad.
HA-HA...
I have a question for you, too.
Do you really need to go to Seattle this Saturday, or do you mind if we do something different?
"We"...
Then... you'll show me what you meant, about the sun?

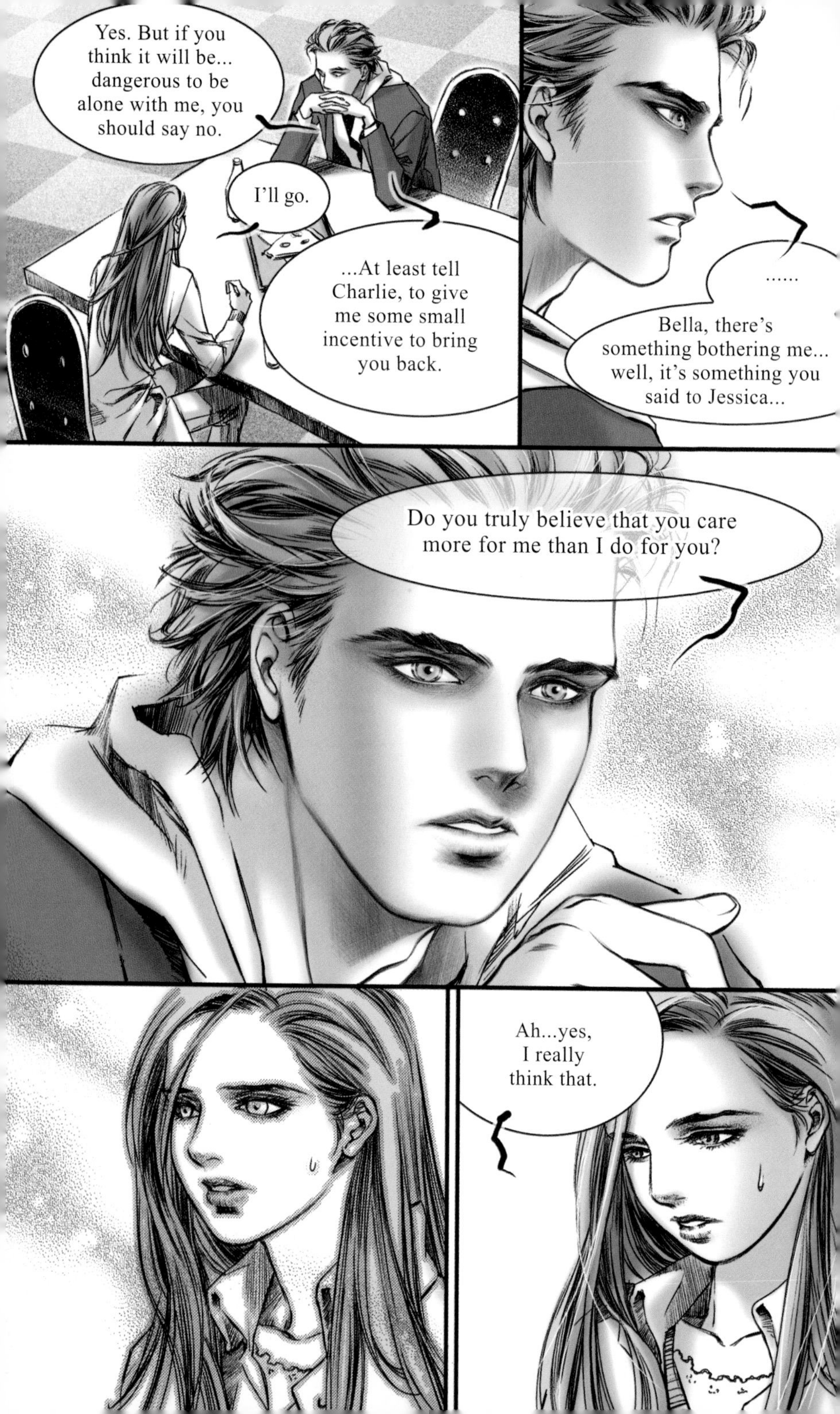
Yes. But if you think it will be... dangerous to be alone with me, you should say no.
I'll go.
...At least tell Charlie, to give me some small incentive to bring you back.
......
Bella, there's something bothering me... well, it's something you said to Jessica...
Do you truly believe that you care more for me than I do for you?
Ah...yes, I really think that.

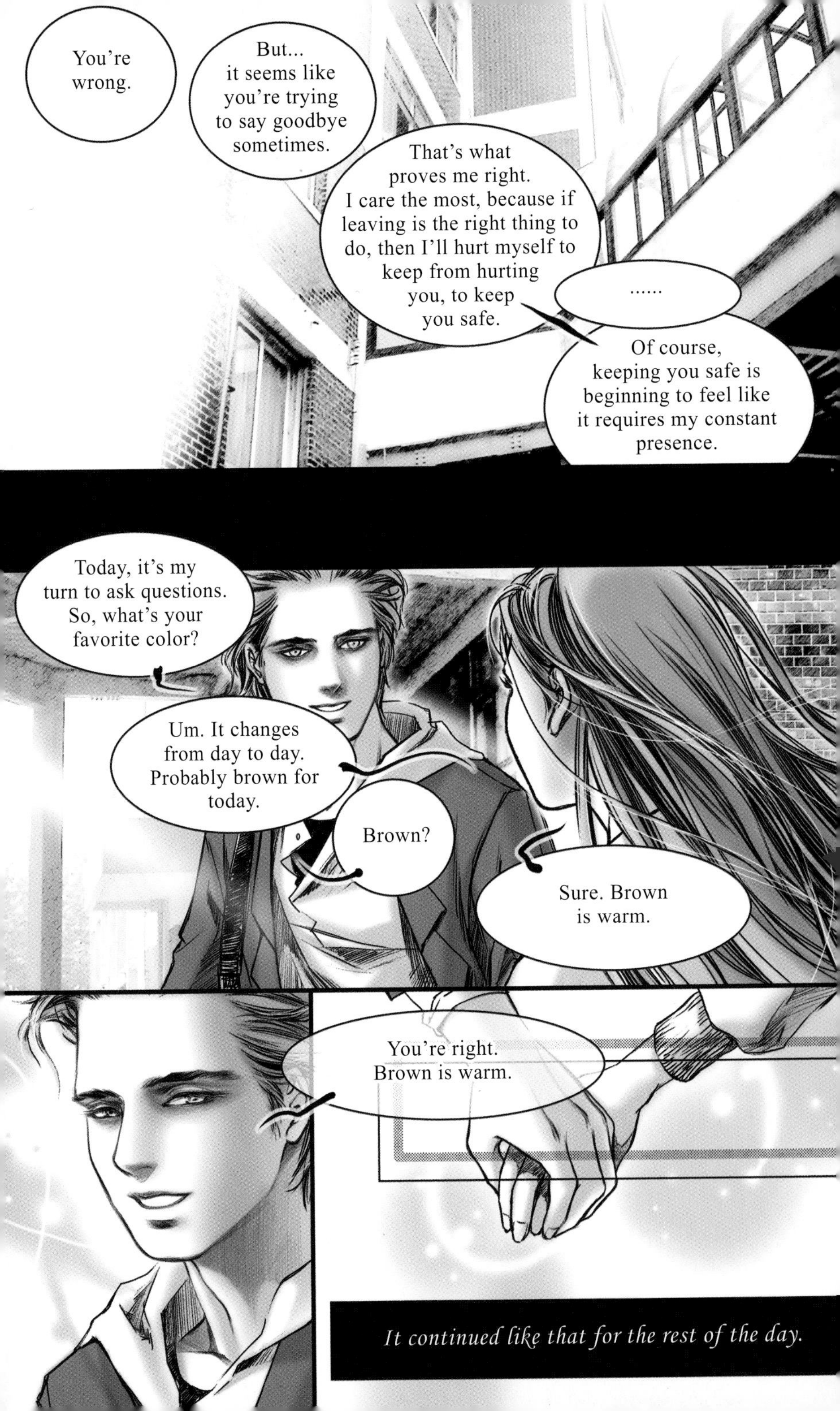
You're wrong.
But... it seems like you're trying to say goodbye sometimes.
That's what proves me right. I care the most, because if leaving is the right thing to do, then I'll hurt myself to keep from hurting you, to keep you safe.
......
Of course, keeping you safe is beginning to feel like it requires my constant presence.
Today, it's my turn to ask questions. So, what's your favorite color?
Um. It changes from day to day. Probably brown for today.
Brown?
Sure. Brown is warm.
You're right. Brown is warm.
It continued like that for the rest of the day.

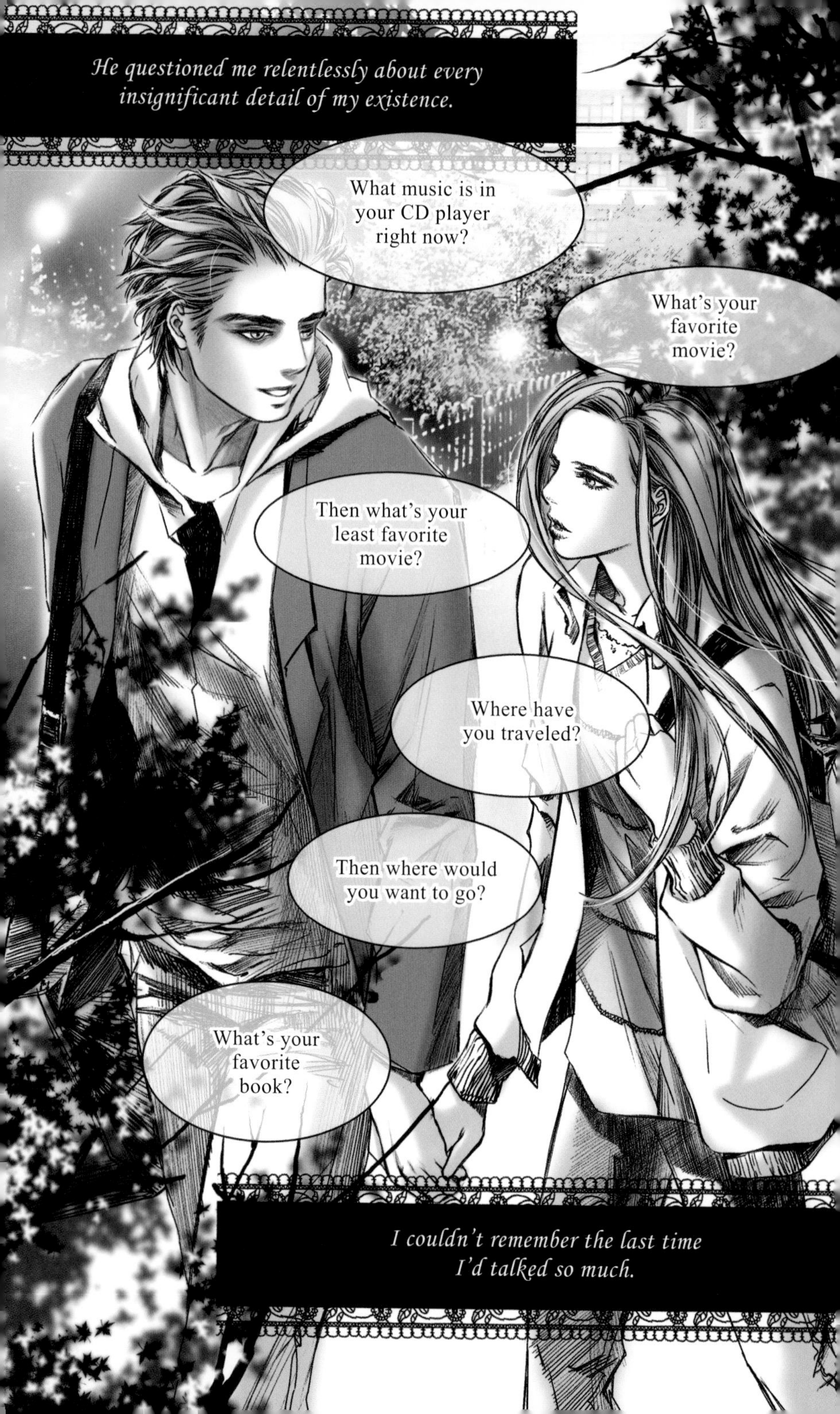
He questioned me relentlessly about every insignificant detail of my existence.
What music is in your CD player right now?
What's your favorite movie?
Then what's your least favorite movie?
Where have you traveled?
Then where would you want to go?
What's your favorite book?
I couldn't remember the last time I'd talked so much.

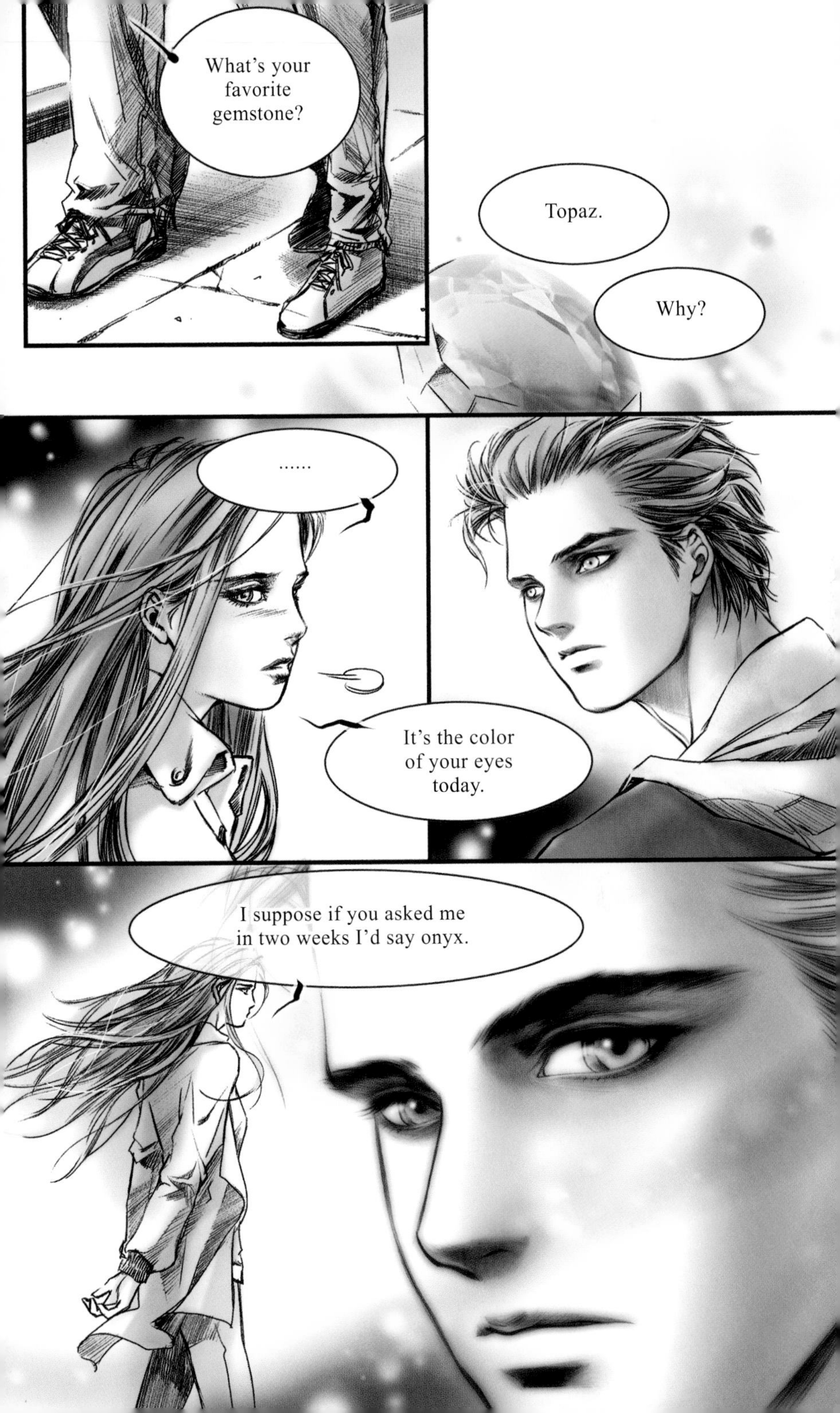
What's your favorite gemstone?
Topaz.
Why?
......
It's the color of your eyes today.
I suppose if you asked me in two weeks I'd say onyx.

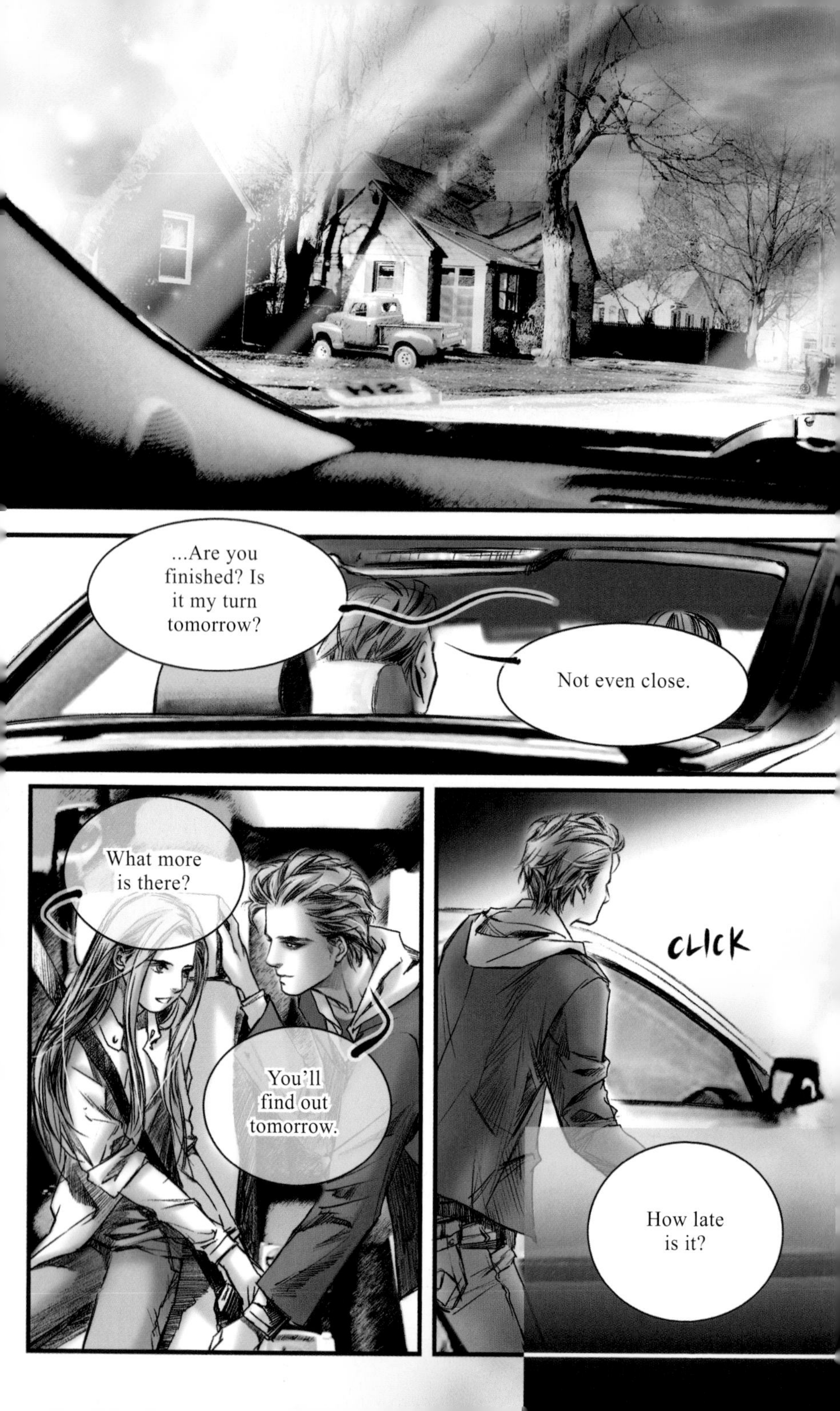
...Are you finished? Is it my turn tomorrow?
Not even close.
What more is there?
You'll find out tomorrow.
CLICK
How late is it?

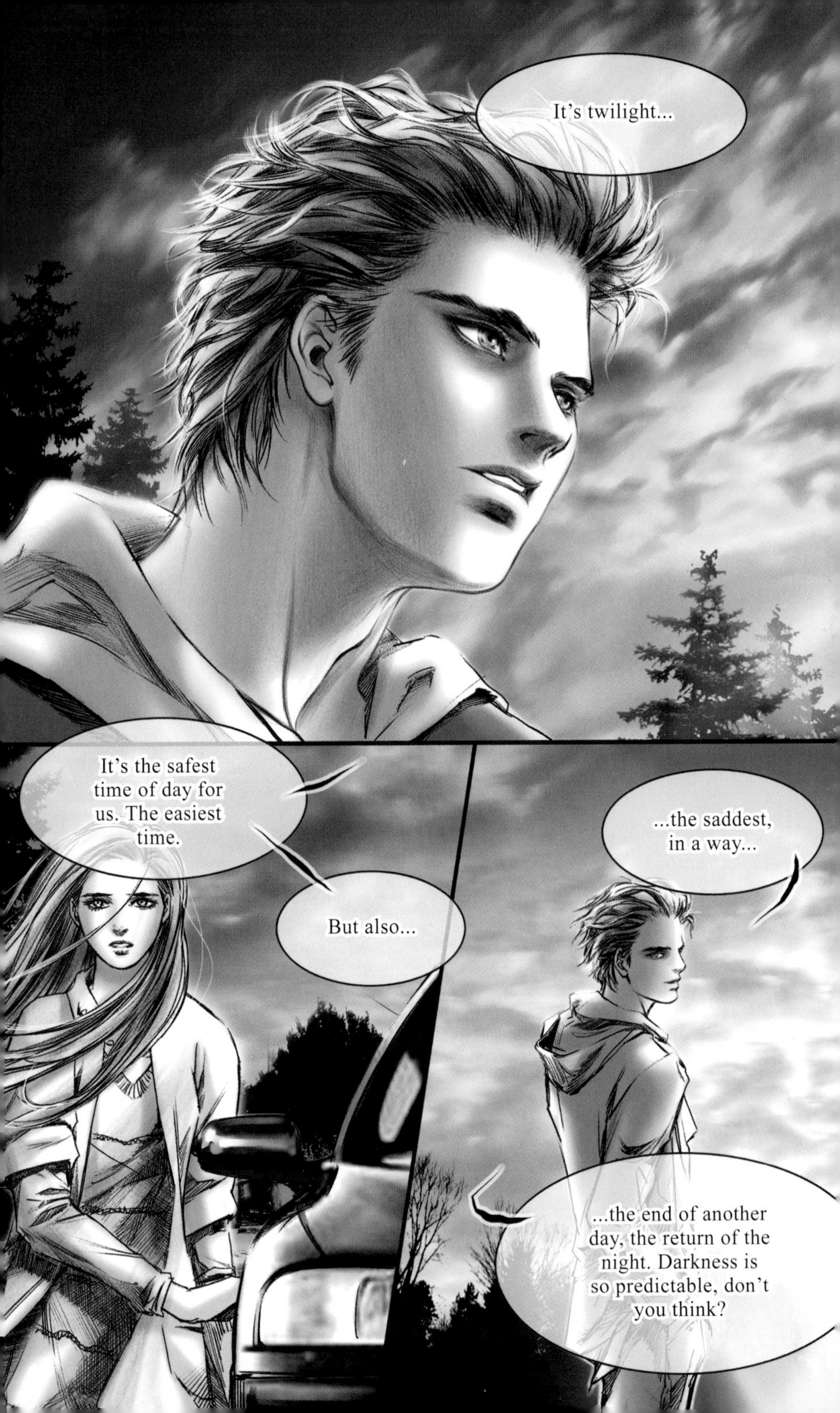
It's twilight...
It's the safest time of day for us. The easiest time.
But also...
...the saddest, in a way...
...the end of another day, the return of the night. Darkness is so predictable, don't you think?

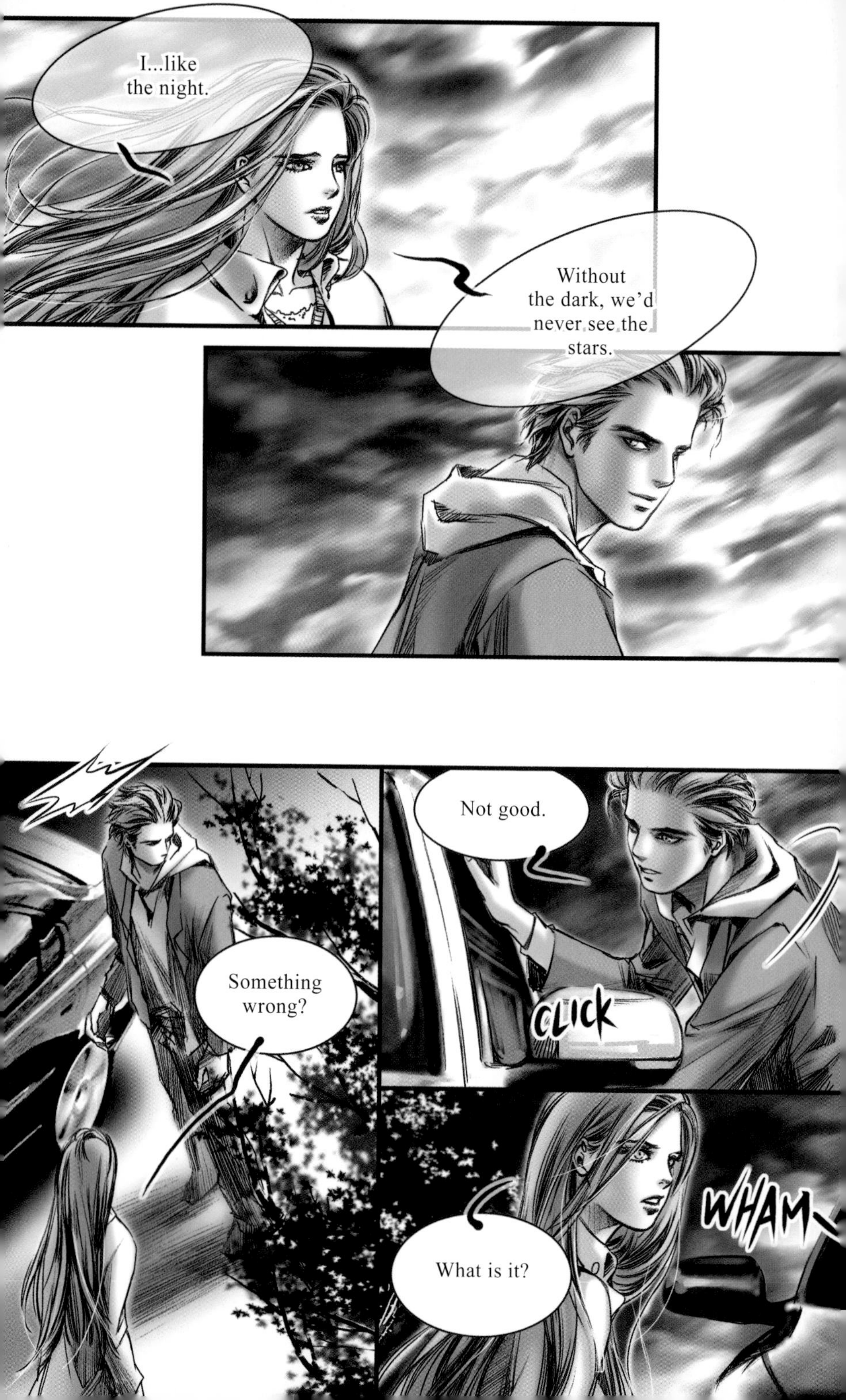

I...like the night.
Without the dark, we'd never see the stars.
Something wrong?
Not good.
CLICK
What is it?
WHAM

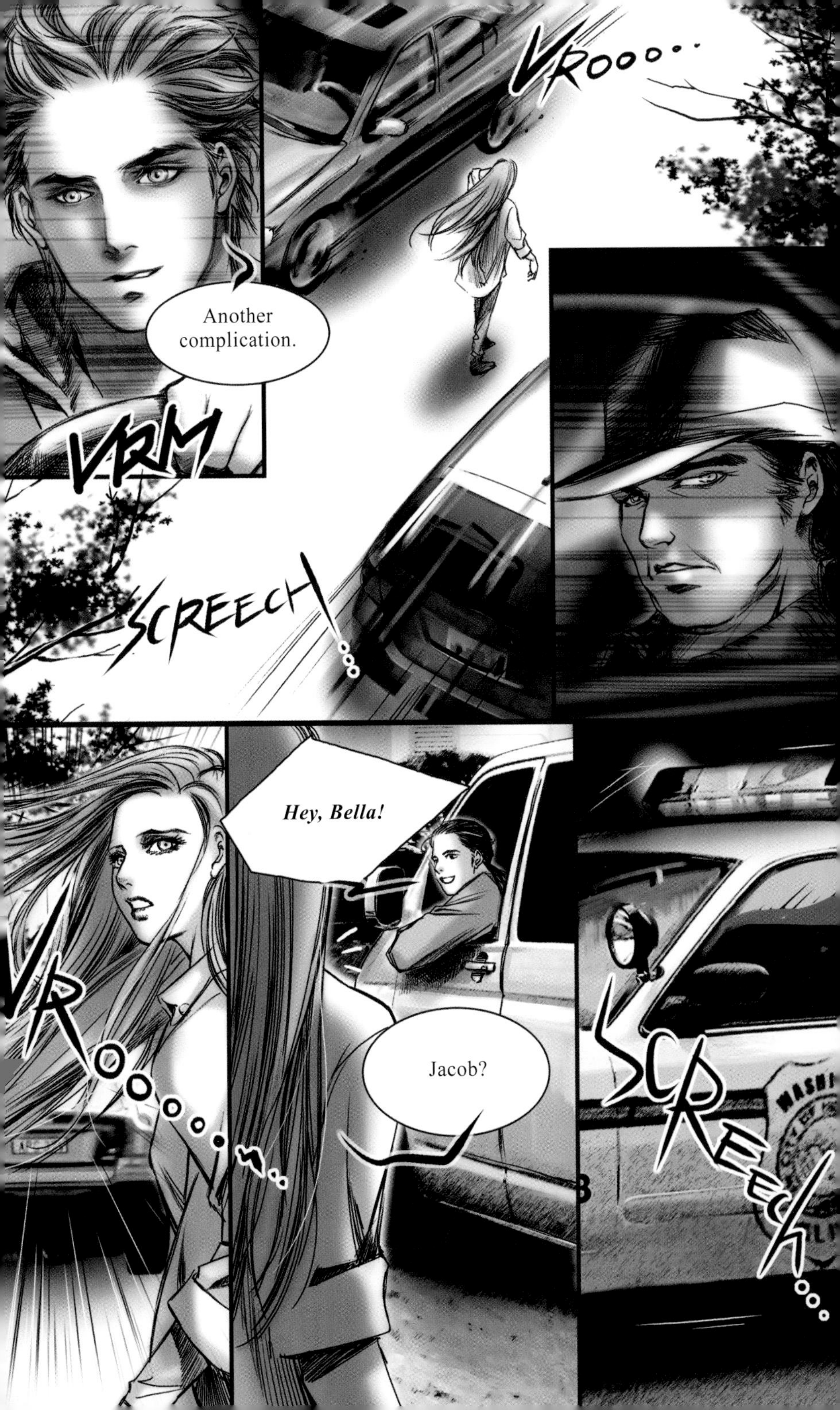
VROOO..
Another complication.
VRM
SCREECH...
Hey, Bella!
Jacob?
VROOOO...M..
SCREECH...

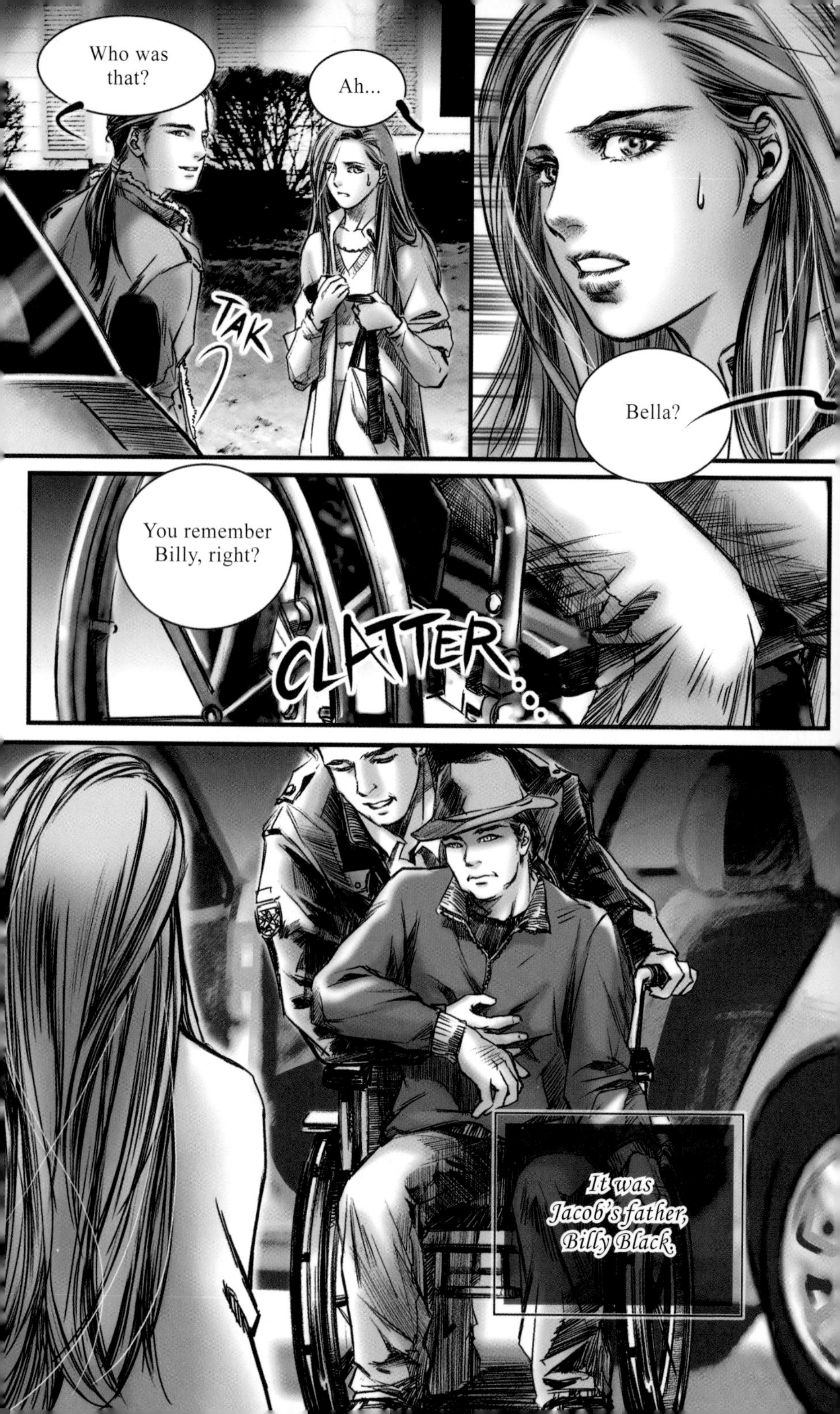
Who was that?
Ah...
TAK
Bella?
You remember Billy, right?
CLATTER...
It was Jacob's father, Billy Black.

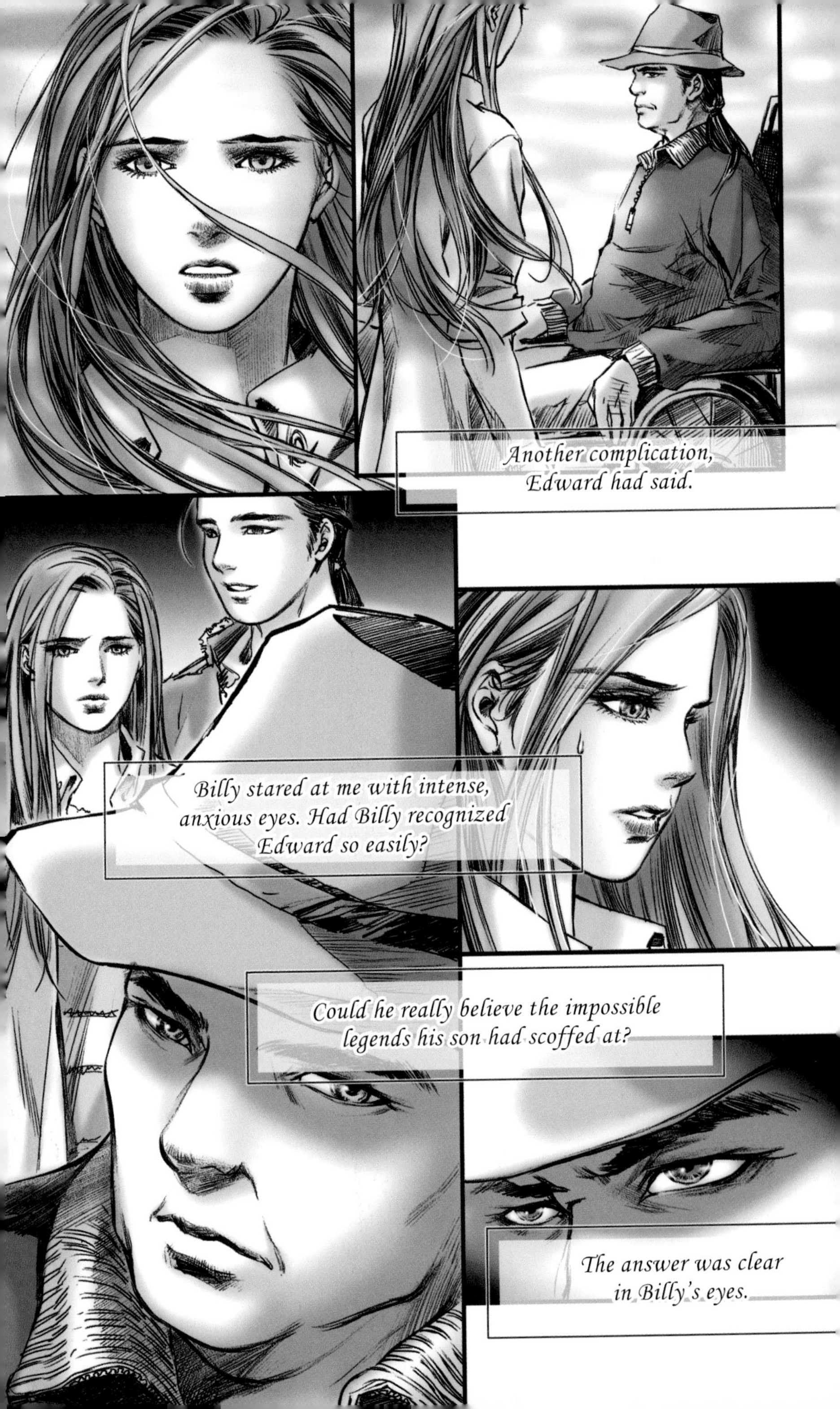

Another complication,
Edward had said.
Billy stared at me with intense,
anxious eyes. Had Billy recognized
Edward so easily?
Could he really believe the impossible
legends his son had scoffed at?
The answer was clear
in Billy's eyes.

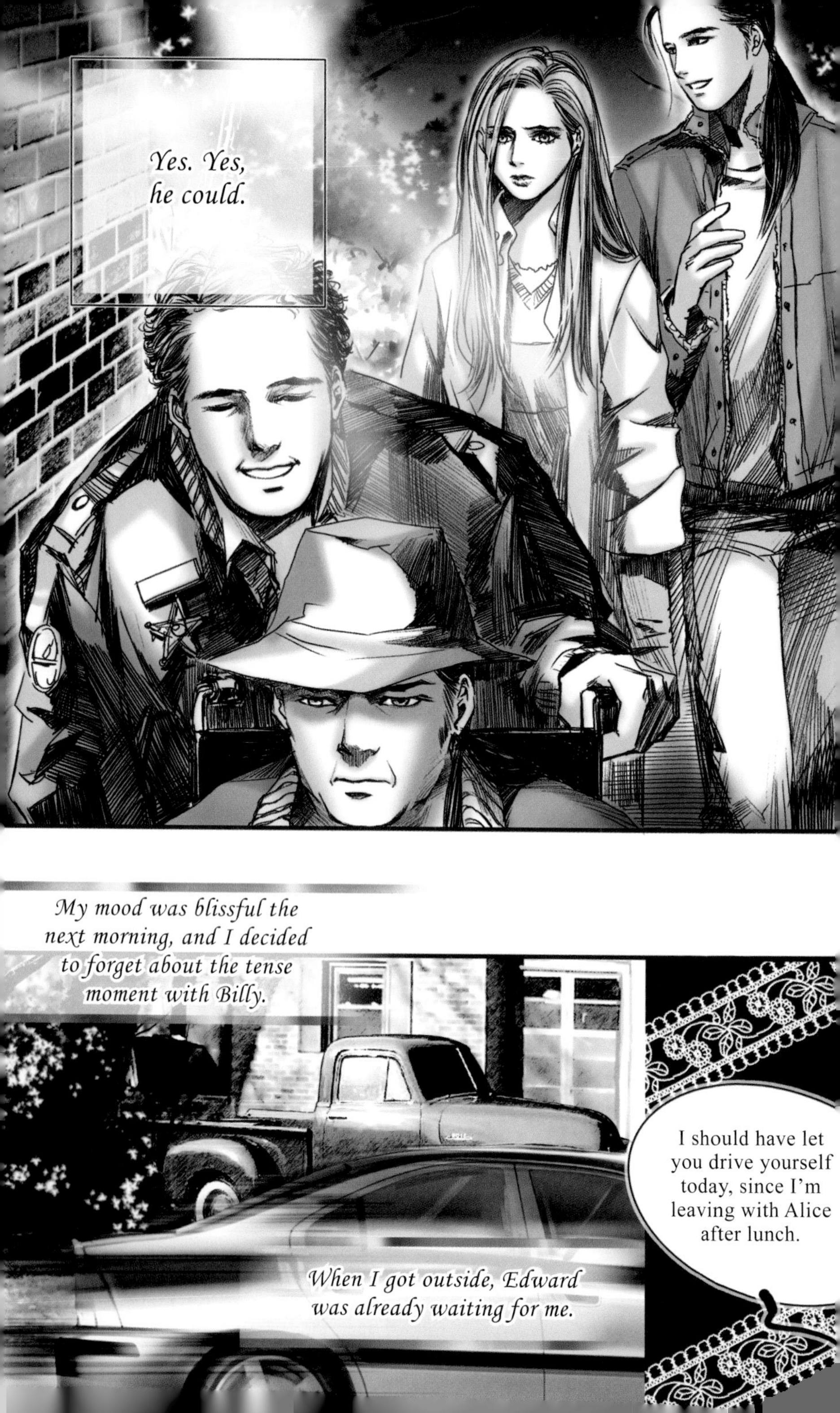
Yes. Yes, he could.
My mood was blissful the next morning, and I decided to forget about the tense moment with Billy.
When I got outside, Edward was already waiting for me.
I should have let you drive yourself today, since I'm leaving with Alice after lunch.

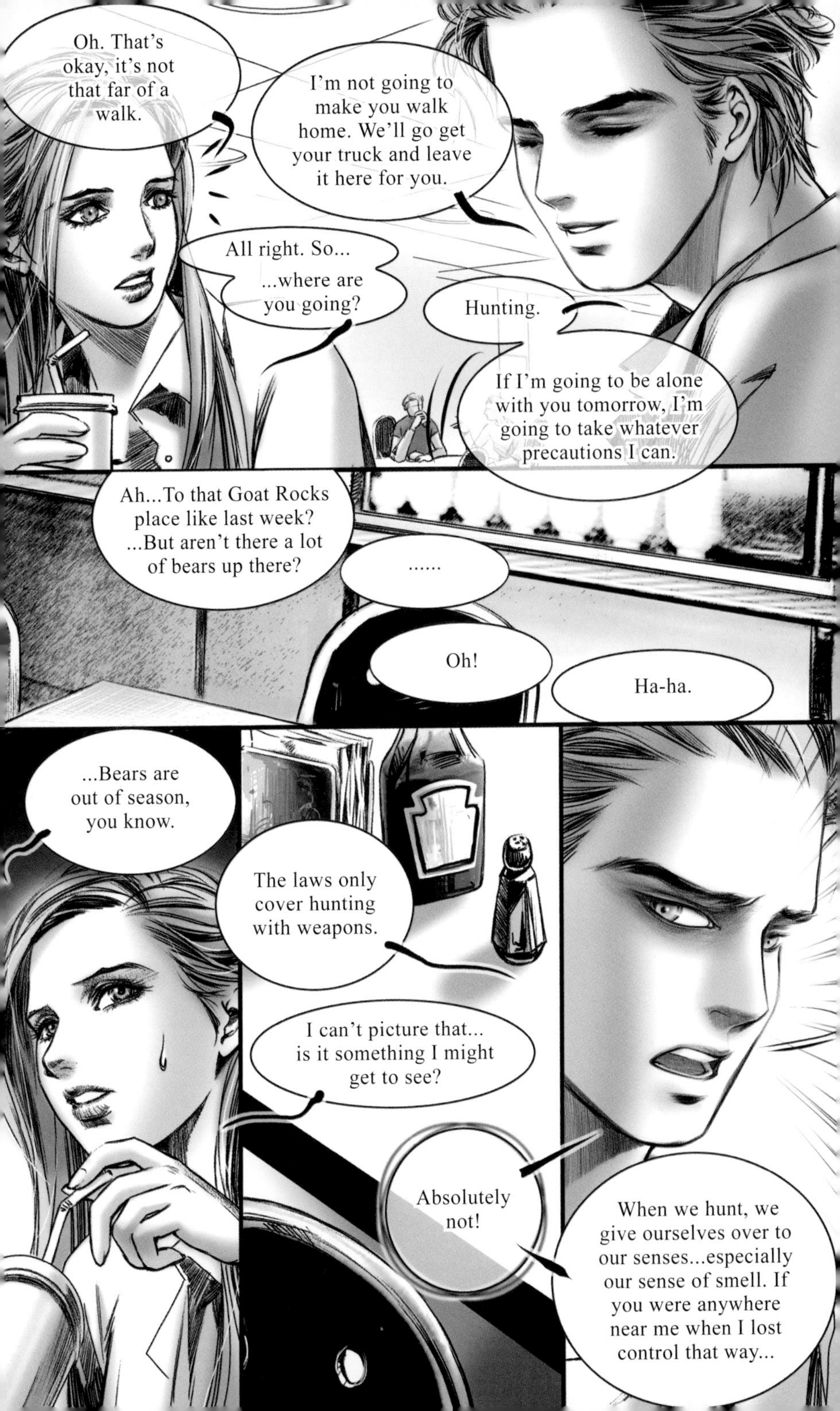
Oh. That's okay, it's not that far of a walk.
I'm not going to make you walk home. We'll go get your truck and leave it here for you.
All right. So...
...where are you going?
Hunting.
If I'm going to be alone with you tomorrow, I'm going to take whatever precautions I can.
Ah...To that Goat Rocks place like last week? ...But aren't there a lot of bears up there?
......
Oh!
Ha-ha.
...Bears are out of season, you know.
The laws only cover hunting with weapons.
I can't picture that... is it something I might get to see?
Absolutely not!
When we hunt, we give ourselves over to our senses...especially our sense of smell. If you were anywhere near me when I lost control that way...

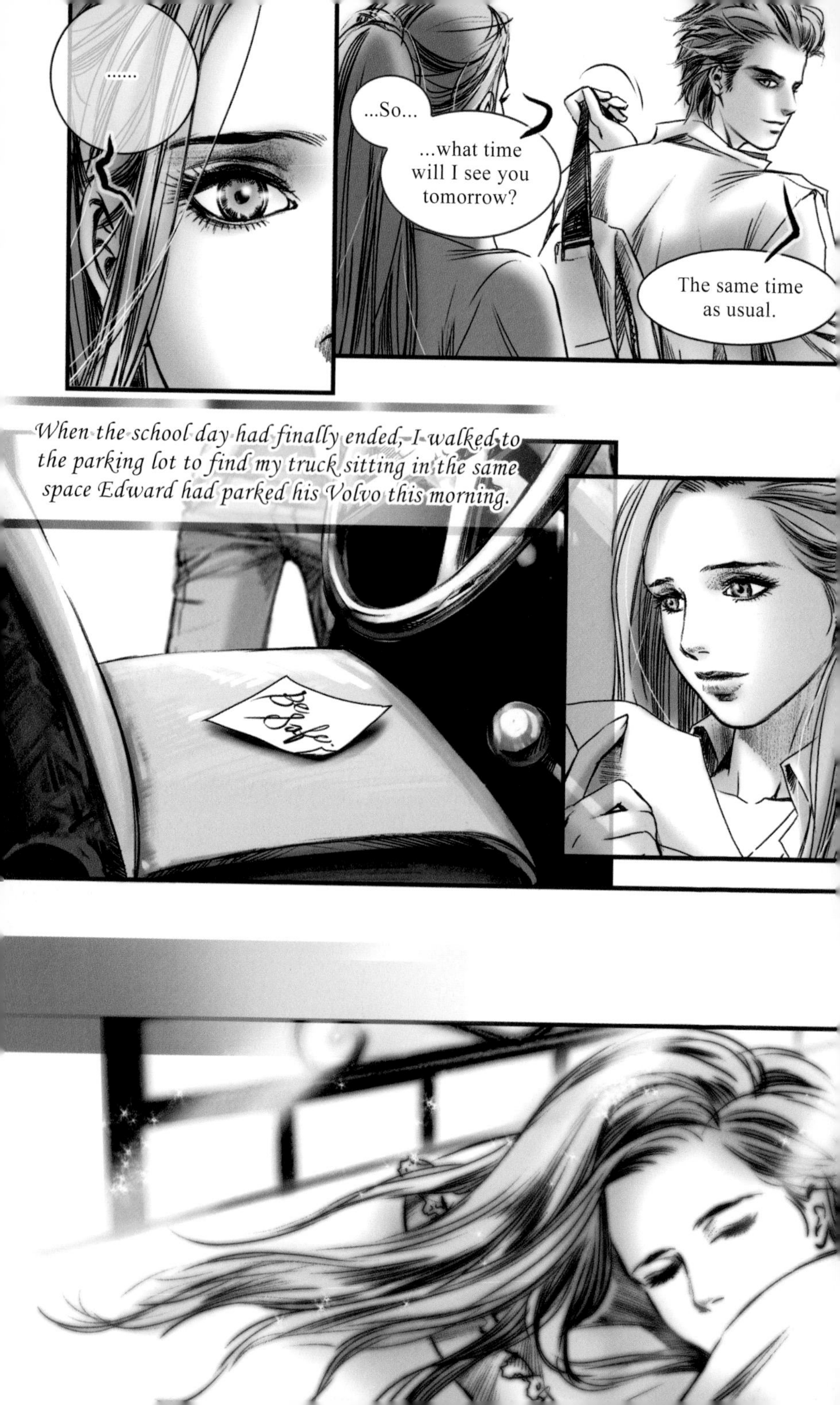

......
...So...
...what time will I see you tomorrow?
The same time as usual.
When the school day had finally ended, I walked to the parking lot to find my truck sitting in the same space Edward had parked his Volvo this morning.
Be Safe.

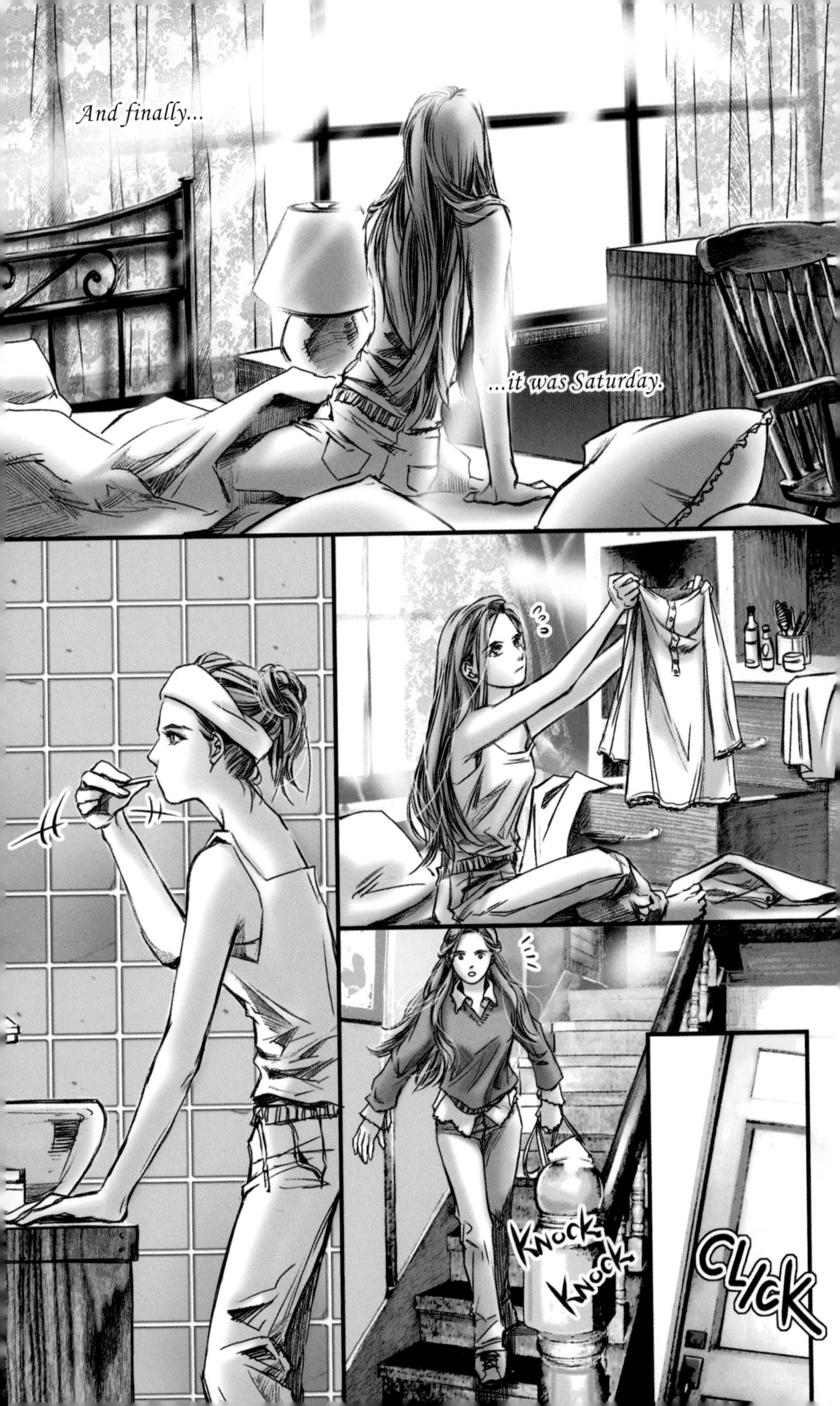
And finally...
...it was Saturday.
KNOCK
KNOCK
CLICK

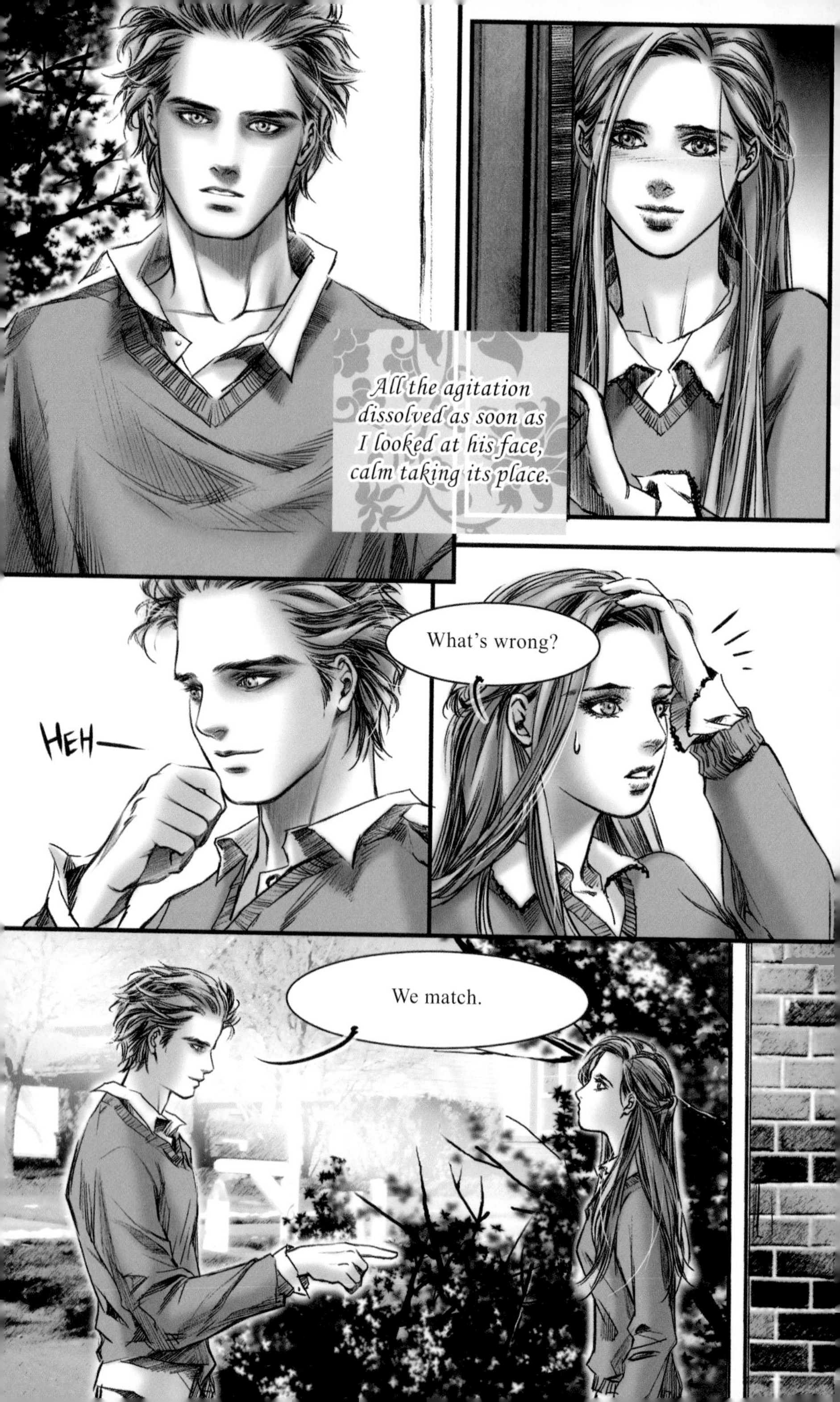
All the agitation dissolved as soon as I looked at his face, calm taking its place.
HEH—
What's wrong?
We match.

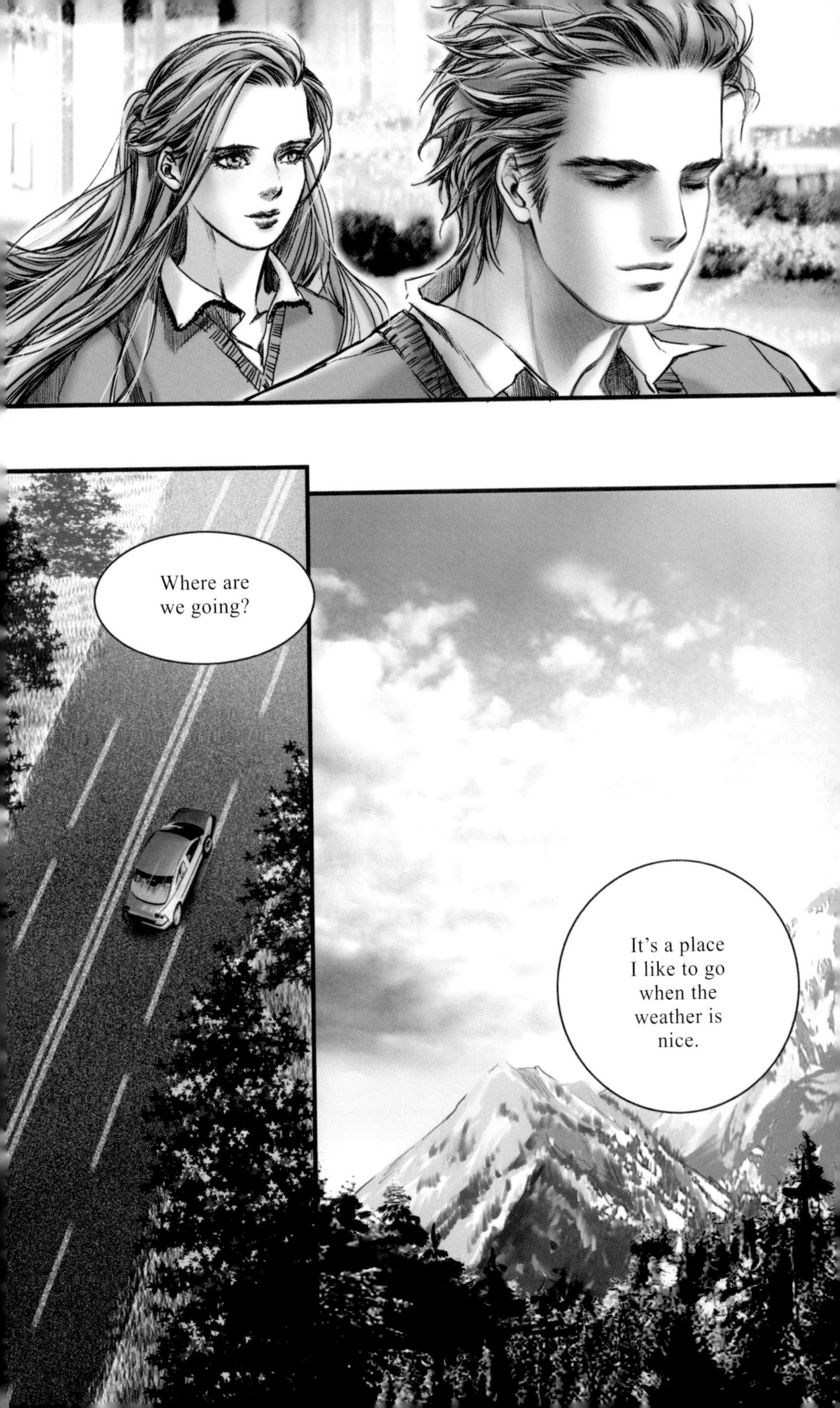

Where are we going?
It's a place I like to go when the weather is nice.

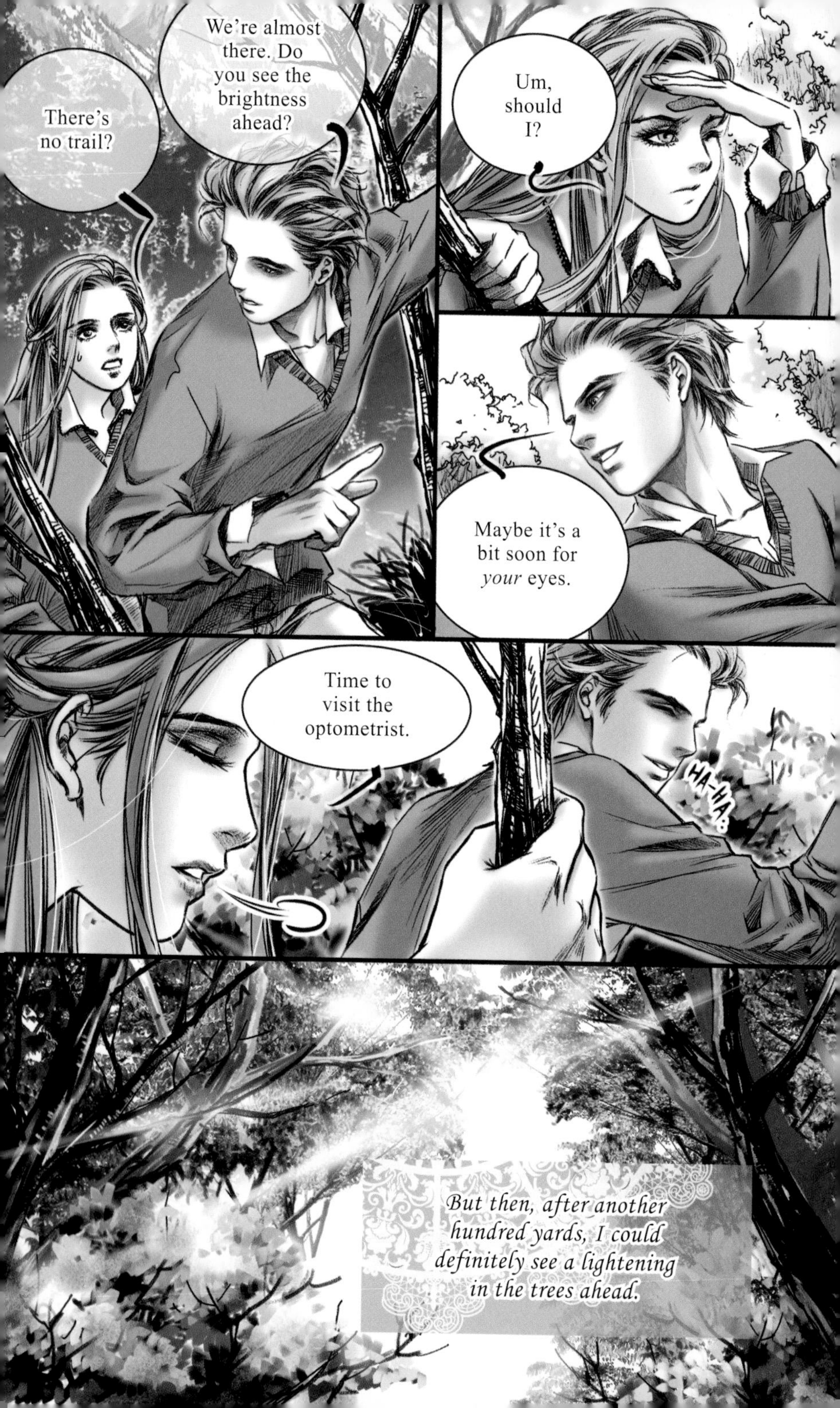
There's no trail?
We're almost there. Do you see the brightness ahead?
Um, should I?
Maybe it's a bit soon for *your* eyes.
Time to visit the optometrist.
HA-HA.
But then, after another hundred yards, I could definitely see a lightening in the trees ahead.

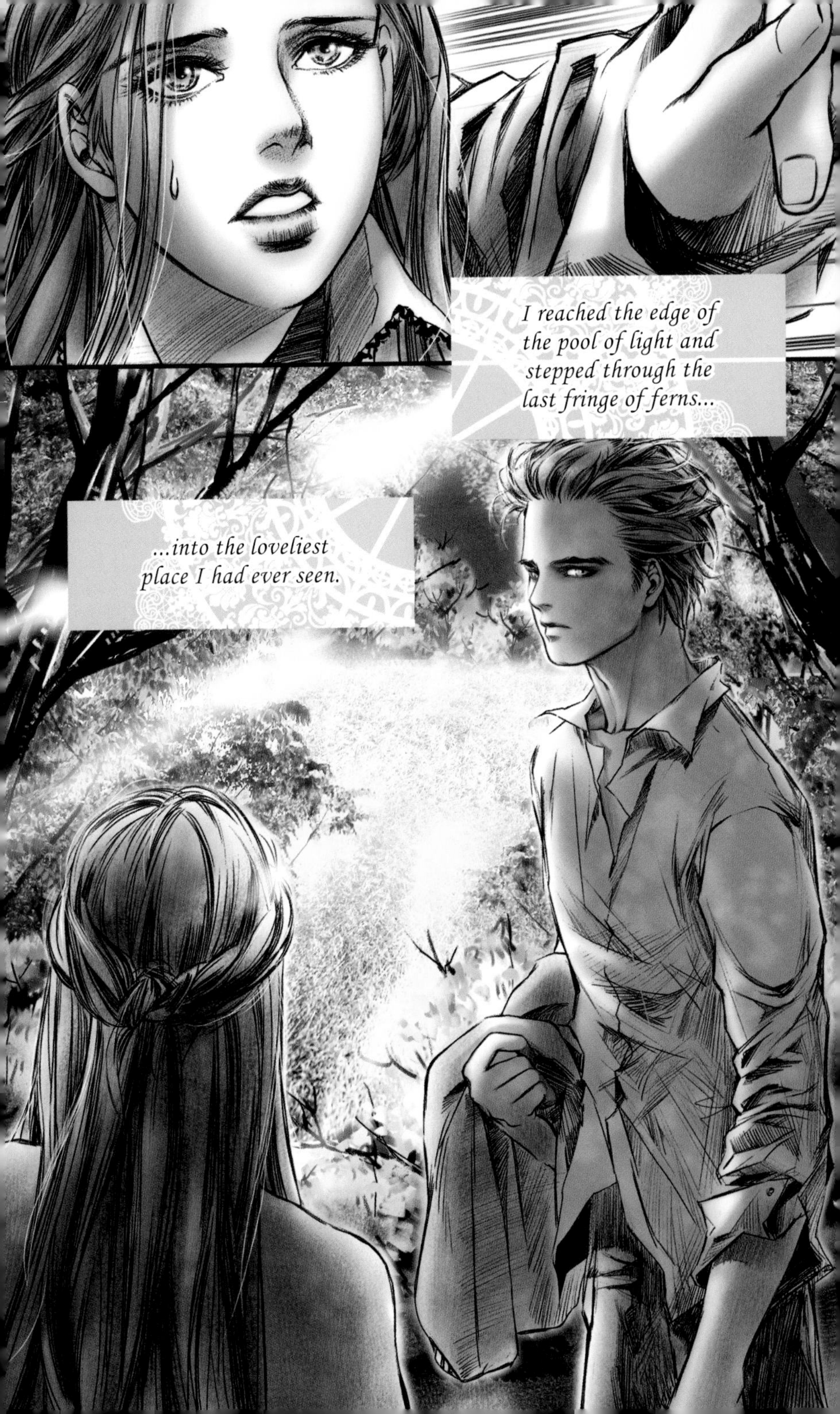
I reached the edge of the pool of light and stepped through the last fringe of ferns...
...into the loveliest place I had ever seen.

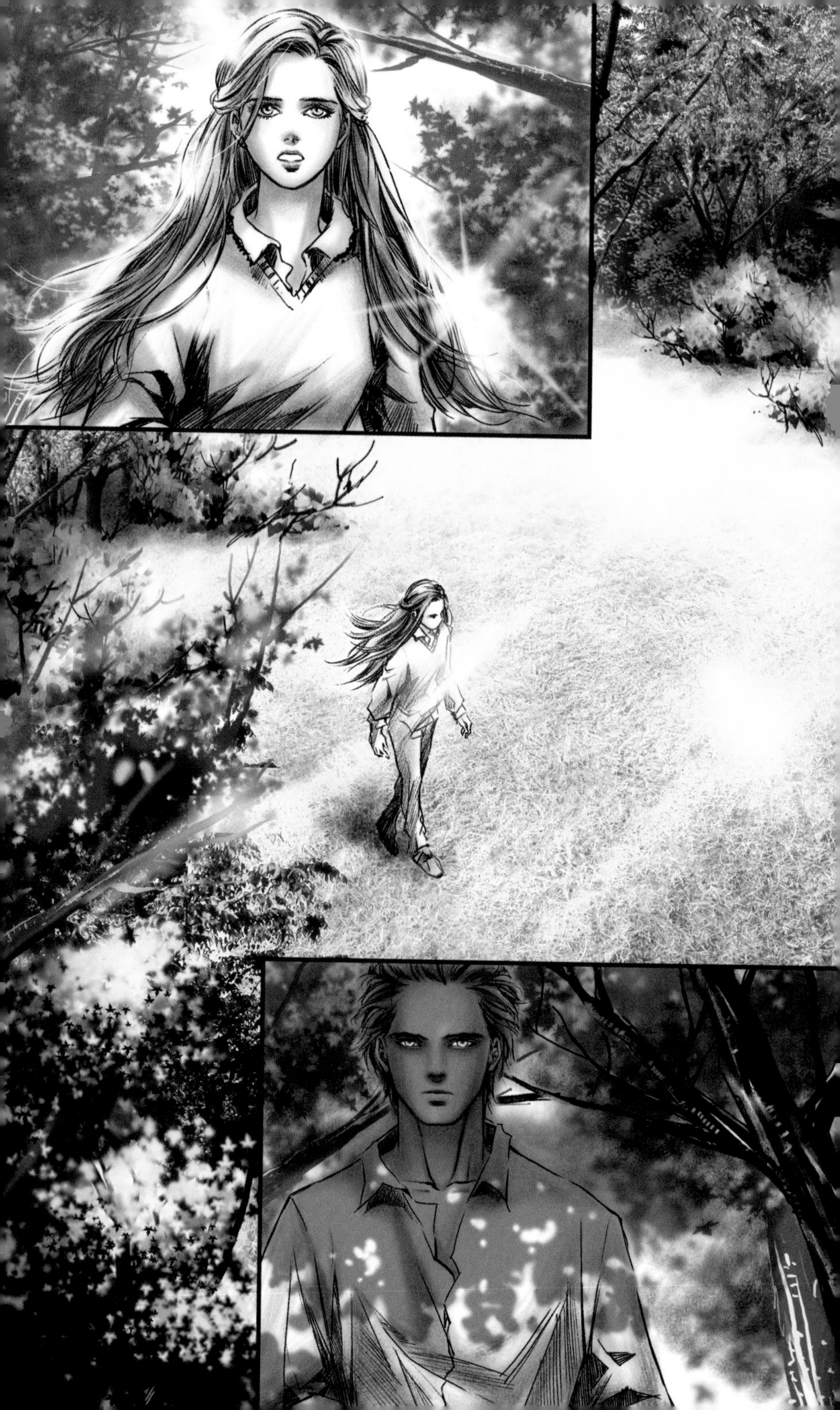

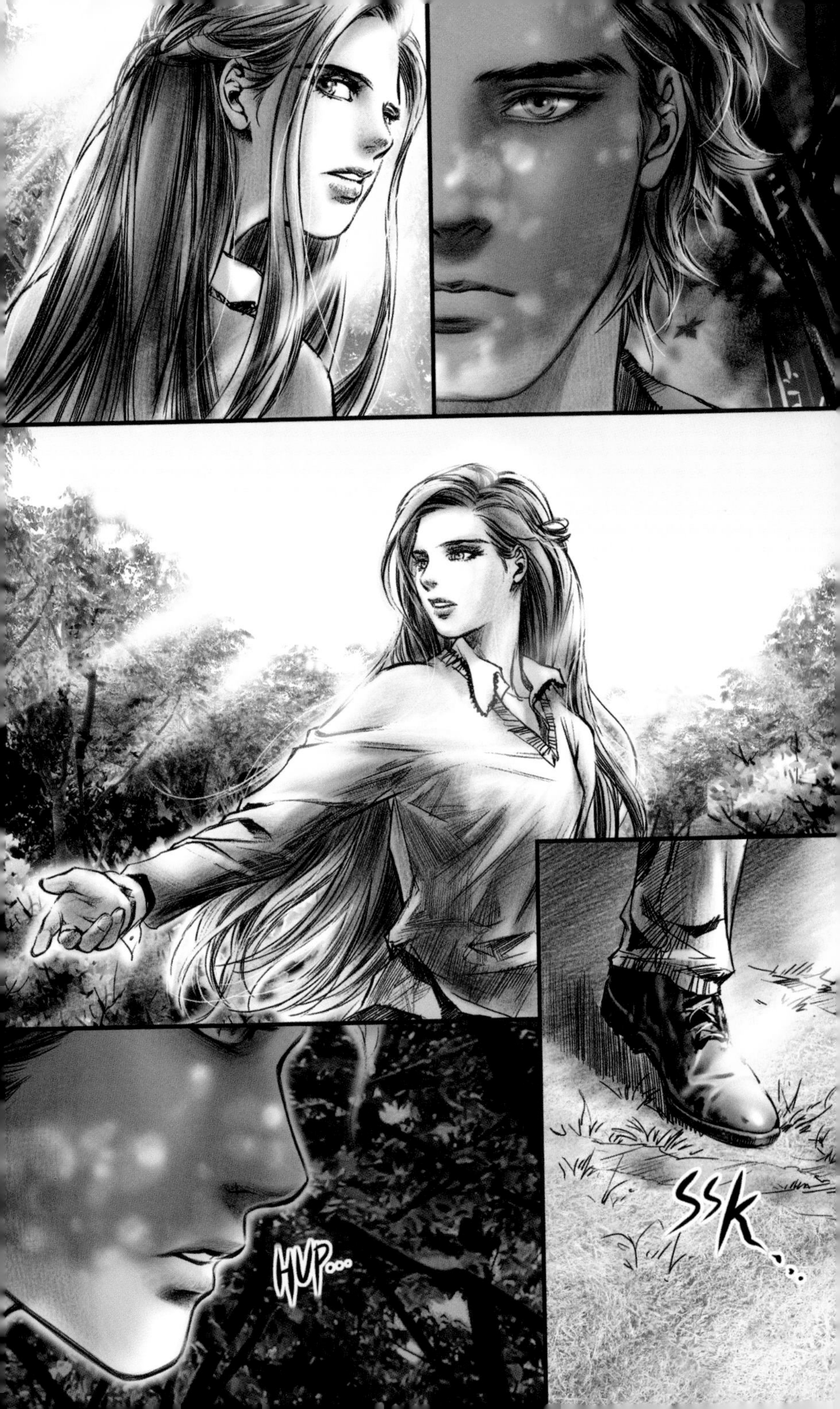
SSK...
HUP...

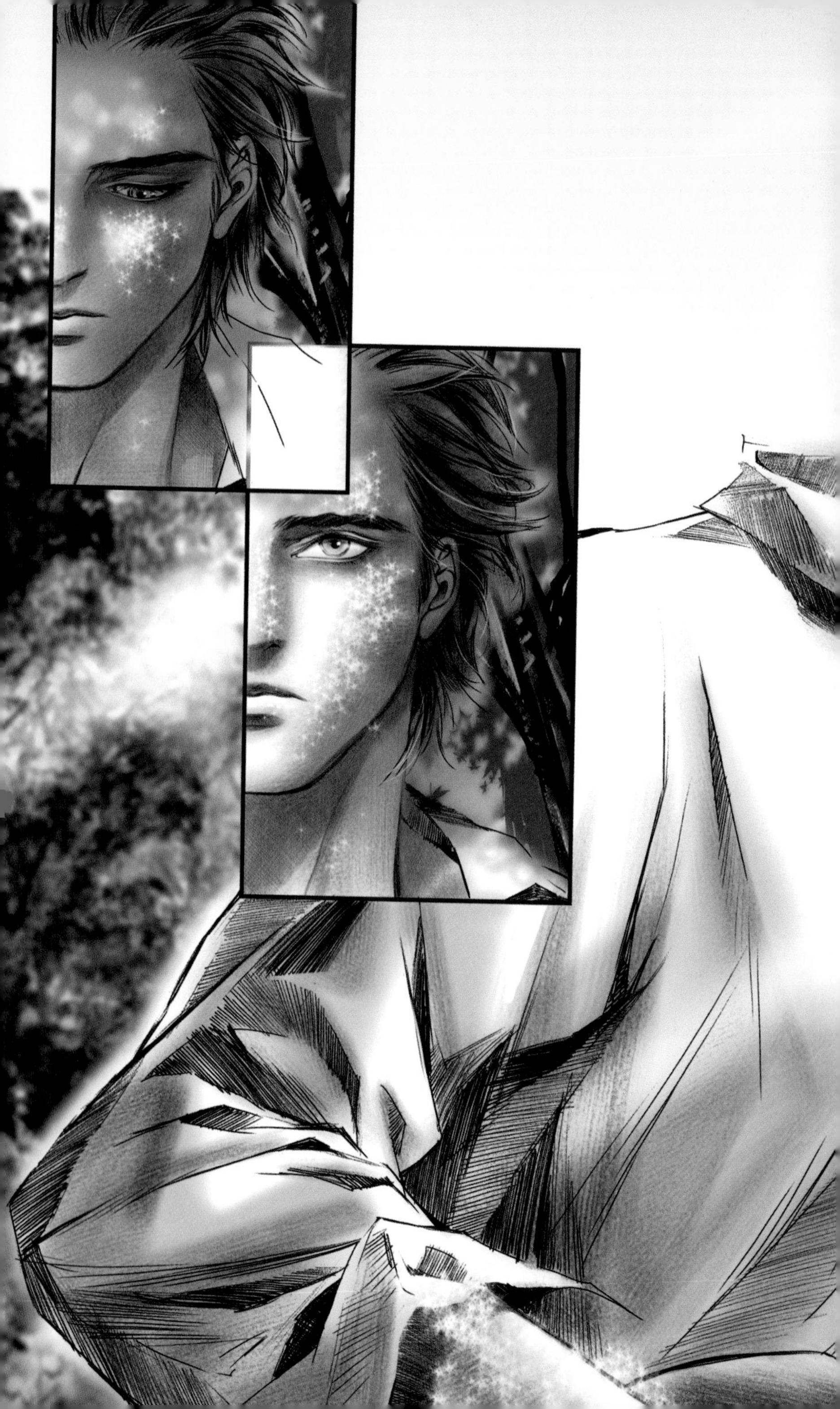

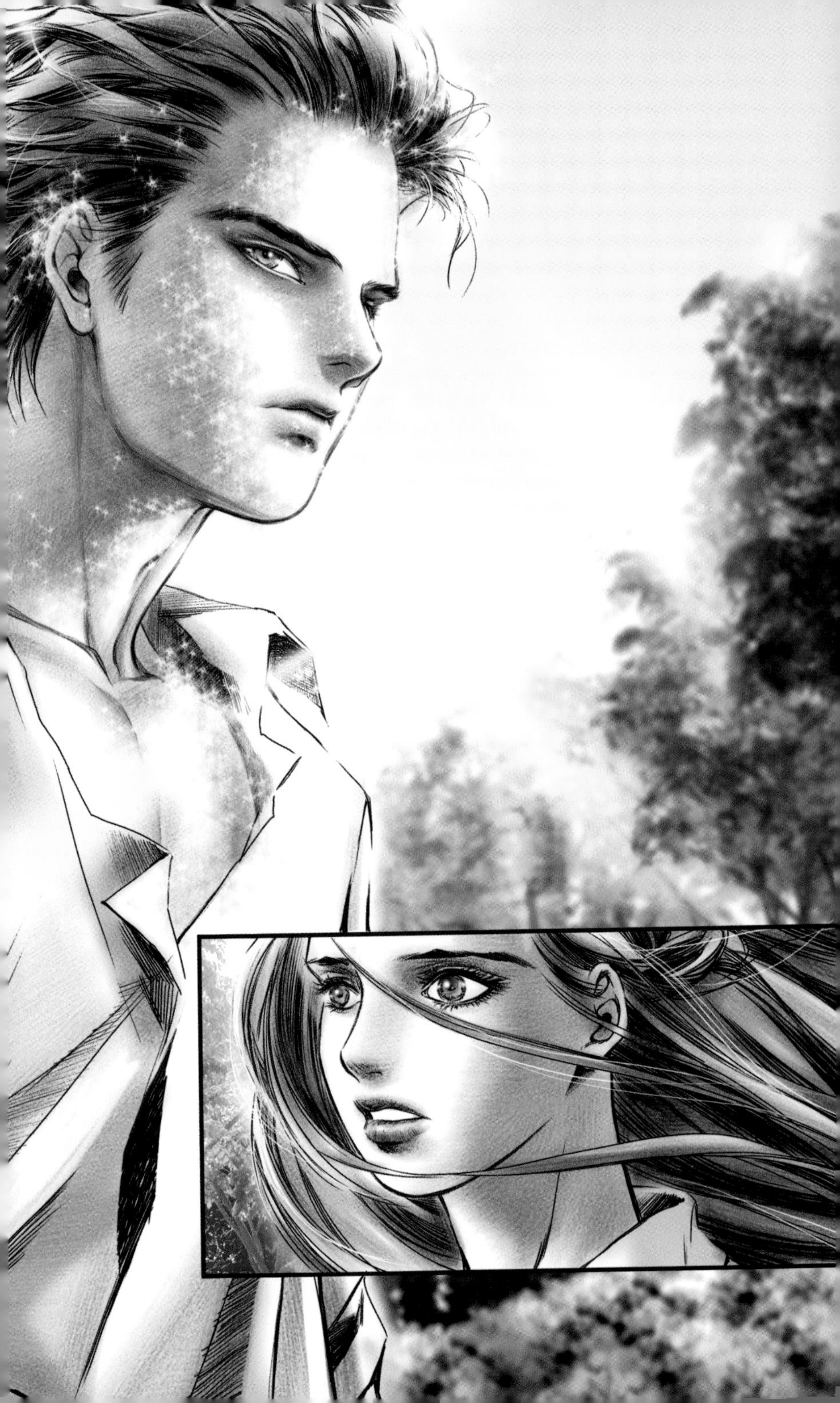

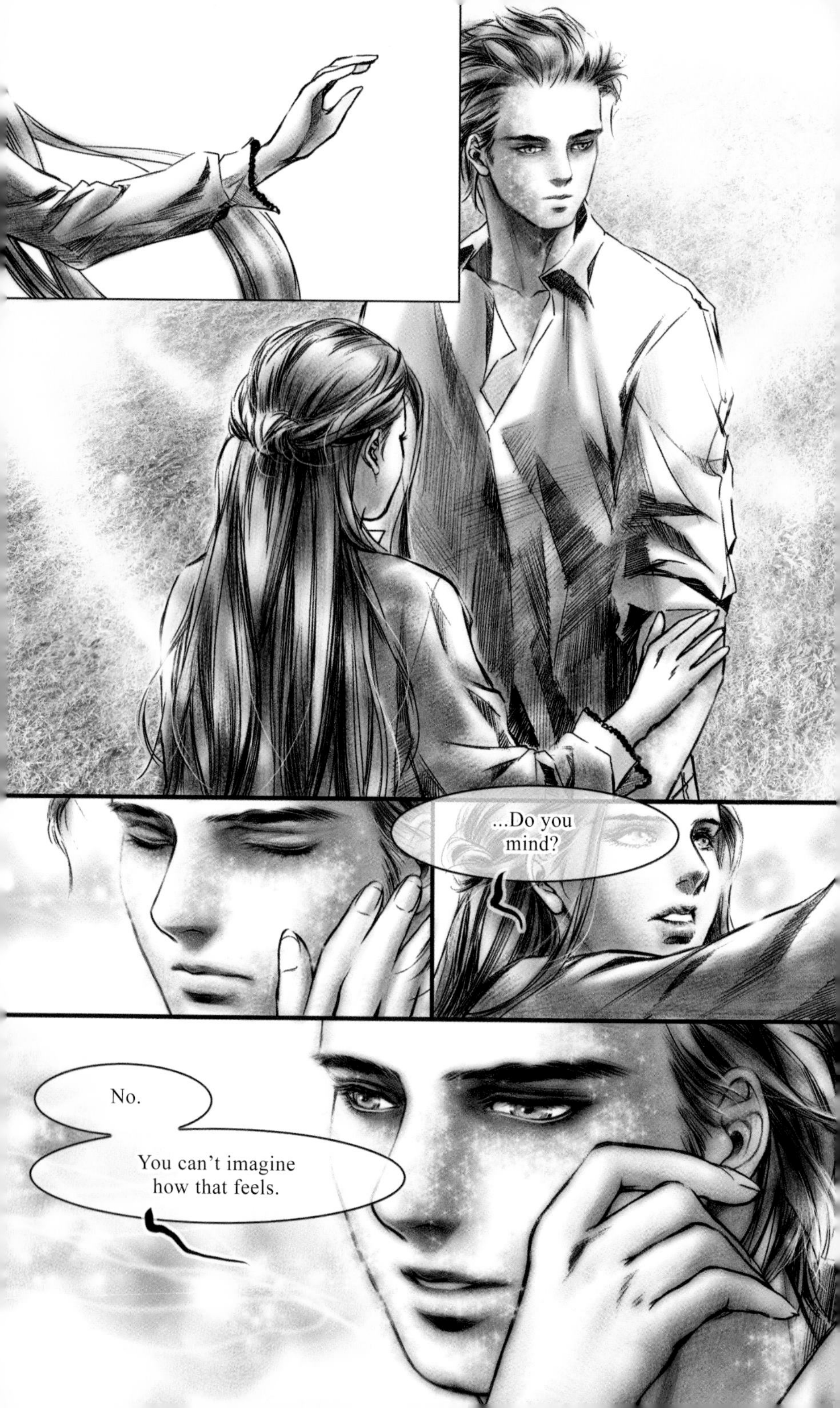
...Do you mind?
No.
You can't imagine how that feels.

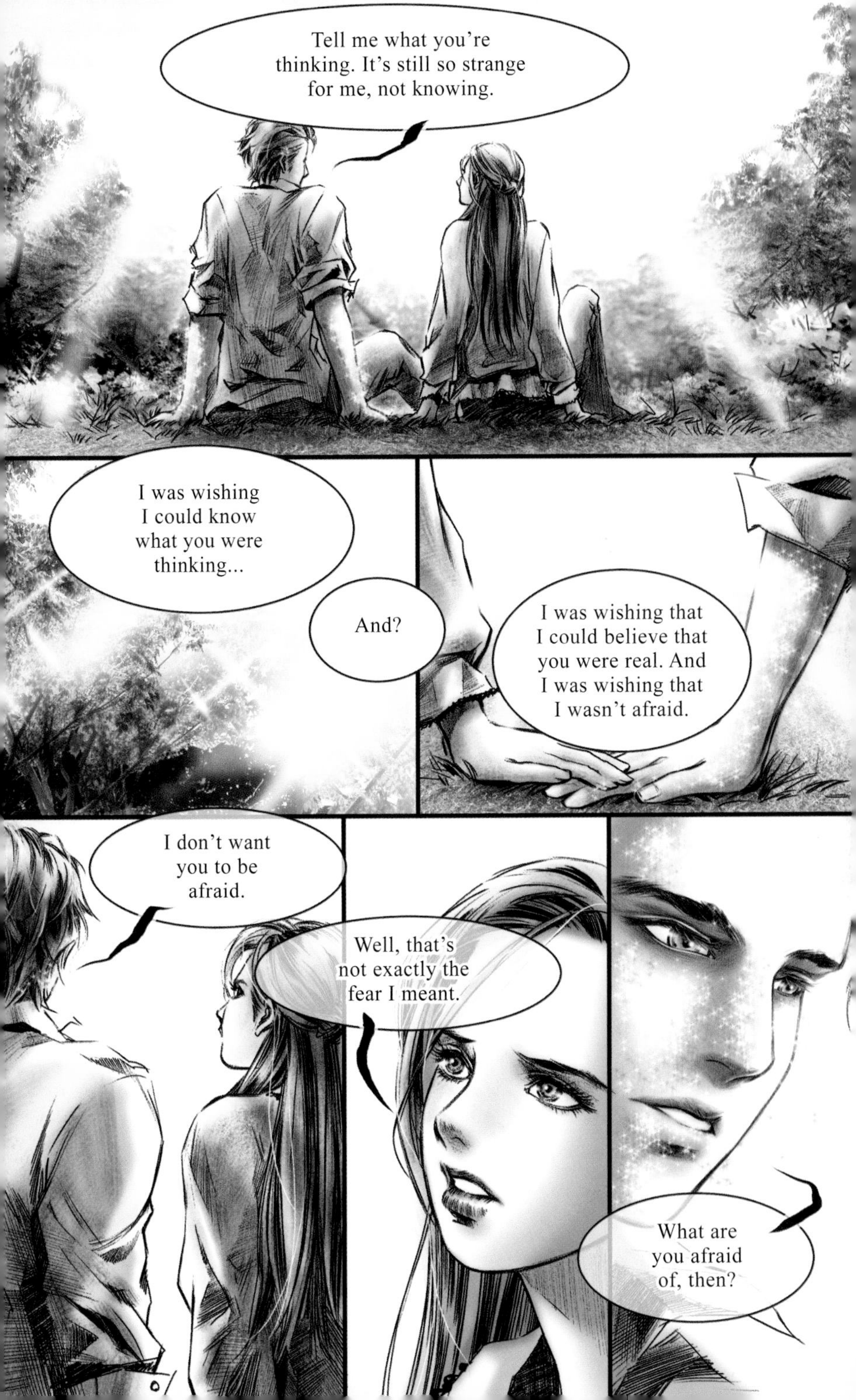
Tell me what you're thinking. It's still so strange for me, not knowing.
I was wishing I could know what you were thinking...
And?
I was wishing that I could believe that you were real. And I was wishing that I wasn't afraid.
I don't want you to be afraid.
Well, that's not exactly the fear I meant.
What are you afraid of, then?

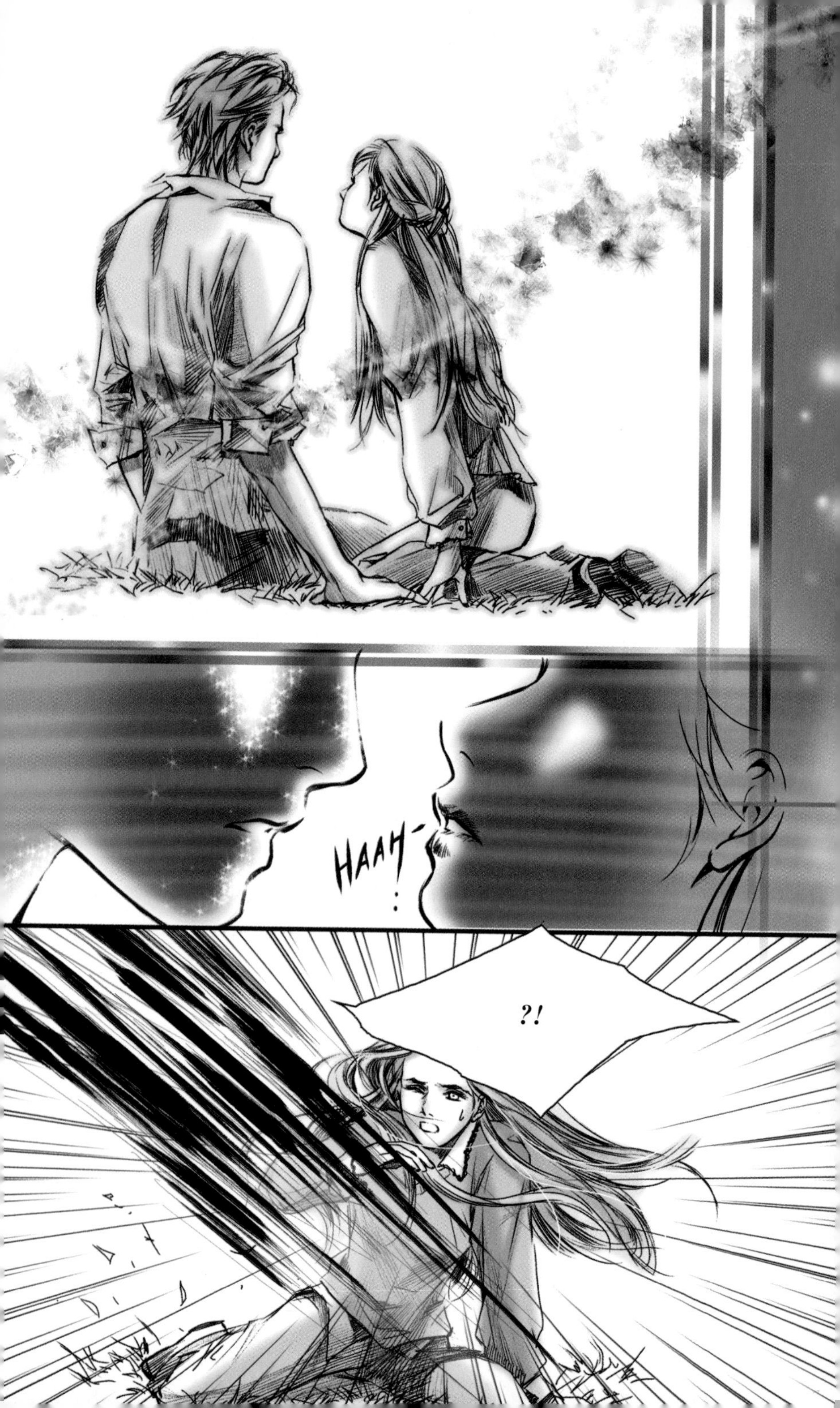
HAAH
?!

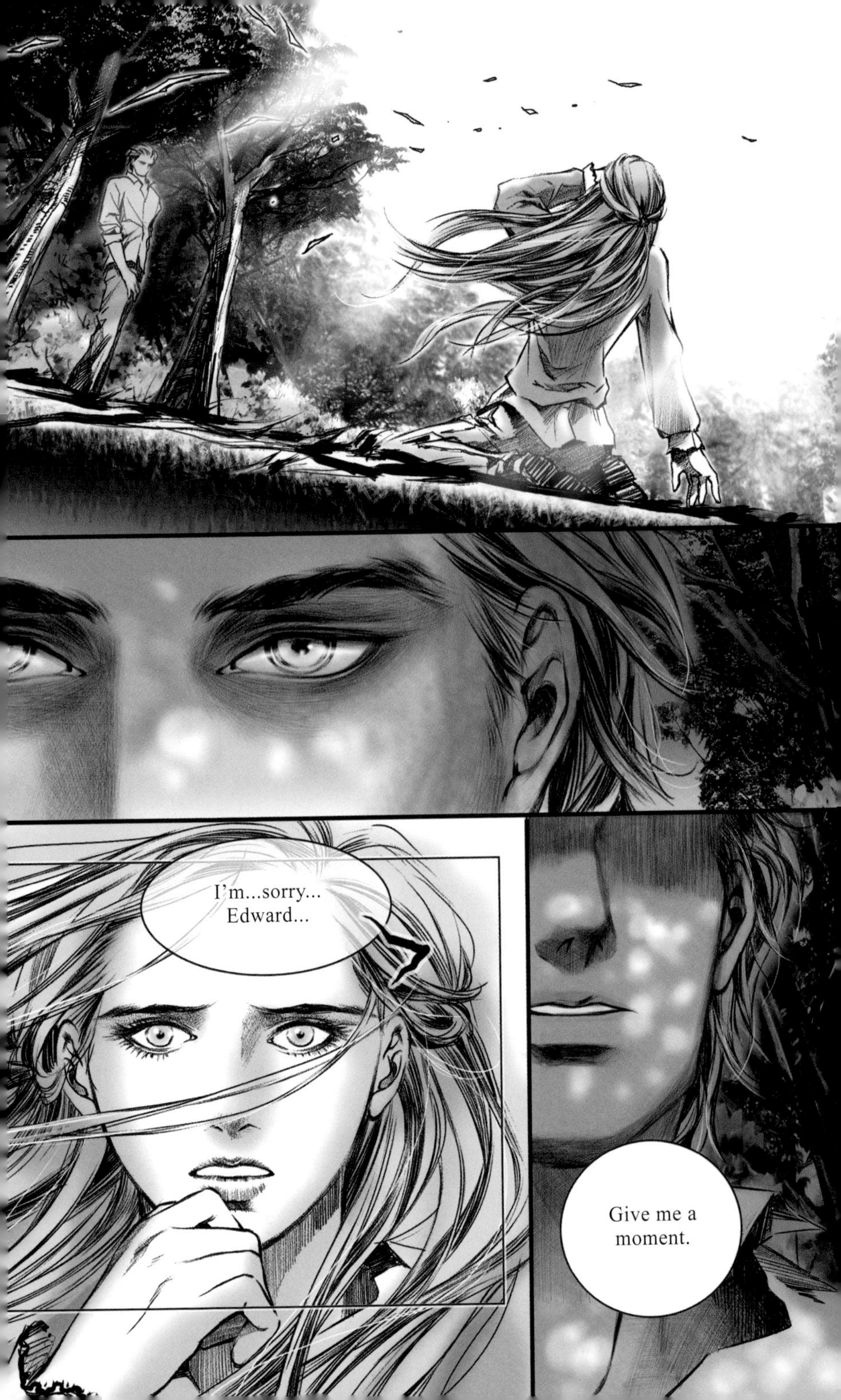
I'm...sorry...
Edward...
Give me a moment.

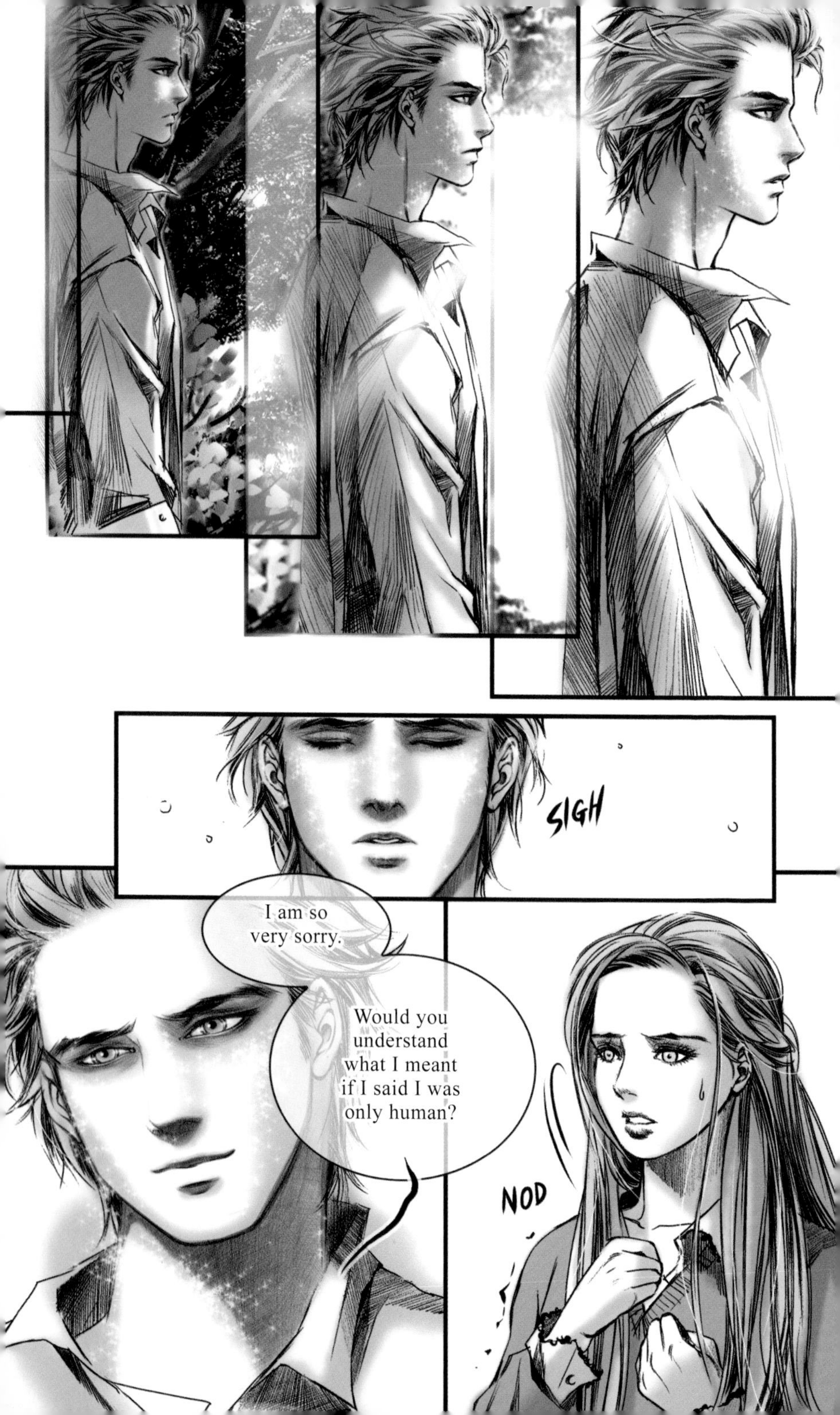
SIGH
I am so very sorry.
Would you understand what I meant if I said I was only human?
NOD

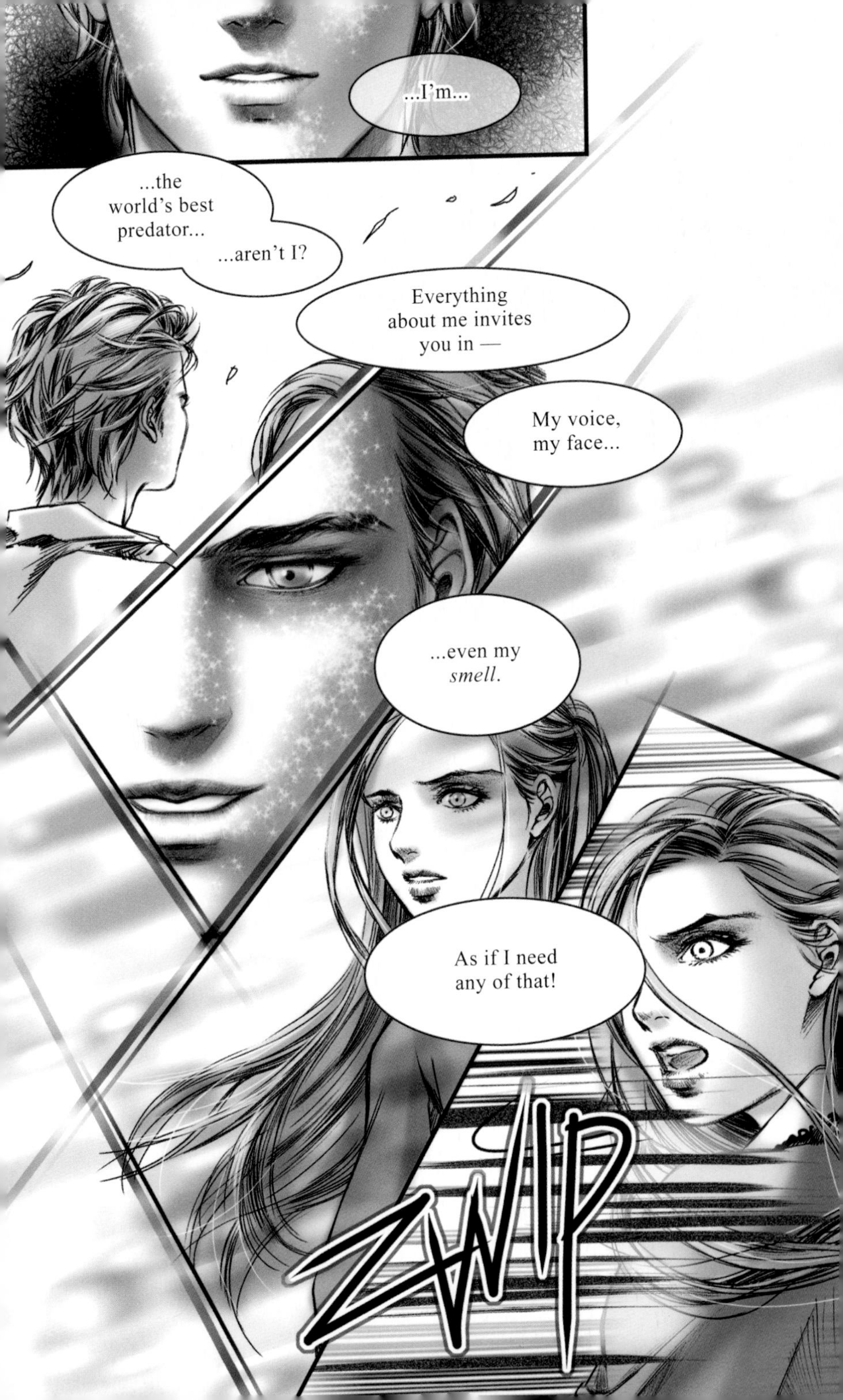
...I'm...
...the world's best predator... ...aren't I?
Everything about me invites you in —
My voice, my face...
...even my *smell*.
As if I need any of that!
ZWIP

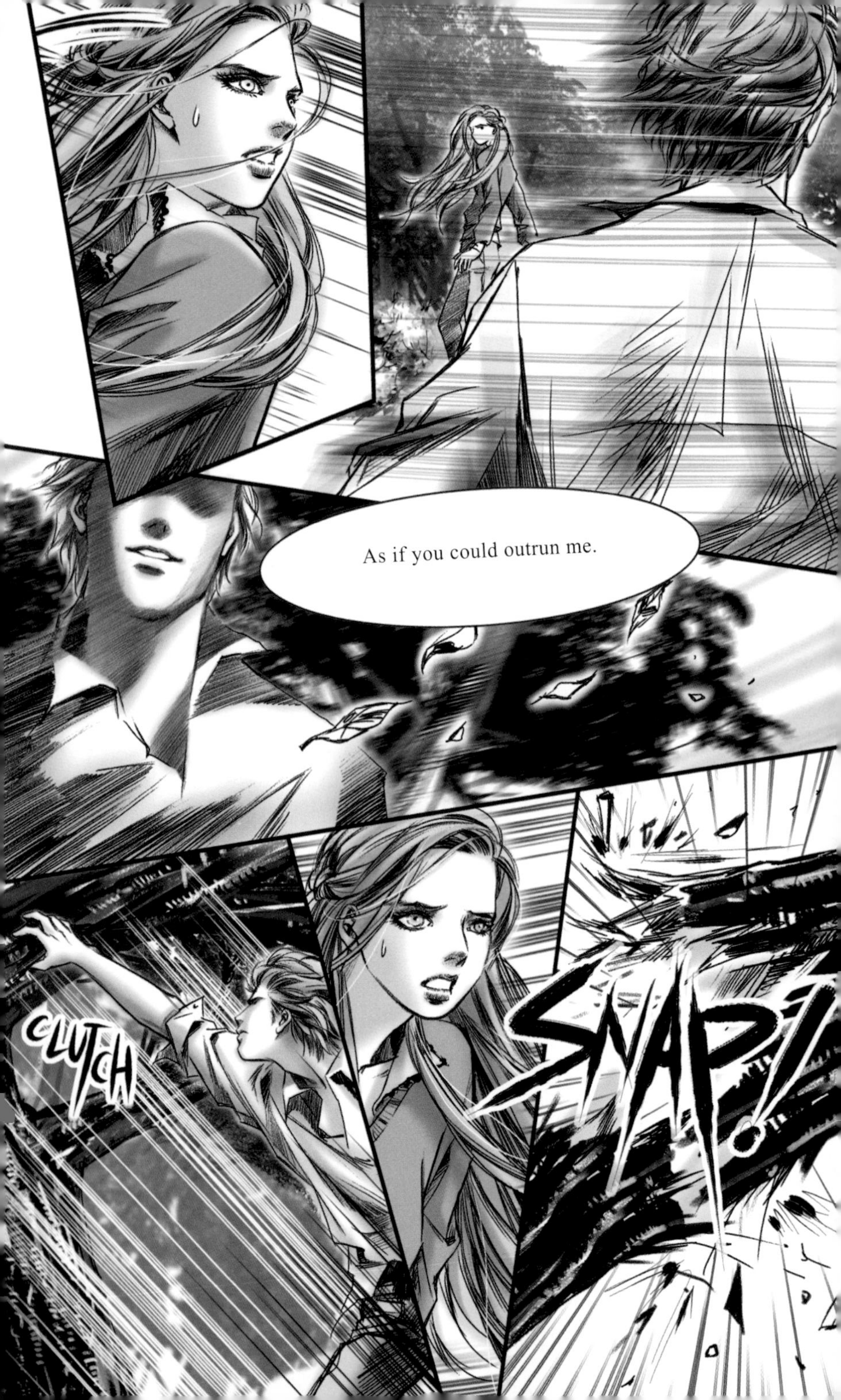
As if you could outrun me.
CLUTCH
SNAP!

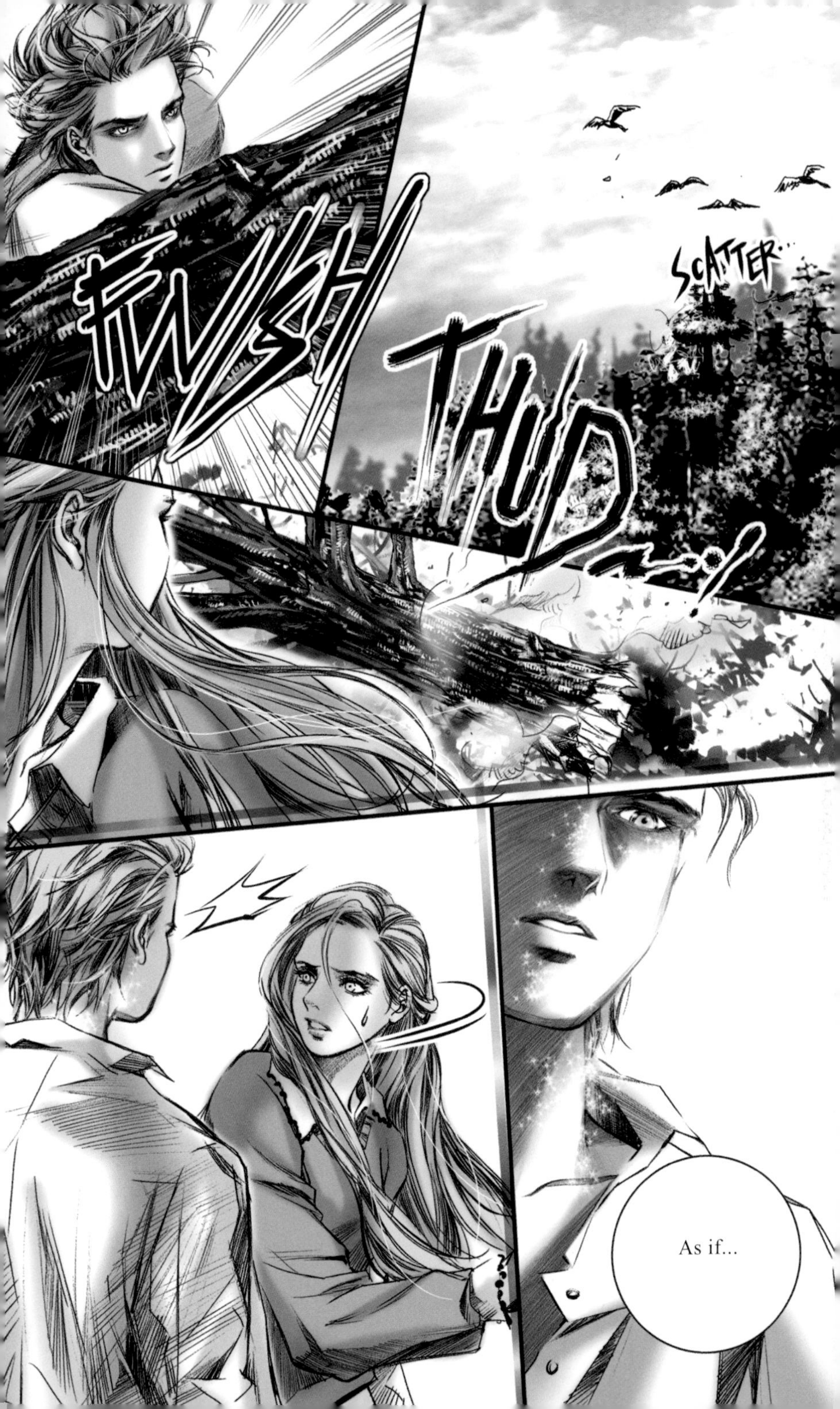
FWSH
SCATTER...
THUD...!
As if...

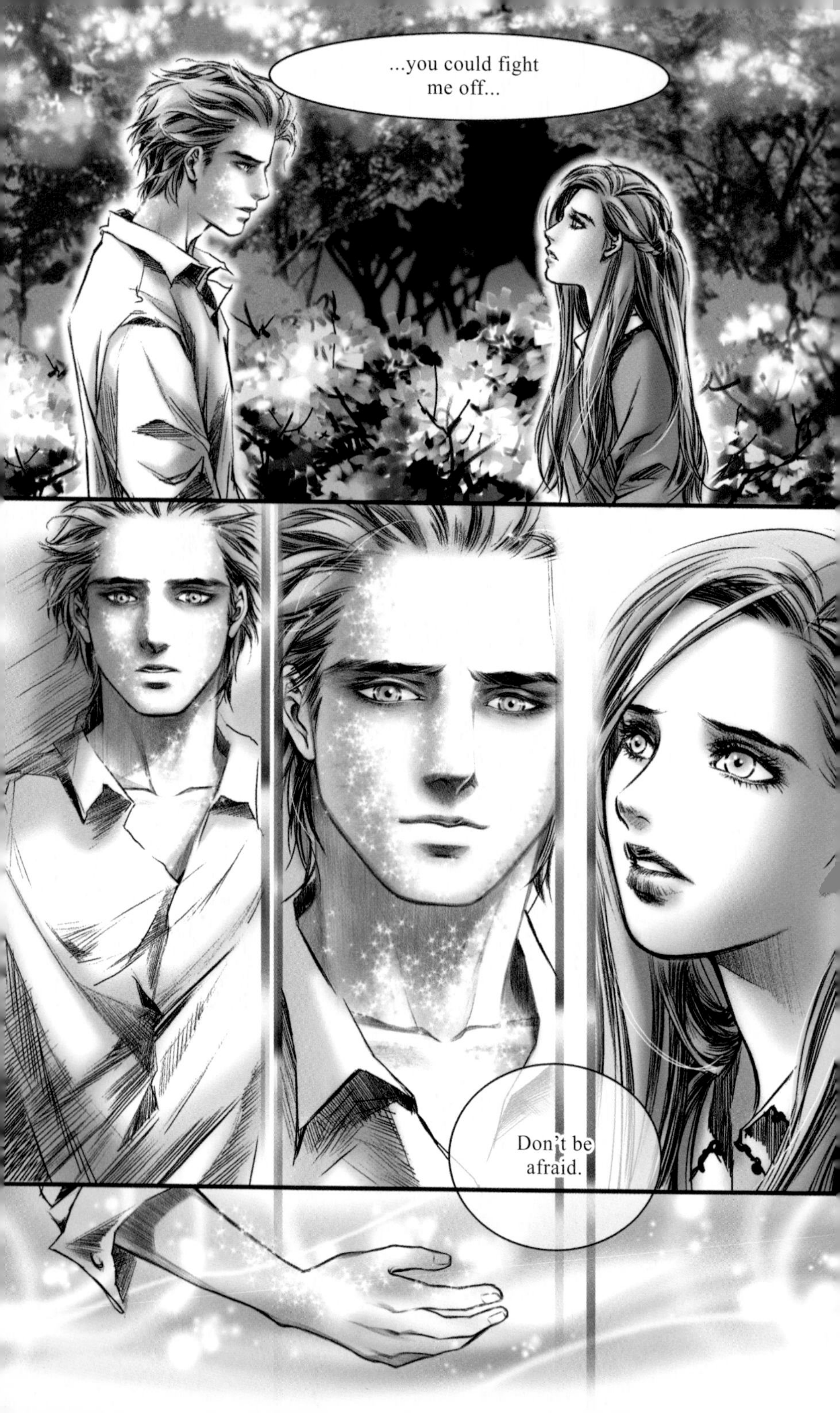
...you could fight me off...
Don't be afraid.

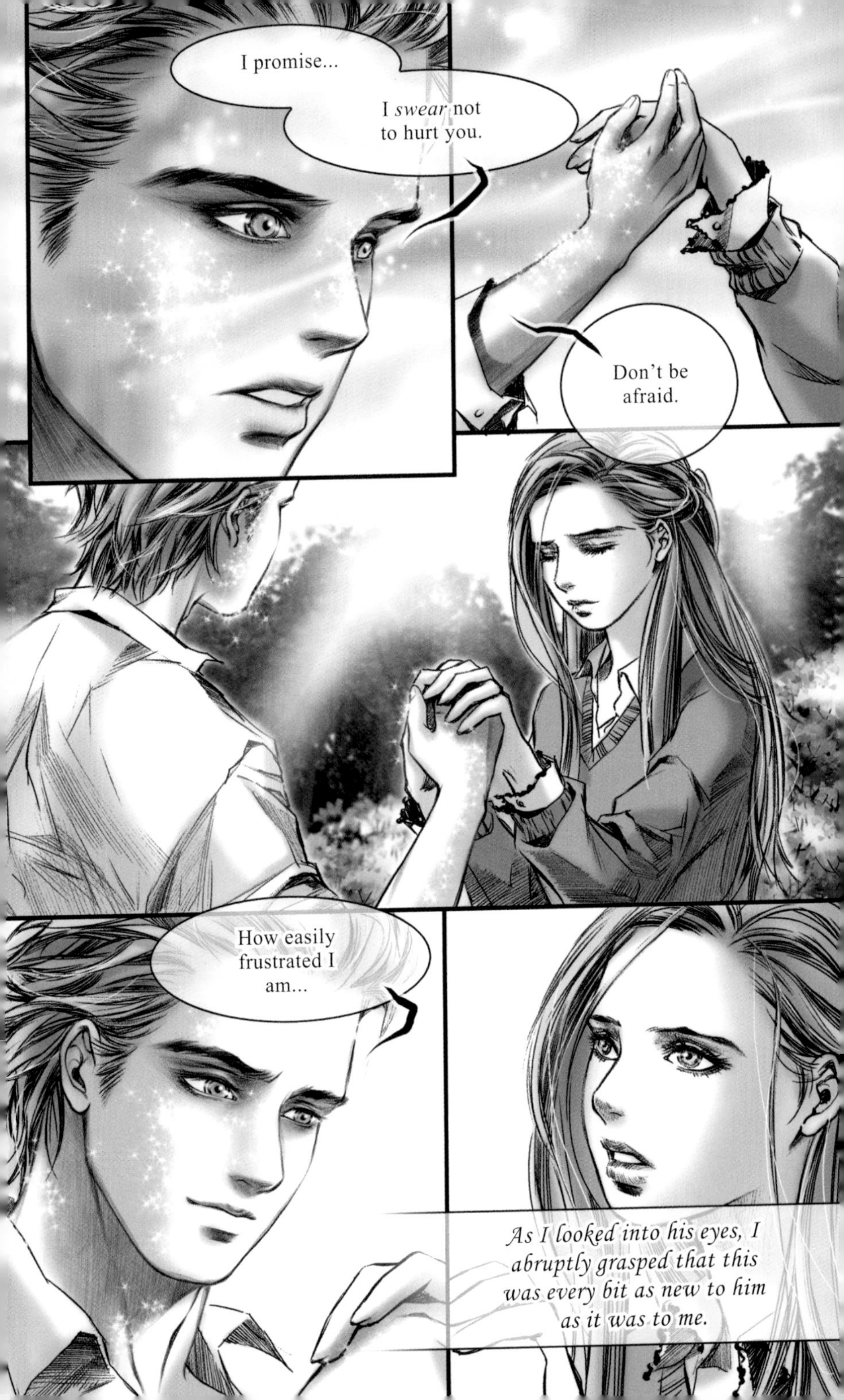
I promise...
I *swear* not to hurt you.
Don't be afraid.
How easily frustrated I am...
As I looked into his eyes, I abruptly grasped that this was every bit as new to him as it was to me.

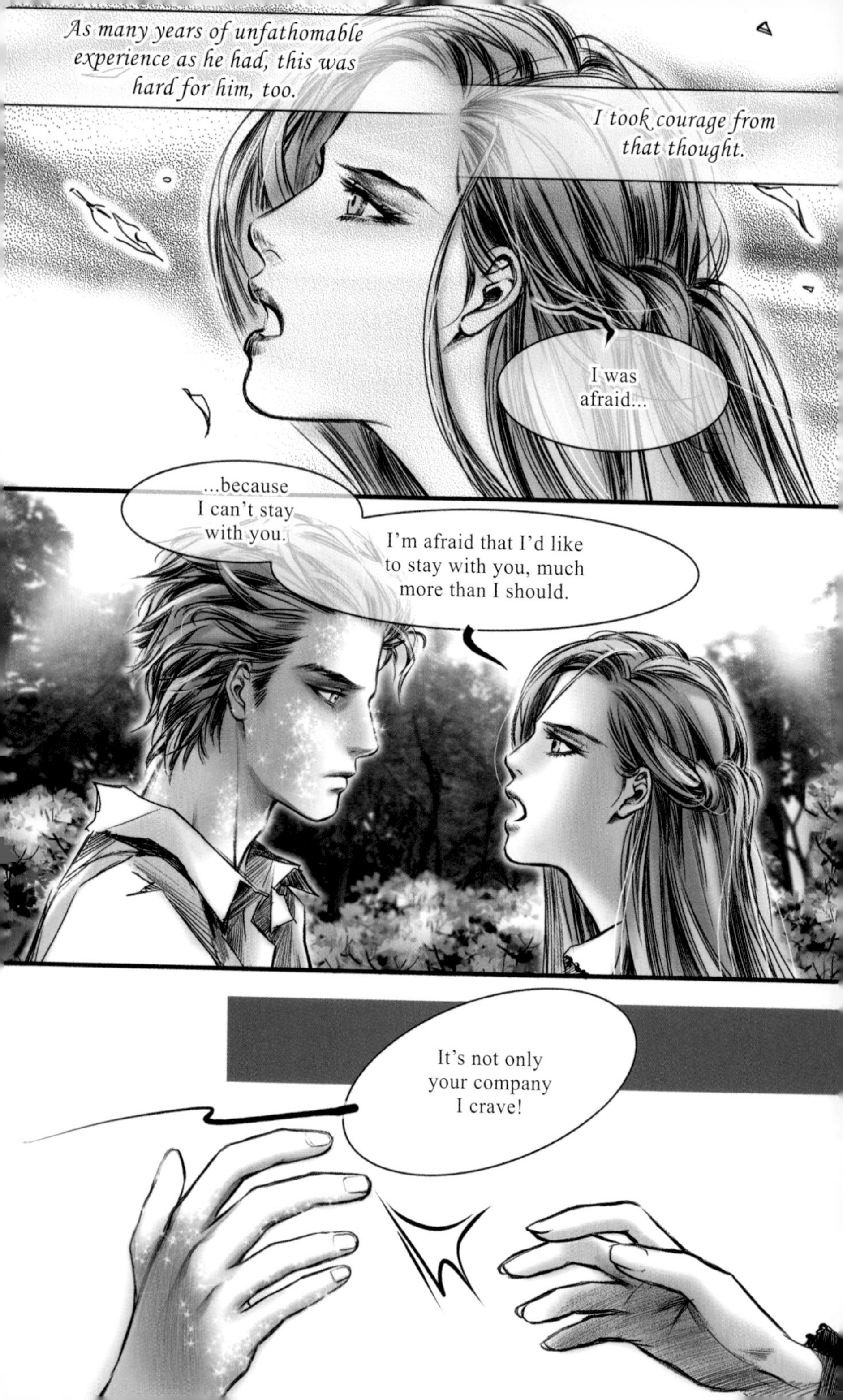
As many years of unfathomable experience as he had, this was hard for him, too.
I took courage from that thought.
I was afraid...
...because I can't stay with you.
I'm afraid that I'd like to stay with you, much more than I should.
It's not only your company I crave!

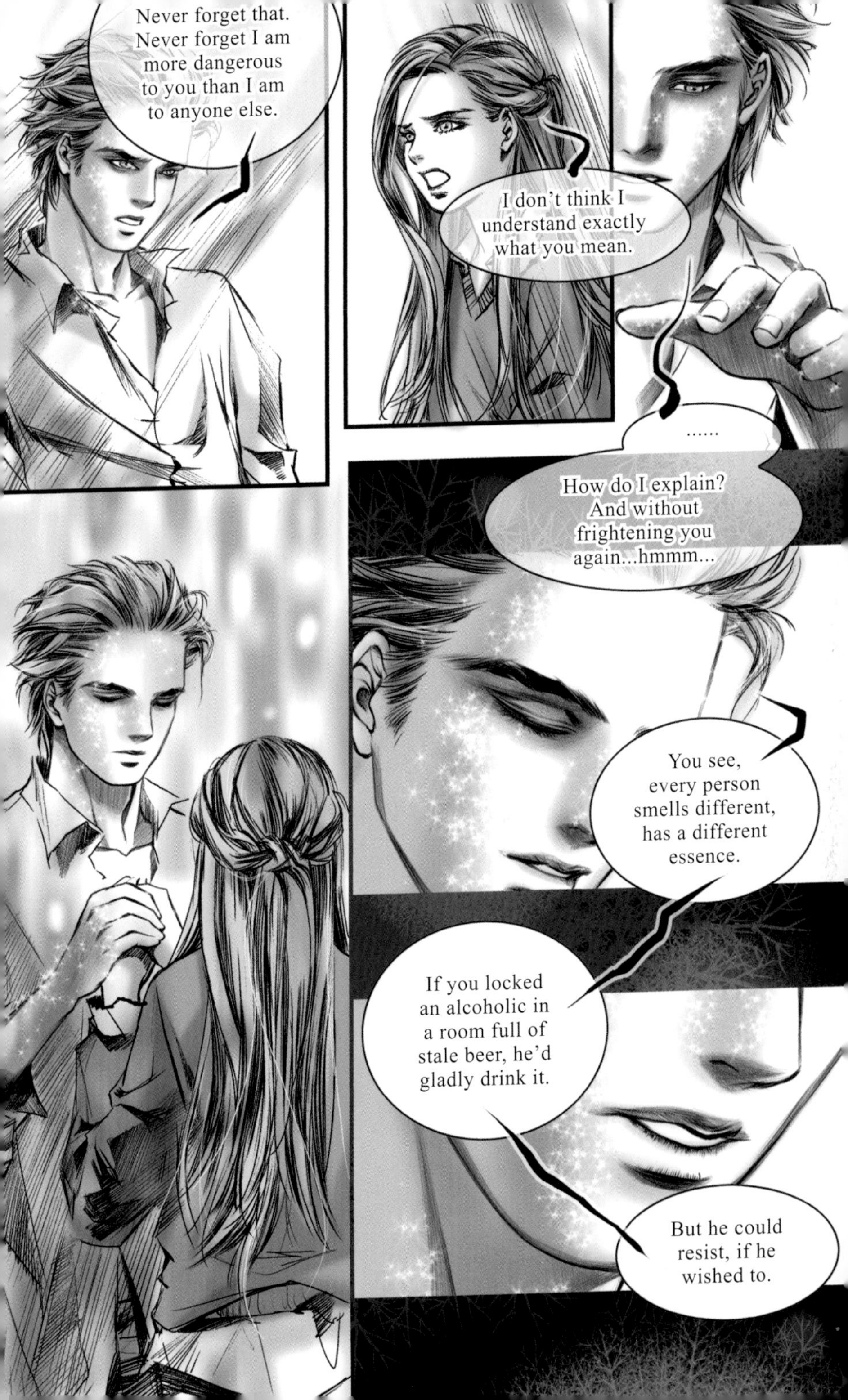
Never forget that. Never forget I am more dangerous to you than I am to anyone else.
I don't think I understand exactly what you mean.
......
How do I explain? And without frightening you again...hmmm...
You see, every person smells different, has a different essence.
If you locked an alcoholic in a room full of stale beer, he'd gladly drink it.
But he could resist, if he wished to.

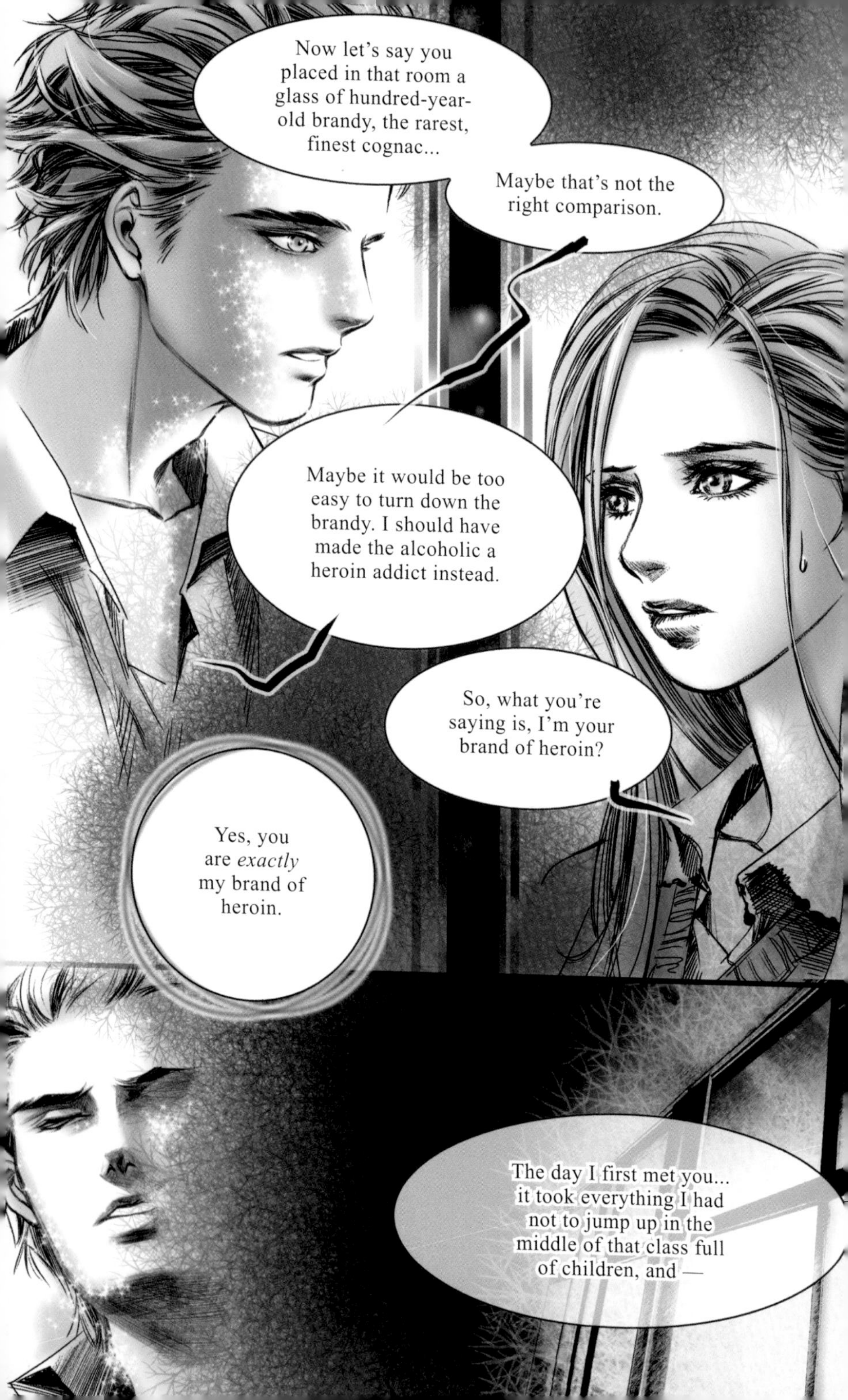
Now let's say you placed in that room a glass of hundred-year-old brandy, the rarest, finest cognac...
Maybe that's not the right comparison.
Maybe it would be too easy to turn down the brandy. I should have made the alcoholic a heroin addict instead.
So, what you're saying is, I'm your brand of heroin?
Yes, you are *exactly* my brand of heroin.
The day I first met you... it took everything I had not to jump up in the middle of that class full of children, and —

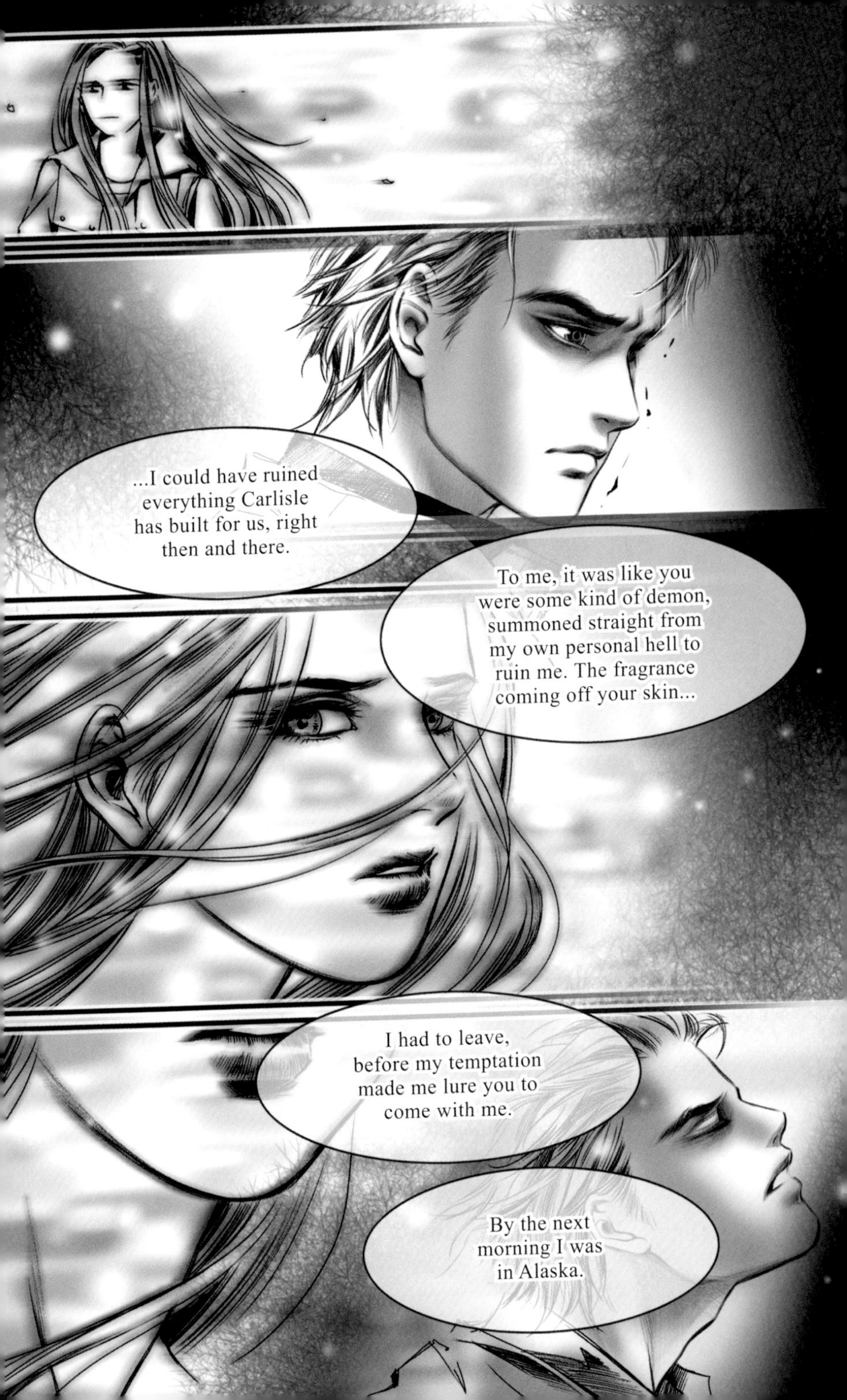
...I could have ruined everything Carlisle has built for us, right then and there.
To me, it was like you were some kind of demon, summoned straight from my own personal hell to ruin me. The fragrance coming off your skin...
I had to leave, before my temptation made me lure you to come with me.
By the next morning I was in Alaska.

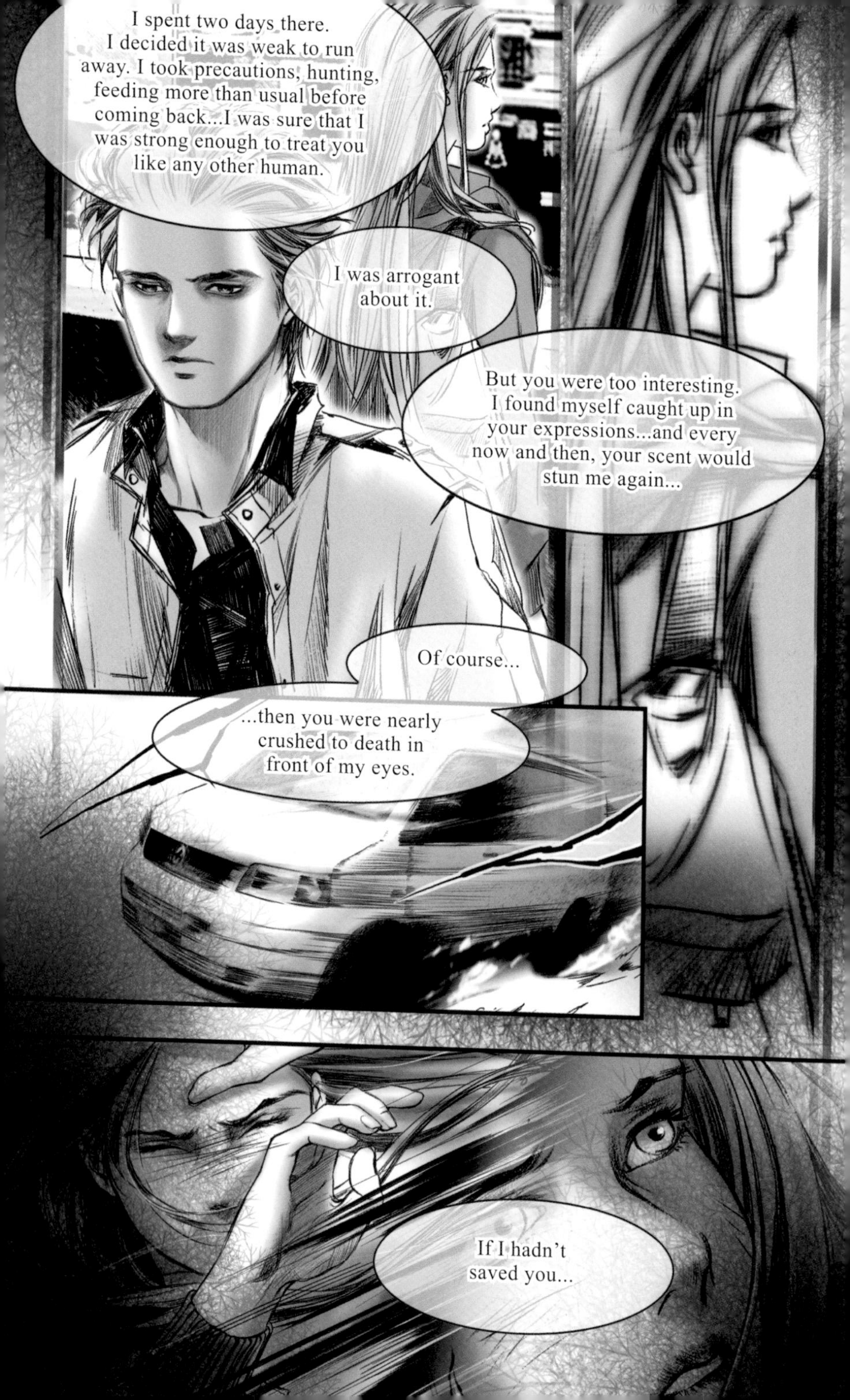
I spent two days there. I decided it was weak to run away. I took precautions, hunting, feeding more than usual before coming back...I was sure that I was strong enough to treat you like any other human.
I was arrogant about it.
But you were too interesting. I found myself caught up in your expressions...and every now and then, your scent would stun me again...
Of course...
...then you were nearly crushed to death in front of my eyes.
If I hadn't saved you...

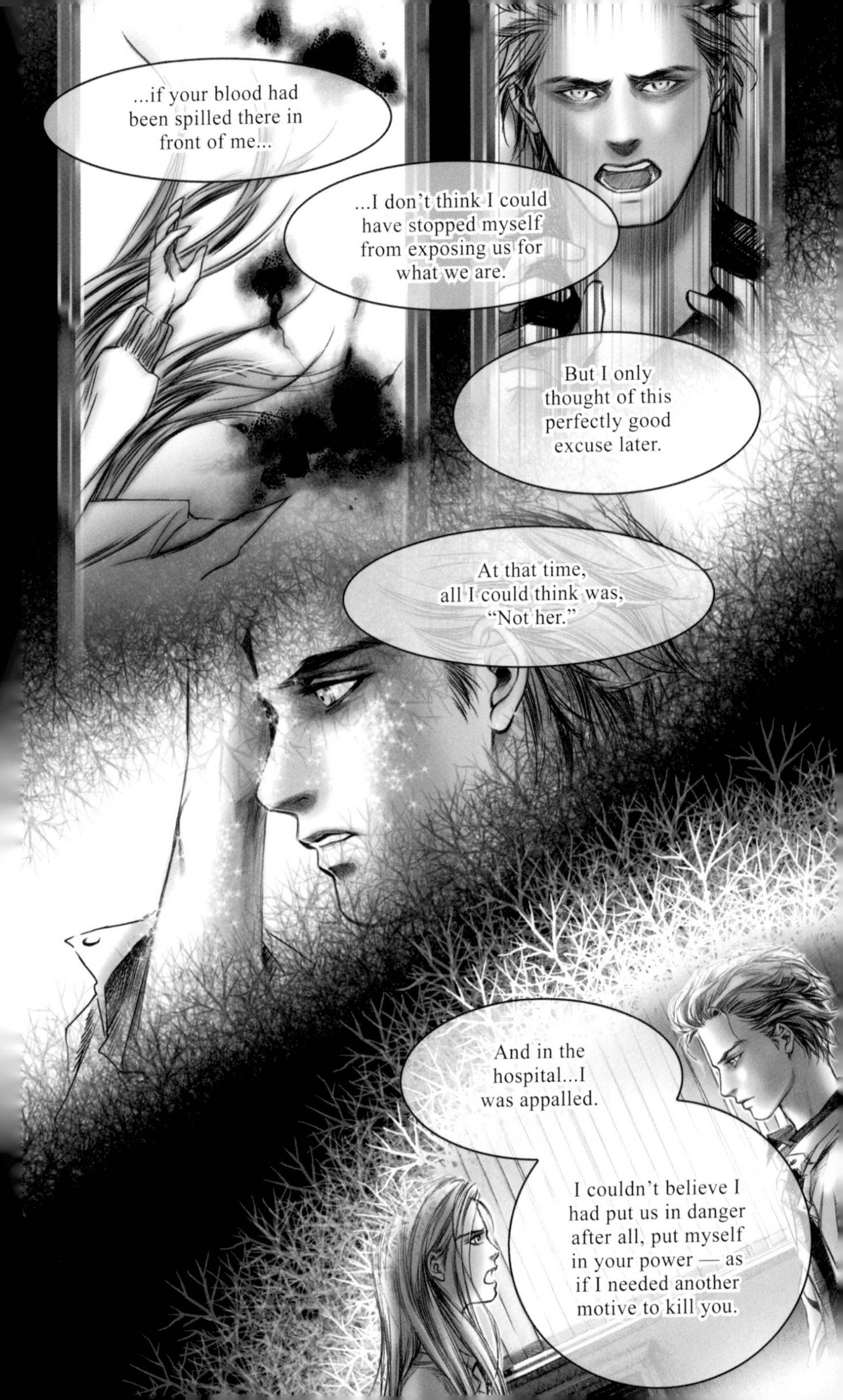
...if your blood had been spilled there in front of me...
...I don't think I could have stopped myself from exposing us for what we are.
But I only thought of this perfectly good excuse later.
At that time, all I could think was, "Not her."
And in the hospital...I was appalled.
I couldn't believe I had put us in danger after all, put myself in your power — as if I needed another motive to kill you.

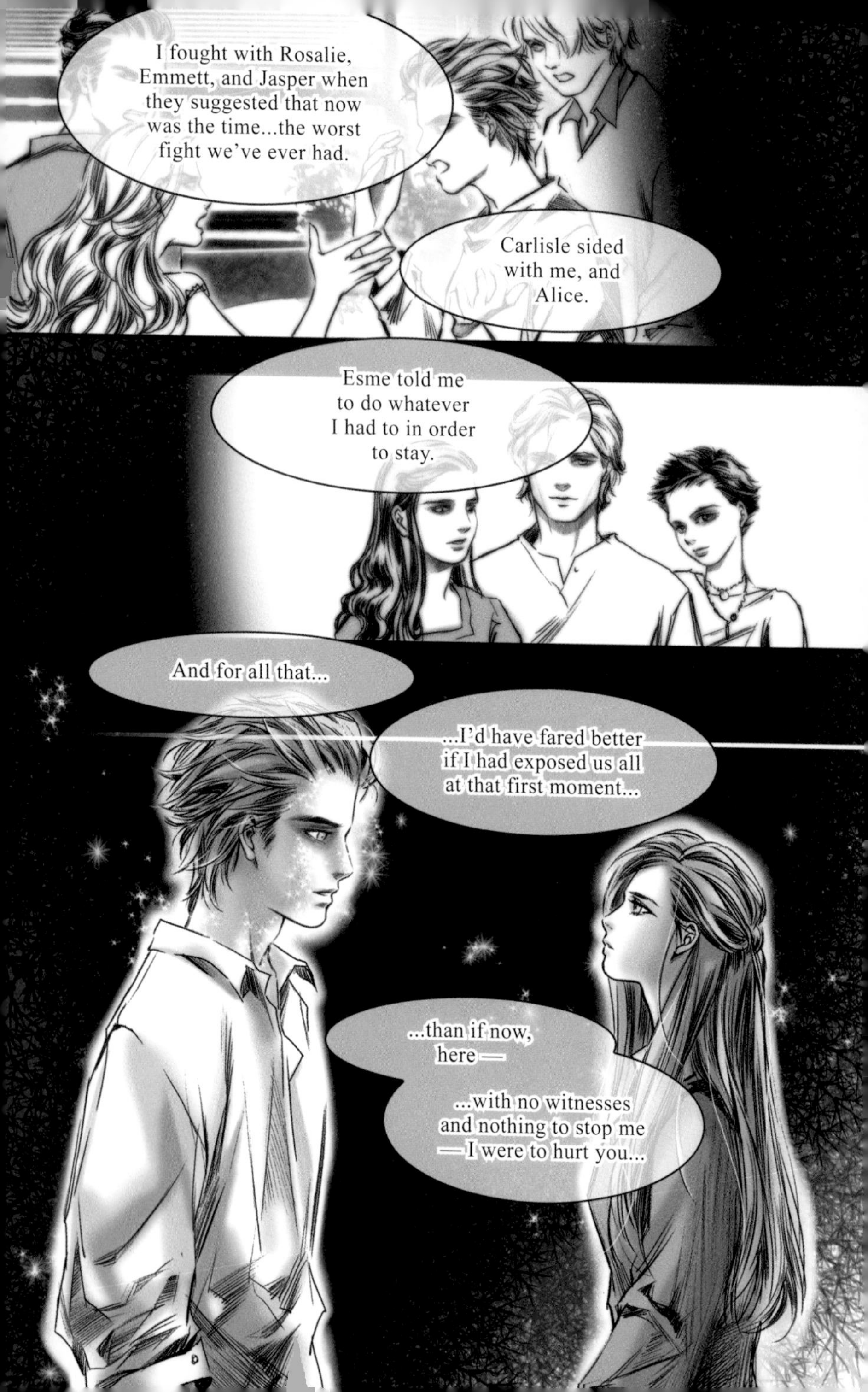
I fought with Rosalie, Emmett, and Jasper when they suggested that now was the time...the worst fight we've ever had.
Carlisle sided with me, and Alice.
Esme told me to do whatever I had to in order to stay.
And for all that...
...I'd have fared better if I had exposed us all at that first moment...
...than if now, here —
...with no witnesses and nothing to stop me —I were to hurt you...

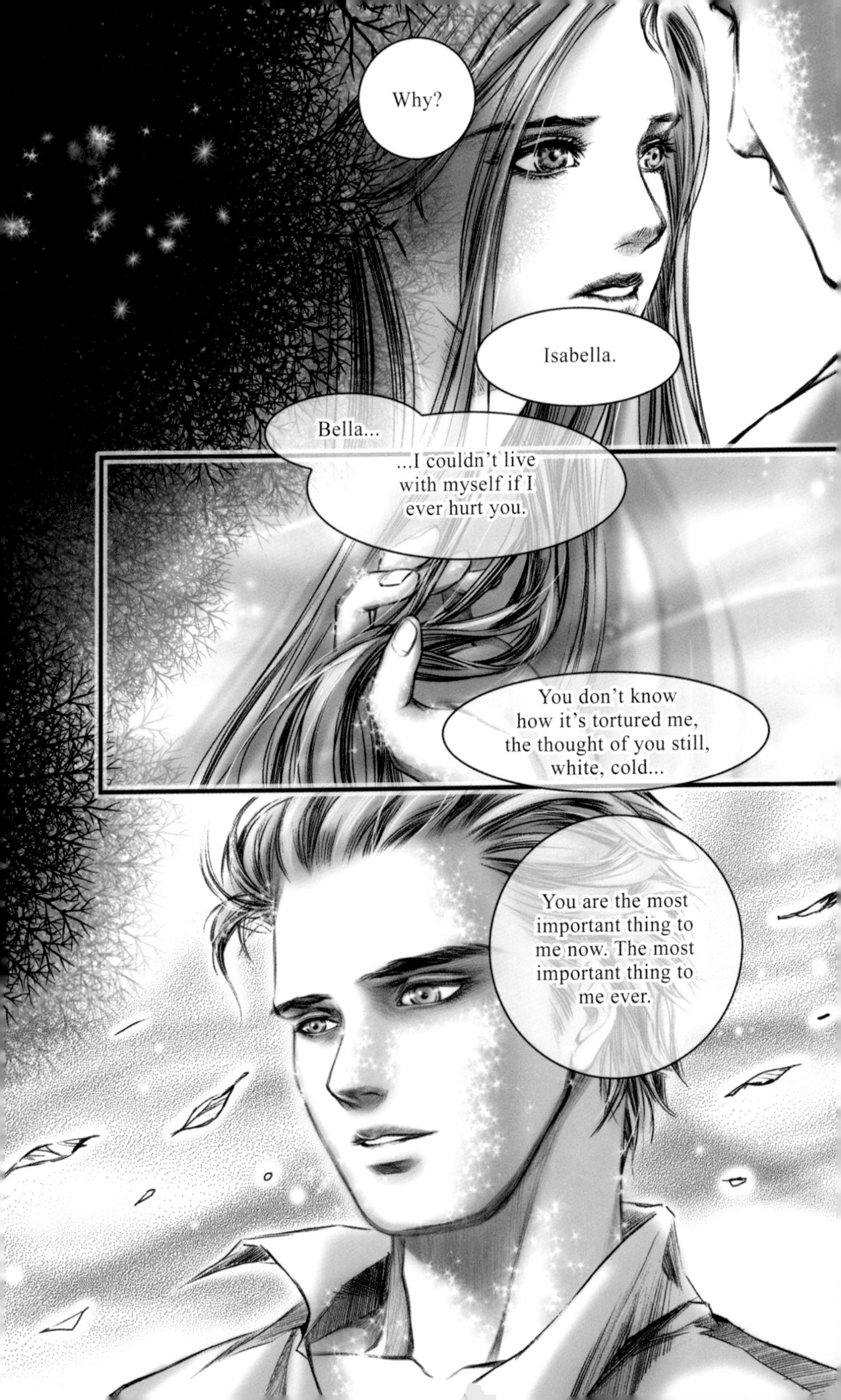
Why?
Isabella.
Bella...
...I couldn't live with myself if I ever hurt you.
You don't know how it's tortured me, the thought of you still, white, cold...
You are the most important thing to me now. The most important thing to me ever.

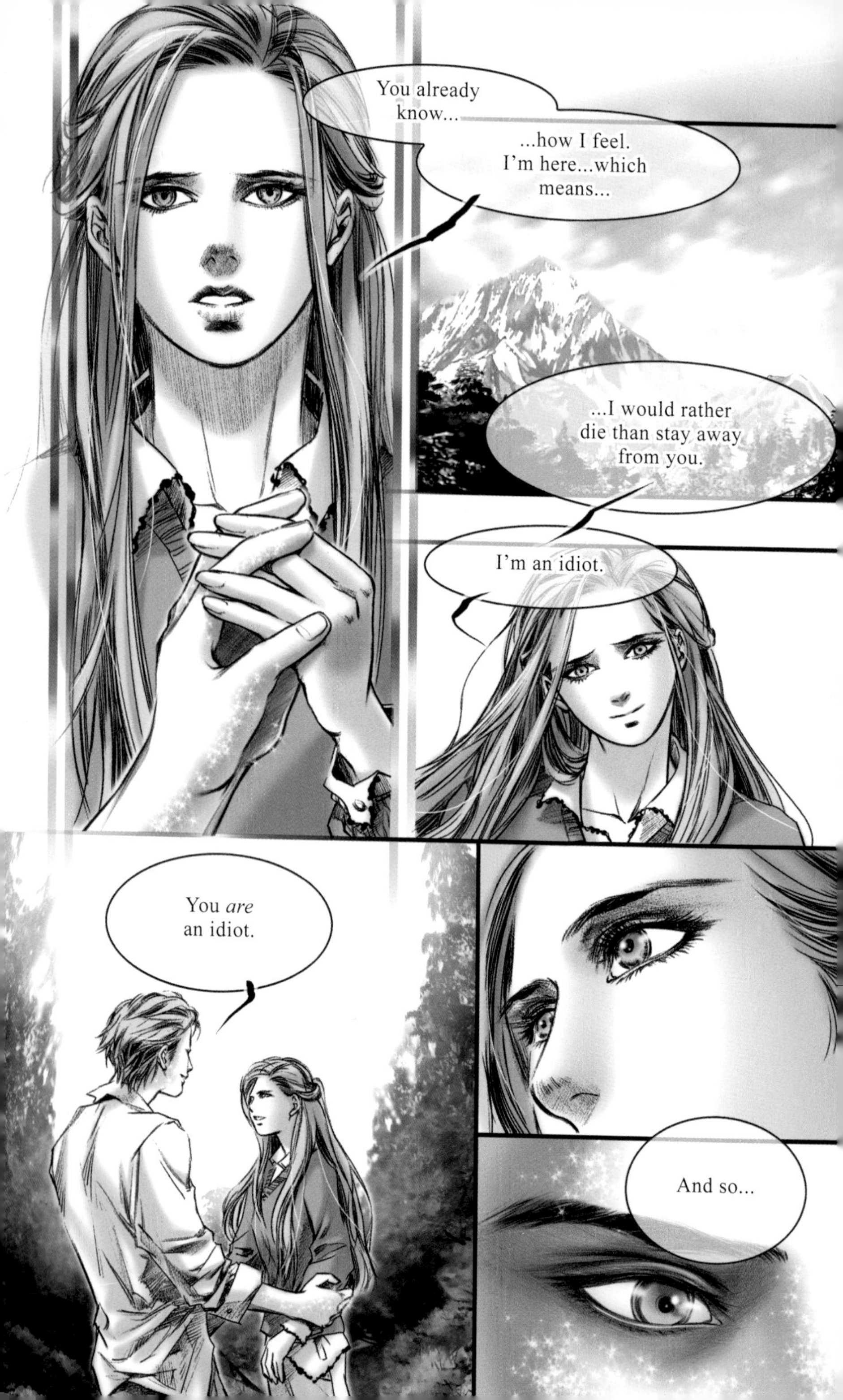
You already know...
...how I feel. I'm here...which means...
...I would rather die than stay away from you.
I'm an idiot.
You *are* an idiot.
And so...

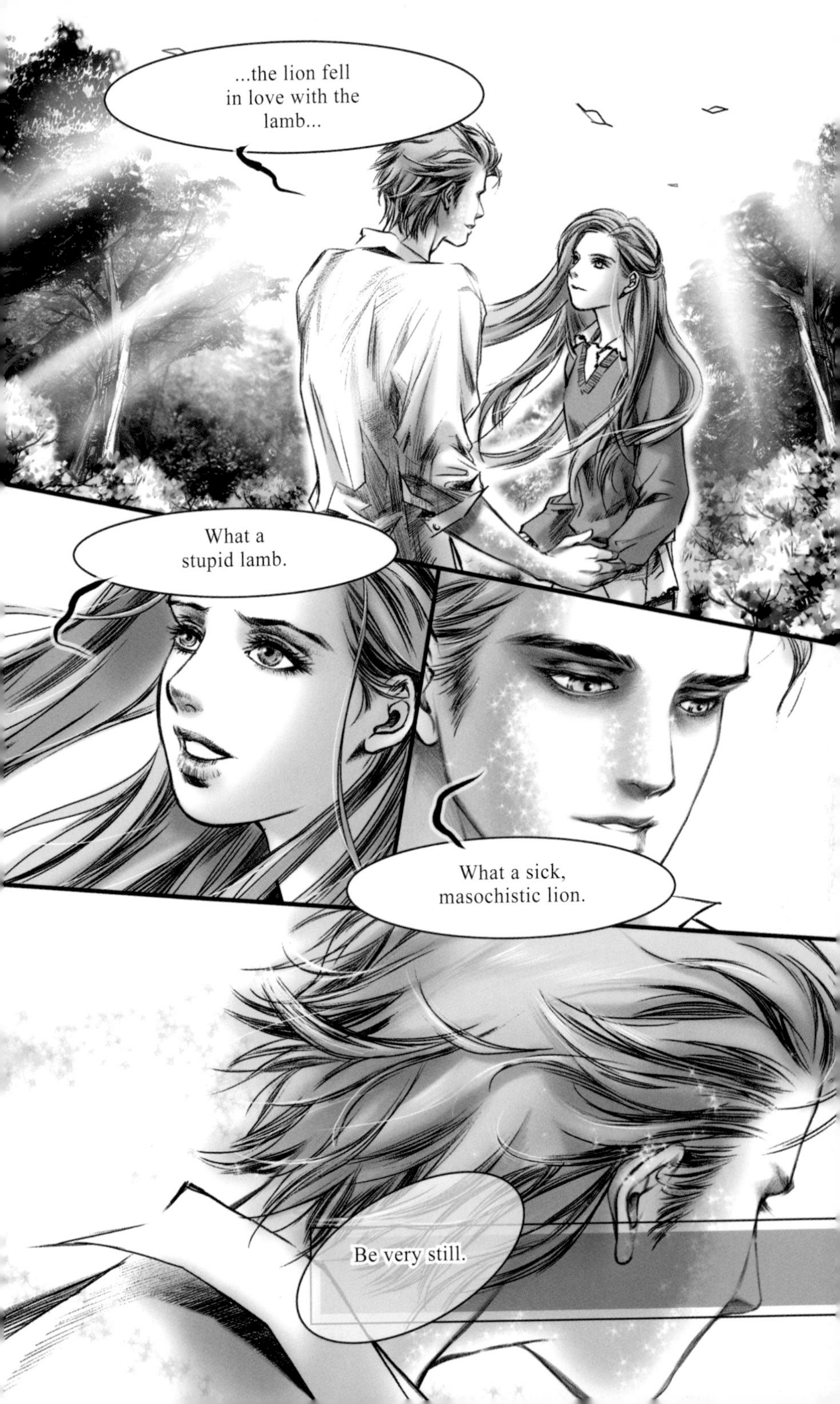
...the lion fell in love with the lamb...
What a stupid lamb.
What a sick, masochistic lion.
Be very still.

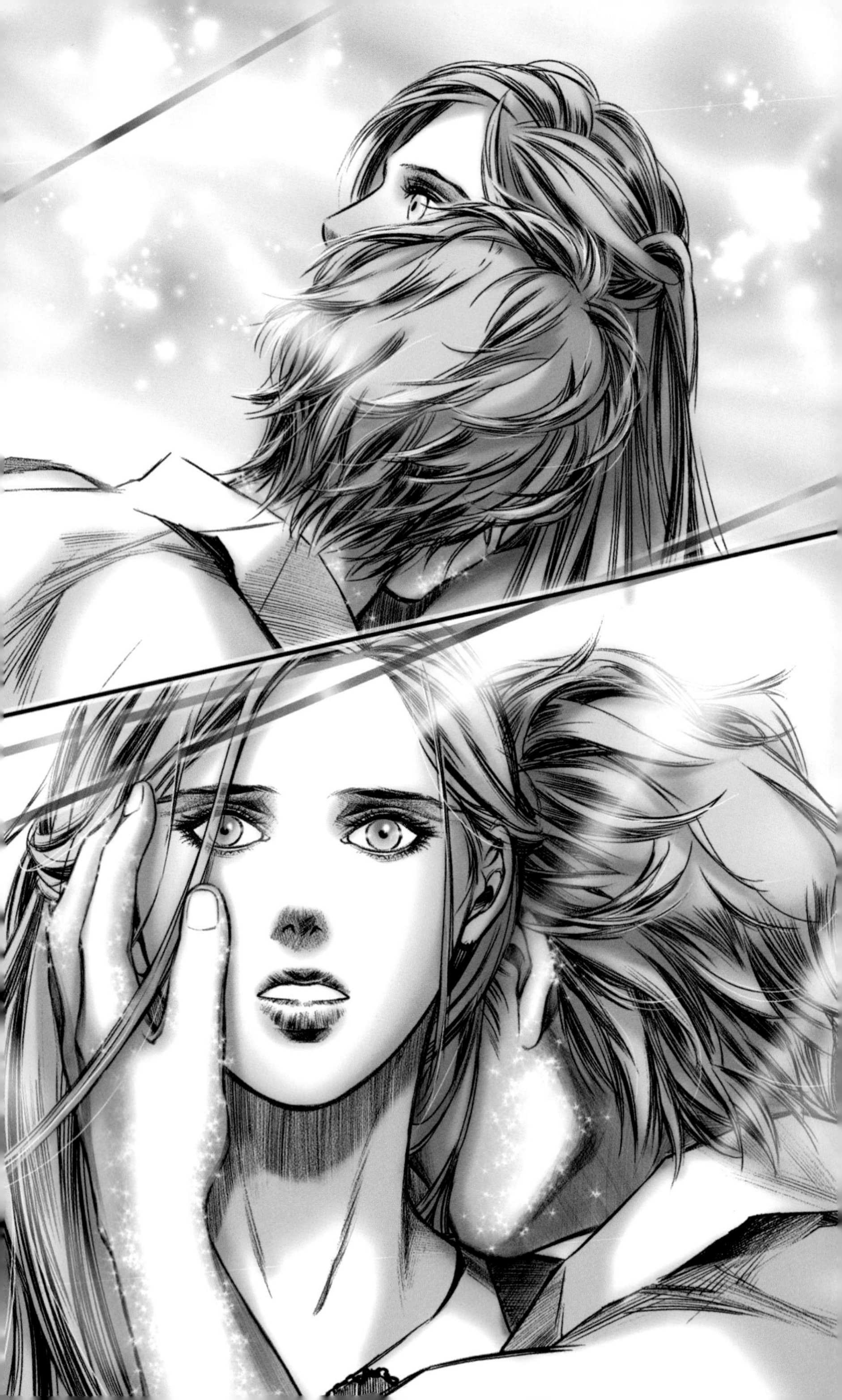

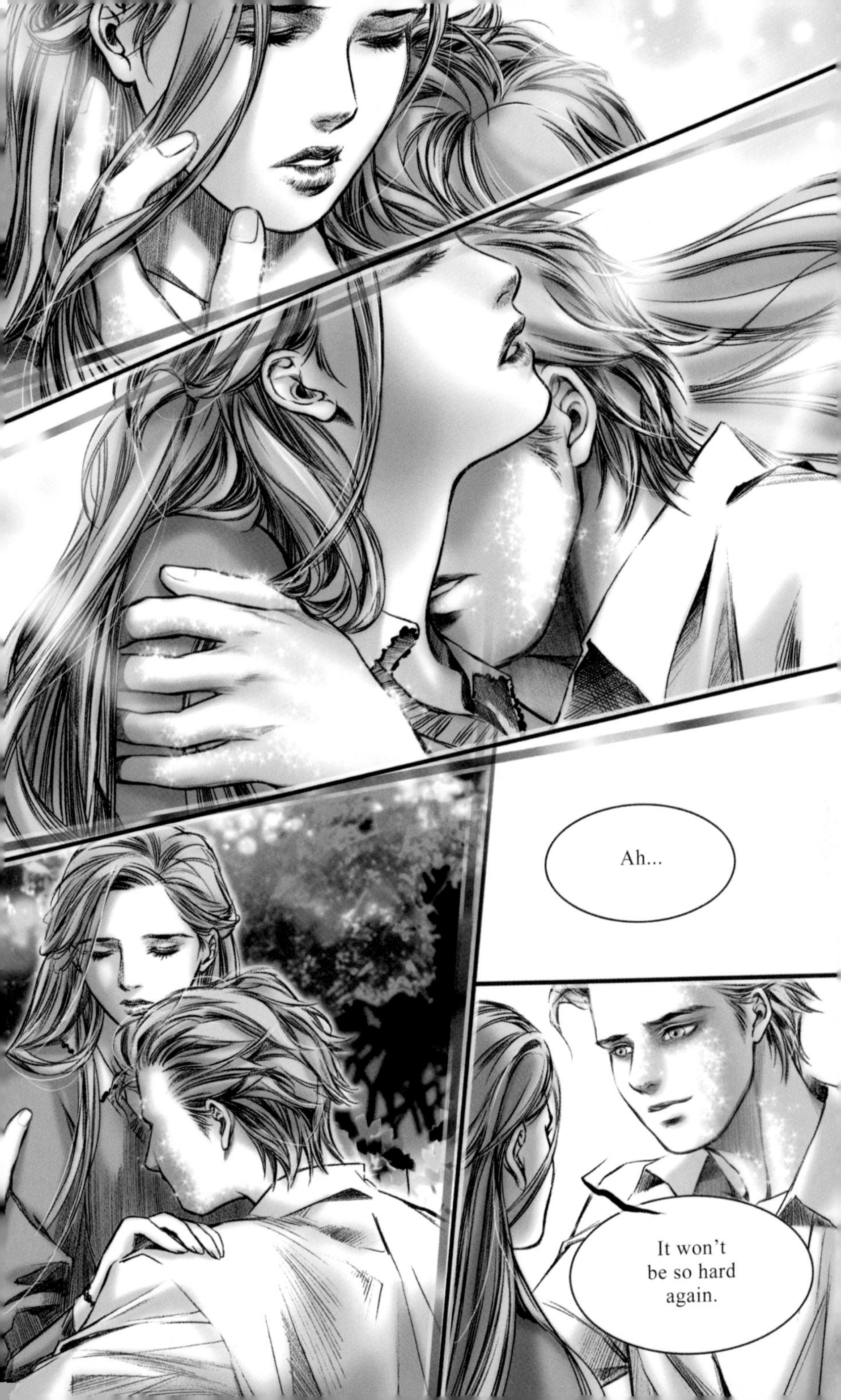
Ah...
It won't be so hard again.

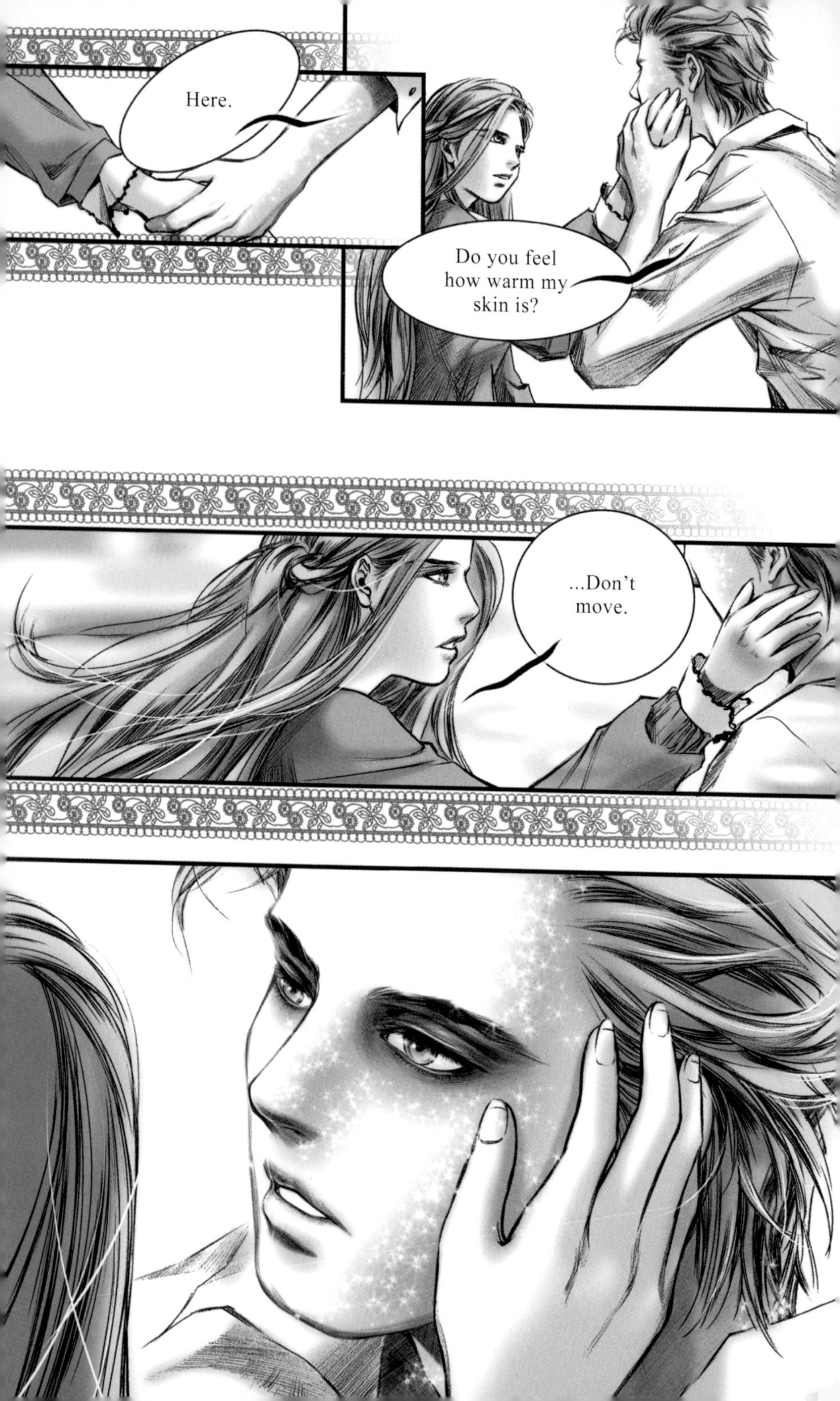
Here.
Do you feel how warm my skin is?
...Don't move.

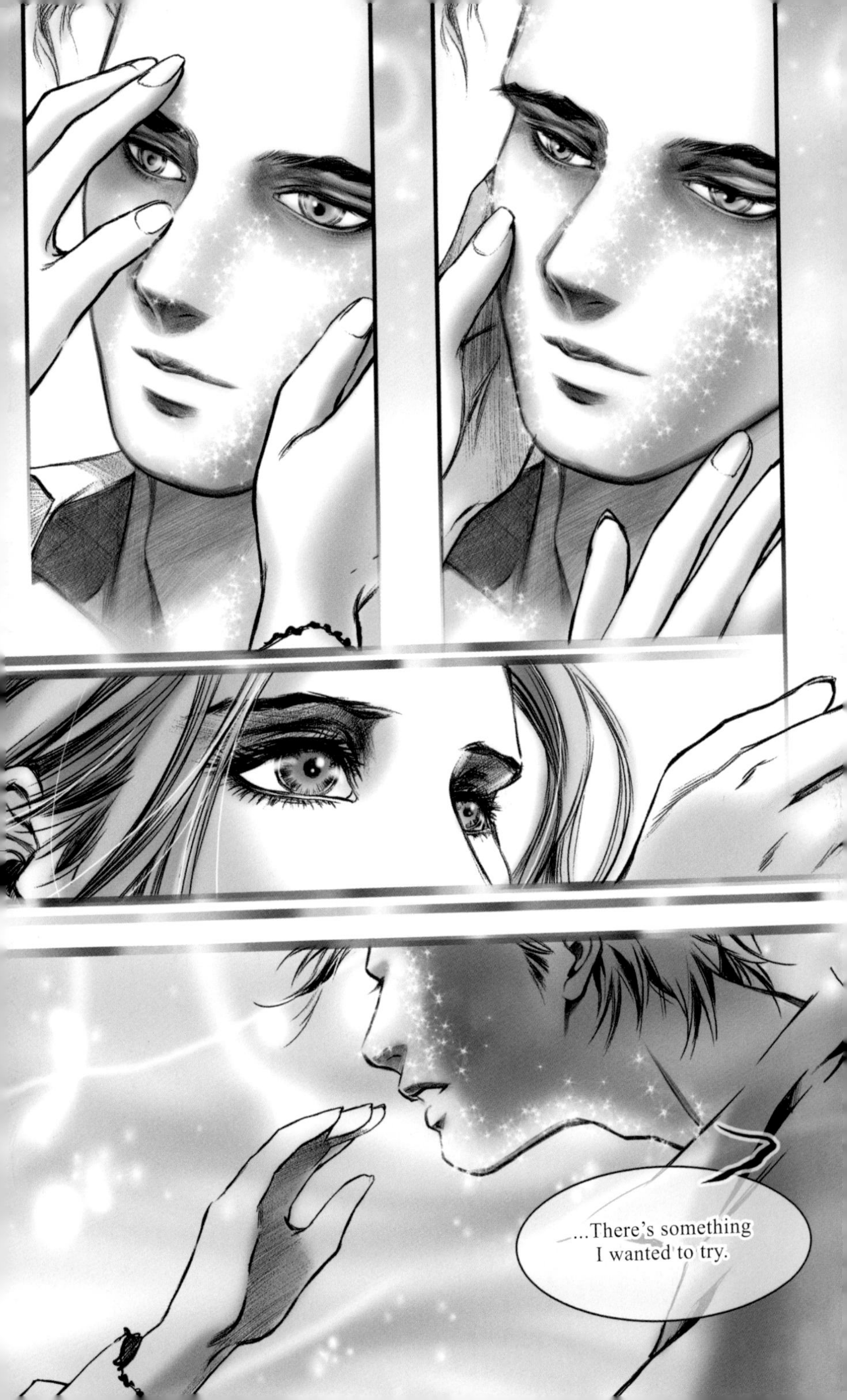
...There's something I wanted to try.

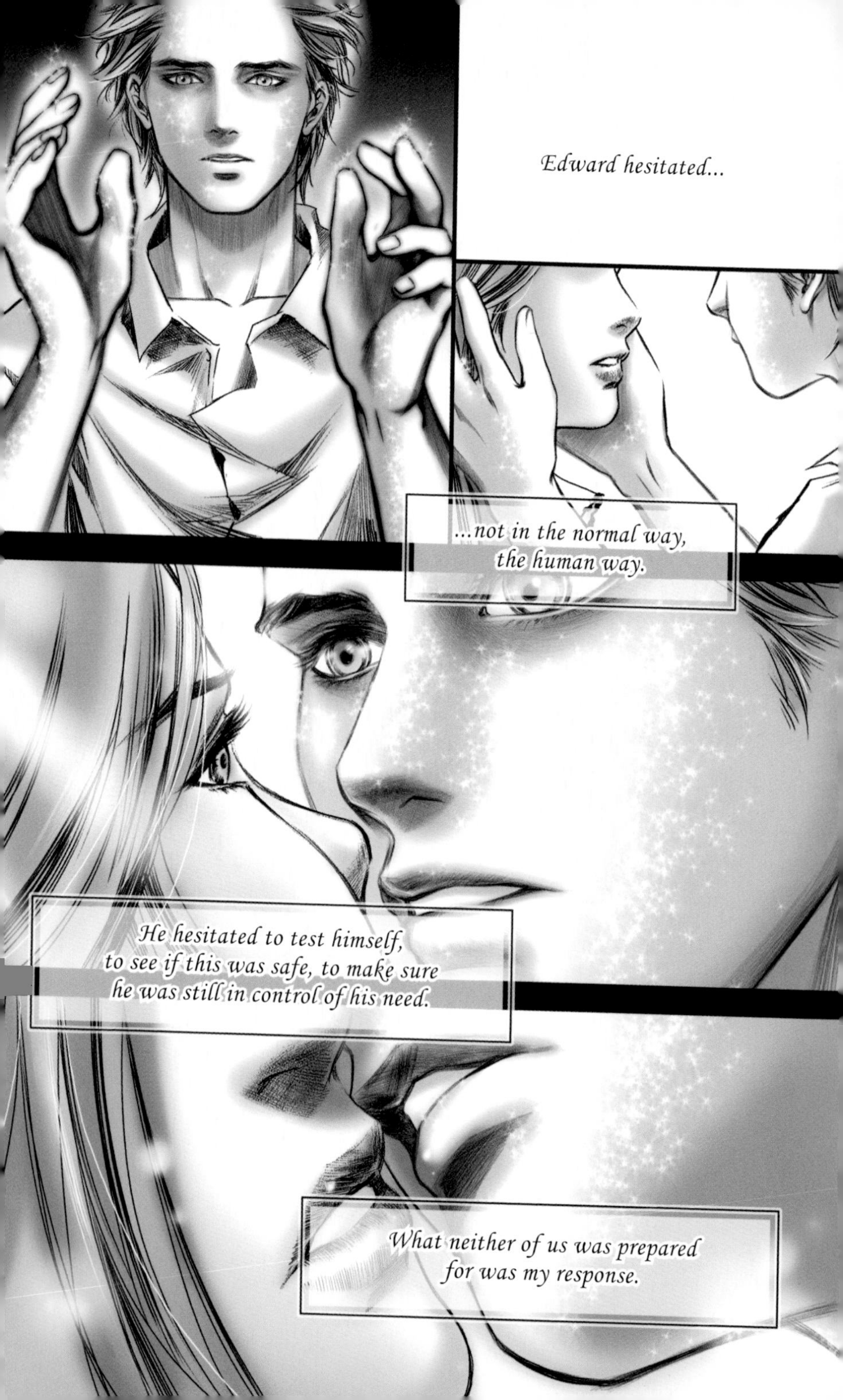
Edward hesitated...
...not in the normal way,
the human way.
He hesitated to test himself,
to see if this was safe, to make sure
he was still in control of his need.
What neither of us was prepared
for was my response.

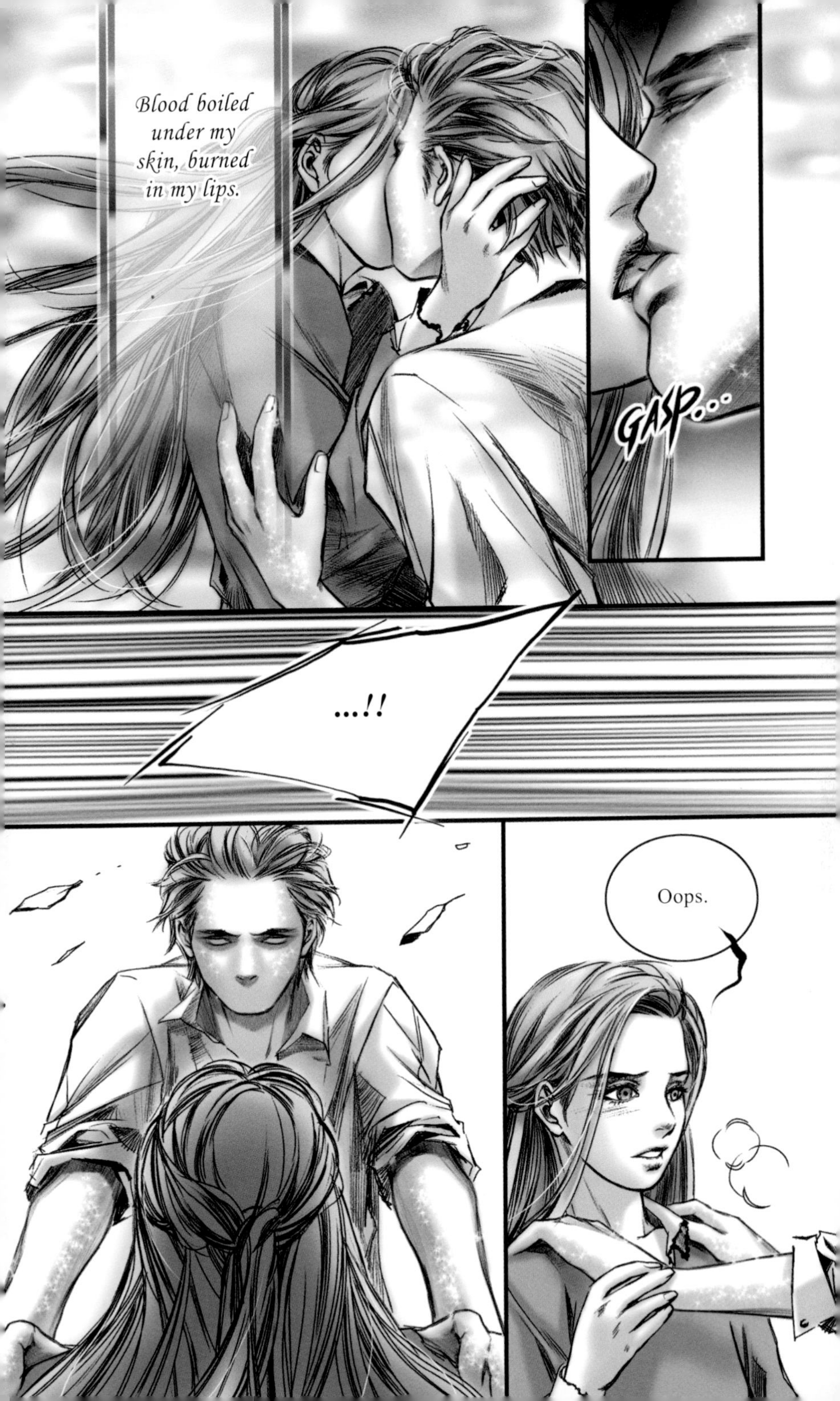
Blood boiled under my skin, burned in my lips.
GASP...
...!!
Oops.

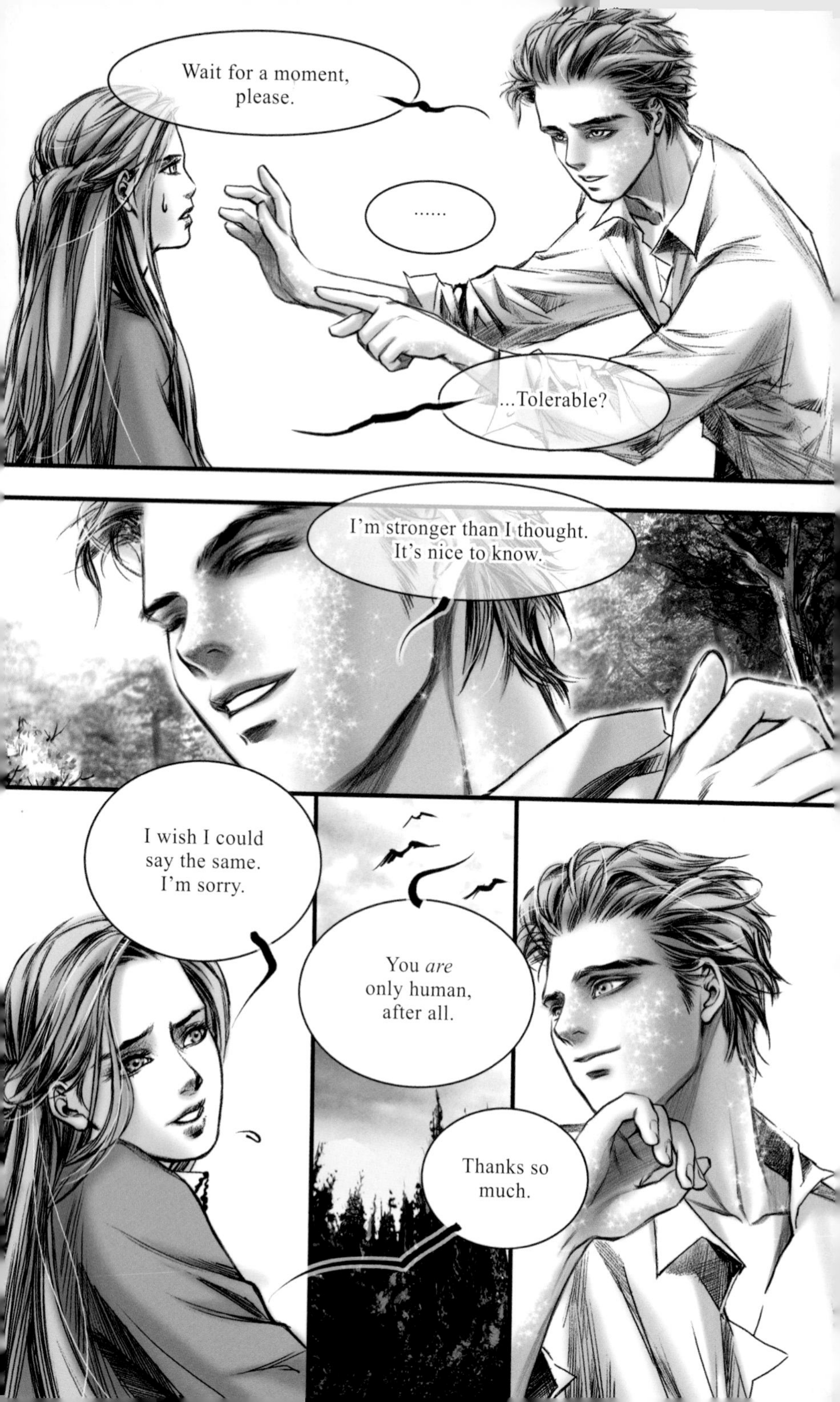
Wait for a moment, please.
......
...Tolerable?
I'm stronger than I thought. It's nice to know.
I wish I could say the same. I'm sorry.
You *are* only human, after all.
Thanks so much.

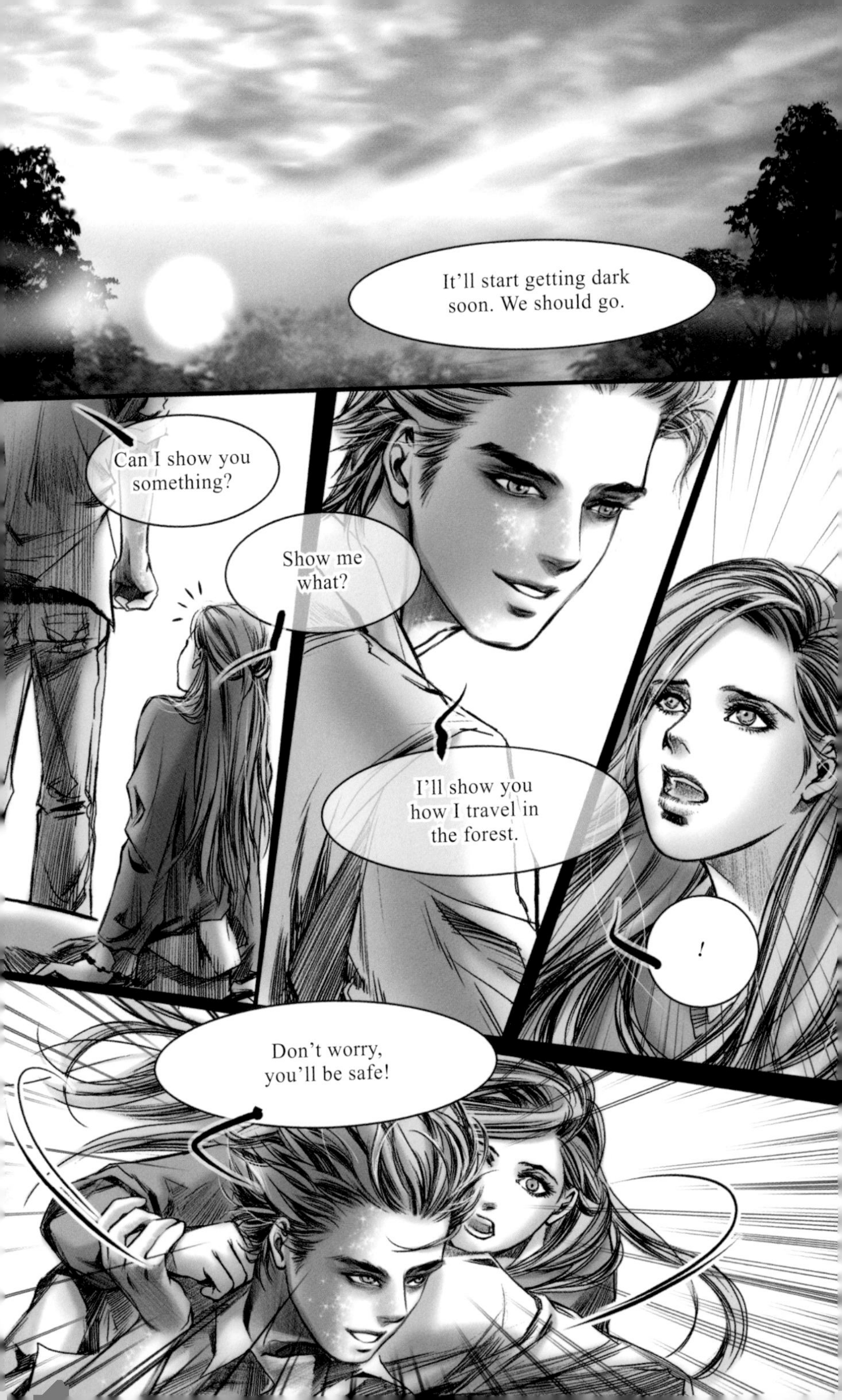

It'll start getting dark soon. We should go.
Can I show you something?
Show me what?
I'll show you how I travel in the forest.
!
Don't worry, you'll be safe!

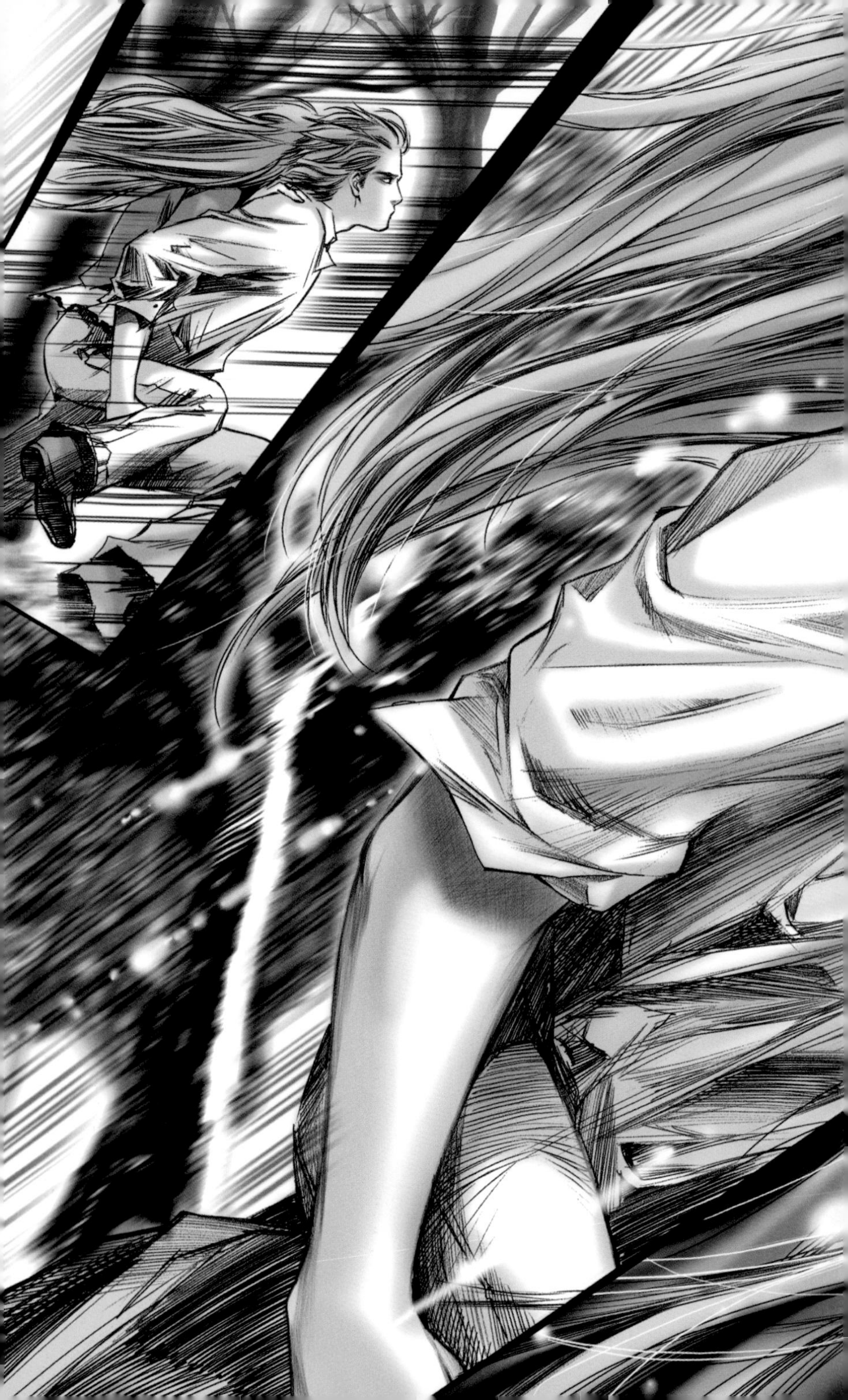

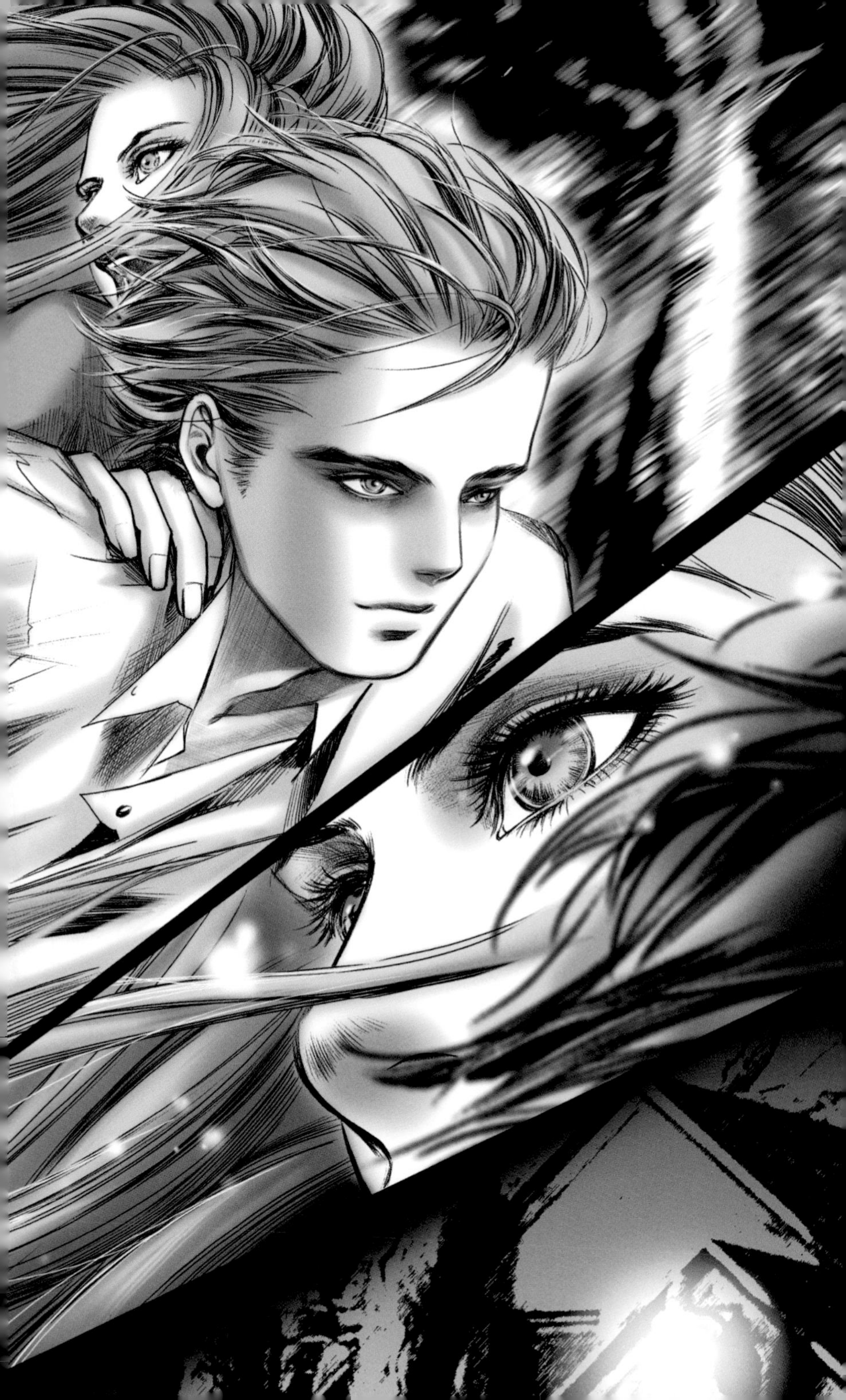

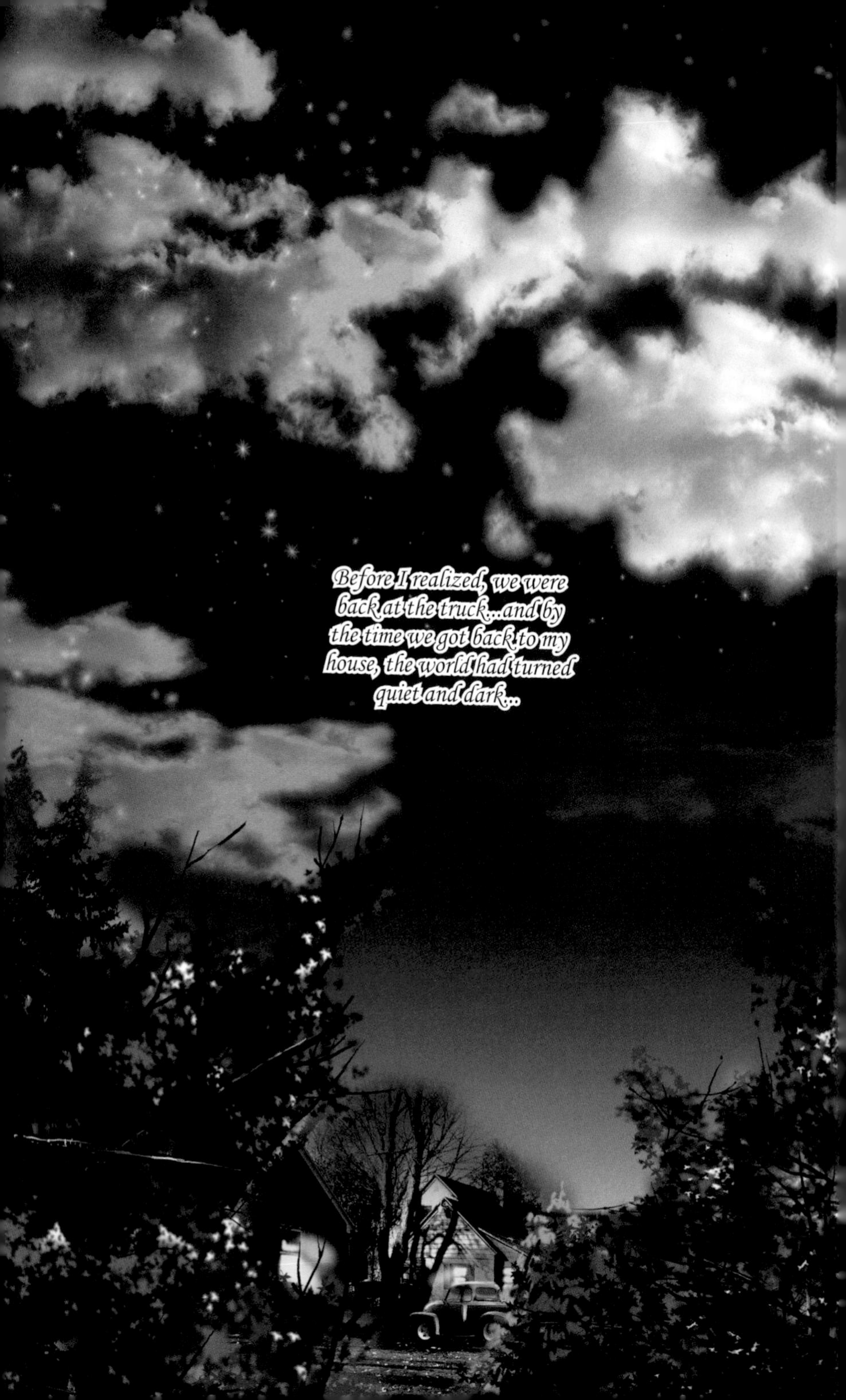
Before I realized, we were back at the truck...and by the time we got back to my house, the world had turned quiet and dark...

To be continued in Volume Two...

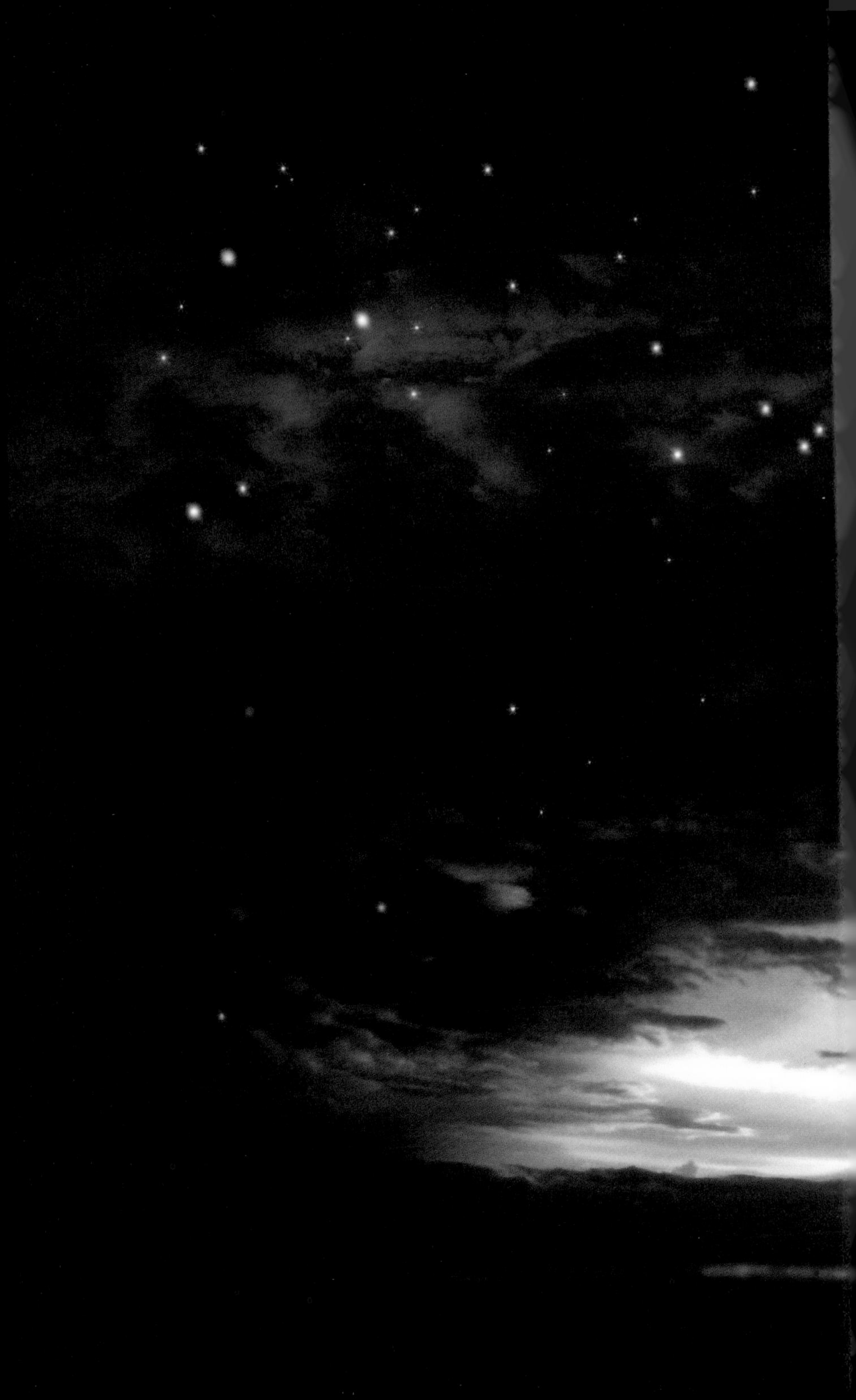

*Thanks to Stephenie Meyer, who supervised each and every page
and provided great guidance.*

*Thanks to my family, whose support allowed me to concentrate on my work,
to Bum, who has been my consolation during the tough times,
and to the whole Yen Press team, who supported me greatly.
And most of all, my appreciation goes out to my editor, JuYoun.
Her patience and encouragement were the driving forces that kept me going.
It's thanks to her that this book is reaching the readers' hands.*

*When the story started out,
neither Bella nor Edward believed that they could find happiness
because they were different from others.
But now, we are beginning to see glimpses that they may indeed
be able to find happiness together.*

*To the reader, I sincerely hope that your own unique nature is loved,
particularly by yourself . . .*

— Young Kim

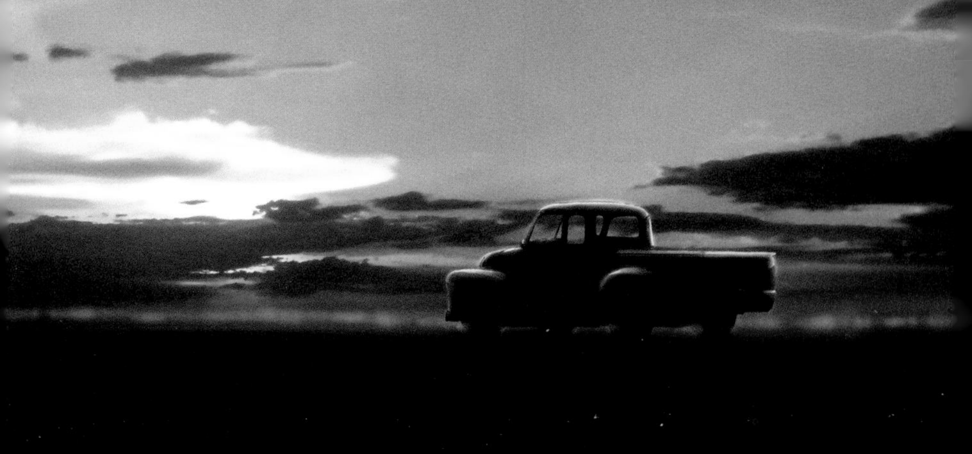